Enjoy!

:)

Maya
Bank
xoxo

Praise for the novels of Maya Banks

"Heated investigative romantic suspense . . . Intense, transfixing."

—*Midwest Book Review*

"Definitely a recommended read . . . filled with friendship, passion, and, most of all, a love that grows beyond just being friends."

—*Fallen Angel Reviews*

"Grabbed me from page one and refused to let go until I read the last word . . . When a book still affects me hours after reading it, I can't help but Joyfully Recommend it!"  —*Joyfully Reviewed*

"I guarantee I will reread this book many times over, and will derive as much pleasure as I did in the first reading each and every subsequent time."  —*Novelspot*

"An excellent read that I simply did not put down . . . A fantastic adventure . . . Covers all the emotional range."

—*The Road to Romance*

"Searingly sexy and highly believable."  —*RT Book Reviews*

"A must-read author . . . Her [stories] are always full of emotional situations, lovable characters and kick-butt story lines."

—*Romance Junkies*

# burn

## maya banks

BERKLEY BOOKS, NEW YORK

**THE BERKLEY PUBLISHING GROUP**
**Published by the Penguin Group**
**Penguin Group (USA) Inc.**
**375 Hudson Street, New York, New York 10014, USA**

USA I Canada I UK I Ireland I Australia I New Zealand I India I South Africa I China

Penguin Books Ltd., Registered Offices: 80 Strand, London WC2R 0RL, England
For more information about the Penguin Group, visit penguin.com.

This book is an original publication of The Berkley Publishing Group.

Library of Congress Cataloging-in-Publication Data

Banks, Maya.
Burn : the Breathless Trilogy / by Maya Banks.—Berkley trade paperback edition.
pages   cm.—(The Breathless Trilogy)
ISBN 978-0-425-26708-0 (alk. paper)
I. Title.
PS3602.A643B87   2013
813'.6—dc23              2013014509

PUBLISHING HISTORY
Berkley trade paperback edition / August 2013

PRINTED IN THE UNITED STATES OF AMERICA

10  9  8  7  6  5  4  3  2  1

Cover photo by Arsgera/Shutterstock.
Cover design by Rita Frangie.
Interior text design by Kristin del Rosario.

*To my "family." Not of blood, but family all the same.*

burn

# chapter one

Ash McIntyre stood on the concrete walkway of Bryant Park, hands stuffed into his slacks pockets as he breathed in the spring air. There was still a nip in the wind, carrying with it hints of winter fading to spring. Around him, people sat on benches and in chairs at the small tables where they drank coffee, worked on laptops or were listening to iPods.

It was an absolutely gorgeous day, not that he usually indulged in things like a walk in the park or even *being* in a park, especially during business hours when he was usually entrenched in his office, on the phone or typing emails or making plans to travel. He wasn't a "stop and smell the roses" kind of guy. But today he was restless and cagey, he had a lot on his mind, and he'd found himself here without really realizing that he'd planned to end up in the park.

Mia and Gabe's wedding was a few short days away, and his business partner was up to his eyeballs in wedding preparations as he sought to ensure Mia had the wedding of her dreams. And Jace? His other best friend and business partner was in a *very* permanent relationship with his fiancée, Bethany, which meant that his two friends were otherwise occupied.

When they weren't working, they were with their women, and it meant that Ash didn't see them except at the office and on the occasions they all got together outside of work. They were still close, and Gabe and Jace ensured they'd stayed solid, including him in their changing lives. But it wasn't the same. And while it was good for his friends, Ash still hadn't quite come to terms with how rapidly all their lives had altered over the last eight months.

It was weird and life-changing, even though it wasn't his life being impacted. It wasn't that he wasn't happy for his friends. They were happy. That made him happy. But for the first time since the beginning of their friendship, he was on the outside looking in.

His friends would vehemently dispute that. They were his family. Much more so than his own batshit crazy family whom he spent most of his time avoiding. Gabe, Mia, Jace and Bethany, but *especially* Gabe and Jace, would deny that Ash was on the periphery now. They were his brothers in all the ways that counted. More than blood. Their bond was unbreakable. But it had changed. So in fact he *was* on the periphery. Still a part, but in a much different, smaller way.

For years their motto had been *play hard and live free*. Being in a relationship changed a man. It changed his priorities. Ash got that. He understood it. He'd think less of Gabe and Jace if their women weren't their priority. But it left Ash out of the loop. The third wheel. And it wasn't a comfortable place to be.

It was especially hard because, until Bethany, Ash and Jace had shared most of their women. More often than not, they fucked the same women. It sounded asinine that Ash wouldn't know how to function outside a threesome relationship, but there it was.

He was restless and edgy, in search of something, he had no idea what. It wasn't that he wanted what Gabe and Jace had—or maybe he did and refused to acknowledge it. He just knew he wasn't himself, and he didn't like that fact.

He was focused. Knew exactly what he wanted at all times and had the wealth and power to make it happen. There were no shortage of women who'd be more than willing to give Ash what he needed or wanted. But what was the point when he himself had no clue what it was he wanted or needed at present?

He scanned the park, taking in the baby strollers being pushed by mothers and nannies. He tried to picture himself with children and nearly shuddered at the thought. He was thirty-eight, almost thirty-nine, a time when most men had already settled down and produced offspring. But he'd spent all of his twenties and a good chunk of his thirties busting his ass with his partners to make their business the success it was now. Without using his family's money, their connections, and especially without their help.

Maybe that was why they hated him so much now. Because he'd thumbed his nose at them and basically told them to fuck off. But the biggest sin he'd committed was in making more of a success of himself without them. He had more wealth and power than even the old man did. His grandfather. For that matter, what had the rest of his family ever done but live off the old man's largess? His grandfather had sold his successful business when Ash was still a boy. None of his family had worked a day in their lives.

He shook his head. Fucking leeches, the lot of them. He didn't need them. Damn sure didn't want them. And now that he had surpassed them—and his grandfather—he sure as hell wasn't going to allow them back into his life to reap the benefits of riding his star.

He turned to go because he had shit to do that didn't include standing around in a damn park self-reflecting like he was in need of a shrink. He had to get his act together and start focusing on the one thing that hadn't changed. Business. HCM Global Resorts had projects in various stages of work. The Paris hotel was a done deal after their having to work fast to replace investors that had backed out. Things were moving along and progressing well. This wasn't the time for him to drop the ball, especially when Gabe and Jace couldn't give work the time they had in the past. Ash was the only one not distracted by his personal life, so he had to step up. Take some of the slack for his friends so they could enjoy having a life outside of work.

As he started to stride back in the direction he'd come, he saw a young woman sitting alone at one of the tables outside of the primary traffic area. He stopped mid-step and let his gaze settle more fully on her, taking in her appearance. Long blond hair that drifted just so with the breeze, revealing a startlingly beautiful face with striking eyes that he could see even from the distance at which he stood.

She was wearing a funky long skirt that swirled with the wind, baring the long expanse of one leg. Blingy flip-flops adorned her feet and he could see the bright pink polish on her toes and a toe ring that sparkled when she moved her foot to shift position. The sun caught on a silvery ankle bracelet, drawing even more attention to her slender leg.

She was busy sketching, her brow furrowed in concentration as her pencil flew over the page, and beside her was a huge bag stuffed full, with rolled-up papers extending from the top.

But what most caught his attention was the choker she wore around her neck. It didn't fit her. He made that instant assessment. It was tight around her neck, resting just at the hollow of her delicate throat. But it didn't *fit* her. It didn't reflect her at all.

It was gaudy on her. A diamond choker, obviously expensive and probably not fake, but it didn't go with the rest of her. It stood out, out of place. His curiosity was piqued because when he saw a piece of jewelry like that on a woman, it meant something far different than it did to most people and he was seized with interest to know if it was indeed a collar, or if it was just an ornament, chosen by her. And if it was a collar, the man who'd chosen it for her had done a piss-poor job. The man didn't know her, or maybe he didn't care to ensure that such an important adornment suited the woman he called his own.

If Ash could make that judgment after mere moments of studying her, then how the hell could the man making love to her not see the same? Maybe the collar was more a reflection of her dominant, which was arrogant and idiotic. A collar should represent his care of his submissive, how in touch with her he was, and it should fit the woman wearing it.

He was making a hell of a lot of assumptions. It could just be a simple necklace the woman had chosen herself. But to a man like Ash, that piece of jewelry meant something more than just an accessory.

How long he stood watching her, he didn't know, but, as if sensing his gaze, hers lifted to meet his and her eyes widened and something like panic entered her expression. Then she hastily slammed her sketch pad closed and began to shove it into her bag. She half rose, still stuffing things into that huge bag, and he realized she was leaving.

Before he was even aware of it, he hurried forward, intrigued. Adrenaline rushed through his veins. The hunt. Discovery. Challenge. Interest. He wanted to know who this woman was, and what that collar she wore meant.

And even as he strode toward her, he knew that if it *did* mean what he thought it did, he was trespassing on another man's territory, and furthermore, he didn't give one fuck.

Poaching another dominant's submissive was one of those unwritten no-nos, but then Ash had never been one for rules. At least the ones he himself didn't make. And this woman was beautiful. Intriguing. And perhaps exactly what he was looking for. How would he know unless he got to her before she bailed?

He was nearly to her when she whirled around, bag in hand,

obviously preparing to walk away, and she nearly bumped head-long into him. Yeah, he was absolutely invading her space, and he'd be lucky if she didn't scream the park down. He probably looked like some stalker about to attack.

He heard her quick intake of breath as she took a step back, banging the bag into the chair she'd vacated. The bag tipped over, coming loose from her grip, and the contents spilled, pencils, brushes and papers flying everywhere.

"Damn it!" she muttered.

She bent immediately, grabbing for the papers, and he chased after one that had been caught by the wind, taking it several feet away.

"I'll get them," she called. "Please don't trouble yourself."

He captured the drawing and picked it up, turning back to her.

"It's no trouble at all. I'm sorry if I startled you."

She let out a shaky laugh as she extended her hand for the paper. "You did that for sure."

He glanced down, taking in the drawing as he started to hand it over to her and then blinked in surprise when he saw himself on the paper.

"What the hell?" he murmured, ignoring her hasty grab for the drawing.

"Please just give it back," she said, her voice soft and urgent.

She sounded scared, like he was going to freak out, but he was more mesmerized by the small expanse of her side that had been bared by the loose-fitting top when she'd reached for the paper.

On her right side he'd glimpsed a tattoo that was vibrant and colorful. Like her. The brief glimpse he'd gotten told him it was flowery, almost like a vine, and that it likely extended a hell of a lot farther up or down her body. Maybe both. He wished like hell he could see more of it, but she let her arm drop and the hem of her shirt settled back to the waistband of that full skirt, depriving him of further view.

"Why were you drawing me?" he asked curiously.

Color invaded her cheeks, making her skin rosy. She had fair skin, just barely kissed by the sun, but with her hair and those gorgeous aquamarine eyes, it looked beautiful. *She* was beautiful. And evidently very talented.

She'd drawn him perfectly. He'd had no difficulty in recognizing himself in the pencil drawing. His thoughtful expression, the distant look in his eyes. She'd drawn him as he'd stood there, hands shoved into his pockets. That moment of self-reflection, and clearly that was evident in the drawing. It made him feel awkwardly vulnerable that a complete stranger had been able to capture his mood in just a few moments. That she'd seen him in that vulnerable moment and had picked up on what he hid from everyone else in the world.

"It was just an impulse," she defended. "I draw a lot of people. Things. Whatever captures my attention."

He smiled, never dropping his gaze from hers. Her eyes were so expressive, capable of swallowing a man whole. And that damn choker stared back at him, taunting him with the possibilities.

"So you're saying I caught your attention."

She flushed again. It was a guilty flush, but also one that was telling. She was checking him out every bit as much as he was checking her out. Perhaps more subtly, but then subtlety had never been one of his strong points.

"You seemed out of place," she blurted. "You have very strong features. I was itching to get them down on paper. You have an interesting face and it was obvious you had a lot on your mind. I find people are a lot more open when they think no one is watching them. If you'd been posing, the picture wouldn't have been the same."

"It's very good," he said slowly as he dropped his gaze to once more take in the drawing. "You have a lot of talent."

"Can I have it back now?" she asked. "I'm late."

He looked back up, lifting his eyebrow in question. "You didn't appear to be leaving until you saw me coming toward you."

"That was several minutes ago, and I wasn't late then. Now I am."

"What are you late for?"

Her brows drew together in consternation and then her eyes flashed in annoyance. "I don't think that's any of your business."

"Ash," he said at her pause at the end. "My name is Ash."

She nodded but didn't say his name. And right then he'd have given anything to hear his name on her lips.

He reached forward, brushing his fingers over the collar at her throat. "This have anything to do with what you're late for?"

She took a step back, her frown deepening.

"Your Dom waiting for you?"

Her eyes widened and her fingers automatically went to the collar where his fingers had been just seconds before.

"What's your name?" he asked, when she remained silent. "I gave you mine. The polite thing to do is return the favor."

"Josie," she said barely above a whisper. "Josie Carlysle."

"And who owns you, Josie?"

Her eyes narrowed then and she clutched her bag, shoving the remainder of her pencils into it. "Nobody owns me."

"Then did I misunderstand the significance of that collar you're wearing?"

Her fingers brushed over it again, and it made him itchy. He wanted to remove it. It wasn't right for her. A collar should be carefully chosen for a submissive. Something that matched her personality. Something made especially for her. And not just any woman.

"You didn't misunderstand," she said in a husky voice that sent shivers down his spine. Her voice alone would seduce a man in a matter of seconds. "But nobody owns me, Ash."

And there it was. His name on her lips. It hit him deep, filling him with inexplicable satisfaction. He wanted to hear it again. When he was pleasuring her. When he had his hands and mouth on her body, drawing whispery sighs of contentment from her.

He lifted one eyebrow. "Then do *you* misunderstand the significance of that collar?"

She laughed. "No, but he doesn't own me. Nobody owns me. It was a gift. One I choose to wear. Nothing more."

He leaned in, and this time she didn't back away. Her gaze fixed on him, curiosity gleaming, and even anticipation. She felt it too. That magnetic pull between them. She'd have to be blind and in denial not to feel it.

"If you wore my collar, you'd damn well know you belonged to me," he growled. "Furthermore, you wouldn't regret for a moment that you gave yourself wholly to me. If you were in my care, you'd definitely belong to me. There'd be no question. And you wouldn't hesitate when asked who your dominant was. Nor would you say it was a gift like it was nothing more than a piece of jewelry thoughtlessly chosen on a whim. It would mean something, Josie. It would mean fucking *everything*, and you'd know that."

Her eyes widened and then she laughed again, her eyes twinkling. "Then it's too bad I don't belong to you."

With that she turned and hurried away, bag over her shoulder and him still standing there holding the drawing she'd done of him.

He watched as she walked away from him, hair sliding down her back and lifting in the wind, a glimpse of the flip-flops and the ankle bracelet that tinkled softly when she moved. Then he glanced down at the drawing in his hand.

"Too bad indeed," he murmured.

## chapter two

Ash sat in his office, door closed, brooding over the report in front of him. It wasn't a business file. No financial chart. No email he had to respond to. It was a file on one Josie Carlysle.

He'd acted quickly, calling in a favor from the same agency he'd used to do a background check on Bethany, which had solidly pissed Jace off at the time. They were good, and, more importantly, they were fast.

After his meeting with Josie in the park, he hadn't been able to shake her from his mind. Hadn't been able to shake his fixation with her, and he wasn't even sure what he'd call it, other than he was acting a lot like Jace had when he'd first met Bethany, and Ash had been quick to call his friend on the stupidity and rashness of his actions then. What would Jace think if he knew that Ash was basically stalking Josie?

Jace would think he'd lost his damn mind. Just as Ash had thought Jace had lost his—and well, he *had*—over Bethany.

According to his report, Josie was twenty-eight. An art grad who lived in a basement studio apartment in a brownstone on the Upper East Side. The apartment was leased to her. Not another man. In fact there was little evidence in the report of this other man's presence, other than him arriving to pick her up at different intervals. The report only spanned a few days, since it had only been since then that Ash had met Josie and immediately requested the information.

More often than not, she spent time in the park, drawing or painting. Some of her work was displayed in a small art gallery on Madison, but nothing had sold, at least in the amount of time since Ash had someone keeping an eye on her. She also designed funky jewelry and had a website and an online shop where she took orders for some of her handmade stuff.

From all appearances, she was a free spirit. No regular work hours. No regular schedule at all. She came and went seemingly on a whim. Though it had only been a few days, it seemed that she was also a loner. His guy hadn't spotted her with anyone other than the man Ash assumed was her Dom.

It didn't make sense to him. If Josie was his, he damn sure wouldn't spend so little time with her, nor would she be alone so much. It appeared to him that Josie was an itch this guy was scratching and that either he, or she, didn't take the relationship that seriously.

Was it all a game?

Not that Ash had anything against people doing whatever the fuck they wanted, but in his world, submission wasn't a game. It was everything. He didn't play games. Didn't have time for them, and they just pissed him off. If a woman wasn't into it with him, then he was out. If she wanted a fucking game where she played at being submissive, complete with cute role-playing and yanking his chain to earn a punishment, he cut her loose quick.

But then most of the women he'd fucked, he'd fucked with Jace. They had their rules. The women were clued in from the start. Bethany had been a complete game changer, and a complete rule breaker. Jace hadn't wanted to share, and Ash got that. He hadn't at first, but he got it now. But it didn't mean that he didn't miss that connection with his best friend.

On the other hand, with Jace out of the way, Ash was solely in control. He didn't have to worry about tripping over his best friend, pissing him off, or playing by anyone else's rules but his own.

That appealed to him. It appealed a damn lot. He'd always known that people misunderstood his personality. Looking at the three of them, Gabe, Jace and Ash, people assumed Ash was the easygoing one. The "I don't give a fuck" kind. Laid-back. Maybe even a pushover.

They were all wrong.

Of any of them, he was the most intense, and he knew that about himself. He'd held back when he and Jace were with the same woman, because he knew he'd take it a hell of a lot further than Jace ever would. So he played it Jace's way and held that part of himself in check. The part that would take over completely. And, well, there hadn't ever been a woman who tempted him to let that part of himself go.

Until now.

And it was stupid. He didn't know Josie. He knew about her, yeah. The report was detailed. But he didn't know *her*. Didn't know if she'd even respond to what Ash would give her. What he would *take*.

That was the biggie. What he would take. Because he'd take a lot. He'd give a lot, but his demands would seem extreme even to someone well-versed in the lifestyle he lived.

He glanced down at the report again, pondering his next move. He already had a man on her. The idea of her being alone so much bothered him. Not that he didn't think it was perfectly okay for a woman to do whatever the hell she wanted in the city. But it bothered him for Josie. A lot. Would her supposed Dom even have a fucking clue where she was during the day? Did he give her protection? Or did he just hook up with her when he wanted someone to fuck?

A low growl rumbled in his throat and he swallowed it back. He needed to calm the fuck down and get his shit together. This woman was nothing to him. But even as he thought it, he knew he was a damn liar. She was something. He just wasn't sure what yet.

His cell phone rang, and he looked down, frowning when he saw the contact. It was the man he had watching Josie.

"Ash," he answered shortly.

"Mr. McIntyre, this is Johnny. Just wanted to let you know what I just observed. With what you told me, I figured you'd want to know what's going down."

Ash sat up in his chair, his frown deepening. "What's wrong? Is she hurt?"

"No, sir. She just came out of a pawnshop. She sold some jewelry. I was in the shop, heard her talking to the pawnbroker. Said she needed the cash to make rent. He asked her if she wanted to sell it or pawn it and she said sell because she doubted she'd have the money to get it back unless something changed. Didn't say what that change would be, but thought you'd want to know what she did."

Anger splintered his mind. What the fuck was Josie doing hocking jewelry in a goddamn pawnshop? If she needed cash, then why the hell wasn't her Dom providing for her? Why wasn't he protecting her better? The *hell* she'd be in a fucking pawnshop if she belonged to him.

"Buy it," Ash clipped out. "Buy every piece. I don't care what it costs. And you bring it to me."

"Yes, sir," Johnny said.

Ash hung up and then leaned back in his chair, his mind working furiously. Then he rose abruptly, his phone to his ear calling for his driver to meet him in front of the office building.

He nearly ran over Gabe in the hallway.

"Ash, you got a second?" Gabe called when Ash continued down the hall.

"Not now," Ash ground out. "Got shit to do. I'll tag you later, okay?"

"Ash?"

Ash stopped, impatience simmering as he turned to look at his friend. Gabe's brows were drawn together in concentration and concern gleamed in his eyes.

"Everything okay?"

Ash nodded. "Yeah, fine. Look, I've got to run. I'll catch up later."

Gabe nodded, but there was doubt in his eyes. No way Ash was sharing what was on his mind. Gabe had enough to keep him occupied with his wedding. Shit, that was tomorrow. Which meant Gabe probably wanted to talk shit about the wedding and the ceremony.

Ash stopped at the very end of the hall and called back to Gabe.

"Everything okay with the wedding? Mia okay? You need anything?"

Gabe paused at his office door and smiled. "Everything's fine. Or at least it will be when the fucking ceremony is done and she's mine. We still on for tonight? Jace is determined to throw me a bachelor party, which is not making Mia happy. I doubt Bethany is any happier, but he swears it's just drinks at Rick's and nothing that will piss either woman off."

Damn it. Ash had forgotten about it all. In his preoccupation with Josie he'd put the wedding and the night out with Gabe and Jace solidly out of his mind.

"Yeah, I'll be there. Eight, right? I'll just meet you and Jace there."

Gabe nodded. "Okay, see you then. Hope everything works out."

Gabe was fishing again, but Ash ignored him and turned for the elevator. He didn't have much time if he was going to make it to the art gallery before it closed.

. . .

Ash walked into the small gallery and quickly glanced around. It was apparent that this was a small dealer with not a lot of well-known artists displayed. He probably dealt with independent artists. Those yet to be discovered. Those displaying in hopes of being discovered.

His eyes settled immediately on a painting on the wall, and he knew without confirming that it was one of Josie's works. It just looked like her. Bright. Vibrant. Carefree. He felt her when he looked at the painting. Saw her, remembered the way she smelled and when she'd smiled, those ocean eyes he could drown in. Yeah, it was definitely hers. He wasn't wrong about this.

"Can I help you?"

Ash turned to see an older man smiling at him. He was dressed in a worn suit with scuffed shoes and wore glasses that drew attention to the lines in his forehead and around his eyes.

"Josie Carlysle," Ash said bluntly. "You display her work here?"

The man looked surprised but then smiled again and turned, gesturing toward the wall. "Yes, I do. She's good. Not focused though. I think it's why she hasn't caught on. She's too all over the place and her style hasn't emerged yet. One that's identifiable, if you understand my meaning."

"No, I don't," Ash said impatiently. "I like it. I like her work. Is that all you have, there on the wall?"

The man's eyebrows went up. "No. Not at all. I have several pieces of hers. I only take a few at a time. I have to utilize the space to display what sells, and I've only sold one or two of her pieces, regrettably. I've actually cut back on the work of hers I display, just because it isn't moving well."

"I want them all."

The surprise was still evident in the man's face but he hurried immediately to the wall to take down the painting that had first caught Ash's attention. It was framed. Not well, and he'd definitely replace the frame with something more worthy of her talent. But first he had to buy up all her work and let the man know that anything else that Josie brought in was *his*.

After a few minutes, the man had taken down the last painting and started toward the desk in front of the gallery. Then he paused and turned, a thoughtful look on his face.

"I have one more. In the back. She just brought it in two days ago. I didn't have the space to hang it, but I didn't have the heart to tell her no. Not when I'd already told her I wouldn't be able to take anything else until I sold something."

"I want it too," Ash clipped out.

"Sight unseen?"

Ash nodded. "If she did it, I want it. I want every piece of hers you have."

The man's expression brightened. "Well, then. Perfect. She'll be thrilled! I can't wait to tell her."

Ash held up his hand, halting the man before he went to the back to retrieve the painting.

"You tell her whatever you want, but you do not give her my name or any information about me. I want complete anonymity or the deal is off. Understand? Furthermore, I'm going to leave you my card. If she brings in anything else, you call me. I want whatever she brings in. I'll pay you double for everything you currently have as long as you make sure she gets her cut. And I will find out if you stiffed her, so don't even think about it. But that extra money also ensures I get first option on whatever else she brings you—and I will buy whatever she brings—so it would be in your best interest to let her bring in whatever the hell she wants."

"O-of c-course," the man stammered out. "I'll arrange it however you like. She won't know anything other than someone took a liking to her work and wanted everything I had. She'll be thrilled. I, of course, will tell her she is free to bring in anything else she has."

Ash nodded. "Good. Then we understand one another."

"Absolutely. Let me just get the painting in the back and bring it out. Would you like to take them all today or have me deliver them?"

"I'll take the one with me," Ash murmured, gesturing toward the first painting he'd seen on the wall. "The others you can have delivered to my apartment."

The man nodded and then hurried to the back, returning a moment later with an unframed painting wrapped in a protective covering.

A moment later, Ash handed the dealer his credit card and watched as the purchases were totaled. He wasn't sure what the breakdown on the commission was, but with what he paid, Josie should have enough to solve any money issues for the short term.

The long term? He wasn't that worried about the long term, because while Josie had no clue of Ash's intentions—yet—he very much intended that the long term would include him.

# chapter three

At ten minutes past eight, Ash walked into the private box where Gabe and Jace were already sitting, enjoying a drink. They looked up when he entered and Jace waved a greeting.

"What's your poison tonight? Your usual?" Jace asked when Ash took a seat next to him.

A woman appeared wearing a sexy smile and propped her arm on Gabe's shoulder.

"So sorry to hear you're off the market," she said in a flirty voice.

Gabe looked pointedly at her arm and when he didn't say anything, she swiftly took it away and then turned to Ash.

"What can I get you?"

He wasn't in a drinking mood, but he didn't want to be a damper on his friend's evening. And it was in fact their last evening as bachelors. Well, it wasn't as if Jace and Ash were married, but Jace would be. It was the last evening with the three of them still single, and it signaled an end to nearly twenty years of living free and playing hard.

His friends would argue that they weren't free or playing hard. He was sure they were doing both just fine. Mia and Bethany weren't any hardship for the men, and they certainly had no hesitations about embracing a permanent relationship.

"Scotch," Ash finally said.

"Was it that hard of a decision?" Jace drawled.

Ash grinned, though it felt more like a grimace. A few moments later, the waitress returned with Ash's drink and he held it up to his two friends.

"Here's to Gabe, the first to take the plunge. Well, the first and the second," Ash amended, referring to the fact that Gabe had been married once before. He tended to forget that and he was sure Gabe would prefer it that way as well. The marriage hadn't lasted that long and it hadn't ended well.

Predictably, Gabe scowled, though he did raise his glass.

"Mia is the only one that counts," Gabe said.

Jace nodded. "Definite upgrade from Lisa. You did good."

"Says the woman's brother," Ash snorted.

Jace lifted an eyebrow in Ash's direction. "You saying Mia's not a good choice?"

"As if. Don't give Gabe any reason to want to kick my ass. Don't want the man wearing a black eye for his big day tomorrow."

Gabe snorted. "Who the hell says it'll be me wearing the black eye? I'll wipe the floor with you, asshole."

Ash rolled his eyes and sank back into the comfortable chair. "So is this what it's come down to for us? Sitting around like old farts the night before the wedding?"

"Yeah, well, you don't have a woman to go home to and explain anything wilder," Jace said dryly. "Mia and Bethany would both have our asses if we had anything resembling a true bachelor party. So yeah, this is as good as it gets. Sorry."

"We're getting too old for that shit anyway," Gabe muttered. "Acting like a bunch of frat boys with their first piece of ass isn't my idea of a good time anymore."

"I'll drink to that," Jace said.

"Well, when you put it that way so will I," Ash added. "Damn, were we ever that bad?"

Gabe laughed. "We were a bit more discerning, but yeah, you can't tell me you don't remember our days in college. Lots of drinking and sex. Not necessarily in that order."

"At least I remember all the women I slept with," Jace said.

"That's because you have Ash to remind you," Gabe shot back. "I don't tag team so I don't have someone to remind me of everyone I fucked because I wasn't fucking them with best friends."

"Now there's an image," Ash drawled. "That's probably the only thing we never tried. A foursome."

Jace laughed. Even Gabe joined in as they continued to give each other shit.

Several drinks later, Gabe kept checking his watch and it amused Ash. The man couldn't wait to get home to Mia. Forgoing any of the traditions of not seeing the bride the night before or day of, Gabe would be going to bed with Mia, waking up with her in the morning and probably make her late for the ceremony by getting a head start on the honeymoon.

"Don't let us keep you," Ash said dryly.

Gabe's head yanked up, guilt flashing in his eyes as Jace laughed.

"How long you and Mia going to be gone on your honeymoon?" Jace asked. "You never said and I didn't see that you'd cleared your calendar at work."

Gabe's expression darkened. "Not working for two weeks. Not even bringing my phone or laptop with me. So if the company goes to shit in my absence, I'm not going to be pleased."

"Fuck you," Ash muttered. "Jace and I do all the work anyway. You just sit back and obsess."

"Surprised you're only going to be gone for two weeks," Jace said. "I figured you'd go off and we wouldn't see you for a month at least."

"Can't say I'm not tempted. But for now, two weeks will do. I plan to be taking a lot more vacation from now on, though. There's a lot of places Mia wants to see and I'm going to make that happen for her."

"You deserve it, man," Ash said sincerely. "You've worked your ass off. Already had one bad marriage. You've got a good woman now and more money than you'll ever spend. Time to go out and enjoy the fruits of your labor. Make sure you don't fuck it up with Mia. She'll love you forever, which is more than I can say for your bitch of an ex."

"Let's not ruin my night by discussing my ex," Gabe growled.

"Any plans for babies yet?" Jace asked. "Has she talked you around on that?"

"She doesn't have to persuade me," Gabe said with a shrug. "I'm not getting any younger. My only concern was whether she was ready for children yet. She's still young. Lot of years ahead of her. I'd wait if that's what would make her happy, but she insists she wants a big family, the sooner the better."

"In other words, you're doing your best to knock her up as soon as possible," Ash drawled.

Gabe tipped his glass in Ash's direction and Jace winced. He visibly shuddered and then took a long swallow of his drink.

"We need to stop now. This is my sister we're talking about. Now I'm going to have to go home and bleach my eyeballs over the images you're invoking."

Gabe rolled his eyes and Ash chuckled. Then Gabe sobered and stared between Jace and Ash.

"Glad to have you both at my back. Means a lot to Mia that you'll be there tomorrow, but it means even more to me. We've been friends a hell of a lot of years. There's no one else I care about having there. Wouldn't give a shit if no one but you and Mia were there. And Bethany, of course."

"Very eloquent speech there, man," Jace said, amusement thick in his voice.

"Meant it," Gabe said simply.

Ash extended his arm with a closed fist to bump Gabe's. "Congrats, man. I'm happy for you. Take care of Mia and you'll never have to worry about Jace and I having your back."

Jace nodded.

"So what was up your ass earlier?" Gabe asked.

Ash blinked, realizing Gabe was talking to him. He shifted uncomfortably in his chair as Jace turned his attention to Ash as well.

"Nothing," he said. "Just had shit to do."

"You looked pretty intense when you damn near knocked me over coming out of your office," Gabe said. "Anything I should know about before I make myself unavailable for two weeks?"

"It had nothing to do with business," Ash said in an even tone. "And that's all you need to worry about."

"Fuck," Jace muttered. "Is it your goddamn family again? Are they still jacking you around? Thought you told them to fuck off for good after the dinner with the old man."

Ash shook his head. "Haven't spoken to any of them in weeks. I saw the old man. Did my good deed. Played the dutiful grandson. Then told my parents to fuck off."

Gabe chuckled. "Would have loved to have been a fly on the wall for that."

Jace was still scowling. Ash appreciated the fact that his friends got so pissed off on his behalf when his family started their crap. Gabe and Jace had always had his back when it came to his family, but more recently, he'd not wanted them involved. He didn't want Mia or Bethany exposed to his family's venom. Especially Bethany, who was a hell of a lot more vulnerable and would have been an instant target for their vitriol.

"You sure they're not giving you shit?" Jace demanded. "Gabe will be out of town on his honeymoon, but Bethany and I are here. You know we'll stand with you."

"I'm a grown boy now," Ash drawled. "I can stand up to mommy and daddy without help. But I appreciate it. And no, they aren't giving me shit. They've been suspiciously quiet. I'm just waiting for the other shoe to drop."

"Well, if everything's okay, and you two are going to be okay running the ship without me for the next two weeks, I'm heading home to Mia. Sooner this night is over with, the sooner she's my wife and the sooner we take off on that honeymoon," Gabe said.

"Speaking of running the ship," Ash cut in before everyone rose to go their separate ways. "You never did say why we dropped Charles Willis like a hot potato. With him out and losing the other two investors, we barely managed to salvage the Paris deal. Anything you haven't shared with us?"

Gabe's expression became shuttered, his lips drawn into a tight line. Jace looked questioningly at Gabe as well. All Gabe had shared at the time was that Willis was out and then the other two dropped without explanation as well, one of whom was a wealthy Texan who they couldn't afford to lose. But with the scramble to replace those investors, neither Jace nor Ash had asked questions. They'd knuckled down, did what had to be done to get back on track.

"He wasn't right for the job," Gabe said darkly. "I knew it in Paris when we met. Knew I wouldn't work with him, no matter his bid. Business decision. It was what was best for the company. My call. I know you're my partners, but we didn't have time to get into the whys and wherefores. We needed to move to get the situation in hand and the plans back on track."

Jace frowned. It was evident he didn't quite swallow Gabe's explanation. It didn't wash with Ash either, but Gabe's face was implacable. And him saying it was a business decision was bullshit. It was personal. Ash didn't know what the hell had gone on in Paris, but whatever it was had turned Gabe solidly against Charles Willis. The man had dropped off the face of the earth after being cut loose from HCM's operations.

Ash shrugged. All he cared was that they'd salvaged the whole bloody mess. He wasn't going to get into what had gotten Gabe's underwear in a knot over the whole thing. It was behind them. No harm, no foul.

"Now if we're done, I'd really like to get home to my future wife," Gabe drawled.

Gabe rose and Jace followed suit. Christ, they really were getting old. It wasn't even ten yet, and they were already folding up the tent for the night and schlepping home. But then, they had women to go home to. In their position, he wouldn't be so eager to spend a night out with friends either.

He walked out with them and watched as Gabe got into his car. Jace turned to Ash. "Want a ride back to your place or is your driver on standby?"

Ash hesitated. He wasn't in the mood to talk, and, no doubt, after Gabe's questions, Jace's curiosity would be piqued. But if he refused the ride, Jace would be even more convinced that something was bugging him. It would be better if Ash just sucked it up and took the ride.

"How's Bethany doing?" Ash asked, when they'd gotten in. He figured if he got Jace talking about Bethany, he wouldn't pry into Ash's business.

Jace's expression eased into a smile. "She's doing good. Excited about going to school."

"What's the latest on Kingston? He still being a dumbass?"

Jack Kingston was Bethany's foster brother. He was also the man who damn near killed Bethany and was currently in rehab. Personally Ash thought Jace had gone far too easy on the other man. Ash would have beat the shit out of him and then nailed his ass to the wall, but in an effort not to hurt Bethany any more than she already had been, Jace had helped Jack get a plea bargain that included rehab and probation.

"We don't hear from him, and I'm good with that," Jace said.

Ash arched an eyebrow. "But is Bethany good with it?"

Jace sighed. "She has good days and bad. When I can keep her focused on me and us, things are good. When she has time to think, she worries. She knows he fucked up, and she hasn't gotten over that. I doubt she ever will. But she still loves him and is sick over what he's done."

"That sucks," Ash murmured.

"Yeah."

They pulled up to Ash's building, and Ash was relieved that Jace hadn't had time to pry into his head. Because he would. Just like Ash would do to him if he sensed something off about Jace. But knowing he'd do the same didn't mean he was lining up to have Jace do it to him. It made him a flaming hypocrite, but oh well.

"See you tomorrow, then?" Jace asked as Ash started out of the car.

"Yeah, wouldn't miss it. You walking Mia down the aisle?"

Jace's face softened. "Yeah."

"Shouldn't we have had a rehearsal or some shit like that?" Ash asked.

Granted, his experiences with weddings had been confined to Gabe's first, but rehearsals were normal for weddings the scale of Gabe's and Mia's, surely.

Jace laughed. "Yeah, man, it was last night. You didn't show. Not that you have to do anything but stand there with Gabe. Mia's going to give you shit about ducking out. I covered for you and said you had shit with work and that you stayed so Gabe could make the rehearsal. That appeased her."

"Christ," Ash said. "I feel like an ass now. I swear I didn't remember. I wouldn't have remembered the wedding was tomorrow if I hadn't seen Gabe at the office earlier."

"You haven't been around much lately," Jace said, curiosity in his voice. "Everything okay with you? Work hasn't been that bad, unless there's something you're not telling me. Things have been pretty damn quiet since Gabe went on a tear trying to get everything worked out before he left for his honeymoon."

"Just been preoccupied, man. No big deal."

Jace leaned forward before Ash could close the door. "Look, I know things have been . . . different. Ever since me and Bethany. I get that. But I don't want things to change, Ash. You're family."

"Things did change," Ash said softly. "Nothing to be done about it. I'm dealing. Don't make it an issue that it isn't, Jace. Be happy and make Bethany happy."

"Are we cool?" Jace asked. "Because you've been off lately. And it's not just me noticing."

Ash cracked a smile. "Yeah, man, we're cool. Stop acting like a goddamn nanny. Go home to your woman. I'll see you tomorrow in my goddamn tuxedo. Only for Mia would I do this shit."

Jace laughed. "Yeah, tell me about it. Bethany and I are so eloping."

"Set a date yet?"

While Jace and Bethany had become engaged at Bethany's twenty-fourth birthday party, they hadn't set a date, at least not to Ash's knowledge. But then, he'd been so far out of the loop lately that it was possible he just didn't know about it.

"Not yet," Jace said. "Was waiting until this shit with Jack blew over. I don't want that hanging over her head when we get married. After he gets out of rehab and gets his shit sorted, I'll plan a trip somewhere and we'll get married on a beach."

"Sounds great. See you tomorrow, okay?"

Ash closed the door and slapped the side to signal the driver to pull away before he turned and walked into his apartment building.

Once inside his apartment, he walked into his bedroom and his gaze fell on the painting the art dealer had pulled from the back. The one that was still wrapped and not on display.

The others he'd put against the wall in the living room, but he'd put this one in his bedroom, intending to look at it when he got home. Now curiosity was eating at him, so he carefully pulled away the wrapping and turned it over.

"Holy shit," he breathed.

It was . . . stunning. Provocative and sexy as hell.

It was *her*.

Or rather her tattoo, or what he imagined had to be her tattoo. Granted he'd only gotten a glimpse when she'd bared a thin strip of her waist, but this was in the right place and it resembled the flowery vine.

The painting was of a nude woman's profile. One hip was presented, arms covering her breasts, but the barest hint of one soft mound peeked tantalizingly from underneath her upper arm. And down her entire side was a colorful, flowery tattoo. It curved over her hip and disappeared between her legs.

It had to be on the inside of one thigh and now he was dying to know if this was an exact replica of her tattoo. The one he'd seen on her body. Jesus, but he was dying to know. Dying to trace the lines with his fingers and his tongue.

He stared at the painting, absorbing every detail. The art dealer had been a fool not to display this one. Had he even looked at it? It was erotic as hell and yet still tasteful.

Long blond hair flowed down her back, the ends lifted as if she was caught in a breeze. Her arms were hugged to her body, her fingertips splayed over the arm pressing down over her breast.

Delicate. Utterly feminine. And so damn beautiful it made his balls ache.

Holy fuck but he was obsessed with a woman he'd only met in person one time. And this painting wasn't helping a damn bit.

Tomorrow this was getting framed and it was going over his bed so he'd see it every time he entered his bedroom. Or, even better, he'd put it on the wall opposite his bed so it would be the first thing he saw when he woke up in the morning and the last thing he saw before he went to sleep at night.

Yeah, he wasn't just obsessed. He was all sorts of fucked up over this woman. He had to get a grip.

Johnny was bringing her jewelry by the office day after tomorrow since the entire business would be shut down for Gabe's wedding tomorrow. Ash then had to figure out how he was going to get it back to her. He could just mail it to her, but then he wouldn't see her. And he definitely planned on seeing her again. Soon.

# chapter four

Ash sat in his office the day after Gabe's wedding and studied the small box containing the jewelry that Josie had pawned. He examined each piece before carefully returning it to the tissue so it wouldn't get damaged.

It was quality. He wasn't an expert but it looked vintage and real. Definitely not fake. It was worth far more than Josie had pawned it for, and the pawnbroker knew it, judging by the price it had cost Ash to get it back.

He didn't like the desperation in that single act. Of pawning jewelry for a fast buck and taking far less than it was worth because she had no other choice. He was going to give that choice back to her. But other choices? Not so much. Not if he had anything to say about it.

It made him arrogant and demanding, but he knew himself to be both, so it didn't bother him. It was who he was. He knew what he wanted, and he wanted Josie. Now he just had to put the ball in motion.

His intercom buzzed and he jerked his head up in irritation.

"Mr. McIntyre, your sister is here to see you," Eleanor, his receptionist, said in a crisp voice that sounded pissed off.

But then it wasn't a secret how Ash—and Gabe and Jace—felt

about his family. Eleanor had been with them for years and it likely hadn't pleased her to buzz him with this kind of information.

What the fuck was Brittany doing here? Had his mother resorted to having his sister do her dirty work for her? He could feel his blood pressure rise, even knowing he had to stop allowing them this kind of power over him.

"Send her in," Ash said grimly.

No way he was going to air family shit outside the privacy of his office. Whatever it was Brittany wanted, Ash would give her a few minutes and then let her know she wasn't welcome at his office. None of his family was, and for that matter, none of them had ever stepped inside the HCM offices. They saved their venom for holidays and family get-togethers.

If they ever set foot inside the HCM offices, they'd be forced to acknowledge his success instead of treating it like a dirty secret no one talked about. They'd be forced to see firsthand that he didn't need them and he'd succeeded without their help or influence. No way they were going to do either.

A soft knock sounded at his door and he voiced a "come in."

The door slowly opened and his sister walked in, apprehension written all over her features. She looked more than nervous. She looked terrified.

"Ash?" she asked softly. "Can I talk to you for a minute?"

Brittany was a replica of his mother. Not that his mother wasn't a beautiful woman. She was. And Brittany was every bit as beautiful, if not more so, than their mother. The only problem was his mother was ugly on the inside and it forever marred his perception of her looks. Because he knew what resided behind that pretty face. It was a cold and calculating mind. He firmly believed she was incapable of loving anyone but herself. It was a mystery to him why she'd ever had children. And not just one, but four.

Besides Brittany, Ash had two older siblings. Both brothers and both firmly under the grasp of their mother and father. Though younger, Brittany was approaching thirty. Or maybe she'd turned thirty already? He couldn't remember and he didn't spare an ounce of sadness over that fact. And she was as solidly under the family thumb as their brothers. Perhaps even more so.

Their mother had handpicked Brittany's husband. An older guy she'd married Brittany off to when she was barely out of college. Wealthy. Influential. All the right connections. The marriage had barely lasted two years and Ash's mother blamed that squarely on Brittany. Never mind that in Ash's digging, he'd found a hell of a lot of skeletons in Robert Hanover's closet.

He was not a man he'd want his sister—or any woman— married to. But Brittany had meekly submitted to her mother's desires despite Ash's warning to her that Robert was not the man he seemed.

At least she'd had the balls to get out of the marriage. That had surprised him.

"What's up?" Ash asked in an even tone.

He gestured for her to sit in the chair facing his desk. She eased into it, perched gingerly on the edge, nervousness and uncertainty evident in her body language.

"I need your help," she breathed out.

He cocked one eyebrow upward. "What's wrong? Get into an argument with mommy dearest?"

Anger flashed in Brittany's eyes as she stared back at Ash.

"Please don't, Ash. I know I deserve your mockery and scorn. I deserve a lot of things. But I want out. And I need your help to do that. It shames me to have to come and beg for help from you, but I don't know where else to go or who else to turn to. If I go to Grandpa, he'd just tell Mom and he probably wouldn't help me anyway. You're his favorite. He can't stand the rest of us."

Surprise gripped him at the earnestness—and urgency—in her tone. He leaned forward, his gaze narrowing at her.

"You want out. What does that mean exactly, Brittany?"

"I want away from them," she said shakily. "All of them."

"What the hell did they do to you?" Ash demanded.

She shook her head. "Nothing. I mean nothing more than usual. You know how they are, Ash. I've always envied you so much. You tell them to fuck off and you've made your own way. All I've done is marry a man my mother wanted me to, try to make the best of a bad situation and fail miserably. I got nothing in the divorce and I was okay with that. I just wanted out. But I have nothing without Mom and Dad's help. And I don't want it anymore. Because their help comes with strings. I'm thirty years old and what do I have to show for my life? No life, no money. Nothing."

The desolation in her voice hit Ash deep. He knew exactly what she meant. It could have easily been him in this same situation. His brothers certainly were. He didn't like the shadows in her eyes and the beaten down look she currently wore. As much as she'd been a bitch before, mimicking their mother, he'd take that over this whipped-puppy look she now had.

"What do you want to do?" he asked quietly.

"Is it pathetic that I don't know? I don't even know where to start. I came to you because I had no one else to go to. My friends aren't friends when the chips are down. They're more than willing to support me when things are good, but I can't count on them for real support."

"I'll help you," he said in an even tone. "Jace owns an apartment that Mia used to live in, and more recently his fiancée lived there. But it's empty again and just sitting there. I can probably buy it from him or at least use it until we get you situated somewhere else."

Her eyes widened in shock.

"Do you have a job?" he asked.

She flushed and dropped her gaze.

"I'm not criticizing, Brittany," he said softly. "I'm asking so I know what kind of help you need."

She shook her head. "No. I've been living with Mom and Dad. It's not that I don't want to work, but what am I good at?"

"You could be good at a lot of things," Ash said. "You're smart. You have a degree. You're just afraid to try and get out there in the real world."

She nodded slowly.

"I can get you a position in one of the hotels, but Brittany, you need to know. It would be a real job with real responsibilities. I can pull strings to get you hired, but if you aren't doing the job, you don't get to keep it. Understand?"

"I understand and thank you, Ash. I don't know what to say. We—I—have been horrible to you." Tears filled her eyes as she stared earnestly back at Ash. "They hate you because they can't control you. And I've let them control me. Now that I'm not going to do that anymore, they're going to hate me too."

Ash reached across the desk and curled his hand around hers, squeezing reassuringly.

"You don't need them, Brittany. You're young and smart. You can make it on your own. You just need a little help to do that. But be prepared. You're going to have to be strong. Our mother is a bitch, and she won't hesitate to use every weapon in her arsenal on you as soon as she figures out what you're doing."

"Thanks," she whispered. "I'll pay you back somehow, Ash. I swear it."

He squeezed her hand again. "The best thing you can do for me is to live your own life and don't let them beat you down again. I'll help. I'll do what I can to shield you from that shit. But it's going to take a lot of strength on your part as well. I'd like to think we could actually be family again."

She curled both her hands around his, her eyes shining as she locked gazes with him. "I'd like that too, Ash."

"Let me call Jace and see where he stands with the apartment. If we can't get you into that one, we'll have to take a look at what else is out there. Do you need me to go with you to get your stuff from Mom and Dad's?"

She shook her head. "I packed everything. My clothes and stuff I mean. Nothing else to pack. I brought it with me. My suitcases are in the reception area here. I took a cab to your office. Wasn't sure what I was going to do if you refused to see me."

"Okay, then let me call Jace and we'll get your bags. For tonight I'll put you up in our hotel. I'm sure the apartment will need restocking. I'll work on that today and also set up an account for you and deposit enough cash to get you through to your first paycheck. Take a few days to settle in and then come back to see me about that job. By then I'll have something lined up for you."

She rose and then was suddenly around the desk, throwing her arms around his neck. He caught her, rising from his chair, still holding on to her so she didn't fall, and he returned her hug.

"You're the best, Ash. God I've missed you. I'm so sorry for the way I've treated you. You have every right to kick me out and never see me again. I'll never forget what you're doing for me. Never."

The fervency in her voice made Ash smile as he patiently waited for the hugfest to be over. Who would have thought today would bring his sister into his office for a family reunion of sorts. Gabe and Jace weren't going to believe this one. Although it would be two weeks before Gabe knew anything.

Jace would likely think he'd lost his mind for helping his sister out. But Ash couldn't just turn his back on her. Even if it was what his family had done to him. Brittany was still his little sister and perhaps this would be a new page for them. Ash didn't like the estrangement between him and his family. But they'd given him no choice. He wanted what everyone else took for granted. A solid family unit. People who had his back. People who loved and supported him unconditionally.

He had that with Gabe and Jace and now Mia and Bethany. But he'd never had it with his own blood. Maybe Brittany would change all of that. Even if they'd never be one big happy family, he and his sister could at least have a relationship.

"I'll have my driver take you to the hotel. I'll ask Eleanor to have him come up and get your bags. She'll also call over to make sure they have a room ready for you when you get there. You'll need to go to the bank to set up your account. I'll have Eleanor help you out with that too. But for now take it easy, try to get some rest and tomorrow we'll move you into an apartment."

He smiled indulgently when she hugged him again. She hastily wiped at a tear as she turned away.

"This means a lot, Ash. It means *everything*. And I swear I'll make this up to you."

"Just be happy and don't let them take you back down," Ash said in a serious tone. "She won't let go that easy, Brittany. You have to know that and you have to be prepared for it. If she pulls any shit, you come to me and I'll sort it out."

Brittany smiled wanly and then started for the door. She paused, her hand gripping the doorknob.

"I've always admired you, Ash. And if I'm honest, I've always been jealous. But you're not what they say you are. I hate them for what they did to you. To me. And I hate myself for letting them."

"They aren't worth your hatred," Ash said quietly. "Don't give them that kind of power over you. Not saying it's going to be easy. But you can't let them knock you down and keep you down."

She nodded and then smiled faintly. "I'll see you soon. I'd like that, I mean. Maybe dinner. Or I can cook something at the apartment for just the two of us."

"I'd like that too," he said sincerely. "Take care of yourself, Brittany. And if you need anything, call me."

As soon as she walked out of his door, he buzzed Eleanor and gave her the rundown on what he needed. After instructing her to assist Brittany in opening a bank account, he told her to give him the account number as soon as Brittany had it so he could wire funds.

What a day. So Brittany had a backbone after all. It had taken her long enough, but better late than never. Their two older brothers had never had the balls or the desire to stand up to their parents and the old man. Ash had no use for them. Both in their forties and neither one able to support himself or his own family. Hell, Ash had nieces and nephews he'd rarely ever seen. He knew nothing about his sisters-in-law other than they were married to weak men still firmly under the thumb of his parents.

That wasn't going to be him. It would never be him. And now, if he had anything to say about it, neither would it be Brittany.

It remained to be seen if she'd really have the fortitude to make a clean break and slip out from under the control of their parents. But he was more than happy to help her if that was truly her goal. She was young and beautiful. She was smart even if she'd made some spectacularly bad choices. She had more than enough time to turn it around and get her life on the right path.

Everyone made mistakes, and everyone deserved the chance to make up for them. He just hoped to hell Brittany would turn it around now and get her head on straight.

He opened his drawer to look at the box of jewelry he'd hastily shoved inside when Eleanor had buzzed him about Brittany's arrival. He brushed one finger over the edge as he thoughtfully stared down at it.

Brittany was squared away, and now it was time to focus on his primary preoccupation.

Josie.

# chapter five

"What do you mean you sold them already?" Josie asked, her voice rising as she stared at the pawnbroker she'd visited several days earlier to sell her mother's jewelry.

He surveyed her calmly. "I sold them. Had a customer who liked the stuff."

Josie twisted her hands in agitation. "Can you give me an address? A name? Phone number, anything? I'd like to buy it back."

"You had the option to pawn it, Miss Carlysle," the man said patiently. "I specifically asked if you preferred a loan with the option of getting your items back."

"But the loan wouldn't have been enough," she argued. "I needed the money *then*. I couldn't wait. But it's different now. I have the money and I have to get my mother's jewelry back! It's all I have left from her. It was my grandmother's. Oh God, I can't believe you sold it so quickly."

The man shot her a look of sympathy but remained silent. Josie was sure he thought he was dealing with a crazy woman.

"Can you give me the information of the person you sold it to?" she asked again in desperation.

"I think you know I can't do that," the man said.

She wiped a hand over her face in agitation. If only she'd waited another day. But how on earth could she have predicted that someone would walk into the art gallery and fall in love with her work—all if it—and buy it for more than the dealer was asking for? It was all so crazy. Not that she wasn't extremely grateful for her good fortune, but if only she'd waited one more day she wouldn't have pawned her mother's jewelry and she wouldn't be standing in a pawnshop desperate to get it back.

"Will you at least contact the person for me and give them my phone number? You could ask them to call me. Tell them I'll pay double what they paid for it. I *have* to get it back."

He sighed and then shoved a piece of paper with a pen across the counter toward her. "I can't promise anything, but write down your info and I'll pass it along. I don't normally do this kind of thing. Once it's sold, it's out of my hands. You relinquished any claim when you sold the jewelry to me."

"I know, I know," Josie said as she hurriedly jotted down her name and number. "I'm not saying it's your fault or that you're to blame. I have only myself to blame for acting so rashly. But I'd really appreciate it if you could just give the person a call and let them know how desperate I am to get the pieces back."

He shrugged as she shoved the paper back to him. "I'll do what I can."

"Thank you," she whispered.

She turned to walk out, her heart heavy. She should have been elated. Her artwork had sold. All of it! And Mr. Downing had told her to bring more, whatever she wanted. He had an interested buyer, and though he hadn't divulged any information about the buyer, he'd told her that the party was interested in whatever else she brought in.

The only thing marring the entire day was the fact that her mother's jewelry was gone. She had no idea where or who had bought it or if she'd ever get it back. She'd been so happy when Mr. Downing had given her that check. Far more than she'd ever hoped for. It was enough to pay her rent and buy groceries for a few months. Plenty of time for her to get other pieces to the gallery. And most importantly, it had been enough money to buy back the jewelry she'd sold, even though she knew it would cost her more than she'd gotten from the sale.

The pawnshop had been the very first place she'd gone after depositing the check into her bank account. And she'd sworn to herself that no matter what, she'd never part with the jewelry again.

Only now it was gone, and so was the last link to her mother.

She left the shop, stepping onto the busy street, uncertain of where exactly she was going next. As she turned to the right, she was stopped by a familiar face. She blinked as she stared back at the man she'd met in the park several days earlier. He was standing there, not looking surprised. In fact, he looked as though he'd been waiting for her. Crazy thought, but she didn't get the impression he was startled at all by the unexpected meeting.

"Josie," he murmured.

"H-hello," she stammered out.

"I believe I have something that belonged to you."

He held out an opened box and as soon as she saw inside, her breath caught and stilled in her chest.

She raised her gaze back to him in confusion.

"How did you get this? I don't understand. How could you have possibly gotten it? How did you know?"

He smiled, but his eyes were steely. No hint of a smile in those green eyes.

"I bought it after you sold it to the pawnshop. I'm guessing since you just came out of there that you want it back."

"Yes, of course I want it back. But that doesn't answer the question as to how *you* got it."

He lifted an eyebrow. "I just told you. I bought it after you sold it."

She shook her head impatiently and it was then his gaze came to rest at her throat. Her bare throat. His eyes glittered with instant interest. She lifted a hand automatically to where the collar had once rested.

He'd know that she'd worn it awhile. There was a thin band of paler skin from where the necklace had been.

"It doesn't explain how you *knew* about it," she said huskily.

"Does it matter?" he asked mildly.

"Yes, it does! Have you been following me?"

"Me personally? No."

"It's supposed to make me feel better that you had someone *else* following me?" she demanded. "That's just . . . *creepy*!"

"Do you want the jewelry back?" he asked bluntly.

"Of course I do," she said in irritation. "How much do you want for it?"

"I don't want money."

She took a step back, looking warily up at him. They were on a public street and there were people all around them, but that didn't mean a whole lot if he was some deranged lunatic out to do her harm.

"Then what *do* you want?"

"Dinner. Tonight. I'll bring the jewelry and you can have it. All I want in return is your company for the evening."

She shook her head. "No way. I don't know you. I know nothing about you."

He smiled patiently. "That's what dinner is for. So you get to know me better. And I can get to know you better."

"You obviously know a hell of a lot about me," she snapped. "Including where to find me and where I've been and what I've been doing."

"Why aren't you wearing the collar?" he asked, his gaze once more raking across her throat.

His stare made her feel vulnerable. Like she was completely undressed in front of him.

This time she laid her splayed hand over her throat as if trying to hide the bare expanse of her skin from his gaze.

"I don't think that's any of your business," she said in a low voice.

"I intend to make it my business."

Her eyes widened. "Do you honestly think I'm going to agree to go to dinner with you? You've been stalking me, or rather you've had me stalked. You're asking personal questions and you're basically blackmailing me for the return of my mother's jewelry."

"So it belonged to your mother," he said softly. "It must be important to you."

Pain stabbed into her chest and she had to suck in a breath to steady herself.

"Yes. Yes, it does," she said in a quiet voice. "I hated having to sell it. If only I'd waited a day. I have to get it back. It's the only thing I have left of her. Tell me what you paid and I'll give you the money. Please."

"I don't want your money, Josie. I want your time. Dinner tonight. Public place. No strings. I bring the jewelry. You just bring yourself."

"And after? Will you leave me alone?"

"Can't promise that," he said mildly. "I go after what I want. If I gave up every time an obstacle was thrown into my path, I wouldn't be very successful now would I?"

"You don't know me," she said in frustration. "You don't want me. How could you? You know nothing about me."

"Which is why I want to have dinner with you tonight," he said patiently.

But she could tell he was fast losing his patience. His eyes simmered with impatience even as his tone remained even. He was clearly a man used to getting his own way. She could tell that just by looking at him. Why the hell would he want her, though? What could she possibly have that he'd want?

He was a man who wouldn't have to look far for any woman. They probably lined up outside his door at any given time. He was obviously wealthy. He had that polished *GQ* look that screamed wealth and privilege. And he had a quiet confidence—arrogance—about him that told her he not only got what he wanted, but that he knew it too.

Arrogance wasn't a quality she was particularly attracted to. But on him, it looked good. It fit him. Just like his clothing and his entire demeanor. And there was something about that gaze that turned her inside out. It had the very first time they'd met. Her stomach had performed somersaults, and he'd made her consider things she'd never considered before. He'd made her *want* things she'd never wanted or realized she wanted before.

And she hated him for that. For overturning her carefully ordered existence. No, it wasn't that well ordered. She didn't have a routine and she liked it that way. But she was comfortable in her life, knew who and what she was. Until him. Until that meeting in the park that had made her question everything about herself.

He was not a man who would be quiet. He'd turn her entire world upside down the minute she allowed him access. She knew that as solidly as she knew anything else in her life. He was someone who liked—demanded—control. It was evident in the way he spoke, the way he carried himself. He'd latched onto the significance of that collar. He'd known what it meant and he spoke as though he had vast experience in the kind of lifestyle that collar signified.

But he wouldn't be like Michael. Nothing like him at all. And that scared her even as it intrigued her at the same time. She was curious—she wouldn't deny that. She wouldn't even deny that he'd made her question everything about herself—and her relationship with Michael. That *he* was the reason why she wasn't wearing that collar any longer.

And now he was standing in front of her, holding her mother's jewelry, demanding dinner with her in return for the jewelry. But his gaze promised a whole lot more. She'd be a fool to think he'd be satisfied with only dinner.

She wasn't an idiot. She'd felt the attraction—that spark— between them. Knew he'd felt it too. As inexplicable as it was that he'd find anything about her interesting, she knew that he was absolutely interested. But for how long? Women like her didn't hold the attention of men like him long term. And she had no desire to be his temporary plaything. A challenge he felt compelled to overcome.

"Josie?" he prompted. "Dinner? Tonight?"

She sighed, dropping her gaze in agitation to the box he still held in his hand. She wanted the jewelry back. It was priceless to her. She should be relieved he didn't want money from her. The money she'd received from the sale of her art would go a long way in helping her over the next months. But instead she found herself wishing that he'd just take the money, give her the jewelry and walk away. Out of her life. Because this was a man who would shake everything up. No doubt about it.

All he wanted was dinner. A simple date. She'd had dates. A night out. Food. A little conversation. She could walk away then and make it clear she didn't want to see him again.

"All right," she finally conceded. "Where and what time?"

"I'll pick you up at seven."

She shook her head. "No. I'll meet you there. Just tell me the place and time."

He chuckled. "So difficult. I'll concede on this point, but I warn you now. It's likely the last concession I'll make where you're concerned."

Her eyes narrowed. "You aren't making a very good case for me to go to dinner with you."

The corner of his mouth lifted. "Just shooting you straight, Josie."

"Time? Place?" she prompted.

"Seven thirty," he answered softly. "Bentley Hotel. I'll meet you in the lobby."

"And you'll bring the jewelry with you?"

He glanced down at the box in his hands and then back up to her, amusement twinkling in his eyes. "If I weren't sure you'd bail on tonight, I'd give you the jewelry now. I have no interest in keeping something that evidently means so much to you. But if it gets you to dinner tonight then I'll keep it as collateral. And yes, I'll bring it. I don't break my promises, Josie. Dinner with me, you get the jewelry. No matter what else happens."

She breathed out, her shoulders sagging in relief. "Okay then. I'll see you at seven thirty."

He reached out to touch her cheek, his fingers just grazing her jaw. "I'm looking forward to it. We have a lot to discuss."

As he said the last, he let his hand drift downward until it touched the hollow of her throat where the collar had once rested. There was no mistaking his meaning. He wanted to know her status. What had happened to the collar. And why she was no longer wearing it.

She sighed and then turned to walk away. How could she possibly explain that *he* was what had happened?

## chapter six

Ash checked his watch as he stood in the lobby of the Bentley Hotel, one of the many hotels owned by HCM. He let out his breath in irritation as his gaze tracked toward the entrance once again.

She was late.

Or perhaps she wasn't coming.

He would have bet any amount of money on her showing up. Her mother's jewelry obviously meant a great deal to her, and while he'd been a complete bastard to blackmail her into having dinner with him, he couldn't muster any real regret. Not if it got him what he wanted.

A few hours in Josie's company.

He had a dozen questions simmering on his lips. He wanted to know why she wasn't wearing the collar anymore. He wanted to know if the guy who'd given it to her was out of the picture now. While it wouldn't change his plans if she hadn't cut the other guy loose, it would certainly make things a hell of a lot easier for him if she weren't in a relationship.

At a quarter to eight, Ash straightened, realization slowly creeping in that she wasn't coming. Disappointment surged in his veins. Not a common sensation for him. But if she thought he would be deterred by being stood up, she was wrong. It only hardened his resolve.

He was about to pick up the phone to call for his driver when Josie burst through the front entrance to the hotel. Her cheeks were red and her hair was askew, as if she'd been hurrying and the wind had played havoc with the long tresses.

When her gaze lighted on him, she paused, standing several feet away as they locked eyes. He found himself walking toward her when, normally, he wouldn't be the first to make a move. People came to him. Not the other way around. And yet, he wanted to close in before she changed her mind and bolted back out the door.

"Josie," he greeted smoothly.

"Sorry I'm late," she said breathlessly. "I was painting. Got caught up in what I was doing and completely forgot the time."

He glanced at the oversized bag hanging from her shoulder and the paint smudges on her fingertips. Then he took in the rest of her, memorizing every detail, right down to her toes.

"That's quite all right. They'll hold our table," he said. "Would you like to eat now or have a drink first?"

She pulled a face. "I'm not much of a drinker. I mean, I don't have anything against it, and I do drink on occasion, but I'm rather finicky and I drink frou-frou girly drinks. But I love an occasional glass of wine."

He chuckled. "You'd fit right in with Mia and Bethany and their girls."

She cocked her head to the side. "Who are Mia and Bethany?"

He reached to take her arm, tucking it over his as he guided her toward the restaurant.

"Mia is the wife of one of my business partners, Gabe, and she's the sister of my other business partner, Jace. Bethany is engaged to Jace."

"Sounds like one big happy family," she murmured.

"Of sorts."

They arrived at the restaurant and the maître d' immediately ushered them to the table always reserved for himself or Gabe or Jace when they chose to eat here.

Josie sat across from Ash, but she didn't fully relax. She was perched on the edge of her seat and her gaze kept darting left and right and beyond Ash. She looked ill at ease and like she'd rather be anywhere but here with him. His ego was taking one hell of a beating. Women didn't normally have to be blackmailed in order to agree to a date with him.

"Would you like wine?" he asked when a waiter immediately appeared.

She shook her head. "No. Water will be fine. Thank you."

"Make that two," Ash murmured to the waiter.

"Don't let me keep you from enjoying wine if that's what you prefer," she said. "I just don't want to drink and then have to get back home. Alcohol makes me pretty fuzzy. Last thing I need to do is be stumbling around Manhattan after dark."

"So you can't hold your liquor and when you do imbibe, you drink girly drinks. I'll have to remember that."

Her lips twitched and her eyes flashed. He'd almost gotten a smile out of her. Was he such an ogre? He was used to women falling for his charm, although in Josie's defense he hadn't exactly been charming in her presence. Something about her brought his caveman instincts roaring to the surface. He was lucky he could form coherent sentences without growling, beating his chest and dragging her back to his cave by her hair.

That would go over well . . .

Not only would she have his balls, he'd never see her again.

The waiter took their orders and then quickly disappeared. Josie glanced up, a question in her eyes as soon as they were alone.

"Did you bring the jewelry?" she asked softly.

He reached into the breast pocket of his dinner jacket and pulled out a small velvet drawstring bag. Placing it on the table, he slid it across to her, but held on when she would have retrieved it.

"The deal was dinner," he said. "I'll give you the jewelry now and hope you don't make a break for it the minute it's in your possession."

She flushed, whether from embarrassment or guilt he wasn't sure. Maybe she had considered it.

"My ego is taking one hell of a beating," he said, voicing his earlier thought. "Am I that unattractive, Josie? I didn't imagine your response to me in the park. You were as aware of our chemistry as I was. But you act like I'm carrying the plague and you don't want to breathe the same air as I am."

Her fingers curled over the bag, brushing against his. Instant warmth traveled up his arm to his shoulder. At just her touch. Such a simple thing. Nothing behind it. It was incidental and yet the air was instantly charged with awareness. No, he wasn't the only one who felt it, but he was the only one embracing it.

"I think you know you aren't unattractive," she said lightly. "I doubt you need me to tell you that. I'm sure you hear it all the time. Women probably fall over themselves to compliment you."

"I don't give a damn what other women are thinking," he said bluntly. "I'm more concerned with what you think."

She carefully drew her hand back, the bag with the jewelry tightly fisted in her grasp, as if she were afraid he'd prevent her from taking it. When he made no move to intercept it, she quickly opened the bag a nd gently pulled out the two rings, a necklace and a bracelet.

Relief was evident in her eyes. The aqua pools lit up as she lovingly traced the lines of the jewelry. A faraway look entered her eyes and when she raised her gaze back to Ash, moisture glistened around the edges.

"Thank you for giving my mother back to me," she whispered. "This is all I have of her. My grandmother too. One day I want to pass it down to my daughter. My grandmother and mother were exceptional women. I want my daughter to have this legacy. Though my daughter will never know them, I want her to know about them. Who they were and how important they were to me."

"What happened to her?" Ash asked gently.

Her lips trembled, but she held herself together, her gaze never faltering, though it grew suspiciously brighter with the evidence of tears.

"Cancer," she said, her voice aching with sorrow.

"Recent?" he asked in a quieter tone.

The last thing he wanted was to upset her, but it gave him absurd pleasure that she'd open up to him. Communicate. It was a start. The start of something more permanent if he had his way. And he had every intention of getting his way. It was just going to require a great deal more patience than he was used to having to employ.

Adrenaline spiked, burning through his veins. She was a challenge. One he looked forward to conquering. It had been a long time since he'd been excited about anything. And Josie definitely excited him.

"Two years ago," Josie said, sadness creeping into those beautiful eyes. "But she was ill for a lot longer. In the end . . ." She broke off, her voice cracking at the very last.

"In the end what?" he prompted gently.

"In the end it was a relief even though I was devastated over having to let go and say good-bye. She was in so much pain. It hurt to see her like that. It hurt her. She hated for me to see her that way, to have to take care of her. She worried for so long that she was taking up too much of my life, that she was holding me back and saddling me with the responsibility of taking care of her. But God, she was my mother. I would have done anything for her. I never regretted a single moment of our time together. And in the end, she was ready to go. She'd fought for so long and so hard. She was exhausted and no longer had the strength to fight. That was the hardest for me. To watch my kick-ass mom slowly fade. I just wanted her pain to be over and for her to have peace. So when she passed away, there was relief. And I know that sounds horrible."

He shook his head. "Not horrible, Josie. Human. She was your mother and you loved her. No one likes to see their loved ones endure pain and heartache."

Josie nodded and wiped at her eye with the back of her hand. Her fingers were shaking when she lowered her hand back to the table.

"Wow, not great dinner conversation, right? Sorry to babble on like that."

"I asked," he said simply. "What about your father? Do you have any siblings or are you an only child?"

She blew out an unhappy sigh. "I'm an only child. My parents wanted more, but my mother couldn't have any more after me. She had cancer once before and with all the treatments, not only could she not bear another child, but she was too weakened by the whole process. I—we—thought she'd kicked it, you know? She went twenty years in remission and then it came back. Much more pervasive this time. She didn't respond to treatment like she did before."

She shook her head. "Sorry. There I go again."

He reached across the table and slid his hand over hers. "We're having a conversation, Josie. It's what two people do when they go out on a date. Stop apologizing. If I wasn't interested, I wouldn't have asked. However, if it's too painful a subject, we can certainly talk about other things. But I'm interested in every part of you. I very much want to hear about you, your life, your family, whatever makes you tick."

She smiled and didn't pull her hand away from his. A fact he was absurdly triumphant over.

"Now, you said *parents*. Did your father pass away as well?"

Her lips tightened and coldness crept into her gaze, turning the aqua color more to blue. It was like looking at a frost-covered windowpane.

"He left her—*us*—the first time she had cancer. Not right away. He waited until she was well enough to make it on her own and then he split. His reason? He couldn't stand the heartache of losing her to cancer. He didn't want to have to watch her die and so he left instead. Isn't that the biggest bullshit you've ever heard? It makes no sense to me. It's never made any sense that he'd walk away from his wife and child, all because he worried she'd die. He lost her either way, but he lost me too. I never forgave him for that. For leaving us both when we desperately needed him. Especially my mother. Who after undergoing extensive treatment then had to find a job so she could support me and pay the bills."

"Yeah, it is bullshit," Ash said darkly. "So you haven't seen him since? How many years ago was this?"

"Eighteen," she replied, her voice tight. No matter her anger—and he didn't blame her for being angry—there was also hurt in her voice. Betrayal. He rubbed his thumb over the tops of her knuckles in a soothing motion, silently urging her to go on.

He had her talking now and hopefully she'd relax and open up further.

"I was ten years old when he left. For a long time he didn't even try to contact her or me. Then when I graduated high school, he called me. He wanted to send me a graduation gift. I told him where to stick his graduation present."

The more she spoke, the cloudier her eyes got and her lips formed a grimace.

"He didn't contact me again until Mom died."

Tears glittered brightly in her eyes and she used her free hand to rub her thumb along the corner of her eye where a damp trail had formed.

"Sorry," she muttered again. "I don't talk about it at all. I mean I never shared this. It's just sort of all coming out and I didn't realize how angry I still am about it all."

"That's understandable," he said. "That's a long time to keep that shit bottled up."

She nodded her agreement.

"So he contacted you when your mom passed away? Did he know she was sick again?"

"He knew," Josie bit out. "He never came to see her. Never called. Never spoke to her. After she passed away, he called wanting to see me. He said he was sorry about Mom but that he wanted us to be a family. I told him that family doesn't do the kind of shit he pulled and that my family was dead. That was two years ago. He's never tried to contact me again. I don't even know where he lives. He moved a lot after he and Mom divorced. His job takes him away quite a bit."

"Do you ever regret not seeing him?"

She looked startled by the question. "No. Not at all. I don't think I could see him without flying into a rage. Especially right after Mom died. If he'd been there, I think I would have just gone off on him. I was furious and heartbroken. And I was pissed. Pissed that he'd been such a coward and that he hadn't been there for my mom when she needed him most."

"I get it. Believe me I do. I don't see my family. Well, most of them. Recently my sister came to see me but until then I've had nothing to do with any of them."

She cocked her head to the side, studying him. Their hands were still joined and he traced several patterns on her skin, from her knuckles to the top of her wrist and back. He liked touching her. Could touch her all night. And it wasn't sexual. He simply enjoyed the satiny softness of her hands. Fingers that were stained with paint, a different color on each tip.

"What did your family do?" she asked softly.

"Long story. I'll tell you about it sometime. Right now, though, I'm much more interested in hearing about you."

She frowned. "That isn't fair. I've told you about my family. I won't say another word unless you reciprocate."

He chuckled and his hand tightened around hers. Her eyes widened and she glanced down at their joined fingers. Yes, she felt it just as much as he did. But she was fighting it and he wasn't.

"Very well then. I'll give you a tidbit and then it's your turn again."

Her gaze narrowed. "That depends on how worthy I feel your information is. You must give a piece of equal value to the one I gave to you."

"Now that's impossible," he murmured. He looked intently into her eyes, that drowning sensation washing over him. "No information I can give you will be as valuable as you sharing yourself with me."

Her cheeks grew pink and she dropped her gaze. Her hand twitched beneath his, but he held it firmly so she wasn't able to draw it away.

"Maybe you think so," she said in a husky voice. "But perhaps I find information about you to be much more valuable. You see, you have me at a disadvantage. You've checked up on me, had me followed. I have no doubt that you know far more about me than I'm comfortable with. So it's only fair that you even the odds by telling me all your deep, dark secrets."

She was flirting with him. In a shy, adorable way, as if she were uncertain of how to do so. He'd never experienced such an intense surge of . . . excitement. There was lust, absolutely. He wanted her like he hadn't ever wanted a woman before. But there was more. He was interested in her. What made her tick. He wanted inside her head every bit as much as he wanted inside her body. Most of all, he wanted her trust, even if nothing he'd done so far deserved such a gift.

Given time he'd prove himself to her. If she only gave him a chance.

"Deep, dark secrets, huh. I fear you're in for disappointment. I'm frightfully boring. I'm married to my business, and I despise my family almost as much as they despise me. My real family are my business partners and their women."

"Except that your sister came to see you recently. Have you reconciled?"

This time he pulled his hand away, leaning back in his chair. His gaze went beyond Josie for a moment before he allowed it to drift back to her face.

"I suppose you could say that. I'm not completely convinced of her sincerity as of yet. I'd like to think she's finally making a break from the wolf pack, but only time will tell."

"What did they do? To you both?"

Ash sighed. "Gave birth to us? Hell if I know. My mother has zero maternal instinct, and yet she had four of us. It baffles me that a woman that self-serving would continue to have children she considered a burden."

Josie's nose wrinkled and her eyes flashed with sympathy.

"Have you never gotten along with them? Even when you were a child?"

"I rarely saw them when I was a child," he said dryly. "We were packed off to school and only came home during the holidays and even then we had a nanny. More often than not, my mom and dad were off doing their thing. Traveling. Involved in the social scene. My grandfather made a lot of money in his lifetime, but we don't come from old money. We would be considered nouveau riche, a fact my mother has never been able to get over."

"Forgive my assumption, but she sounds horrible."

"It's no assumption. She and my father are both lousy people. Not just lousy parents, but lousy in every aspect. I firmly believe the only reason she had so many children is because my grandfather came from a large family with several siblings, and he wanted my mother to give him several grandchildren. And if nothing else, my mother will not piss off the old man because she depends on him too much for support. So she had us, but he paid for our up-bringing, such as it was. The only times she or Dad ever had time for us was if the old man was present. I don't know what was worse. Them being lousy parents or them acting like caring parents around others."

"That sucks," Josie said. "I adored my mother. And my grand-mother. They were wonderful women. So what happened with your sister? And how old is she?"

"Brittany is the youngest. She's thirty now. My mom married her off right out of college to a much older man who had the right pedigree. The marriage lasted two years and Brittany bailed, get-ting nothing in the divorce settlement. That pissed my mother off even more because in her words, she'd worked damn hard to land a husband for Brittany and the least she could do was suck it up and remain a dutiful wife until her husband died, leaving her a rich widow and the means to funnel money to her parents."

"Wow," Josie whispered. "That's insane. I mean that's stuff from some historical saga. I didn't think there were really people like that in this day and age."

He smiled. "Sorry to burst your bubble."

"So what prompted Brittany's visit?"

"She wants out," he said quietly. "As I said, she got nothing in the divorce and she's been living with my parents ever since. She has a college degree but has never had a job. She came to ask me for help. Primarily financial help, but I think she was looking for an ally. Emotional support as well."

"And did you help her?"

"Of course. I set her up in an apartment, got a bank account opened for her with enough cash to last until she starts work. In a few days she'll take a position in one of my hotels. The rest is up to her. I gave her the means to start a new life, but it'll be up to her to make it successful. My mother is going to give her shit. She'll want Brittany back under her thumb where she pulls all the strings. I just hope Brittany has the balls to stand up to her."

"I think it's wonderful that you did so much for her. She must have felt like she had no one to turn to."

Ash shook his head. "She didn't. And regardless of how shitty she may have treated me in the past, I do realize that she didn't really have a choice. Mom wouldn't have allowed anything else. She seems sincere now, and if she is, then I'll do whatever I can to help her. I don't care what my parents and other siblings think of me. Brittany hasn't gotten to that point yet, but she will."

"Other siblings? How many do you have?"

"Three including Brittany. I have two older brothers who are both in their forties and neither one of them can support their families without help from my parents and the old man."

"That's sad. So if you don't have anything to do with them, how did you make it? I mean you're obviously successful."

"I think it's your turn," he pointed out. "I've spilled my guts and so far all I know about you is that your dad is an asshole and your mother passed away after a long battle with cancer."

"I'll let you ask a question as soon as you answer my last one."

He arched an eyebrow at her. "Then I get two because you're already over quota."

Her lips twitched in amusement. "Do you have any idea how sterile this conversation is with all the talk of keeping score?"

"It doesn't have to be. And okay, I'll answer, but this is the last one until you catch up."

"Deal," she said with a smile.

"I became friends with Gabe Hamilton and Jace Crestwell in college. Jace's parents were killed in an accident when he was twenty and he had to take over caring for his much younger sister. Our focus changed after that. Before we had a fuck-it attitude and while we made the grades, we were more concerned with beer and women. We formed our business as soon as we were out of college. We started with a single hotel. Poured our heart and soul into it, and every penny we could scrape up or borrow. We waited a year before we expanded. Using the first hotel as collateral, we were able to secure financing for another property. From there, using the early hotels and their success, we expanded rapidly and began to have an easier time finding investors."

"So your family had nothing to do with your success, then."

"None whatsoever," he bit out. "I wouldn't take a dime from them. Didn't want the strings attached. And I wanted them to have no part of my business."

"Guess they didn't take that very well," she murmured.

He grinned. "Nope. They were pissed that *A*: I made it without them and *B*: I don't give them money. It's kind of like if your dad showed up tomorrow and wanted you to be one big happy family."

Her eyes grew stormy and her lips tightened at the mention of her father.

He leaned forward, sliding his hand across the table to cover hers once more. A muscle jumped in her arm and she shivered, chill bumps forming and racing across her skin.

"Now it's my turn to ask you twenty questions."

"Hey, I didn't ask you twenty."

"Close enough," he muttered.

She sighed. "Okay, okay. Ask away."

His gaze immediately went to her neck. To that pale ring where the collar had rested. It had been the first thing he'd noticed when she'd walked out of the pawnshop, and he hadn't dared to get his hopes up. But the fact that she'd accepted his dinner invitation, even if he'd blackmailed her, and that she didn't wear the collar tonight as a barrier between them, told him that she was at least intrigued by this thing between them. Whatever the hell it was.

"Why aren't you wearing the collar?" he asked softly.

Her free hand went immediately to her neck, and consternation shone brightly in her eyes. But she remained quiet, lips firmly pressed together.

"Josie? Why aren't you wearing the collar?"

She sighed. "I'm not seeing him anymore."

He had to work hard not to react to that piece of news. He'd suspected as much, but he hadn't wanted to jump to any conclusions.

"What happened?"

She pulled her hand away from his, dropping it into her lap. She looked down, refusing to meet his gaze. He waited, not letting her off the hook. This was too important. He wanted to know everything.

"Did you break it off or did he?" he finally asked.

"I did."

"Want to tell me why? What happened, Josie?"

Her head popped up, her eyes flashing. *"You're* what happened, Ash. *You.*"

# chapter seven

There was no faking Ash's surprise. She'd definitely caught him off guard with her outburst. His eyes narrowed and he leaned farther over the table. He was still holding one hand, and he covered her free one, his palm sliding over the tops of her knuckles.

The man was lethal. With every touch, he seduced her, and she doubted he even knew it. Or maybe he did. Maybe he knew *exactly* what he was doing.

"I didn't happen," he said in a low voice. "Because if I did, you'd be in my bed right now."

His voice was a husky growl, sliding over her skin until the hairs at her nape stood on end.

She tried to pull her hands away, but he held firm, not allowing her to escape.

"You happened," she refuted. "That day in the park. You made me question everything. And I didn't like what I discovered as a result."

"And that being?"

She shifted, uncomfortable with his close scrutiny. She didn't want to be having this conversation. It was too intimate. It was too . . . revealing. Ash was a man that if you gave him an inch, he'd take a mile.

"What did I make you question, Josie?"

It was equally clear that he wasn't going to back down.

"What that collar signified," she said, finally relenting.

"What do you mean by that?" he prompted gently.

She blew out a deep breath. "The things you said, what the collar meant to you and what it *should* mean to me. I realized that. After. I thought about it a lot. And when I went to see Michael to find out what that collar meant to him, he didn't even notice I wasn't wearing it. Now, maybe I'm wrong, but I'd think a man wouldn't like the fact that a woman took the collar off. I mean if it's supposed to mean everything you implied."

"You're not wrong," Ash said.

"It's a game for him. Maybe it was for me too," she whispered. "He told me I was taking things too seriously. That the collar was fun, but meaningless. It's like he was role-playing and none of it was real. And when I realized that, I also recognized that I didn't want a game. But at the same time, I don't know if I want it to be real. I think . . . with you . . . that it would be very different. With a man like you, I mean."

"It's not meaningless," Ash growled, his face drawn into a scowl. "And hell yes it would be different with me. But you know what? It would be real. And it would mean something."

"What would it mean?" she asked, her lips trembling as she stared back at the intensity in his eyes.

"It would mean you belong to me. Only to me. That you would submit to me. That I'd take care of you, provide for you, make love to you."

He could have no idea the effect his words had. That they reached deep inside her and called to a part of her she hadn't known existed. With Michael, it had been a game. She could see that now. Two people playacting. Going through the motions for a thrill. There was nothing wrong with that, but it wasn't what she wanted.

But the thought of being with Ash, of belonging to him in the sense he was talking about, scared her. He was overwhelming in every sense of the word.

"I think you know I want you, Josie. I certainly haven't made it a secret. The question is whether or not you want me and what I can give you. But you also need to think about all I would take. Because I take a lot. I give more, but I take everything."

She swallowed, her hands trembling beneath his. He curled his fingers tighter around her hands and squeezed gently.

"I don't know what to say."

"Say you'll think about it," he murmured. "At least give me that."

She licked her lips, her chest rising and falling with her rapid breaths. Saying she'd think about it wasn't a commitment. There was nothing to say that she had to go through with anything. And she did need time to consider what she was getting herself into.

"I'll think about it," she finally conceded.

Satisfaction, no, *triumph* gleamed brightly in his eyes. He acted as though she'd already agreed. Maybe he thought she had by saying she'd think about it. Or maybe he just didn't like taking no for an answer.

The waiter returned bearing their entrees. Ash quieted until the plates had been served and the waiter retreated.

"Now, tell me more about you. You're an artist, obviously."

She nodded, not even tasting the food she put in her mouth. The steak smelled delicious and was so tender she could cut it with her fork. But the moment she put it on her tongue, the taste didn't register. She was too preoccupied with Ash, and the proposition he'd put before her.

"Are you able to make a living at it?" he asked.

It was a personal question, but then Ash didn't seem the sort of man who worried too much about propriety or boundaries.

"More so now," she said ruefully. "I've been able to make it. It's not always easy. But I've tried regular nine-to-five jobs. I don't have a passion for it. Not like I do for my art. I've sold a few pieces here and there and I design jewelry and sell it over the Internet. I make enough to pay my rent. Most times," she added with a grimace. "This month was lean for me. Internet orders, which are usually steady, were down and I hadn't sold any of the art I display in a gallery in the last six weeks. That's why I went to the pawnshop to sell my mother's jewelry. I hated it, but I didn't see another way of paying my bills. I could have gotten a loan, but that doesn't do me any good if I don't have the money to pay it and the interest off."

"Where the hell was Michael in all of this?" Ash demanded.

She blinked at the ferocity in his gaze, the anger she saw brimming in his eyes.

"I'm not sure I know what you mean."

Ash's lips twitched in annoyance. "You were having financial trouble, which forced you to choose between selling your mother's jewelry, something that obviously means a lot to you, or not being able to pay your rent and ending up without a place to live. Michael should have helped you."

She shook her head. "No. It's not like that. I don't want him to support me. He makes good money, but our relationship wasn't about that. I couldn't take money from him. It would be too much like he was paying me for sex."

Ash looked even more annoyed. "You have some fucked-up reasoning, Josie. If it was a choice between you being on the streets or taking money from a man who damn well should have protected you better then there's no question that he should have provided for you. You shouldn't have had to ask. If he was involved with you, if he was your Dom and he knew what he should about you then he would have known that you were in trouble. He should have known you were in a fucking pawnshop hocking jewelry to make ends meet. And he damn sure should have stepped in and taken care of you. If he treated you like he was supposed to, you wouldn't feel uncomfortable with him helping you. You should have complete trust in the man you've given yourself to. And he should cherish that gift by making sure you have no worries, financial or otherwise."

"Guess I never looked at it that way," she murmured.

"You will," he said.

The determination in his voice made her go still. He was so sure of himself. Of her. Of there being an eventual "us."

"How is your food?" he asked, shifting the conversation in a completely different direction.

She stared down at her plate, realizing the steak was half-finished and she had no memory of eating what was gone.

"It's good," she said quickly. "Excellent actually. I've never eaten here before. It's too rich for my blood. What made you choose it?"

The corner of his mouth lifted. "I own the hotel, so it's only natural that I'd have a restaurant in it that I love to eat at. I'm glad the steak was to your liking."

Her jaw went slack. "You own this hotel?"

His eyebrow went up. "You sound surprised. I told you that my partners and I own several hotels."

"I guess I thought you meant like a hotel chain or something small. This hotel is . . ." She grasped for the right word to keep from sounding like a complete moron.

"It's what?" he asked.

"It's so glitzy and obviously caters to the wealthy. I guess I thought you owned something on a much smaller scale," she murmured.

"Does that bother you?"

She shook her head. "No. It just took me by surprise. I mean you look like you're wealthy, but maybe I wasn't thinking you were *this* successful."

"And you think that if you agree to what I've proposed that it makes you a gold digger?"

He nailed it with one shot. The man was far too adept at reading her mind.

"Let's just say that I'm not in your league. Anyone looking at the two of us would immediately label me an opportunist. No one would ever believe that I wasn't with you for the money."

"And would you be?" he asked bluntly.

She couldn't suppress her reaction. Her lips thinned and the corners dropped down in a frown.

"Of course not! I don't want or need you to support me, Ash. I don't want your money. I want . . ."

She broke off in horror at what she'd almost said. But Ash didn't miss it and his gaze became all the more intense.

"What do you want?"

"You," she whispered. "Just you."

Satisfaction gleamed in his eyes and a slow smile worked over his mouth.

"Then you need to deal, Josie. Because with me comes all that I can give you, and it will not make me happy if you refuse anything I choose to give you or do for you. As long as you and I know the score, I don't give a fuck what anyone else thinks and neither should you."

She licked her lips, his earlier words coming back to her. She had wanted to question him then, but the moment hadn't seemed right and then the food arrived. But the question was burning on her lips, and she had to know.

"You said earlier . . . I mean, when you said you'd give but that you'd take. A lot. What did you mean by that?"

"Everything," he said bluntly. "You in my bed. You in my space. You under my protection. I'd take everything, Josie, and you'd give it."

"That doesn't seem very equal," she murmured.

"Nothing I can ever give you could compare to your gift of submission. The gift of your trust. Nothing is more valuable than that, and you can't put a price tag on that kind of gift. I'd spend all my time catching up, because hell no it's not equal. What you'd give me far surpasses anything I could give you."

"Wouldn't you also be giving me yourself? I mean you said I'd give myself to you, but you'd give me you in return, right?"

He paused a moment, still staring intently into her eyes. "You get me. All of me. What I choose to give you. Nothing more. And you have to understand that. If that bothers you, then you have to deal or make a decision because I can't give you more."

She digested his words for a long moment and then glanced back up at him, her brow creased as she plunged ahead with her next question, or rather, condition. He might not take it very well, but she couldn't even consider this if he refused.

"I won't share you with another woman," she said. "I mean if we do this, I won't tolerate you being with another woman. I don't know how this works. If you have other women like me. But I don't want to ever worry that you're with someone else. Because if I give you everything you're demanding, especially my trust, then I'd expect you to be faithful to me for however long this lasts."

"I have no intention of sleeping with another woman or even being with another woman if I have you. Why would I need someone else if you've submitted to me and are in my bed? I'd never give you that kind of disrespect, Josie. Of everything else I give you, respect would be the uppermost. I'd care for you, protect you and cherish you. No other woman would get those things from me."

She wasn't at all sure what to say to that. He sounded so . . . decisive. As if their relationship were already a fait accompli.

He leaned forward, his gaze growing more intense, his tone . . . persuasive. As if he wanted very much for her to render her decision now instead of taking time to think it over.

"One thing you need to realize. I'm not more than you, Josie. I get that there is an inequality in power in the relationship. The scales are tipped in my direction. But that doesn't mean I'm more. Never more. You are *everything* in this equation. You don't lower your gaze. You don't ever feel like you're less, because that's going to piss me off. You don't kneel unless that's what I want when you're sucking my dick. I make the decisions. You submit to me. But that doesn't make me more and you less. It makes you everything. And your power over me is far greater than any perceived power I have over you. You talk about what I give you and what you give me. Without me, you'll be fine. You can make it on your own. You've proven that. But without you, I have nothing because money, wealth, power, it doesn't mean anything without someone to share it with. So maybe my need of you is greater than your need of me. But that doesn't mean I'm not going to do everything in my power to make you need me every bit as much as I need you."

Her eyes widened at his impassioned speech. Holy crap, did he mean that? All of it? "You need me?" she whispered.

He released her hand and leaned back, dragging his own hand through his hair in agitation. "I can't explain it. This thing, whatever it is between us. But yeah, I need you. I'm not even sure *need* is the right word because it's such an inadequate word for the insane urge I have to be with you. To have you. To have your submission.

It's never been like that with another woman. It's something I want. It's something I desire. It's something I enjoy. But with you I need it and if I don't have it, I'm going to lose my fucking mind. So yeah, I need you, Josie. And that's putting it mildly. And if that scares you, I'm sorry, but I can't be any other way with you. I'm shooting you straight. I'll try not to overwhelm you, but I only know one way with you. Full-on, no holding back."

She was speechless. She had no idea how to even respond. This was crazy. All of it. They'd only seen each other twice before tonight. How could he possibly have determined that she was someone he needed when they knew next to nothing about each other? For that matter, how could she feel like she needed *him*?

"Another thing you need to know," he said before she could respond. "I don't deal in fantasies, Josie. I deal with reality. And maybe your fantasy *is* my reality and that's okay as long as you realize at the end of the day the fantasy becomes reality. What we do is real. It's here. Solid. It's not going away tomorrow or the next day. You need to be sure you can deal with that because yeah, I'll give you the fantasy but it's going to be real. No made-up shit you only dream about in your head. Are you prepared for that? Can you deal with this being real and permanent?"

"But how? I mean I understand where you're coming from about the line between fantasy and reality. I get that Michael obviously wanted a game. It wasn't real with him, and I realized I didn't want to play a game. But if I'm not even sure of what I want, how can *you* be expected to know?"

He smiled and reached over to slide his palm over her hand again. "That's my job. Yours is to submit, to give freely of yourself. My job is to be in tune with your needs and desires, to know them better than my own."

"It sounds too good to be true," she admitted. "You say this isn't fantasy. That it would be real with you, but it *sounds* like fantasy."

"You won't know unless you take the plunge. But believe me when I say this is no game. If you submit to me, you'll know it's real. No playacting. No silly games. You'll feel that to your bones. I guarantee it."

It was on the tip of her tongue to say yes. To *take the plunge* as he labeled it. But it would be stupid of her not to take time to think about it, preferably when he wasn't sitting across from her seducing her with every look, every touch and every word that came out of his mouth.

There was no doubt that he called to a part of her soul that had never been stirred. He made her want things she'd never considered. She knew without a doubt that a relationship with him would be far different than what she'd had with Michael. And she wasn't entirely certain she could handle that. Ash was an overwhelming presence. He in turns frightened her and intrigued her.

"I'll think about it," she said in a quiet voice. "I need time, Ash. This is . . . heavy. It's a huge decision and one I can't make lightly. I wouldn't want to disrespect you by agreeing and then immediately balking at the terms of our relationship. If I agree then I have to know that I'm capable of giving you all the things you want."

"I'll give you time," he said. "I hope that you won't take too long, but also know there is no time limit on your decision. I'm not going to take up with another woman in a week because you haven't given me your decision. You need to know there *is* no other woman. No one I'm considering. The other thing you need to know is that I don't make this offer lightly. In fact, I've never asked another woman for this kind of relationship."

Her brow furrowed. "But you said this is who you are. What you are. How can you never have asked another woman for these things? I doubt you've been celibate forever."

He laughed. "No, indeed not. The women I've been with all

knew the score. What I expected and what I'd take. But I never considered those actual relationships, because going in, she and I both knew it was very temporary. Hardly what I'd call an actual relationship."

"So I wouldn't be temporary?" she asked, voicing perhaps her biggest fear. That he'd grow tired of her in a week's time and simply move on to someone else.

But then what was she expecting? What was she even asking for? Something long-term? How could she ask that of him when she wasn't sure she wanted something more permanent? It was a huge leap to be making. It was possible that she wouldn't be able to handle the demands he made. And yet, the idea of him only wanting a temporary fling unsettled her.

"I can't say with any authority what you'll be, Josie," he said in a quiet voice. "But what I can say is that no, you most certainly will not be temporary. I intend to keep you for a very long time. And if it makes you feel better, I've never asked a woman for anything longer than a few weeks, and none of those women had the hold on me that you already have."

Warmth traveled through her veins, sending pleasure into her chest. It was silly. This giddy feeling that she was somehow more to him than any other woman. But what woman didn't like to feel that way about the man she was with?

No matter what the future had in store for them and any relationship they entered, she was comforted by the thought that for whatever reason, he felt for her what he hadn't felt for another woman.

"I won't take long," she said. "Just give me a few days to sort it all out in my head."

He nodded. "That's fine. I'll give you my cell number. When you've had time to consider everything I've said, call me and we'll have dinner in my apartment. Then, if you've agreed, we'll go over the terms, or rather my expectations."

She frowned. "Shouldn't we do that *before* I make my decision?"

He smiled. "That's where trust has to enter, Josie. Consider what I've told you, how it will be, and then when you say yes, we'll go over the more intimate details of our arrangement."

# chapter eight

Ash wasn't someone who liked waiting around. Especially for something he wanted. He was too used to getting what he
wanted, when he wanted. *No* wasn't a word in his vocabulary and
the more time that passed since his dinner with Josie, the more on
edge he felt.

Not even the situation with Brittany had been able to distract
him from his preoccupation with Josie.

His sister had settled into her apartment and had reported to
work at the Bentley in their administration. So far she seemed to be
doing well. He received regular reports about Brittany from the
manager, who was satisfied with her performance so far. He'd commented that she was punctual, a hard worker and seemed eager to
make her job a success.

Tonight he had dinner plans with Brittany, and he would have
looked forward to it were it not for the fact he had yet to hear from
Josie. It had been a *week* since their dinner, and he'd been very confident that he'd hear from her in a matter of days. He'd seen the look
in her eyes. She was intrigued. She was obviously attracted to him.
And the things he'd offered seemed to appeal to her.

So why was it taking so damn long for her to respond? Or did
she even plan to? Maybe she'd gotten home and immediately talked
herself out of a relationship with him.

He knew he should have pressed for an answer the night they'd gone to dinner. She'd been precariously close to consent. He'd seen it in her eyes and in her body language. Whether she consciously realized it or not, she wanted him and she wanted the kind of relationship he proposed.

This was new territory for him. Never had he been in a position where he had to wait for a woman to make up her mind whether she wanted to be with him. The women he'd been with in the past hadn't hesitated even a minute. They'd been all too eager to hook up with him, no matter how long things lasted.

And in fact, there had been several who hadn't gotten the message that they were over. The last woman he and Jace had been together with—not counting Bethany—had not taken the end of her fling with him and Jace well at all. She'd been pissed and acted very much the woman scorned even though he and Jace had made it abundantly clear that it was a temporary arrangement.

He replayed the evening Josie and he had dinner. Yes, he'd definitely been blunt and straightforward. Maybe that scared her. Maybe he'd come on too strong too quickly. But he didn't want to mislead her. He wanted her to know exactly what she was getting into with a relationship with him.

"Hey, man."

Ash looked up to see Jace standing in the doorway of his office. Ash motioned him in and Jace sauntered toward the desk, closing the door behind him.

"You've been quiet lately. Anything wrong? How has the fallout over Brittany's defection been?"

Ash rolled his eyes. "Predictable."

"Meaning what?"

Jace took a seat across from Ash and pinned him with an inquisitive stare.

"Oh, you know my dear old mother and father. Dad is too much of a spineless wimp to do or say much of anything. He just toes the line with Mom and whatever she says goes."

"They been giving her shit?" Jace asked with a scowl.

"Well, they showed up at the apartment you're letting her use. Ordered her home and told her to quit being a child. This is a thirty-year-old woman my mother was dressing down, mind you. When Brittany refused, Mom wanted to know how she afforded the apartment she was living in and how she was making it on her own. Brittany told her it was none of her business how she got the apartment and that she was making it like most people made it. By working."

Jace chuckled. "Good for her. Wouldn't have thought she had it in her to stand up to the wicked bitch of the east."

"Me either to be honest," Ash admitted. "But she seems determined to make a break from the family. I'm proud of her. Mom can be intimidating and you have to understand until recently Brittany has always done what Mom wanted her to. No questions asked."

"Must be a hard adjustment for her," Jace said in sympathy.

"I'm having dinner with her tonight. You and Bethany want to join us? I'd like Brittany to meet Bethany. Brittany hasn't associated with the best female friends. They were never her real friends and Brittany knows that. When the chips are down, they aren't riding to her rescue. They dropped her like a hot brick."

"Sure. I'll call Bethany and make sure we don't have other plans."

"Thanks. Will be nice to take my mind off other things."

Too late he realized how telling that statement would be, and the last thing he wanted was to discuss it with Jace, who would most definitely latch on to it and wouldn't let it go.

"Anything you need help with?" Jace asked, his brow wrinkled with concern.

"Nah. Not unless you have a way of making a woman acquiesce to your demands."

At that Jace's eyebrow lifted. "A woman? Do tell. This has to be worth the price of admission."

"It's complicated," Ash muttered. "She's being difficult."

Jace laughed. "Show me one woman who isn't!"

"Bethany," Ash pointed out. "You're a lucky son of a bitch to have her. She'd give you the moon and you know it."

"So what's the problem with your woman du jour?"

Ash scowled. "That's just it. She's not just any woman. I don't know, man. She hits buttons that a woman has never pushed for me."

"Oh shit. It's happened," Jace crowed. "The smug son of a bitch who gave me and Gabe so much grief has finally fallen hard and from the sounds of it she isn't exactly reciprocating."

Ash flipped up his middle finger. "It's too early for that. She just intrigues me. I want her," he said bluntly. "And I'll do whatever it takes to get her in my bed. The problem is, she isn't exactly tripping over herself to get there."

"Now this is hilarious. Women kill themselves to get next to you. You're the charming one. Not as hard-ass as Gabe and I are."

Ash barely held back the snort. His friends were sadly mistaken on that score. He might give the appearance of being the easygoing, laid-back one, but when it came to women, what he wanted, what he needed? There was no charm, no being laid-back. It had been years since he'd let that part of himself go with a woman. He still remembered her fondly. He'd just turned thirty. She was a few years younger than him. They both wanted and enjoyed the same things and when he'd actually let her see him for what he was, she hadn't balked.

He still thought of Cammie from time to time. Wondered where she was. If she was married with children. And wondered if she'd found a man to satisfy her submissive streak.

She and Ash had parted as friends. She'd wanted more than he could give her. At the time he was solidly married to his career, try-ing to make HCM into what it was today. She wanted to settle down, have a family, live the American dream. And Ash hadn't been prepared to do that.

It wasn't that he minded the idea of marriage to her. She was a beautiful woman, fun to be with. He could have grown to love her. He knew that. But he'd wanted to wait. He hadn't wanted to marry her when he wasn't absolutely certain he could provide for her every need.

Now? Marriage and commitment seemed to be the next logical step. Gabe and Jace had taken the plunge. They were all at a point in their careers where they could step back, relax, focus on things other than business.

But while Gabe and Jace had found that perfect woman, some-one who embraced and accepted the kind of men they were and loved them in spite of their imperfections, Ash hadn't yet met a woman who fulfilled the parts of his heart that weren't satisfied by his career and good friends.

"She wants me," Ash said. "She wants what I can give her, but as much as I can see that she wants it, she's hesitant."

"I know patience isn't one of your virtues, but perhaps this is one time you need to get acquainted with the concept."

The heavy amusement in Jace's voice just made Ash grumpy. Patience? Definitely not one of his virtues. And he definitely wasn't going to start getting up-close and personal with the idea now of all times. Not when he wanted something as badly as he wanted Josie.

And he still couldn't explain it. Obsession. It was a word he'd associated with Jace when it came to Bethany, and Ash had come down hard on Jace for it. He hadn't understood it. He'd even tried to talk Jace down, going as far as doing a background check on Bethany and then warning Jace off.

It wasn't one of his better moves, because Bethany had been the best thing that had ever happened to Jace. It was a good thing his friend hadn't listened to Ash's advice, and now that Ash found himself in a similar predicament, he could well understand Jace's uncharacteristic reaction to Bethany.

"Let me ask you something," Ash said, his tone serious. "In the beginning with Bethany. Did you sit back and wait or did you move in, take charge and take over?"

Jace winced, his face contorting with a grimace.

"I tried at first to be patient, take things slow. But that lasted a very short period of time. I wanted to give her time to adjust. I mean, her circumstances were different than most. It made me crazy to think of her not having a place to sleep, and when I moved her into Mia's old apartment it made me crazy because she wasn't with me all the time even though we were together every day. But I wanted her in my apartment. As long as she was living somewhere else, I didn't feel like she was completely mine. It sounds nuts but I wanted to know where she was every minute. It makes me sound like a fucking stalker, and maybe that's what I was. Hell if I know. I just knew that I wanted her with me. Every day. In my apartment when I got home. In my bed every night. Not in another apartment where she could bolt at any time even though I had men on her."

"Yeah, that didn't work out too well if I remember right," Ash said dryly. "Didn't she bail on them and disappear for a few hours?"

"An entire day," Jace muttered. "Hell, I thought she'd left me or walked out, but all she did was go find Jack, and I still get tense just thinking of all that could have happened to her in those few hours."

"I didn't get it then," Ash admitted. "I thought you'd lost your mind. But I get it now, because I feel the same way about Josie. And it's crazy. We've only seen each other a few times and had only one date where we actually spent more than a few minutes in each other's company. I'm still kicking myself for not pressing her harder at dinner. She was so close to agreeing, but the dumbass that I am, I backed off because I didn't want to overwhelm her, so I granted her wish for time to think. Well, that was a fucking week ago and I haven't heard shit since our dinner."

Jace's face crinkled in sympathy. "So what are you going to do?"

"Well, I have plans tonight with Brittany, and you and Bethany if you can make it, but tomorrow I'm employing a full-court press. I'm done sitting back and being patient. If she's going to tell me no, I at least want to hear it from her lips instead of enduring this prolonged silence."

"Good luck man. I hope it works out for you. And at the risk of being a total hypocrite since I got in your face for checking up on Bethany, have you checked Josie out?"

Ash nodded. "Yeah, I did. After our first meeting in the park. No skeletons in her closet that I uncovered anyway."

"Okay, well, if there's anything I can do, you know you only have to ask. If you get her to agree, we'll have to hook up, and when Gabe and Mia get back from their honeymoon, we can all get together. You can introduce Josie to Mia and Bethany. They have a good group of girlfriends, and I'll tell you from experience, when they have their girls' nights out?" He broke off and a shit-eating grin attacked his face.

Ash held up his hand with a groan. "I know, I know. You've already regaled me with the details of drunk, sexy women in fuck-me shoes wanting to be fucked in those fuck-me shoes. No need to torture me further."

Jace laughed and then rose. "Let me go call Bethany. I'll let you know about tonight. Where we eating and what time? I just need to give her a heads-up so she can be ready."

"How about the Bryant Park Grill right after work?"

Jace nodded. "Sounds good. We'll see you there."

# chapter nine

Brittany was noticeably nervous at dinner, though Bethany was a complete doll, easing the awkwardness and treating Brittany like a long-lost friend.

The Bryant Park Grill was hopping, as it was every day right after work hours. It was filled with suits, businessmen and women enjoying cocktails after a day at work. It was a popular after-work haunt, but that wasn't why Ash chose it.

He'd chosen it because he thought he might see Josie there. But according to the man Ash had assigned to keep tabs on Josie, she hadn't been out of her apartment at all for several days.

Maybe she was working furiously to finish a new piece of art for the gallery. Maybe she wasn't giving his proposition a moment's thought. He'd told Jace he'd give her until tomorrow, but he was only half paying attention to the dinner conversation because he was tempted to go to Josie's apartment unannounced.

Patience. Jace had said to have patience. Ash nearly snorted over the hypocrisy of that statement, even if Jace had admitted it.

Their food was served, and Brittany had finally relaxed, even smiling in Ash's direction. At one point she leaned toward him so only he would hear and said, "Thank you, Ash. You can't know what this means to me. You're the only family I have now. The others have cut all ties. They treat me like I'm some sort of traitor for wanting to have my own life. You understood what I wanted and needed and you didn't judge me for it."

Ash smiled. "Join the outcast club. It's not so bad really. The longer you remain away from them, the more perspective you'll gain and you'll realize that this is something you would have been happier doing a lot sooner. But you've done it, and that's all that counts. It'll get easier. I promise."

"Does it bother you?" she asked in an earnest voice. "I mean does it bother you that they treat you like an outsider? That they have such disdain for you and your success?"

Ash shrugged. "It did in the beginning I suppose. I haven't given it much thought over the last few years. I have good friends and they're my family. And now you."

Her face lit up, the shadows chased from her eyes in a flash. "I'm glad we can be family, Ash. I really mean that. I'm not going to let you down. I know I didn't get the job on my own, but I'm not going to make you regret giving it to me."

They were interrupted by the ringing of Ash's cell phone. He reached automatically for it, holding his breath without realizing at first that he was doing so. It could be Josie. He'd waited a damn week for something, anything from her.

But when he looked at the incoming name, he frowned. It wasn't Josie. It was the man assigned to Josie.

"Excuse me, I have to take this," Ash said as he rose, already pushing the button to accept the call.

He walked away from the table to a quieter area near the restrooms.

"Ash," he said shortly.

"Mr. McIntyre, I know my reports have been much the same all week. Miss Carlysle hasn't left her apartment until now and I knew you'd want to know what I saw."

"What?" Ash demanded.

"She's sporting one hell of a black eye. Split lip. Looks like someone took a shot at her. I could be wrong. It could have been an accident, but I doubt it. And it could be why she hasn't left her apartment."

Ash swore. "Where is she headed now? Are you on her?"

"Yeah, I'm following her now. Looks like she's headed to the gallery. She had several canvases when she got into a cab. I'll keep you posted."

"Do that," Ash murmured as he hung up.

He stood for a moment, his mind filled with rage at the idea that someone had abused Josie in some way. And then he cursed the fact that he hadn't asked his man if Josie had been anywhere or if she'd had visitors. Surely he would have reported it if she had. But then he hadn't had her shadow back on the job until two days after their dinner. He'd thought she would have contacted him by then and when she hadn't, he'd put his man back on her to monitor her activities.

Obsessed? Yeah, that was one word for it. Demented was another. He was acting like a crazed stalker, the kind most women would do well to steer clear of. Only he wasn't going to harm Josie. But he was kicking himself for not keeping his man on her, because someone had hurt her, or at the very least she'd been injured in some way.

Why hadn't she called him? Why hadn't she come to him for help? She had to know after their conversation that he would take care of her.

With a muttered curse he returned to the table where Brittany, Jace and Bethany all looked up at him. Concern immediately flashed in their eyes. His expression must have been grim for them to have picked up on his mood so quickly.

"I'm sorry to cut this short, but I have to go. Brittany, I'll make it up to you soon. Promise. Jace and Bethany, thank you both for coming, and please, all of you finish your dinner. I'll see you all later."

As he turned to walk away, Jace called out to him.

"Ash? Everything okay?"

Ash sent him a look he knew Jace would pick up on. He'd know it had to do with Josie, and he'd understand. Jace nodded once and then turned back to the women, smiling and engaging them both in conversation.

Breathing a sigh of relief and knowing he owed Jace for taking over, he picked up the phone to call for his driver. If Josie was going to the gallery, she'd probably go right back home since she hadn't been anywhere else in the last several days. He'd take care of buying the art she'd taken in later, but right now he was going to be at her apartment waiting for her to return and then they were going to have a serious come-to-Jesus moment.

# chapter ten

Josie breathed a sigh of relief as the cab pulled to a stop at the corner of the cross street her apartment was on. She hadn't wanted to venture out at all, but she'd wanted to get more of her artwork to Mr. Downing. While the money from the sale of her previous works would tide her over for the next few months, she'd wanted to get more to him so the buyer wouldn't lose interest or think she didn't have anything else to offer.

As she paid her fare and stepped out of the cab, she self-consciously put a hand to her bruised cheek and winced when her fingers brushed over the corner of her mouth where her lip had been split. Head down, she hurried down the sidewalk toward her apartment, only wanting to be back inside and out of view of anyone.

Though she had nothing to be ashamed of, she still felt embarrassed over what had happened. Shocked. Completely and utterly shocked that Michael had come to her apartment and lost his temper, something that had never happened before. She was still in disbelief over it all. She should have pressed charges. She should have done a lot of things, but she'd been too numb to take it all in. So instead she'd sequestered herself in her studio apartment and worked feverishly to take her mind off the events of the last week.

She knew she owed Ash a response. An explanation. Something! She'd told him she wouldn't take long, but how could she go to him with bruises inflicted by a man who'd been her dominant?

Of course, it was laughable now. He wasn't a true dominant. He'd been playing at it. It was an ego trip for him. He'd become someone completely different the moment he realized she was serious about ending their relationship. Her mistake had been mentioning Ash at all, not that she'd called him by name, but she'd told Michael that he couldn't give her the things another man had promised her.

Now she wasn't so certain. What if Ash was no better? She knew next to nothing about him. She'd been ready to commit, had actually made up her mind to call him the same day Michael had come to her apartment. After that fiasco, she'd harbored doubts and self-preservation had kicked in.

If Ash was more intense than Michael—and it was evident he definitely was—then could she expect the same kind of treatment at his hands? Or even worse?

Her head spun with the possibilities and she knew she was in no emotional state to be making such a huge decision. To place her trust, her well-being, her entire self into the hands of a man like Ash. And so she'd remained silent, mulling over her decision, going back and forth.

The fact was, she was afraid. And that fear had prevented her from either accepting or declining his proposition. And she hated that fear. It wasn't how she wanted to live her life or make her decisions. She needed a clear head before taking that huge step in trusting another man who could very well turn out just like Michael.

She heaved an unhappy sigh and reached into her pocket to retrieve the keys to her apartment. Her head was still down when she reached the steps and she saw an expensive pair of shoes directly above the first step leading down to her door.

Startled, she glanced up to see Ash standing there. As he looked her over, fury blazed in his eyes and she took an instinctive step backward.

"What the hell happened to you?" he demanded.

He was seething, anger bristling from him in waves. Gone was any semblance of charm or laid-back calm. He was one huge ball of pissed-off alpha male.

"Please, not here," she whispered. "I just want to go inside. Let me by and then leave."

His expression of complete *what the fuck* made her pause as she attempted to push by him. He grasped her shoulders, his grip firm but extremely gentle, his fingers against her skin, but not pressing into her flesh.

"I want to know who the fuck did this to you," he growled.

Her shoulders sagged and she nearly dropped the keys that dangled precariously from her fingers. She tightened her grip and then pushed her chin upward.

"Let me by," she said through clenched teeth.

To her surprise, he dropped his hands and let her go down the steps, but he followed closely behind, giving her no option to go in and shut the door to prevent his entry.

She sighed as she unlocked her door and pushed it open. She felt better the moment she was inside. Her own space. It was laughable that she felt safe here after what had happened with Michael. But now that she knew just what he was capable of, she'd never make the mistake of letting him within a mile of her.

She dropped her purse by the door and walked into her tiny living area. Ash closed the door, sliding the deadbolt into place, and then he too entered her living room. A room that suddenly seemed way smaller with him in it. He stood there, staring at her, his gaze relentless as he did a thorough up-and-down of her body, stopping once again on the bruise on her cheek.

His eyes grew cold and she shivered.

"I haven't heard from you," he began.

She flushed guiltily and lowered her gaze, not wanting him to see all she wanted to hide.

"And now I'm thinking there was a reason you haven't called me."

Slowly she nodded, still not meeting his gaze.

"Josie, look at me."

His voice was soft. Gentle even. But it was definitely not a request. It was a command. One she felt compelled to obey.

Slowly she lifted her head so their eyes met.

"Who did this to you?"

Gone was the gentleness, replaced by an edge of steel to his tone. His entire body vibrated with fury and it made her hesitant to tell him what had happened. How she'd ever thought him not dangerous or perhaps charming or affable she had no clue. Because the man standing in front of her right here, right now, looked capable of terrible things.

And it wasn't that she was afraid of him. No, she knew instinctively, even as she was shrouded in fear over what had already happened to her, that this man would not hurt her. But he was angry. Angry didn't even begin to describe what she saw in his eyes. And he absolutely looked capable of killing someone. She found herself not wanting to tell him, because she feared not him, but what he'd do.

"Josie, answer me," he said through his teeth. "Who. Did. This. To. You."

He wasn't going to allow her not to tell him. And though she didn't fear reprisal, she knew she absolutely had to obey him. He wouldn't allow her to duck the question. She firmly believed he'd stand here all night, do whatever it took to get what he wanted.

She closed her eyes and exhaled in a long, weary sigh, her shoulders sagging in defeat.

"Michael," she whispered, her voice so low she could barely hear it herself. Maybe she hadn't even really voiced it.

"Say that again?"

The words whipped from his lips, snapping through the air with enough force that she felt them. She chanced a glance up and immediately flinched at the look on his face. It was . . . terrifying.

"You heard," she whispered in only a slightly louder voice.

"You're telling me that motherfucker put those bruises on your face? That he split your lip?"

He advanced and she rapidly took a step backward, which only seemed to piss him off even more.

"Goddamn it, Josie, I'm not going to hurt you! I'll *never* fucking hurt you."

The words were explosive. Not exactly soothing and yet she took comfort in the vehemence with which he made the vow. So much so that she took a step back toward him so they now only stood a foot apart.

His entire body still vibrated with rage. His green eyes were nearly black, the green just a thin ring around the dilated pupils. And then he raised his hands, slowly, as if he feared frightening her. He cupped her face in his palms, his touch infinitely gentle, and she didn't know how he could possibly pull that off when the rest of his body was taut with fury and his expression was so black.

But that touch was so exquisitely tender that she literally melted into his hands. She felt no pain even though her face was still painful to touch several days after the incident. He brushed his fingers over the bruise and then traced the split at her lip, so lightly that she nearly didn't feel it.

"I'll kill him."

Ash's voice was absolute. The resolution in his voice made her blood chill in her veins because she believed him. In this moment, she believed him absolutely capable of killing the man who'd hurt her. Her pulse leapt and her breathing accelerated as panic shot down into her belly.

"No! Ash, please. Just let it go. This is why I didn't want to tell you. Why I haven't called."

She would have said more, but he put his finger over the uninjured part of her mouth to silence her.

"Let it go?"

His tone was deadly.

"You want me to fucking let it go when that motherfucker put his hands on you? What the fuck happened, Josie, and I want every goddamn detail. Nothing left out. I want to know when this happened. I want to know how many times he hit you. And above all, I want to know why the hell you didn't immediately come to me or call me, the *instant* this happened."

Her mouth went slack against his finger. And then, as if he changed his mind entirely, he pulled away, turning to survey her living room, glancing toward the open archway to her bedroom.

"I'm taking you to my apartment," he said firmly. "You're moving in with me."

"Wait. *What?* Ash, I can't—"

"This isn't negotiable, Josie." His eye glittered with purpose and his stance was rigid, brooking no compromise. "You're coming with me. Now let's go into your bedroom. You're going to sit on the bed and tell me what you need packed for tonight. Tomorrow we can go over what you have to have or want moved to my place and I'll arrange for someone to come in and have everything brought over. But when we have this conversation about that son of a bitch—and we *are* having that conversation—it's going to be in a place where you feel absolutely safe. A place where you know no harm will come to you. That's in stone."

Her mouth dropped open even farther, but even amid the utter shock of his proclamation came . . . *relief.* Comfort. But mostly overwhelming relief. The decision had been wrested from her hands, and at the moment she embraced that. Her worries—fears—surrounding Ash seemed silly now. That she'd even entertained that he might be like Michael or that she would be entering an even worse situation than the one she'd just come from seemed absurd.

"I can pack my own things," she whispered.

There was a sudden fire in his eyes. Satisfaction over her capitulation. Maybe he'd expected her to fight it more or even to outright refuse, though she could see he had no intention of backing down.

"Didn't say you *couldn't* pack. What I said was that you're going to sit on your bed while I do this for you. All I need from you is to tell me what you want for tonight and maybe tomorrow. The rest will be taken care of after you and I have talked later tonight."

Wow. Okay. This was moving at supersonic speed. She felt like she'd just gotten off an insane roller-coaster ride and was still trying to gain her bearings.

He held out his hand to her, not moving to her or taking it on his own. He simply held it out, waiting. Waiting for her to accept. To take his hand and to enter his world.

Taking a deep breath, she reached out, sliding her palm over his upturned one. He gathered her fingers gently in his hand and then squeezed, holding firmly. Like he was forging an unbreakable bond between them.

Then he pulled her gently toward her bedroom, and she followed, allowing him to lead her inside where he sat her on the edge of the bed as if she were incredibly fragile. Something precious and breakable.

He backed away and did a quick survey.

"Do you have an overnight bag?"

"In the closet," she said huskily.

She watched in stupefaction as he briskly began to pack under her quiet direction. Didn't they have it all turned around? He was doing everything for her. What had she done for him? But then, he had said he'd give a lot. But he'd take everything.

She shivered lightly, wondering just how much he'd take, and if she'd have anything left when he'd taken his fill.

# chapter eleven

Ash wasn't a stupid man. He knew he'd pressured Josie, given her no time to breathe, analyze or react to his arrogant demand. And it *had* been the height of arrogance to sweep into her apartment and order her to move into his.

So it was with brisk efficiency that he hurried about his task, because the longer she sat on that bed looking overwhelmed and befuddled, the more time she'd have to reconsider her quiet agreement. Which meant he risked her not coming home with him.

And that was *not* an option.

He packed an overnight bag, called his driver to make sure he'd be waiting outside Josie's apartment, and then he hustled her toward the door, not giving her any further time to process the whirlwind event.

After urging Josie into the car, he closed her door and paused only a moment to call his doorman and ask him to go up to Ash's apartment and take down the painting of Josie from his bedroom and store it, along with the others in his living room, until Ash retrieved them. He didn't want Josie to know he was the one who'd bought her work. Not yet.

When he got into the car next to her, he relaxed and then glanced sideways, taking in her pale, shaken face. The bruises pissed him off. Enraged him. The split at the corner of her mouth stood out, a reminder that another man had put his hands on what Ash already considered his. That the man would have put his hands on any woman in such a manner. Not just Ash's woman, but any woman. But most especially his woman.

"I don't know if this is a good idea, Ash," she said quietly, speaking for the first time since she'd given him hesitant instructions on what to pack for her.

"It's a very good idea," he said firmly. "You would have already come to me if it weren't for that asshole. You know it and I know it. Now, we still have to address the matter of Michael, and we'll do it when we're in a place you feel safe and secure, and you'll do it in my arms, where you know nothing bad is going to touch you. But know this. What he did doesn't change one thing about you and me. We're inevitable, Josie. From that first day in the park, we were inevitable. Fighting is a waste of time and mental energy. I'm not fighting it and I don't want you fighting it either."

Her mouth parted in surprise. Her eyes flashed, not in anger, but in recognition. Good. They were getting somewhere because she was starting to see what he saw. What he *knew*.

"Not happy that you kept this from me," he continued. "That you didn't come to me the minute this happened. But we'll work on that. You weren't mine yet even if I knew you were. But you are now. And you'll come to me any time you have a problem."

Slowly she nodded, and satisfaction—triumph—gripped him.

He held out his arm, not liking the distance between them, but not wanting to push her too hard. Not yet. He'd already pushed enough. He wanted her next move to be of her own doing, and so he waited, arm outstretched toward her.

She came readily, with no hesitation, and he liked that. She slid next to him, burrowing into his side so he could wrap his arm around her. And he did. Anchoring her against him. She laid her head against his chest, the top resting just underneath his chin. He liked her tucked there.

She gave a soft sigh and then seemed to melt into him, her body sagging as if a great weight had been lifted off. Relief.

The scent of her hair tantalized him. Soft and sweet, like her. He ran his hand up the length of her arm, enjoying the feel of her skin and knowing that soon, he'd discover all of her flesh. But for now she needed comfort. Safety. A sense of security. She needed to know that he would never hurt her. Never raise his hand to her as Michael had done.

He pressed his lips to her hair and inhaled even as he pressed the kiss to her head.

Deep. Yeah, he was in deep. He didn't even have a fully thought-out plan. He'd acted on instinct. Knew he had to have her. Knew he had to have her in his space. And he knew if he didn't press now, that he'd likely lose her.

Overwhelming her seemed the best idea, even if it made him a total bastard. But he wouldn't compare himself to Michael. He wasn't that man. He might not be the most understanding, patient and considerate person. And he definitely did not back down when he wanted something. But he'd never, ever raise his hand to a woman. The idea appalled him.

But he absolutely had no such problem meting violence out on the bastard who'd hurt Josie.

He shoved that thought aside, because he knew it had to be dealt with later—and it would be dealt with. But Josie came first. Her needs. Her comfort. Starting right now.

The drive was silent, and Ash did nothing to disturb it. He knew Josie was processing the evening's events. Knew she was probably having second and third and fourth thoughts. But she was here in his arms, and as long as she was here and not in her apartment, he could fight dirty.

Instead he simply stroked her skin, sliding his palms up and down her arms, offering her comfort the best way he knew how.

"I'm sorry, Ash," she said quietly, her words nearly lost against his chest.

His hands stopped their upward progress and he tilted his head downward so he could better hear her.

"Why are you sorry?"

"For not calling you. For not responding when I said I would. I was just so freaked out."

He slid his fingers underneath her chin and turned her face, tipping it upward so her gaze met his. Then he put a finger over her lips.

"Not now. And you won't apologize to me. There's nothing to apologize for. We'll talk this out, Josie. I want to hear every word. But not here. For now just sit here with me, and let me hold you. When we get to my apartment, we'll talk. But even then you won't apologize for something that was not your doing. I may not have liked that you didn't reach out to me when you needed someone, but I understand."

Her smile was tremulous and warmth entered her eyes, removing some of the uncertainty and anxiety that had taken residence in the aquamarine pools.

"There, that's better," he said. "You have such a beautiful smile. I'm going to ensure that you do it more often, Josie. I'm going to make you happy. That's a guarantee."

She cocked her head, a baffled expression crossing her face. "I'm at a loss, Ash. Things like this just don't happen. They *don't*. A part of me thinks I've entered the *Twilight Zone*. It's all . . . crazy."

He smiled indulgently. "In my world, they do. Or at least they do now. Can't say this has ever happened to me either, so we're both entering new territory. But it's your world too, Josie. There are no rules but the ones we make ourselves. Can't say I've ever been much of a traditionalist anyway. I'm too much of a 'do it my own way and fuck the rest of the world' kind of guy."

Her smile broadened, her teeth flashing and an adorable dimple forming in her cheek. It fascinated him. Made him want to trace the indention and then follow it with his tongue.

"I'm kind of getting that about you. I pity the person that ever tells you that you can't do something."

"Yeah, that doesn't go over too well," he admitted.

"I'll try not to be the person who pisses you off by telling you no, then."

His smile faded and he stared intently into her eyes. "I hope to hell I never give you reason to tell me no. But if you do, Josie, understand. I won't ignore that word. Unless it has something to do with your safety or well-being. Or if it means you walking away from me. *No* is a deal breaker. It means I stop whatever I'm doing. So use it wisely and only if you mean it. Because I take that word very seriously."

Her eyes went soft and she leaned further into him, her body molding so very temptingly to his. His balls ached, his dick was stiff as a board and his teeth were clenched tight as he sought to control his physical reaction to her nearness.

This woman did it for him. He had no explanation for why. He barely knew her, but he knew he had to have her. Knew he *would* have her. Knew they were going to be tangled up and that he had no desire to extricate himself. He also knew that this woman was different from all the women who'd come before her.

That part scared the shit out of him and excited him all at the same time.

What if she was the one? That woman who, when a man saw

her, he was instantly struck with the knowledge that he was done for. Like Mia was for Gabe. Like Bethany was for Jace. The *one*.

He couldn't even wrap his mind around it. Wasn't even going there. It was too soon. The entire situation was crazy. He was moving her into his apartment. He was taking over her life. He hadn't thought beyond that to "what next?"

Because what the hell was next?

Other than getting Josie in his bed, under his hand, submissive, fully submissive to his every need and desire. Just as he would see to her every need and desire. Wasn't that enough? It had to be because he wouldn't let himself think beyond that.

His driver pulled to a stop on the side street to his apartment building and then got out to open the door for Ash.

Ash stepped out first, sliding away from Josie and then extending his hand to help her from the backseat. He tucked her into his side and then collected her overnight bag from the driver before hurrying toward the entrance.

"You live by the Hudson," Josie said faintly, staring in the direction of the river.

"Yeah. Nice view from the top. Come on up. Let's get you inside."

They rode the elevator to the top floor and he carried her bag inside, guiding her toward the bedroom. She stiffened slightly when they entered the master suite, and she glanced sideways, caution reflected in her eyes.

He tossed her bag onto the bed and then pointed toward the bathroom.

"I'll give you time to get changed into what you're sleeping in. I'll be in the kitchen fixing you a glass of wine. Take your time."

"Where am I sleeping?" she murmured.

He put his hands to her shoulders and let his palms glide down her shoulders. "In my bed, Josie. With me."

Anxiety crept into her gaze.

He leaned forward and pressed his lips to her forehead, feeling particularly tender toward her. Perhaps it was the vulnerability. The worry and fear he could see in her eyes.

"When we talk, Josie. It will be in my bed. You in my arms. You safe. And you'll know that. But you're only sleeping. It's why you're changing into your nightclothes. You won't wear them again, but tonight, you need that barrier because you're still not sure of me. After tonight, you will be."

He kissed her one last time and then he turned, leaving her in his bedroom alone to change.

He went into the kitchen, taking his time as he took down two glasses and opened a bottle of wine. He remembered that she didn't drink much in the way of alcohol, but she had mentioned she liked an occasional glass of wine, and it would most certainly help her relax tonight. He didn't know for certain, but he imagined her to prefer red wine. She'd want something with color. Vibrant and flavorful. Nothing devoid of warmth like white wine.

He frowned when he realized his own dinner had been interrupted, and since he'd gone straight to Josie's and met her upon her arrival, it was likely she hadn't eaten either.

He rummaged in the fridge for fruit salad and several wedges of gourmet cheese. He arranged a tray, pulling bread and crackers from the pantry to accompany the cheese and fruit. And something sweet. Didn't all women enjoy chocolate?

His housekeeper often left him delectable homemade treats, and this week's offering was chocolate mousse with a cream cheese topping. There were five individual dessert dishes on the top shelf of the fridge, so he pulled two of the single-serving containers out, added them to the tray and then yanked spoons from the drawer.

Satisfied that he had all the bases covered, and that he'd given

Josie enough time to prepare for bed and to get over any nerves she was feeling, he headed back toward the bedroom.

When he walked in, she was sitting cross-legged in the middle of the bed, and he was absurdly taken by the image of her in his bed. Comfortable, bare feet, like she belonged.

She was wearing silky, hot pink pajamas. Long-legged and long-sleeved, covering her entire body. Buttoned to the neck.

He'd give her this tonight. That barrier. But after this, she would come to their bed with nothing. She'd sleep next to him, her skin against his.

Her eyes widened when she saw the tray he carried and she scrambled up, scooting back off the bed so he could set the tray down.

"Pull back the covers," he directed. "We'll get into bed and I'll put the tray on the nightstand. You can eat in bed next to me."

She hastily pulled back the comforter and the sheet and even plumped the pillows before crawling back onto the mattress.

As he said, he set the tray down on his side of the bed and then strode toward his closet to strip out of his clothing.

He faced a dilemma, because he never wore anything but boxers to bed. Then he shrugged. It wasn't as if he was completely nude, and he'd promised her that she'd only rest in his arms. He wasn't putting the moves on her, so his boxers would do.

When he walked back out, he felt her gaze on him even as she tried to hide the fact that she was watching him. It was adorable the way she peeked from underneath her lashes and the color heightened in her cheeks when he crawled onto the bed beside her.

He offered her the fruit and cheese first and then slipped a glass of wine in her free hand. He offered her bites, enjoying the slight brush of her lips over his fingertips. And she seemed to derive as much pleasure from eating from his hand as he did in feeding her this way.

A dreamy, contented look entered her eyes, some of the earlier shadows chased away as she relaxed. Tension drifted from her shoulders, and they settled, her entire body going slack.

"Hungry?" he asked huskily, entranced by the provocative image she presented.

Finally. In his bed. Just inches away. His body screamed at him to take her, to take what was his even as he mentally chastised it for being an impatient asshole.

"Starved," she admitted. "I haven't eaten well over the past few days."

His expression darkened and anger vibrated once more from his body. "You'll take better care of yourself from now on. I'll take better care of you," he amended.

She smiled. "It's not solely because of . . . Michael . . . and what happened. I've been busy with work."

He knew well why, but he asked anyway, because it would seem odd not to, and she was offering information, relaxing around him, and he wanted that. Wanted easy communication. No hesitancy or reserve on her part.

"What have you been working on?"

Color tinged her cheeks and he glanced curiously at her.

"I've been working on an erotic series of paintings. Not too over the top. Tasteful. Sexy but still classy."

Excitement gleamed in her eyes as she sat back a moment, refusing further food from his hand.

"I sold all my work that was exhibited in the art gallery where I sell on consignment! It was the most incredible thing. Mr. Downing had told me he couldn't take anything else of mine because nothing had sold and I had already brought him the first painting in the series I'm working on. Then he called to tell me the news that not only had he sold everything but that he wanted more! And that a buyer was interested in whatever I brought in. I've spent the week working on the rest of that series."

She ducked her head self-consciously and then peeked back up at him from underneath her lashes.

"They're self-portraits. I mean, not that you can tell who it is, but I used my likeness in a series of nude poses. I have a . . . tattoo, one I designed myself, and it features prominently in the paintings. I . . . I like them. I think they're good. I hope the buyer will like them too."

There was a note of anxiety at the end of her statement that made his heart clench. Hell yes he'd like them, and he'd be damned if anyone else even got to see them. They would be his. Only his. And only he would see her without her clothing. That was for him and him alone.

No doubt, Josie was a beautiful woman, and there was also little doubt that men and women alike would be drawn to the paintings. She had talent, no matter what the moron gallery manager had said about her style. It was only a matter of time before others discovered that talent. Ash was just glad he got to those paintings before someone else did. The idea of anyone else having something so intimate of Josie's made his teeth clench.

"I'm sure your buyer will love them," he said. Even as he spoke, he made a mental note to call Mr. Downing first thing Monday morning and make damn sure he wrapped and delivered the paintings to Ash's office. "I'd love to have seen them myself."

She blushed but smiled and then said, "Perhaps I can take you down to the gallery to see them. I only just dropped them off. Maybe the buyer won't have bought them yet. They may sit there for days."

He leaned in, touching her cheek and letting his fingers travel down her jaw to her neck where he pushed back the long blond strands of her hair. "I'd rather you draw me something new.

Something no one but me will see. Perhaps even something a bit more erotic than your other paintings?"

Her eyes widened and then her brow furrowed as if she were visualizing the painting already. Her lips parted and her breath escaped in an excited rush. He could literally see her painting it in her mind.

"I have ideas," she said. "I'd love to do something more personal. I mean, as long as you never displayed it."

He shook his head solemnly. "No one but me will ever see it. I'll treasure whatever you paint for me, Josie. But if you give me you, the sexy you, you can be damn certain it will only be for me and nobody else."

"Okay," she murmured, her face flushed with color and . . . arousal.

"Have you had enough to eat?"

She nodded and handed him the half-empty glass of wine. He set it aside and then took the tray to his dresser and left it before returning to the bed. And Josie.

He climbed in, holding his arm out so she could nestle beside him. They were leaned up against his mound of pillows, her body anchored against his.

"Now tell me about Michael," Ash said in an even tone.

She stiffened against him and for a long moment she was silent. Then she sagged and blew out her breath.

"I was so wrong about him," she whispered. "I never imagined him capable of something like this. Even during our relationship, when he exerted his . . . dominance . . . it was always done in a restrained, careful manner. He always treated me very carefully. Like he was determined never to hurt me."

"Where were you when this occurred?" Ash demanded. "Did you go see him?"

She shook her head. "No. He came to me."

Ash swore. "You let him into your apartment?"

She pushed up and off him, turning so she could look him in the eye. "Why wouldn't I have? Ash, we were lovers. He never gave me any reason to believe he'd hurt me. He never lost his temper. Not once. I never even saw him angry. He's always been very calm and restrained. He came to see me because he didn't believe I was serious about ending our relationship. He brought the collar back, apologizing, saying that it evidently meant something to me and that he would be aware of that going forward."

Ash frowned but didn't interrupt her.

"When I told him it was over, he demanded to know why."

She broke off, glancing away, folding her hands in her lap as she presented her profile to him. He pulled her tighter against him, molding her to his body. He could feel her pulse, how agitated she'd become.

"What happened then?" he asked softly.

"I told him that he couldn't give me the things another man had promised me," she whispered.

Ash's hold tightened further. "Go on."

"He freaked. I mean completely lost it. The words were barely out of my mouth when he slapped me. I was so shocked that I didn't even know what to do. And then he was standing over me, where I'd fallen, and he hit me again. He wrapped his hands in my hair and accused me of cheating on him. Told me that he'd handled me far too gently. That if he'd been the way he should have with me this would have never happened, that I would have never cheated."

"Son of a bitch," Ash ground out. "I'll kill him for this."

She shook her head violently. "No! Ash, leave it alone. It's done with. It's over."

"The hell it is!"

He calmed his breathing and forced the rage from his mind and eased his grip on her arm where his fingers had dug into her skin.

She would wear no marks from him. None that weren't given in passion and tenderness. None that she wouldn't want to wear.

"I should have gone to the police," she said in a low voice. "I should have pressed charges. Had him arrested. But God, I was just in shock. And then I felt so . . . stupid. How could I not have seen this in him? That capacity for violence? How could I have had sex with him and never known what lay underneath his façade? When I think of what could have happened. I trusted him. Implicitly. I gave him full access to my body. He could have done anything to me. It's why . . ."

She broke off, going silent against him. He pushed her hair from her battered cheek and then pressed a kiss to the bruised flesh.

"Why what?" he asked gently.

She closed her eyes. "It's why I didn't call you. Why I didn't come to you. Why I didn't accept what you offered. I was . . . afraid."

He tensed, his gaze focusing intently on her. "Afraid of *me*?"

She nodded miserably.

He sucked in his breath. He understood. He didn't like hearing it, but he understood.

"I get it," he said, stroking his hand up her arm. "You thought because you misjudged him so badly that you couldn't trust your judgment of me and my intentions."

She nodded again.

"I understand, but Josie, you need to get this. I am *not* Michael."

She glanced back up at him, hope stirring in her eyes. She wanted to believe him. Wanted to trust herself and her instincts where he was concerned.

"I will never hurt you," he said, the vow coming solemnly from his lips. "If we have issues, we work them out. And it does not involve me raising my hand to you. Ever."

"Okay," she whispered.

"Come here," he murmured, stretching his other arm to her.

She didn't hesitate and promptly buried herself against his chest. He wrapped both arms around her and held her close, breathing in her scent.

"Pisses me off that you'll wear those bruises for several more days. I don't like seeing them, but more than me not liking to see them is *you* having to see them and remember him hurting you."

"I'm okay," she said against his chest.

"You're not. Yet. But you will be," he promised. "Give me that, Josie. Give me the chance to show you that we're right together. I get that you're gun-shy right now and that you're doubting yourself, but give yourself into my care. Give me that chance. You won't regret it."

She was silent for a long moment, one that had him on edge as he waited for her acceptance.

Then she gave it. One simple word, laced with uncertainty but quiet determination.

"Okay."

His own chest caved in a bit. He breathed in and out for several seconds before squeezing her to him.

"Sleep now, Josie. Tomorrow we'll decide what to do about your apartment."

He held her just as he was doing until her body went lax against his and the soft, even sounds of her breathing filled his ears. And still he waited, tense, replaying every word she'd said earlier. The fear in her voice. The self-condemnation. The image of her lying on the floor, Michael standing over her while he hurt her made it impossible for him to sleep.

It was well past midnight when he quietly picked up his cell phone from the nightstand and punched Jace's number from his contacts list.

"What the hell?" his friend mumbled into the phone. "This better be good, Ash."

"I need an alibi," Ash said.

There was a long silence.

"Jesus. Fuck! What the hell, man? Do you need help? What's going on?"

Ash glanced down at Josie, her eyelashes resting on her cheeks, the shadow of a bruise still on her face.

"Not now. But soon. Right now Josie needs me. She needs comfort and peace. And she needs to know that I will never hurt her. For now, I'm going to spend every minute making sure she knows this. But then I'm going after the bastard who put these bruises on her face and I'll need you to help provide an alibi if it becomes necessary."

"Christ, Ash. What the fuck? Someone hurt Josie?"

"Yeah," Ash bit out. "And I'm going to make sure he never touches her or any woman ever again."

Jace blew out his breath over the phone as he grew quiet.

"Whatever you need, man. You have it. Never have to ask."

"Thanks, man," Ash murmured. "Talk to you later."

# chapter twelve

Josie stirred and tried to stretch but immediately ran into a hard body. Her eyes flew open and she blinked rapidly as confusion ran through her mind. Then she remembered. She was in bed with Ash. In Ash's apartment. In his arms.

Her gaze met the hard wall of his chest, saw the rise and fall of that beautiful male flesh. She inhaled, savoring his smell. Her lips were so close that she could easily press her mouth to his skin. And she was tempted.

But they weren't lovers waking up after a night making love. They hadn't had sex at all. Yet. They didn't know each other at all beyond a few pleasantries and one conversation over dinner.

And yet she was here in his bed after agreeing to move in with him.

She closed her eyes and wondered again if she was making the right decision. Her mind and heart argued incessantly, and she still wasn't sure who was the clear winner. Maybe there wasn't one. She was going to have to wing this, because there was no clear and easy "right" decision.

Hesitantly, she lifted her gaze, holding her breath as she looked up to see if he was awake. Her eyes met his and she felt the jolt all the way to her toes. He was definitely awake and he was staring intently at her. As if he could reach in and pluck her thoughts right from her head.

"Good morning," he murmured.

She dipped her head as heat crept over her cheeks.

"Josie?"

She glanced back up to see the question in his eyes.

"What's wrong?" he asked gently.

She swallowed. "This is hard."

He slid his hand up her body, over her arm and then up to tangle in her hair before brushing his fingers over the curve of her cheek.

"Never said it would be easy. Nothing good ever is."

That was true enough. And no, Ash would definitely never be easy. Nothing about him was simple or uncomplicated.

"Like waking up, you in my arms."

The statement rumbled from his chest and warmth seeped into her blood, traveling through her body.

"I liked it too," she whispered.

"Want you to feel safe here," Ash said in a serious tone. "Safe with me."

"I do."

"Good. Now give me your mouth so I can tell you good morning properly."

She tilted her chin upward and placed her hand against his chest. He flinched beneath her touch, his muscles tight and quivering. She withdrew hastily, but he caught her hand and guided it back to his chest.

"Like you touching me," he murmured. "I'll want it often. Just like I'll be wanting to touch you anytime you're near me. If we're in the same room, Josie, I'm going to be touching you."

And then he kissed her, his warm, sensual mouth working exquisitely over hers.

It was gentle. Undemanding. Coaxing, almost.

She sighed into his mouth and relaxed, going limp against him, trapping her hand between their bodies.

"Been waiting for this," he murmured. "You in my bed. Your mouth on mine. You the very first thing I taste in the morning. The last week has driven me crazy, Josie. Waiting for you. For this. And I finally have it. I'm not letting it go."

"I've been waiting too," she admitted. And she had. She'd dreamed about it. Wondered how it would feel. And now she knew. It felt . . . right.

Her earlier worries evaporated. Her questions. Her fears. The idea that she was making the wrong decision. They were gone in a perfect moment of absolute rightness. This was what she wanted. What he could give her. And she wasn't going to fight it or herself any longer.

He rolled her onto her back, coming up and over her, his body looming big and strong. He kissed her again, deepening it this time. Allowing his urgency to bleed into her mouth.

His lips moved strongly over hers, demanding, taking. He stole her breath. She couldn't breathe because he didn't let her.

"I was determined to wait. To be patient," he rasped out. "Can't do it, Josie. I have to have you now. Tell me you're with me. You have to be with me. I can't be the only one feeling like I'm going to die if I don't get inside you."

His impassioned words cut to her core. She arched into him, inviting him without words. But he stopped, his eyes boring intently into hers. He wanted the words. He demanded them.

"Tell me," he demanded. "Tell me you're with me, Josie. I want to hear you say it so there's no doubt that this is what you want. As much as I want you, as much as I have to have you, if you're not with me, this stops now."

"I'm with you," she said breathlessly, her heart surging, adrenaline spiking through her veins.

"Thank fuck," he breathed.

He kissed her again, as if he couldn't stand to have his mouth away from hers for even a moment. Then he reluctantly dragged his head away, his eyes brimming with lust and arousal.

"Need to get a condom. We'll talk about alternatives later, but for now, you have to be protected. And we have to get rid of those pajamas. Pink is you. Definitely your color, but right now, I'm dying to see that tattoo."

She smiled as he rolled off her and rummaged in his nightstand drawer. Then he came back to her and pushed his hands underneath her pajama top to the waistband of her bottoms.

"Been dying to see it ever since that first day in the park where I got just a glimpse when your shirt came up."

"You saw it already?" she asked in surprise.

He smiled, pausing in his downward push of her bottoms. "Yeah. Drove me crazy. I've been thinking about it. I want to see just how far it extends."

She lifted her butt so he could pull her pajamas the rest of the way off. He tossed the bottoms aside and then began working his way up from the last button, slowly opening her top to reveal the rest of her body.

When he loosened the last button, he pushed the material apart and over her shoulders. She hitched herself upward, wanting to be rid of the top every bit as much as he did. This time it was she who sent the piece of clothing sailing across the room to hit the floor near the bathroom.

His gaze was riveted to the tattoo. She watched as his eyes tracked downward, following the line of the design to where it flowed over the top of her thigh and disappeared between her legs.

She shivered at the intensity in that stare. There was a brooding possessiveness. A look that screamed, "Mine!"

Ash turned Josie gently on her side, wanting to see the entirety of the tattoo. It was startling in its vibrancy, a shock of color against pale skin. Done in pinks, oranges, aqua blues that matched her eyes and shades of purple and green.

It was, as he'd suspected, a flowering vine, but it was rendered in exquisite detail. This was no simple tattoo done in a few hours time. He couldn't imagine the time it had taken. The patience exerted in getting the design done just right.

He let his fingers trail over her skin, tracing the lines to where it flared over her hip and then across the top of her thigh before dipping lower, on the inside of her thigh. He turned her again, to her back this time, his fingers resting next to the golden curls covering her mound.

"Show me," he said in a low growl. "Spread your legs, Josie. Show me the tattoo and that sweet little pussy."

Her eyes blanked and widened, the pupils flaring and then constricting. But she obeyed instantly, her legs going slack and slowly parting to bare herself to his gaze. He stroked the soft curls, approving of her easy acquiescence.

"Beautiful," he said, the words thick in his throat. The tattoo, all that sweet, pink, feminine flesh. Josie was beautiful.

The intricate design curved around the inside of her thigh, coming to a stop just at the back of her leg. It was a bright, floral blanket over her skin, vibrant like her, a perfect reflection of her personality and artistry.

There would be plenty of time to exert his dominance, to have her submit in all manner of ways. Today was about their first time together and establishing trust. It was about him taking care of her needs. Pleasuring her. He would be infinitely gentle, because before it was over with, he knew he'd take everything. He'd demand everything. So for this one time, he would give her an experience that would become the basis of their bond.

He leaned down, pressing his mouth between her breasts. She

arched into him, seeking more of his mouth. So he gave her more, kissing a line down to her belly. A soft moan escaped and her stomach clenched and quivered beneath his mouth.

The anticipation of tasting her intimately had him doing his own amount of quivering. He was walking a razor's edge. The urge to spread her wider and plunge into her was overwhelming. He wanted to claim her. It was a primitive instinct, one that had ruled his thoughts since the moment he'd laid eyes on her. And now she was here, naked, in his bed. His to do with what he wanted.

He was going to damn well savor the gift and appreciate it for what it was worth. She'd given him her trust, and he knew how huge that was, given the circumstances.

He pressed a kiss to the silky hairs over her pussy and then nuzzled deeper, inhaling her scent as he spread her further to his advances. He stroked his fingers through her velvety folds, spreading moisture from her opening up to her clit so his fingers slid more easily and he wouldn't irritate the sensitive flesh.

"Ash!"

His name exploded from her mouth. He loved the way she said it, the sound of his name on her lips. And he knew he could make her even crazier with desire just as soon as he got his mouth where his fingers were.

Using his fingers to open her to him, he pushed in, swiping his mouth from her entrance to her clit, her wetness like honey on his tongue.

A ragged moan tore from her throat and suddenly her hand was in his hair, fingers clenching over his scalp. He sucked lightly at her clit, exerting just enough pressure to send spasms of pleasure through her legs. Then he licked downward again, wanting more of her silken, hot dampness.

His tongue slid inside her, fucking her in slow, sensual strokes. While he may have decided that this time would be all about her and her pleasure, making her writhe beneath him was also his pleasure. He was hard and aching, so aroused that his head was spinning.

"Give me one," he said huskily, raising his head to look up her body. "In my mouth, Josie. Come all over my mouth. I'll work you back up again. I'll make it good for you."

Her eyes were glazed with passion, her lips red and swollen from his kisses and the fact her teeth had found purchase there while he'd eaten her.

"You like my mouth, Josie?"

"Oh yeah," she breathed. "You've very good with your tongue."

"You inspire me," he said with a chuckle.

She moaned again when he slid his tongue back inside her liquid heat. Tasting her from the inside out.

Deciding to up the tension and get her off with his tongue inside her, he slipped his thumb over her clit, rolling as he continued to lick and suck, acting like his tongue was his dick.

Her ass came off the bed, bucking upward at the pressure he exerted with his thumb. She went even softer around his tongue. Hot, sleek, spilling into his mouth. He lapped hungrily, greedy for her orgasm.

With his free hand, he inserted one finger, moving his tongue only long enough to reach inside her, stroke the silky walls and then press deep. She clutched at his finger like a greedy fist, holding on when he withdrew and replaced it once again with his tongue.

"Now, Josie," he growled. "Get there."

He stroked her with his fingers and his tongue and she went wild beneath him. She let loose a torrent of energy as she quaked around him. Her legs closed against his head, anchoring him in place as he continued to lap hungrily at her. And then a sudden burst of heated honey on his tongue.

She rolled her hips and bucked as wave after wave of her orgasm washed over them both. Goddamn but his dick was going to be permanently imprinted on the mattress. It was rigid and straining underneath him, hungry for what his mouth was currently getting.

He rose up when he sensed her orgasm had faded to the stage where she was too hypersensitive to his continued ministrations. Hunching over her, palms planted on either side of her head so his weight wouldn't press down on her, he leaned down, angling his head to kiss her. So she could taste herself, so he could share it with her.

"Your passion. Your sweetness, Josie. Never tasted anything sweeter. It's you on my tongue and now on your own."

She groaned, and it sounded nearly pained but she kissed him back every bit as hungrily. Her nipples were rigid peaks, jutting upward as if begging for his mouth just as her pussy had. He'd get to those next. But first he wanted to sample her mouth and her neck. Then he'd work down to her delectable breasts.

"Can I touch you?" she whispered.

"Never have to ask that," he murmured against her ear. He licked the shell, eliciting a shiver through her body. "I want you touching me often. I'll never not want it. If you're with me, I want you touching me. Even if it's not sexual. I'm a feely person, Josie. Don't know if that bothers you. Hope to hell it doesn't. And I don't give a shit if it's in public or not. I have no problem with the world knowing you're mine."

She sighed and slid her hands over his shoulders and then down his back. He goddamn near purred as her nails dug into his skin.

"I like that," she said.

"What part?"

"All of it. Michael wasn't like that."

Her eyes became troubled, almost as if she realized that it wasn't likely a good idea to bring him up, especially when Ash was about to get his dick inside her for the first time.

He made certain his face softened, not wanting her to think she'd made him angry.

"Wasn't like what?"

"Demonstrative. He wasn't into affection. Touching me. Except when we had sex. But only then, and even so, it was very . . . impersonal. But the way you say it sounds . . . nice. Like you want me to be close to you. To touch you."

"Hell yes I do," he said. "Don't give a fuck who knows it either."

She smiled and then shivered again when he bent to graze his teeth over the skin just below her ear.

"I'm liking this, Ash," she whispered. "All of it. And that scares me because it sounds too good to be true."

"Glad it appeals, Josie. Would suck if it didn't, because this is who I am and what I offer. It's not too good to be true. It's just good. Now let's focus on the matter at hand. Because if I don't get my dick inside you soon, it's going to become very painful for me."

She looked alarmed, but he grinned, letting her know he was only half kidding. Because it was pretty damn painful. It had been a long-ass time since he'd sported an erection this long without doing something about it. And eating her sweet pussy while his dick was poking the damn mattress was not an experience he wanted to repeat anytime soon.

He'd much prefer a sixty-nine, with her sucking him off while he feasted on her. But as with all of the other fantasies he had, it would have to wait. And now that he had her exactly where he wanted, he had all the time in the world to explore every sexual kink he could possibly ever want to pull out of his repertoire.

He turned his attention to her breasts, and they were perfect breasts. Small without being too small, but not too big either. Just enough swell to make his mouth water, and her nipples were absolutely perfect, pink confections.

He ran his tongue around one puckered ridge, tracing every

detail, licking the point before sucking it strongly into his mouth. Her entire body went rigid, her gasps filling the air and sliding over his ears with a warm buzz.

"Ash."

The way she said his name, he knew she wanted to ask something. He looked up, connecting with her gaze, watching in fascination as the color turned electric, a shock of blue-green awash with desire.

"I want to taste you too," she whispered. "I want to make you feel as good as you made me feel."

He smiled tenderly at her and then leaned down to kiss the corner of her mouth. "You will. But right now is about you, and me making you go over as many times as I can. Believe me when I say, you'll get my dick in your mouth soon."

"Looking forward to it," she said in a hazy murmur.

"Me too," he said before lowering his mouth back to her breasts.

He lazily toyed with her nipples, alternating between them, licking them into hard points before sucking hard with just enough bite to make her let out the most erotic sounds. She wasn't a quiet lover. She was extremely vocal, a multitude of sounds slipping from her lips, all sexy as hell, the ultimate sounds of female pleasure.

He groped for the condom he'd taken out, tore the wrapper and then reached down to roll it on. He winced when his hand made contact with his dick. He was so hard and so close to coming that even his own touch was painful.

"Are you all right?" she whispered.

"I will be in just about three seconds," he murmured back as he slid a finger inside her to gauge her readiness.

She was still swollen and snug from her orgasm and he broke into a sweat imagining how fucking sweet she was going to feel all closed around his cock, squeezing and milking it for every drop of his release. Shit but he had to get it together or he was going to come in the condom right now.

Taking deep breaths, he positioned himself over her, nudging her entrance with the head of his dick as he planted his hands on either side of her head.

"Reach down and guide me in," he said hoarsely. "Wrap your fingers around me and put me inside you, baby."

He caught her reaction to the endearment, approval and delight flashing in her eyes. He tucked that little piece of information away and then closed his eyes when her hand found him.

Her fingers circled his width, stroking up and down as she positioned him at the mouth of her pussy. Sweat broke out on his forehead and he clamped his lips together in an effort to keep it together.

"Take me," she whispered. "You're there, Ash. Come inside me now."

Readily, he pushed in, ensuring that he wasn't too forceful and that she was able to accommodate him easily. She was damn snug, but she stretched, enveloping him as he thrust deeper and harder this time.

"Now, move your hands and put them above your head against the headboard," he said.

She twitched and pulsed in reaction, her pussy going wetter and hotter around him. Slowly, she did as he directed, lifting her hands and then putting them over her head.

He reared up and then slid his hands underneath her ass so he could hold her and position her so he could get even deeper inside her. He glanced down, drawn by the sight of his cock sliding in and out of her pussy. Then his hands glided from her ass up her legs until he hooked them behind his back, opening her further so she was completely accessible.

"How close are you to coming again?" he asked, breathing through his nose as he sought for control.

"Close," she whispered. "But I need . . ."

She bit her lip and broke off, her gaze falling from his.

"Look at me," he bit out.

Her gaze snapped back to his, her eyes wide.

"What do you need?"

"Uhm, for you to touch me." Color flooded her cheeks and suffused her body, making it delectably pink. "I've never been able to come from just penetration."

He lowered himself, coming to rest on his forearms so his face was just above hers, their mouths precariously close.

"A lot of women can't come without clitoral stimulation," he said gently. "Doesn't mean there's anything wrong with you. Furthermore, even if it was an oddity, you don't ever hesitate to tell me what you need in bed. Got it? I can't please you if I don't know what turns you on and what doesn't. And I want you to be pleased because that makes me happy."

"Got it," she returned softly.

"Use your hand," he said, carefully reaching up to tug one of her hands down between them. "I'm going to go hard, baby. I'm about to explode here. Build up's been too long. Once I start going, I can't stop, so you need to make sure you get there with me. If you need a minute, go ahead and start touching yourself now. Just let me know when, okay?"

She slid her fingers between their bodies, and he could tell when she touched her clitoris. There was an immediate burst of satisfaction in her eyes. They went dreamy and hazy, cloudy with desire.

"Go now," she whispered.

"Be sure, Josie. This isn't going to last."

She nodded, her face already strained with her impending orgasm.

It was like setting the bloodhounds free.

He withdrew, enjoying the sensuous slide from her body. Then he slammed forward and began thrusting hard and deep. Faster. Harder. His eyes rolled back in his head. He'd never felt anything so goddamn good in his life.

A roar began in his ears. His blood thundered through his veins. Josie went dim in front of him and the room faded as agonizing pleasure bloomed, unfurling like a tightly closed bud in the first rays of spring sunshine.

"Jesus," he gritted out. "This is going to kill me."

"Me too," she gasped. "Oh God, Ash, don't stop, please!"

"The hell that's happening."

He pounded into her, the force of his thrusts shaking the entire bed. Her breasts jiggled enticingly, her nipples so hard and beaded that it looked painful. But then hell, he was banging away at her like some rutting pig.

Need splintered through him. Razor sharp, his orgasm swelled and boiled low, gathering in his balls and then shooting straight up his cock, exploding outward in a painful spurt. He wasn't breathing. He was just thrusting, riding the wave. Immersing himself in her warm clasp over and over.

"Josie," he whispered, her name nearly a groan.

"I'm with you, Ash."

Her words cut the last thread and he spiraled downward like a snowflake in the wind. Crazy. Fluttering madly. His entire body sizzling like a blown fuse. Hell, he probably had blown a few circuits. His mind was mush. Completely overtaken, sated, satisfied.

He collapsed down on her, no longer able to keep his weight off her. He lay there, gasping for breath, her body beneath his. For a long moment he remained there, but he knew he was smothering her and he also had to get rid of the damn condom.

He couldn't wait to have her bareback. He'd stay inside her all damn night. They'd wake up a sticky, wet mess, but he didn't give two fucks. He wanted his come in her and on her.

Levering himself upward, he kissed her forehead and then smoothed the hair from her face before kissing her lips.

"Was that good for you?" he asked.

"If it was any better, I'd be dead," she said ruefully.

He smiled and then got up just long enough to discard the condom. Then he crawled back into bed, pulling her into the shelter of his body.

"Think I could go back to sleep for a while," he murmured.

"Mmm hmm," she agreed.

"Then let's sleep. I'll arrange something for us to eat when we wake up."

She snuggled deeper into his embrace and then threaded her leg through his so his was looped over hers.

"Works for me," she whispered.

# chapter thirteen

"I want you to wear my collar, Josie," Ash said in a low voice.

She turned in his arms, surprised at the blunt declaration. The two were stretched out on Ash's couch, a lazy morning after their lovemaking and short nap earlier. After they'd woken up again, Ash had brought her breakfast in bed and then he'd taken her into the bathroom where he'd washed every inch of her skin and hair in the shower.

He'd dried her, brushed out her hair and then wrapped one of his robes around her before taking her into the living room where they'd been on the couch ever since.

Ash stared intently at her as if gauging her response. His gaze flickered over her face and then back up to hold her eyes.

"Know you wore Michael's. Also know it didn't mean a damn thing. It means something to me, Josie. I want it to mean something to you too."

"Okay," she whispered.

"I want to choose it especially for you. I don't have it yet, but I will. And when I get it, I want you to wear it. Will you do that for me?"

She nodded, already imagining wearing his jewelry, the knowledge of what it would mean to him alive in her mind.

"Got a lot of other things to talk about today," he continued. "A lot we need to work out. I'd rather get it all out today so we can move on, knowing what we need to know. And you'll know what you need to know."

"Okay, Ash. I'm ready."

He squeezed her arms, satisfaction brimming in his eyes. "Means a lot for you to trust me. Especially after what happened with that prick. I won't ever hurt you like that, Josie. You may not know it right now, but you'll know it soon."

"I know you won't hurt me," she said, lowering her mouth to his. "I trust you, Ash. I do. I'm not just saying that. You have to know how hard this is for me. But I'm good with my decision. I know it's the right one. You don't have to prove that to me."

"Yeah, I do," he refuted. "Every day. I have to show you every day what you'll mean to me. That's on me. And we'll get there. This—you—are important to me. I'm going to make sure you know that at all times."

She leaned in, laying her head on his shoulder, her body settling over his. He felt so good. So solid and strong. He didn't have to work at making her feel safe. She did feel safe. Just being close to him.

"First thing we need to talk about is medical exams and birth control."

She lifted her head back up, one eyebrow raised in question.

"I don't want to use condoms. Not with you. I want to be able to come inside you, on you. In order for us to do that, you need to have an alternate method of birth control and we also both need tests so we know we're both clean, although I'll tell you now, Josie. Not sure what you did with Michael, but I use condoms. Never haven't. And it's been a while for me. Not since . . ."

He broke off and shook his head. "That will come in a bit."

She cocked her head to the side. "What will come?"

"The circumstance surrounding the last time I had sex with a woman," Ash said in a serious tone. "I'll get to that. But right now there are other things we need to get settled."

The way he said it made her concerned. Her brow furrowed and he reached up, curling his hand around her nape to pull her down so his lips settled against her forehead.

"Michael and I used condoms," she said quietly. "He's the only man I've been with in two years. And I'm already on birth control."

"You good with my word or you want a copy of my last medical exam?" he asked.

She frowned, wondering if this was some kind of a test. If she said she wanted a copy of his medical report, would it seem that she didn't trust him? Was he asking her if she trusted him this far? But if she didn't ask for it, if she said his word was good enough, that was taking a huge leap. And her life was too important to take those kinds of risks.

"I'd like the copy," she said.

He nodded, seemingly unbothered by her request.

"I'll make sure you get it this afternoon."

"What about me?" she asked. "Do you want me to be tested? The last time I saw a doctor was three months ago. Obviously I've had sex since then."

"I'll arrange it for this afternoon."

Her eyes widened. "I can't get an appointment with my doctor that quickly."

"We'll use mine. He'll see you," Ash said confidently.

She nodded.

"Now we need to discuss our arrangement here. At this apartment."

"Okay."

She hadn't meant it to sound hesitant. But things seemed much simpler in the abstract. Now that they were actually hashing out specifics, she was nervous and on edge.

"No way to do this except to be blunt," Ash said, his voice soothing. "I know you're nervous, but we'll talk it out and then deal."

She took a deep breath and then nodded.

"This apartment is not convenient to public transportation. Which is just as well, because I'd prefer having the security of knowing you're safe when you leave here. Which means that my driver will take me to work in the mornings and pick me up in the afternoons. Between those times he'll return here and be at your disposal. But, and this is not me being a controlling asshole, I want to know where you go, when you go, and I want to know you're safe while you're doing it.

"Now we need to sort your apartment out and get what you need from there. You'll move it here, whatever you need. I have an office and extra bedrooms. You can use whatever space you like to paint or draw. I thought the living room might be the best choice simply because you'll have more light and you'll have the view of the river."

She felt light-headed. Like everything around her was moving at the speed of sound while she stood stock-still, trying to take it all in.

"I'll want and need you to be flexible, because when I get home every day, I want you here. Which means that I'll stay in touch with you and you'll do the same with me. My schedule varies. Some days I'll be home early, and those days I'll let you know. Others I'll be late. If I travel—and I don't have immediate travel plans—I'm going to want you with me. Is that something you can deal with?"

She sucked in a breath and then smiled shakily. "Do I have a choice?"

He paused a moment. "No. Those are my expectations."

"Well, then I suppose I'll be home when you are," she said lightly.

He breathed out, his shoulders dipping slightly in relief. As though he'd expected her to refuse. She wondered what he would have done if she had balked? Tossed her out? Or would he have tried to reach a compromise?

He'd readily admitted his need of her. He wanted her, no doubt. But how inflexible was he really? She was curious, but she wasn't ready to push back. Not yet. Not over something she had no real issue with. If and when the time came when he posed something she couldn't embrace, then she would test the boundaries of their newly forming relationship.

"Just so I understand your . . . expectations . . . you basically want me here when you are. Or where you are. And you want me to tell you where I'm going and when and where. And you want me to check in with you frequently."

It didn't sound that demanding to her. It sounded reasonable. She didn't want him worrying about her. Didn't want to be a distraction for him. If he worried—and it was obvious he did—she wanted to do whatever she could to alleviate that stress.

"Yes," he said, his eyes growing more intent. "But, Josie, you need to understand. You make it sound light. It's not. I will be pissed if you flake. This isn't an 'oh sorry I completely forgot to tell you where I was going' thing and laugh it off. I expect you to tell me everything."

"Okay, Ash," she said quietly. "I get it."

He nodded. "Now, there are things you need to know about me. I don't want this shit coming up later and surprising you or making you feel awkward. It's better if you know everything from the start so you can deal and it doesn't become an issue down the road."

She lifted an eyebrow. He sounded so serious. Like he was about to drop some earth-shattering bomb on her. She wanted to joke and ask him if he was about to admit to being an ax murderer, but he was too serious and he wouldn't appreciate her attempt at levity. So she remained silent, waiting for what he had to say.

He shifted upward, grimaced a moment and then leaned

forward so he could shove a cushion between his back and the arm of the sofa. She sat forward so he had room but then he promptly snaked an arm around her waist and pulled her solidly back to him so she was once more nestled against his body.

"Any serious conversation we have is going to be with you in my arms so I'm touching you," he said. "Never you across the room from me. That is not going to make me happy. Warning you now that if you get pissed and we're having a discussion, you won't be putting distance between us."

She smiled against his chest and nodded. That sounded fine to her. One of the things she had disliked the most about Michael was his aloofness when it came to her. The distance—emotional distance—between them. Michael was more of a sit-down-across-the-room-from-each-other-and-discuss guy. For that matter, the only time he ever touched her was when they were having sex. He wasn't demonstrative or affectionate. And Ash couldn't seem to keep his hands off her for two seconds. She liked that. She liked it a *lot*.

"Is this going to be a serious discussion?" she asked, no longer able to keep the teasing note from her voice.

There was no doubt that Ash radiated seriousness today. And it was starting to feel suffocating. She needed to lighten the moment, even if for a brief second. It wasn't in her nature to take everything so seriously. And Ash was an intense guy. Maybe he'd eventually lighten up around her, or maybe he'd always be this . . . broody . . . when it came to her.

His hold tightened around her. "Yeah. It's serious. Everything about me and you is serious. I get that this seems heavy, especially today when we hash it all out. It won't always be this . . . intense. But today, yeah. Need to get whatever out that has the potential to hurt you, because that I will not allow going forward."

Her brow furrowed again and she pushed up so she could see his eyes. So serious and intent. On her. Watching her every reaction.

"What is it, Ash?" she asked. "What is it you think is going to hurt me?"

He sighed. "Don't know if it will or not, but it could. If you don't understand it from the start. I just don't want you blindsided. If you're prepared and you know everything, then it doesn't have the power to catch you off guard."

She reached up to touch his jaw, running her fingertips over the slight stubble. He hadn't shaved this morning, and the dark blond formed a shadow on his jaw.

"Then tell me. I'll understand."

He caught her hand and kissed it, pressing his mouth into her palm.

"Jace Crestwell is my best friend. He and Gabe Hamilton. But Jace . . . We share a bond. Gabe is my best friend, no doubt. But Jace and I have always had a closer friendship. He's my brother in every sense of the word. I trust him. He has my back and I have his. Always. We used to share everything, and by that I mean women. I've had a lot of threesomes over the years with Jace."

Her brow crinkled, her eyebrows bunching as she stared into his eyes. And to think she'd been worried that she'd be expected to share him with other women. This she hadn't expected. She couldn't imagine as possessive as Ash had been with her so far that he'd want her to have sex with another man while he watched or participated. Furthermore, it wasn't something she wanted.

"Is that something . . . I mean, is that what you'll want to do with me? Share me with another man?"

"Fuck no."

The denial was explosive, the words rushing from his mouth in a puff of air she felt on her chin. Relief hit her hard and she relaxed, waiting for him to continue.

"I didn't get it then," he muttered. "How Jace was with Bethany. I didn't understand it. But I do now."

"You're losing me," she said patiently. "I don't understand what you're talking about."

"As I said, Jace is my best friend. He's involved with Bethany. They're engaged. We'll see them a lot. I'll want to share you with them. Their friendship I mean. They're important to me and you're important to me. So we'll spend time with them. And what you need to know is that in the beginning, the first night that Jace and Bethany were together, I was with them."

Her eyes widened. "Are you . . . do you still have . . . three-somes . . . with them?"

Ash shook his head. "Hell no. Jace didn't want it the first time. I didn't know it at the time. It's fucked up and complicated, but what you need to know is that I've had sex with Bethany. And you'll see her. And Jace. And I don't want it to be awkward for you. It was awkward as hell the first few times we were all together after that night. But we're cool with it now. Bethany's cool with it and so is Jace. It's not something that gets brought up. But it's there. And I don't want it to hurt you when you look at her and know that I've had sex with her. Because there's nothing there, Josie. Nothing but deep friendship. Bethany's a great woman. I think you'll like her. But she is no threat to you."

"I understand," she said quietly. "I appreciate you telling me. Being up front with me about it. I can see how it would be awkward, especially if I didn't know and somehow put my foot in my mouth in front of them."

His gaze focused on her, studying her intently. "Is that going to be a problem with you? Spending time with a woman I've fucked and that I care a great deal about?"

"Not if you tell me it shouldn't be a problem for me."

He shook his head. "No, it's not a problem. Like I said, I didn't get where Jace was coming from then. His possessiveness where Bethany was concerned. We'd never had a woman come between us like that. There'd never been one who mattered. But I get it now because I know I don't want to share you with anyone, and especially not my best friend, even if he was single and not in a relationship. And as for other men, that is not something you ever have to worry about. I've had threesomes with Jace and another woman. A hell of a lot of times. I won't lie. We've fucked our way through countless women over the years. It's not something I'm proud of but it's not something I lose sleep over either. It is what it is. But there will be no threesomes with you, Josie. It's only going to be you and me. I'm going to be the only man making love to you from now on."

It all sounded so final, and yet she knew they were just words. How could they be anything else? They'd known each other such a short time. They'd only had sex once. And he was talking like this was a done deal. That they were permanent and in a committed relationship long-term.

While she didn't doubt his commitment, or even her own, there was no way she could look down the road with any authority. There were too many what-ifs.

"Now tell me what you're thinking," he prompted.

She smiled. "I'm not sure how you expected me to react, Ash. Did you think I'd change my mind because you've had kinky sex with a bunch of women? You're what, thirty-five? Thirty-six? It's not realistic to think you hadn't had affairs."

"I'm thirty-eight. Almost thirty-nine," he corrected.

"Okay, well, so you're thirty-eight. I've just told you that I had a relationship—and sex—with a man as recently as a few weeks ago. I can hardly condemn you for having similar relationships."

"But we won't be seeing the man you fucked," Ash pointed out.

She sighed. "I won't say it'll be fun to look at her and mentally compare our performance, or even imagine you and your friend both making love to her. But I'll deal, Ash. And if she's as nice as you say she is, then I'll like her and hopefully we can be friends. I'll just have to not torture myself by visualizing you in bed with her."

"It was only one time," he said gruffly. "Don't want you thinking about it at all when we get together. Because know this, Josie, no matter who was in the past, you're my present and my future. And those women have nothing on you."

A smile curved her lips and she leaned in, pressing her forehead to his. "I'll do my best not to think about it at all, then."

"Good. Now, it's almost lunchtime and we still need to sort out your apartment. Want to go grab a bite to eat and then swing by your apartment so you can get all your art supplies? If you make a list of stuff while we're there, I'll have someone go over and get it all packed for you. Don't want you worrying about anything other than settling into my place."

"That sounds fine to me," she said.

He kissed her hungrily. "We'll see the others in time. But for now, I want you all to myself. I'm tempted to call in to work Monday and spend the week with you."

Her heart fluttered. It was a tempting visual. An entire week in Ash's bed. In his arms.

"Unfortunately, with Gabe on his honeymoon and the deals we have working, Jace and I can't miss."

"I understand," she said easily. "I have work to do too."

"Like the idea of you working in my space," he murmured. "When I'm at the office, you'll be here. I like that image. And then you here when I get home. Wearing nothing, Josie. I'll call you when I'm on my way home each day, and when I get here, I want you naked and waiting. Unless I tell you different, that's the way I want it."

"Okay," she whispered.

# chapter fourteen

Jace was waiting for Ash when Ash got into his office Monday morning. Not that Ash had any doubt his friend would be chomping at the bit to pick his brain after Ash's late-night phone call Saturday night.

Jace was sitting in Ash's office when Ash walked in. Jace's worried gaze found him.

"You get everything sorted out?" Jace asked, not even giving Ash time to sit down.

Ash tossed his briefcase onto his desk and then flopped down into his chair, glancing over at his friend whose eyes were dark with concern.

"I'm working on it," Ash murmured. "Made a few calls on my way into work. Need to get a man on the asshole, monitor his movements, figure out the best time to strike."

"Jesus," Jace muttered. "You're serious about this."

Ash's eyebrow went up. There was a stack of notes on Ash's desk. Missed calls that needed returning. Documents that needed his signature. But he left them untouched, leaning back in his chair as he calmly surveyed Jace across his desk.

"Have I given you any reason to believe I'm anything but dead serious? He hurt her, Jace. He put bruises on her face. No way in fuck I'm letting it go. She was too scared and shocked to report it.

But I'm glad she didn't because I can make the bastard suffer far more. He would have been out of jail in two seconds, and it's doubtful anything would have come of it. You know how this kind of shit gets brushed underneath the rug. Especially when you have the money and connections to make it go away."

"He has all that?" Jace asked.

"Some, yeah. No match for me, though. I'm going to make damn sure he gets the message. Josie is mine and if he ever fucks with her again, he's a dead man."

"How is Josie taking all of this?" Jace asked quietly.

Ash paused. "Okay I think. I didn't really give her time to process much. When I hit her apartment after bailing on dinner Friday night, I didn't give her any options. I packed her shit up and told her she was moving in with me. It was an asshole move. She needed gentle handling, but I knew if I gave her space she might never come to me. So I pressed my advantage when she was overwhelmed and shaken and I moved in quick."

A smile quirked the corners of Jace's mouth. "You? Asshole moves? Aren't you supposed to be the charming, nice guy? Thought being an asshole was mine and Gabe's job."

Ash grimaced. "Why the fuck does everyone think I'm such a laid-back pansy?"

Jace snorted. "Never said that, man. But you're usually Mr. Polished when it comes to women. Never known you to be off your game."

"The other women didn't matter," Ash said simply. "Josie does. Can't afford to play it safe with her. Have to press my advantage when I have it."

Jace took in a long breath, his gaze intently studying Ash. After a moment, Ash shifted uncomfortably underneath his friend's scrutiny.

"Are you thinking long term here?" Jace asked. "You say she's different and already I've seen just how different you are about her. You're talking about breaking the law and doing God only knows what to the asshole who beat her up. But just how different are we talking here, Ash?"

"Think about how you felt when you met Bethany," Ash said in an even tone.

"Shit," Jace breathed. "Say no more. I get it. And congrats, man. Never thought it would happen for you this fast. You've always been so determined to live by our motto, 'play hard and live free.'"

"Yeah, well, so were you," Ash said dryly. "And don't congratulate me yet. Too much shit to sort out, and while I may have Josie where I want her right now, it's definitely not in the bag."

"But knowing how I felt about Bethany, and you saying it's like that? You're done for, man. If you feel even half what I felt for Bethany in the beginning, this is it for you. And knowing you the way I know you, if Josie is what you want, you're damn well not going to let her go."

"Fuck no," Ash muttered. "If she's not with me for the long term, it'll be because she fought me tooth and nail and won. And I don't lose."

"You thinking marriage? Absolute commitment? What are we talking here, Ash? I need to know so I can give you shit after all the insults you hurled mine and Gabe's way when our balls were twisting in the wind over Bethany and Mia."

Ash flipped up his middle finger. "I don't know yet. Marriage is a big step. It's permanent. And it's too early to be thinking about marriage and babies and shit. All I can focus on is Josie and making sure she's as into me as I'm into her."

Jace nodded. "Yeah, I get it. But just so you know, I'm going to start planning that bachelor party now."

Ash chuckled. "Whatever, man."

Jace's expression grew more serious and he leveled a hard stare in Ash's direction. "Now what about the man who hurt Josie? You said you needed an alibi, and you know I'll do whatever you need, but I need details here. Can't say visiting you at Riker's is on my top-ten list of shit to do for kicks and giggles."

Ash sighed and ran a hand through his hair. "I'm checking into it, as I said. But I want to move quickly on this. I want to get Josie settled, and part of that is me knowing that this asshole won't be threatening her anymore. I got some preliminary info on him and his movements. He's pretty predictable. Keeps to the same schedule. If that holds true, then I plan to address the situation Friday night."

Jace's eyes narrowed and he sat forward in his seat. "You as in you personally? Or are you having the issue taken care of by a third party?"

"Both," Ash said, taking in his friend's reaction.

"Jesus, Ash. Don't fuck up, man. I doubt Josie wants to visit you in jail anymore than I do."

"Not going to be an issue," Ash said evenly. "The guys I have in mind are good. Cover all the bases. They'll swear they don't know me and I'll swear I don't know them. Don't want to put you in a bad position and definitely don't want Bethany involved, so I'd prefer if my alibi was only you and not the two of you together."

Jace nodded. "Yeah, you know I don't mind going to the wall for you. Ever. But I don't want this touching Bethany. And whatever you need, man. You know that, right?"

"Yeah, I know. Appreciate it, Jace."

"Let me know, okay? Don't keep me in the dark. I'll want details, and if you get into trouble, you better fucking call me. And don't do this alone, got me? If you can't arrange it with whatever men you plan to hook up with for the job, then you call me and I'll go with you."

Ash grinned. "Yes, Mother. Want to wipe my ass for me while you're at it?"

"Fuck you," Jace said rudely.

Ash chuckled and then sobered as he stared back at Jace. "Don't want this touching Bethany or you. You providing me an alibi is enough. It's more than I want to ask of you. I'd never do anything to jeopardize your relationship with Bethany."

"Yeah, I know. But also know that you're my brother, Ash. You're family. Not those shitheads you share blood with. Me and Gabe and by extension Mia and Bethany. Don't care what I have to do to help you. I'll do it. No questions asked."

"Christ, man. Stop it already or we'll be a bunch of pansy-ass girls reaching for the fucking tissues."

Jace threw back his head and laughed. "Okay, now that we have that squared away, when do I get to meet Josie?"

Ash huffed out a breath. "Soon. I want you and Bethany both to meet her. After I get this shit with her ex taken care of then I can breathe a little easier. Maybe we can have dinner Sunday night."

Jace nodded. "Sounds good to me."

"She knows about Bethany." Ash made a face. "I told her everything. Didn't want it to catch her off guard, not that I think it would ever come up, but I didn't want to take any chances."

Jace winced. "How she'd take it? I can see how that would be awkward as hell when we're all together. Especially now that she knows."

"She was cool about it. I doubt any woman loves the idea of hanging with a woman her man slept with in the past. But I assured her that you had no intention of ever sharing Bethany with anyone ever again, and that furthermore, I wasn't going to be involved in any threesomes and I sure as hell wouldn't want to have a threesome with her and another guy."

Jace scowled. "Fuck no I'm not sharing Bethany with anyone. Bad enough there was that one time with you."

Ash held up his hands. "Don't get all worked up. I didn't bring it up to piss you off. I just wanted you to know that Josie knows. I was straight with her about everything regarding my sexual history."

"Bet that took a while," Jace said dryly.

"About as long as it took you to explain to Bethany," Ash shot back.

"Touché," Jace said with a grin. Then he stood, heading toward the door. "If that's everything, I'm going to get to work. I have calls to make and a conference call in half an hour. You got lunch plans?"

Ash checked his watch. "No, but I plan to head home early today. Didn't like leaving Josie on her own so quickly after I got her moved in. I have people bringing her shit over to my apartment and I told her I'd help her sort it all out when I got home. So I'll probably skip lunch, get my desk cleared and then head out around two."

Jace nodded. "Okay. Keep me posted. Especially about Friday night. We need to get our stories straight."

"Will do," Ash replied.

# chapter fifteen

Josie put down her paintbrush and scrambled to wipe her hands before picking up her ringing cell phone. They shook slightly as she saw it was Ash calling. A flutter began in her belly, rising up into her throat.

"Hello?"

"I'm on my way home."

Ash's simple words sent a tingle down her spine.

"Okay," she murmured. "I'll be ready."

"Good. You didn't forget, then."

"No," she said softly. "I know what your expectations are."

He paused. "But is it what you want, Josie? Or are you only catering to my desires?"

"I want it too, Ash. I'm a little nervous, but it's because this is all new and we're still getting to know each other. But I wouldn't be here if I didn't want to be. No matter what kind of woman you think you hustled to your apartment, I'm not her. I'm not weak or spineless. Granted, I didn't handle the situation with Michael like I should have, but I'm not easily walked over."

He chuckled, the sound warm and vibrant in her ear. "I never thought for a moment that you were weak or spineless, baby. It takes a strong woman to take on a man like me. Never doubt that."

A broad smile attacked her face and her belly clenched in delight at the soft endearment. It wasn't the first time he'd called her baby, and she'd loved it then. There was something about this man's voice softening, the tenderness when he used the pet word, that made her heart skip a few beats.

"I need to go if I'm going to be ready for you when you get here," she said. "I don't want to disappoint you on your first day home to me."

There was another pause and then his voice low and sweet, sending a brisk thrill coursing through her veins.

"You won't disappoint me, Josie. Don't want you thinking that. Don't even want it in your head. If you're there when I get home, naked and waiting for me, I'm not going to be disappointed. I've looked forward to it all day. I'll let you go so you can get ready. See you soon."

"Bye," she whispered.

As soon as she ended the call, she surged to her feet, frowning when she saw the scattered supplies all over his living room. She knew his housekeeper was coming in the morning, but she didn't want to be an added burden. For that matter, all her stuff was in boxes, neatly stacked against the living room wall. She hadn't bothered unpacking them yet because she'd wanted to work, eager to get more of her paintings to the art gallery.

Hopefully Ash wouldn't be annoyed at the mess and at the chaos she'd brought into his immaculately kept apartment.

She rushed to the bathroom, wondering if she had time for a quick shower. But she'd taken one this morning. She was clean. Just her hands and her arms had paint splatters and she could clean those off in short order.

Still, she paid careful attention to her appearance. She brushed out her long, blond hair and surveyed her reflection in the mirror.

No makeup today, but then she rarely wore more than lip gloss and mascara.

Satisfied that she didn't look an absolute mess, she went into the bedroom and stripped out of her clothing. She folded the jeans and the shirt, not knowing if she'd dress afterward or if Ash would keep her occupied until bedtime. She'd tackle that particular issue when the time came.

But what now? Did she wait in the bedroom? Should she sit in the living room and wait for him there? She frowned pensively. They hadn't gone over the particulars, just that he wanted her naked and waiting for him.

He'd been specific in that he didn't want her to kneel unless he wanted her there because she was sucking his cock. Her cheeks flamed in remembrance of that statement. Michael had liked her to kneel. Liked her subservience. At the time it hadn't bothered her. It was a part of their relationship, one she'd readily agreed to. Now she felt foolish for offering the jerk her submission.

She walked into the living room, deciding this was where she'd wait for him. He'd liked the idea of coming home and finding her naked and waiting, which told her that he'd probably like to see her as soon as he walked in. If he had to look for her, then she wasn't waiting for him very well. And she liked the idea of being the first thing he saw when he got off the elevator.

Since she wasn't going to kneel, she opted for the plush leather couch, but she put one of the throws down so it would be comfortable against her bare skin. And then she pondered over whether she should sit up? Recline? Laughter bubbled from her throat. She was so overthinking this.

She was an artist and visuals appealed to her. She knew all about provocative poses and Ash would appreciate one of those surely. She wanted to wow him the first time he came home to her.

Warmth entered her chest as those words settled over her. Coming home to her. How easily she fell into his life, his apartment, and adopted it as her own. Was she really considering this home now? And that she had a man coming home to her every day?

Not deliberating over whether she was crazy for entertaining such thoughts, she settled onto her side, arranging her hair to hang over her shoulder, partially obscuring her breasts. It wasn't that she had any inhibitions. But less was often more. Men responded to what they couldn't see often as much or even more than what they could see.

It was what made her paintings provocative. The hint of flesh. Just a glimpse of the forbidden.

She rested her head against the arm of the couch and let her gaze drift toward the elevator door. Her skin tingled, anticipation licking over her body as she imagined what Ash would choose to do when he got home.

Arousal hummed low in her body. She was tempted to slide her fingers between her legs and stroke herself to a quick orgasm. It wouldn't take much. She was worked up just thinking about Ash's arrival. But she didn't want to take away from whatever he planned.

So she waited, each second seemingly an hour.

When she heard the elevator, her breath hiccupped and stuck a moment in her throat. Her mouth went dry and she hastily licked her lips just as the doors slid open, revealing Ash in the suit he'd worn to work.

One hand shoved into his slacks pocket, his pose casual and arrogant. He exuded wealth, charm and . . . power.

She shivered as their gazes met and held. His eyes burned over her, flaring when he took in her pose. Appreciation gleamed, and she was glad she'd opted for seductive instead of just sitting and waiting.

He strode toward her, his jaw tight, eyes blazing. She lifted her head, tracking his progress.

"Hello," she said huskily. "And welcome home."

He surprised her by dropping to his knees in front of the couch. He swept in and fastened his mouth to hers in a heated rush that took her breath away. His hand tangled in her hair, yanking her closer so there was no space between them.

"Fucking beautiful," he growled. "Been thinking about this all day. Me coming home, seeing you waiting. But nothing could have prepared me for the reality."

He traced a finger down her cheek, stroking gently as he sucked in breaths to catch up from their kiss.

"Really glad you're here, Josie."

"I'm glad too," she murmured.

"Had a dozen different ideas on the way home. Thinking of how I'd take you when I got here. The minute I saw you, I forgot everything but the way you look perched on my couch."

"I'd love to hear all those ideas. I'm intrigued now."

He smiled, his eyes gleaming with amusement. "Some of them are probably illegal."

"Even better."

He laughed, low and husky, the sound vibrating over her skin. "I like your enthusiasm."

"Should we write them all down and draw one out of a jar to decide how we have sex?" she asked with a grin. "Or can I count on you to be decisive in the matter?"

"My darling is being cheeky today," he drawled. "I might have to punish you for that."

Heat rushed into her cheeks. One of his eyebrows lifted.

"You like that idea."

She cleared her throat, unsure of what to say. Ash had said he wasn't into games. Wasn't her playing the naughty submissive to earn a punishment a game?

Ash's gaze narrowed and he slid his fingers underneath her chin, forcing it upward so she met his gaze.

"What the hell are you thinking right now?"

She sighed. "It's silly. I guess I was worried about how to respond to that. And how it would make me sound if I did say that the thought of you punishing me turned me on. You said you weren't into games and you wanted to keep it real."

He brushed his thumb over her lips to silence her.

"First of all, never ever hesitate to tell me anything. Especially what turns you on, what you want, what you need from me. Sexually, emotionally, whatever. Second thing, your desires aren't a game. I get that what I said may have caused some confusion. What I meant was that you and me, we're real. Not a game. Doesn't mean we can't play together. As long as you get that what we do is real."

"Clear as mud," Josie said, amusement thick in her voice.

"We haven't talked about punishment. Have to tell you, I'm not much into the discipline thing. I'm not your father and you're not a child. But there are things I like, and there's a big difference between thinking you need punishing and me wanting to redden your ass because it turns me on. Get where I'm coming from?"

"Yeah," she said breathily.

"I'm guessing that idea appeals to you too."

She nodded. "I like it. I mean it's a turn-on. There's something hot about a mouthwatering alpha male spanking me. Or exerting his will over me. That probably sounds stupid."

Ash sighed. "You're not getting me, baby. Nothing you think or feel is stupid. Understand? If it turns you on then it's not stupid. If it turns you on, I want to know about it because I want to bring you pleasure. I want to make you feel good. Now, what I want at this exact moment is you on your knees, my dick in your mouth. But after? We're going to have a discussion about your kinks. And mine for that matter. Hopefully they'll match up pretty damn well."

She swallowed and licked her lips in anticipation.

He groaned and then pressed his mouth to hers, devouring her hungrily.

"You drive me crazy," he said into her mouth.

"Good," she whispered.

He reared back, pushing up to his feet. Then he extended his hand down to help her up. After reaching over for one of the pillows from the couch, he dropped it onto the floor and then urged her down on her knees on the cushion.

His hand went to his fly, unfastening it and then lowering the zipper. He reached in, pulled his straining erection from the confines of his pants and fisted it as it jutted forward toward her mouth.

"Lick it," he rasped out. "Tease the head and then suck me deep."

She flicked out her tongue, circling the broad head and teasing the sensitive underside. She loved the way he sucked in his breath and the way it escaped in a long hiss in reaction.

His fingers delved into her hair, twisting around the strands before his knuckles came to rest against her scalp. His hold wasn't gentle, and she liked that. With his other hand, he cupped her jaw, opening her mouth as he pushed inside.

His thrusts weren't any more gentle than his grip in her hair, and she loved that too. She loved the raw power barely restrained underneath the surface. He was like a lion poised to pounce. All predatory, delicious male.

She levered up higher so she could take him deeper. She wanted him deeper. Wanted his taste, loved the way he took control, the fact that she had no power except what he gave her.

"Jesus," he breathed. "Never felt anything better than your mouth around my cock, baby."

She shivered in delight over his words. Her nipples hardened, puckering into taut crests. She gasped when he reached down and took both nipples between his thumbs and forefingers, twisting gently, exerting just enough pressure to drive her insane without causing her pain.

She licked leisurely from base to tip, letting the head rest precariously on her lips before sucking him back in and sliding her mouth down until her chin rested against his sac. She swallowed, milking the head with the back of her throat. He groaned, rewarding her effort with a twitch, and his fingers grew more aggressive at her breasts, eliciting a groan of her own.

"I've imagined you so many ways," Ash said in a strained voice. "Tied up, ass in the air, my mark on your skin. On your hands and knees, me taking you from behind, in your ass, in your pussy. You on top of me, riding me. Me eating your sweet pussy while you suck my dick. You name it, I've imagined it."

She shuddered, her body trembling almost violently as the images he provoked fired through her mind.

"I won't always be this easy, baby," he murmured. "It's hard to hold back, but I don't want it to be too much too fast."

She tore her mouth away from his cock and stared up at him, her fingers wrapped around his erection. "I don't want you to be easy, Ash. That's not why I'm with you. I want what you can give me. I *need* it."

He cupped her face in his hands and looked down, his expression tender. "I love that you want that from me, Josie. I just want to make sure you're ready for it. You've been through a lot and the last few days have been hectic and stressful for you."

"Yes, they have," she agreed. "But do you know today was the best day? The first day in longer than I can remember where I was utterly content. I was happy, Ash. Because of you. Because I was here. I sat in your living room painting, and all I could think was how content I was to be here, working, anticipating the moment when you called to let me know you were on your way home."

His eyes softened and went liquid green, the color almost electric. "You take my breath away."

"Now," she said, rocking back on her heels as she positioned her mouth to take his cock again. "When do we get to the kinky part?"

# chapter sixteen

Ash was nearly undone by the sight of Josie on her knees, her mouth around his dick, just like he'd imagined so many times since seeing her that first day in the park. Now she was his. In his apartment. His life.

He knew she'd given him a precious gift. He didn't look beyond the fact that she offered him her trust. She'd placed her body and heart in his hands, and he'd do whatever it took to protect both. He'd never take for granted what this beautiful, courageous woman was giving him.

He slid his hands through her hair, curling the strands around his fingers as he leaned into her. Deeper. Each stroke the most exquisite pleasure he'd ever experienced.

He'd had many women. He'd been honest with Josie about that. But she was different. And he couldn't even say why definitively. There was something about her that just spoke to him on a different level. Made him think about permanency when that had never been an issue in his past relationships. But then, him and Jace fucking the same women could hardly be classified as actual relationships.

It had been years since he'd spent any time with a woman one-on-one, and he found the idea appealed to him now. Josie appealed to him.

She was on her knees before him, utterly submissive, and not only submissive, but she wanted the same things he wanted. Enjoyed the same kinks he enjoyed. There wasn't a more perfect woman for him. Of that he was certain.

He sank deep into her mouth, twitching at the back of her throat before sliding back out, enjoying the rasp of her tongue over the sensitive underside of his dick. Then he withdrew, watched as her eyes, aquamarine pools clouded with desire, found his.

Wordlessly, he extended his hand down for hers to help her to her feet. As soon as she'd risen, he pulled her into his arms, crushing her against his chest. He kissed her, almost forgetting in his urgency to possess her mouth that he should take care. She still wore bruises. Her mouth was still tender. Yet it hadn't stopped him from fucking her mouth, even as gentle as he'd been.

"Let's go into the bedroom," he said gruffly. "I've been hard on your mouth. For now I'll focus on other portions of your delectable body."

Her eyes flared with heat and anticipation. She'd asked him for kinky. He sure as hell could accommodate her there. His hands itched to redden her ass, to see his marks of possession on her body. It was a primitive urge that completely overtook him. He wanted to own her, for there to be no question as to his ownership.

But as he guided her toward his bedroom, he acknowledged that he didn't want just to own her body. He wanted to own her heart. And while he would possess her body in short order—as he'd already possessed her once—it would take much more effort and time to own the parts of her she held most dear. Her heart, mind and soul.

He wanted them all. Wouldn't settle for anything less than all of her.

Now he just had to convince her.

"Get on the bed. Lie on your stomach, hands behind you at the small of your back. I'll come to you as soon as I prepare everything."

She caught her breath and color suffused her cheeks. He could see her breathing had sped up and excitement reflected in her gaze. Her hand slid from his, leaving him bereft of her touch. Then she walked to his bed and positioned herself as he'd directed.

He collected the items he needed from his closet. A leather strap. He was confident it would bring her—and himself—great pleasure. A length of rope.

He dropped the rope on the bed and then positioned his knee between her splayed thighs. He gathered her wrists in one hand and then began coiling the silken rope around them, binding them together.

She gasped softly. He could feel the tension coiling in her body. When he had her wrists securely tied, he stepped back.

"Up on your knees," he said firmly, injecting a bite of command into his tone. "Ass in the air. Cheek against the mattress."

She struggled upward, and he reached underneath her, splaying his hand over her soft belly. He helped her upward until her knees found purchase in the mattress and she rested her face against the bed.

Satisfied with her position, he stepped back again to retrieve the leather strap.

"Have you done this before, Josie? I don't want it to be too much. You need to let me know what you can take."

"Yes," she whispered. "And I can take a lot, Ash. Don't hold back. I . . . need it. I want it."

He leaned forward, blanketing her with his body. "If it's too much, at any time, you say stop. Understand? It all ends with that word, darling."

A shudder rolled through her body. She liked endearments. He liked her reaction every time he used them.

Then he stepped back once more and smoothed a hand over her plump ass.

"Twelve," he said. "Twelve marks you'll wear on your skin. When I'm certain you're with me, we'll graduate to more. But for now, we start at a dozen."

She nodded, her eyes closed, her lips tight with anticipation. He didn't make her wait any longer.

The first snap of leather against her skin was loud in the silence. She jumped, the red immediately blazing across her ass. Then a soft moan escaped her lips, the sound intoxicating to him.

Again he expertly delivered the blow, the other cheek this time. Red shimmered, coloring her skin, the contrast between the paler,  where the leather had kissed beautiful and

tlessly as he administered the third, fourth , she was softly begging. More. Harder.

sie. They'll be harder. And then I'm going to hink you can take that?"

His name came out a moan. A desperate plea. Yeah, she was with him. More than with him. He was holding back, and she didn't want that.

He allowed more power into the tenth stroke, watching her closely, how she took the pain. It was there, at first. But just as quickly as the pain registered, she converted it, pushed it away and embraced the pleasure.

Her eyes, open now, were soft and dreamy, as if she'd escaped into another world.

He wasn't used to tempering his movements, to holding himself back. He'd held back with Bethany, that night he and Jace had been with her together, because Jace wouldn't allow him to do anything but. But Josie was important. Different. He wanted to cherish her. Be gentle and patient, even when she herself exuded impatience with his reserve. There would be plenty of time for him to give her everything. For now he wanted to make sure she was with him every step of the way, that he didn't cross the line and cause her more pain than pleasure.

He gave her the eleventh and then paused, savoring the last, wanting her edgy and needing. She twisted restlessly, arching back. He didn't even know if she was cognizant of the way her body begged for more.

"Twelve, Josie. Take the last. Give it to me. Everything you have."

He brought the strap down, harder than the previous times, taking care not to hit the same spots he'd hit before. The crack sounded. Her surprised yelp faded into a moan. A soft, sweet sigh of pleasure that prickled the hair at his nape and dove deep under his skin. His dick was rigid, so hard it was painful. He wanted inside her body. Deep in her ass. It was the one part of her he hadn't possessed yet, the final hurdle in his complete ownership of her body.

He dropped the strap, impatient to be inside her. But he held himself back, forcing himself to take the care he needed to ensure she could take him with no pain.

He took his time applying the lubricant, stretching her opening, adding one finger and then two, applying the gel inside and out. Then he squirted more into his hand and rubbed it down the length of his erection.

A groan escaped him. His dick hated his hand. It wasn't what it wanted. His cock wanted inside her.

He pushed forward, cupping her rosy buttocks in his palms before spreading them so her opening was bared to him. Then he circled his erection with one hand, palming the base, and guided it against her entrance.

She presented the most erotic image, kneeling, ass presented, her hands bound and secured at the small of her back. Utterly helpless to do anything but take whatever he gave her.

He tucked the head of his cock to the puckered opening and

began to press forward, taking his time and exerting patience he hadn't known he possessed.

She moaned as he began to push inward, stretching her tight ring around the thick width of his dick.

"Don't fight it, baby. Push back and let me inside," he soothed. "It's going to feel so good when I'm inside you."

He reached underneath her, circling her waist, his fingers splayed wide against her belly. Then he lowered his fingers, delving into the damp curls to find her clitoris. As soon as his finger brushed over the taut bud, she jerked in reaction and he took advantage of that burst of pleasure to thrust hard.

She gasped as her body opened, surrendering to his invasion. He closed his eyes and breathed harshly through his nose as he fought off his release. God, she was so tight around him, gripping him like a fist. And he was only halfway in.

He stroked once more over her clit, exerting just the right amount of pressure, and when she began to buck back toward him, he used his strength to push himself the rest of the way in. To the balls. She enveloped him, swallowing him whole. His thighs rested against her ass as he heaved for breath.

"I'm close," she whispered desperately. "I can't hold it off, Ash. Oh God."

He moved his finger, just for a moment, waiting for her to catch up. He didn't want her to come yet. It would make his possession too painful. She needed to be with him the whole way. The minute she orgasmed, the edgy build-up would be lost and he'd hurt her.

"Not until I do," he commanded, withdrawing a bit so he could push back into her. "And I'm not ready yet, baby. You feel so damn good. Going to enjoy this sweet ass a little longer before I come inside you."

She moaned again, her ass clenching hard around his cock.

He withdrew and thrust forward again, careful to keep his

fingers from her clit. Then he touched her again, testing just how close she was to falling over.

The moment her body tightened, he took his finger away again, earning him a desperate sound of agitation and impatience. He smiled. So responsive. So fucking beautiful. And all his.

He was balls-deep inside her ass, no part of her body untouched by him. She wore his marks on that beautiful ass. And still she wanted more. Fucking perfect.

He began to thrust harder. Rhythmically. A drive to completion. As soon as he felt his balls draw up and the rush begin to hurdle over him, he began to stroke her clit again, wanting her with him. Wanting them both to fly over that edge together.

With his free hand, he curled his fingers around her bound wrists, gripping the rope, holding it and using it to pull her back hard against him to meet his thrusts. She let out a sharp cry, one that worried him for a moment because he feared he was hurting her. But she was thrusting back against him, desperate for more.

"Get there, Josie," he rasped out. "Come for me, baby. I'm there. I'm coming. Fuck me."

His fingers never left her clit, even as his own orgasm swarmed over him. The room blurred around him. He closed his eyes as he strained into her, as he yanked her back to meet his demanding thrusts.

The first spurt of his release was painful. Edgy. Overwhelming. Still, he continued to thrust, bathing her insides with his hot semen. Until it seeped from her opening and ran down the inside of her leg.

The visual spurred his orgasm to further heights. Seeing the evidence of his possession on her body was supremely satisfying. He'd never been so gratified before.

His name tore hoarsely from her mouth. Her entire body tightened. Her fingers balled into tight fists underneath his hand. Her body shook and trembled and then she slid down, her knees losing purchase on the bed. He went with her, his hand sliding from between her legs to brace himself on the bed so she didn't bear his full weight. But he let her have some of it. The feel of her beneath him, of the way he blanketed her body, hit him hard. He loved it.

Nothing was more satisfying than her beneath him, him deeply embedded in her body.

When it became evident that his weight was likely too much and that she struggled to catch up in her breathing, he shifted, causing them both to moan as he began to retreat from her ass.

Gently he pulled the rest of the way out, holding himself up on his palms as he looked down at her reddened ass, the distended opening where he'd been just seconds before, and the traces of his semen on her skin.

"Fucking beautiful," he murmured. "Never a more beautiful sight, baby."

She sighed, her eyelashes fluttering against her cheek. Then he loosened the bonds at her wrists and leaned in to scoop her into his arms. She nestled against his chest as he carried her into the bathroom. He set her down on the commode only long enough to turn on the shower and wait for the water to heat. Then he pulled her into the shower with him and washed every inch of her skin with gentle hands.

"Too much?" he murmured as he stroked a hand over her cheek.

She looked up at him, her eyes still glazed with passion. And she smiled. A beautiful, gut-tightening smile that made him want to take her all over again.

"Never too much," she whispered. "It was wonderful, Ash. I loved it."

He leaned down to kiss her as the hot spray rained down on them both. "Glad to hear you were with me, sweetness. Because it's definitely something I want to do again. Never going to have enough of you."

She circled his neck, hugging him as she returned his kiss. He reached up behind her to turn off the water and then he ushered her out to wrap a towel around her so she wouldn't get cold.

After she was dry, he wrapped his robe around her and tied the ends so she was completely covered.

"It's early yet. You want to go out and get something to eat or would you prefer me to order in and us eat here?"

She paused a moment, her hands thrust into the pockets of the robe. The towel he'd wrapped her hair in was perched atop her head, and she'd never looked more beautiful than she did right here, wearing his robe, in his bathroom while they discussed their plans for the evening.

"I'd like to eat in. Here, with you, if that's okay," she said. "This is our first night together. I mean not exactly, but it's the first day of you going to work and coming home. I'd like to spend it alone with you."

He smiled, because he understood what she was saying. He had no desire to share her with the world yet. It suited him just fine to stay behind the doors of his apartment, prolonging the inevitable, when they both would go out together.

He wanted to introduce her to Jace and Bethany. Gabe and Mia. He wanted to share her with his friends. Hoped they'd become her friends as well. But for now, he was content to let it remain only the two of them for as long as they could hold off the outside world.

He leaned in to kiss her, brushing his lips long and sweet over hers. "That sounds perfect to me. I'll order the food and you can show me what you worked on today."

# chapter seventeen

Ash fingered the choker he'd had designed for Josie as he waited for Jace to make his appearance in Ash's office. He'd known exactly what he wanted for Josie, but finding someone who could custom design it in a matter of days had been challenging. But he found, as with everything else, if you had enough money, nothing was impossible.

He'd chosen bronze because he loved the contrast of the golden metal against Josie's fair skin and it matched well with the golden streaks in her hair. But the stones, he'd been adamant that they match her eyes. Aquamarines, rarely found on the market, were embedded in the metal, creating a dazzling jeweled choker that would look stunning against her skin and provide a perfect accompaniment to her gorgeous eyes.

He could have chosen blue topaz, but they weren't as rare or as expensive, and he wanted only the best for Josie. Smaller diamonds crusted the edge, providing a glittering border around the choker, and in between the aquamarines were smaller emeralds, just to provide a richer array of color.

He'd wanted vibrant. Something that reflected her personality. Not just some dull, colorless piece of jewelry chosen without thought or care for the person receiving it.

The result, he had to admit, was stunning. He knew, without her seeing it first, that she would love it.

And the timing was perfect. Because he hadn't felt as though he could take this step with Josie until after the situation with Michael had been addressed. Tonight he would be taken care of and then Ash's focus would be solely on Josie. Michael would no longer be a threat.

The entire week Ash had been adamant that Josie remain in his apartment. He hadn't wanted her going out, and the one time she had—a trip to the gallery to bring Mr. Downing more artwork and also to pick up her check for the last pieces—he'd sent his driver with her, and his driver had accompanied her inside. Ash hadn't wanted to take any chances that Michael would by lying in wait for her or that he'd make a public scene, which Ash knew would appall Josie and embarrass her.

He hadn't explained to Josie why he'd been so forceful in his expectations, or why he'd told her that the next week she would be granted more freedom to do as she liked. He could hardly tell her that he had to first take care of the asshole who'd put his hands on her. None of what he had planned would touch Josie. He'd make damn sure of that. And neither would Michael ever touch her again.

A sound at the door had him looking up to see Jace coming through. His friend's expression was grim and worried, but then Ash had already told him why he needed to see him.

"I've got everything set for tonight," Jace said quietly.

"Bethany's out, right?" Ash asked. He'd been explicit. While Jace would be involved, at least in the capacity of providing an alibi for Ash, he hadn't wanted Bethany to have any part in lying for him. Just as none of this would ever touch Josie, neither did he want it to touch Bethany. She'd had enough hardship in her life and Ash wasn't about to pile on more.

Jace nodded. "I told her, just as you've told Josie, that we have an important meeting here at the office. I've set up the conference call with investors. You'll be here at the start so they all get a good look at you. You'll get up a few minutes in and excuse yourself to go to the bathroom. Mute the call for a period. But then it gets a little tricky, because you'll have to continue to conduct the conference call while you're on your way. If I angle the monitor just right, I can make me the primary focus and have your guy come in and sit in the background. Your coat, him there, but you on the actual call. Make sure they hear you periodically. I've arranged for the building's security monitors to 'go down' right before the time you leave, so no cameras will catch you departing. I have an extra security badge you can use to buzz out, so according to the logs you'll still be here with me and if necessary I'll use your badge to leave when I go. I can only make the call go on for so long, so once you go silent to handle your situation, you need to make it quick and then pipe back in so it appears you were there for the entire call. It would be best if you come straight back here so we can both leave together once the cameras all go back online."

Ash nodded. "Thanks, man. Means a lot. And just so you know, if shit goes down, you're clean. I won't let this fall back on you."

"Just make sure shit doesn't go down," Jace said in a dry tone. "I still think you should have someone else handle this. You're risking a fuck of a lot by doing this yourself."

Ash's lips tightened. "I want my point made, and the best way to do that is to deliver the message myself. I want this fucker scared shitless. I want him to know that I have him by the balls, and after I beat the shit out of him, I want him to know that I can easily ruin him if he ever steps out of line again."

Jace's smile was rueful. "Have to admit, you have a point. Also have to admit that if some fucker messed with Bethany, I'd beat the hell out of him myself and not rely on others to do the dirty work for me."

"You understand me, then."

Jace nodded. "Yeah, I get you. Don't have to like it, but I get you. I'm worried, Ash. Don't want this shit falling back on you. Not when you've found . . ."

He broke off and Ash pinned him with a look. "When I've found what?"

Jace's smile was crooked as he stared back at his friend. "Your kryptonite."

Ash didn't flinch. Was that what Josie was? Yeah, he could see it. He'd given Gabe and Jace no end of grief over falling head over ass for a woman and going against their *play hard and live free* motto. But now that he was in a very similar situation, he didn't object one bit.

A sense of peace settled over him.

"You've been a lot more calm. Settled lately," Jace said. "I like it on you, man. After Bethany . . ." He broke off again with a sigh, almost as though he hated bringing it up after they'd sworn not to go back there. "After Bethany, I was worried. About you and me. Hated what happened even though I don't regret it. I hope to fuck that makes sense. I didn't like what it did to us and I didn't like how shitty I was to you and Bethany after that night. But I also don't regret the decision I made not to share her with you."

"I don't regret it either," Ash said with a smile. "I'm good with it, Jace. You need to stop dwelling on it. We're good. You got over being a dick. Bethany makes you happy. Now I've got Josie, and she makes me happy."

"Glad for you, man."

"Yeah, I know you are."

"No word from your family? How are things with Brittany?"

Ash sighed. "Nothing this week, and that makes me nervous, because it's not like them to just give up and sit back. Brittany's happy in her job. She hasn't done much more than work and go home, but she'll get there. I want her to meet Mia and Josie and hook up with Mia's girls. They'd be good for her. Josie is more Brittany's age, so maybe the two of them will hit it off."

"You sound positively domesticated with all the girlfriend-arranging you're trying to do," Jace teased.

"Fuck you, man."

Jace's expression grew serious. "So nothing from the Wicked Bitch of the East? She laying low? And what about the old man? Can't believe he wouldn't have anything to say about Brittany's defection. Not when he's so high on family bonds, no matter how fake they may be."

Ash sighed. "Yeah. Nothing this week. But I don't expect that to last."

"Well, when the shit hits the fan, I expect you to let me know. No way I'm letting you into that viper's nest without backup."

Ash chuckled. "You make it sound like a sting operation."

"Hell, an evening with your family qualifies."

Ash checked his watch. "Want to grab a bite to eat before our conference call? I want to call and check in with Josie. Make sure everything's all right with her and remind her that I'll be late."

"Yeah. Want to hit the Grill again?"

Ash nodded. "Thanks again, Jace. Know I don't say it enough, but you and Gabe always having my back . . . Don't have words."

Jace grinned. "After tonight, how about you let your lady off the leash and let her mingle with the rest of us?"

Ash laughed. "Yeah, I know, I've kept her to myself this week. It's been nice. But yeah, I want her to meet you and Bethany. Gabe and Mia will be back by Sunday. Would be nice to get together with them too."

"A year ago would you have ever thought that the three of us would be so tangled up with women? Gabe married, me engaged and you head over ass for a woman you only just met?"

Ash shot him a glare. "You're one to talk about being head over ass for a woman after only just meeting."

Jace's grin was unrepentant. "Only takes one time, man. When it's the right woman, you just know. I would have never thought it would go down like that, but then when I saw Bethany, I just knew."

"Yeah, I hear you. I wasn't much of a believer myself, but then I met Josie and something just clicked. Can't even explain it."

"Don't need to. I get it," Jace said as they walked out of Ash's office. He stopped outside the door and turned to Ash, his eyes serious. "Just remember this, man, and it's applicable and so true on so many levels. Take it from me, because I did my best to fuck it up. Falling in love is the easy part. It's everything else that happens afterward that's hard and takes work."

"Christ. You've turned into a pyschobabbling pussy," Ash said in disgust.

Jace flipped him off. "Fine, don't listen to some friendly advice, but don't come crying to me when you fuck things up."

"Yeah, whatever," Ash grumbled.

"Want to walk or take the car?"

"Walk," Ash said. "I'll call Josie on the way."

Ash stared stonily down into the bloody face of Michael Cooper while the other men who'd accompanied Ash stood to the side, their gazes alert, watching for any sign of discovery.

Ash flexed his fingers, working the stiffness from his knuckles, the gloves he'd worn torn across one hand and smeared with the other man's blood.

"You forget Josie Carlysle exists. Understand? If I hear of you coming within a mile of her, you'll regret it."

Michael nodded his head, spitting blood from the side of his mouth. "I understand. Jesus. She's not worth it."

"Wrong, asshole. She's worth it. More than you could ever imagine. She's mine now and I protect what's mine. Furthermore, if you even think of going to the police like she should have done when you laid hands on her, I will make your life hell. I'll be watching you, Cooper. Don't ever forget it. If you try to start trouble over this, I'll ruin you. You'll have nothing left. And if you don't think I have the money, power and connections to make it happen, just try me. When I'm finished with you, you'll be living in a cardboard box begging for money so you can eat."

Michael nodded again, fear and panic blazing in his eyes. He was a pathetic, ball-less worm.

Ash let go of Michael's shirt and shoved him to the ground where he lay panting for breath, quiet moans of pain slipping from his battered mouth.

"This is what you did to her, you son of a bitch," Ash said, fury lacing his every word. "You hit her and then held her down on the floor while you hit her again. Count yourself lucky that this is all I'm doing to you. Forget my warning, and I'll come down on you so hard that you'll feel me when you're taking a piss. For that matter, I'm watching you, Cooper. If I ever hear of you hurting *any* woman again, you'll go down."

"Need to go," one of the men said in a low voice. "Few minutes was all you said. It's dangerous to be out here any longer."

Ash nodded. "I'm done with this asshole."

Ash and the others turned, leaving Michael along the side of the building where they'd ambushed him. It was a path he took every evening and, luckily for Ash, it was well out of sight of the main streets. Still, he was taking a huge risk. If the wrong person happened upon them, all hell would break lose. He couldn't afford to be seen, couldn't afford any witnesses that would counteract his alibi if Michael pulled a really dumb move and went to the police.

He pulled up the collar of his long coat, one that would be

discarded and never used again, one he'd purchased specifically for tonight. Satisfied his face was shielded by the cap he'd pulled low over his hair and the lapels that covered his cheeks, he hurried off, leaving Michael lying on the ground, the victim of an apparent mugging. He'd been more than willing to let the other men take what they wanted.

Ash slipped the man on his right a wad of cash and muttered his thanks.

"No problem, McIntyre," C.J. murmured. "If you need us, you know where to find us."

Ash nodded and strode in the opposite direction from them when they reached the street. He was only a few blocks from the office building and he had to hurry to make it back before the cameras came back online. He grabbed his phone, the call still open, and brought it to his ear. He still had the mute button punched and left it so the sounds from the streets couldn't be heard.

He listened in as Jace effectively held the conversation, giving no opportunity for Ash to have interjected anything. When he reached the door of the office building, he hurried in, making sure his face was obscured. He ducked into a bathroom on the first floor and stuffed the coat into the gym bag he carried and ripped off the cap. After checking his appearance and ensuring there was no blood on him anywhere, he punched the mute button on his phone and headed toward the elevator.

A few minutes later, he stood in the doorway of Jace's office and motioned for the other hired man to step away. They traded jackets, the other man quickly disappeared and Jace joined the wrap-up, thanking the investors for their time and fielding a few last minute questions. Jace looked inquiringly at him, his gaze sweeping up and down Ash as if to gauge whether there was any indication of what he'd done.

Ash just nodded in his direction as they ended the call.

There was silence a long moment before Jace finally broke it. "Any problems?"

Ash shook his head. "No. Fucker is taken care of. He'll wear the bruises longer than Josie did. And he'll think twice before raising a hand to another woman again."

"Glad it's done with. This shit stresses me out, man. Would love to know when the fuck you fell in with the kind of guys you pulled in for this job. Hell, for that matter, how you knew the men you had take care of Bethany's problem with the man Jack owed money to."

Ash shrugged. "Does it matter? They aren't people I'll ever invite to dinner or people you, Gabe and especially our women ever have to meet."

Jace sighed. "Just makes me wonder what kind of shit you've been into that I didn't know about."

"Nothing illegal," Ash drawled.

"Until now," Jace said quietly.

"Until now," Ash agreed. "But it had to be done. Not going to allow anyone to fuck over my woman. Won't hesitate to do it again if there's ever the need."

Jace rose, blowing out his breath in a deep exhale. "I'm ready to get home to my woman, and I'm sure you're ready to get home to yours." His gaze drifted over Ash again, concern bright in his eyes. "You okay, man?"

"Yeah, I'm good. Fucker didn't touch me. My hand's sore, but nothing serious."

Jace shook his head. "Let's get out of here and make damn sure we're seen leaving together.

# chapter eighteen

It was the first night all week that Ash had been late coming home from work, and it sucked. Despite them only being together a week, Josie had grown used to Ash coming home to her before dark. They'd fallen into a comfortable routine. She worked during the day. He worked during the day. But then he came home and she was waiting for him. Every day. On the couch, naked. And when he walked through that door, the air immediately changed.

She'd asked for kink, and Ash had certainly delivered. Her ass was still sore from last night's interlude. The first spanking on Monday night hadn't been overwhelming. It had been perfect. Then he'd laid off the rest of the week, opting for other explorations that didn't involve him taking a crop to her ass.

But then last night?

She rubbed a hand over her bottom, enjoying the tingling sensation from the still-raised welts. He'd used a crop, and he hadn't been as gentle as he had that first night. But then she'd begged him for more. More edge. More of that fine line between pain and pleasure.

What did he have in mind for tonight? Or would he be too tired after a long day at work and a late meeting?

Her phone rang, and she pounced, her eyes lighting up when she saw it was Ash calling.

"Hey," she said softly.

"Hey baby. I'm on my way. Be ready for me. Been a long day. Just want to get home to you."

A thrill shot through her chest. It made her ridiculously giddy that this man looked forward to coming home to her so much. Ash was a man who could have any woman he wanted. And he wanted her. There wasn't a woman alive who wouldn't enjoy a stroke to the ego like that.

"You got it," she said. "I'll be waiting, Ash."

She already had in mind the way she wanted to greet him tonight. Granted, they did things his way. His control. His authority. He called the shots. But he hadn't asked her to suck his cock since that first night either, and she knew he enjoyed it. A lot.

Tonight, she wanted to do that for him. Take control just long enough to give him pleasure after a long, exhausting day. Somehow she didn't think he'd mind giving her that tiny bit of control.

She shrugged out of her clothes, brushed her hair and then checked her appearance, just as she did every day when she expected him. Then she went into the living room to wait for him on the couch.

She didn't seem to have as long to wait this time, which either meant he'd waited longer to call her or perhaps she'd relaxed enough in their routine that each minute didn't feel as though an hour was passing.

As soon as she heard the elevator open, she swung her legs over the couch and slipped to her knees on the thick, fur rug in front of the sofa.

When hers and Ash's gazes connected, she felt a jolt at the intensity in those brilliant green eyes. They were hard, but appreciative. Dark, so dark it made her shivery. If his expression was anything to go by, this hadn't been the best day in the world, but he seemed very satisfied to find her waiting on her knees, even if he'd told her he didn't expect her to kneel.

He stalked toward her, discarding his briefcase with a thump on the floor. He also pulled off his suit jacket and tossed it toward the armchair and immediately began unbuttoning his sleeves.

When he stopped in front of her, she put her hands up, sliding them to his fly, and his eyes flared in surprise.

"What are you up to?" he asked softly.

She smiled. "I'm welcoming you home. Just stand there and enjoy it."

"Oh hell," he breathed out.

She unzipped his pants and impatiently shoved them down over his hips and then dove into his boxers, gently pulling his rigid erection free of confinement. She licked her lips, anticipating that first taste of him. The feel of so much hard flesh over her tongue.

"Jesus, Josie. You licking your lips like that is about to drive me crazy."

She smiled again just as she guided the broad head of his penis to her mouth. "That's the idea."

He sucked in his breath, a sharp inhalation that was audible in the quiet. She licked the head and then tucked it inside her mouth, sucking gently as she pulled him deeper inside.

"I've missed you today," she whispered as she let his cock slide free momentarily. "Been waiting all evening for you to come home. Wanted to make it special. Something you won't forget."

"Guaranteed I'm not forgetting this, darling. Never. Love coming home to you. This week has been the best week of my life."

Again that giddy thrill attacked her, spreading warmth through her entire body. She loved that he was so open with her. There was no doubting how he felt, that he wanted her. No silly guessing games. No games period. But then, he'd told her that. That he didn't play games. That they were real. What they did was real. Maybe she hadn't fully appreciated that at first, but he'd proven to her that he meant those words.

Every day, he didn't hesitate to tell her how beautiful she was, how much he wanted her, how much he liked having her in his apartment. That he adored her gift of submission and that he treasured the fact she'd given him her trust.

In a week's time, this had surpassed any relationship she'd ever had in the past. In just one week, Ash had become more deeply entrenched than any other man had. With Michael, their times apart hadn't felt interminable. She didn't watch the clock, anxious for the next time she'd see him.

Her heart hadn't been involved. And now it was. Ash didn't just own her body. He owned her heart and soul and he'd conquered it in less than a week.

It sounded crazy. Things like this only happened in books or movies. Relationships were tricky things you had to work at. They didn't just happen. Love didn't just happen. Did it?

But it had.

She couldn't love him so soon, could she? Not when they were still learning each other, exploring the boundaries of their relationship.

She was in lust. Definitely. She was definitely in "like" with him. She liked him a hell of a lot. But did she love him? Did she feel as though every minute apart was the most agonizing torture?

It made her crazy, because she knew she was falling hard for this man, but she fought the idea, knowing it was too soon. Knowing there was still too much she didn't know about this man. She hadn't even met his friends. His family. Though she doubted that would ever come. He hated them. He'd made no secret about that.

She couldn't imagine hating her family. She'd adored her mother and mourned her after her passing. But she hated her father, so who was she to judge Ash? But then, she didn't count her father as family. Because family didn't bail on you. Not true family.

No, her father was a sperm donor and nothing else.

"Baby, you're not here."

Ash's gentle reprimand brought her abruptly back to the present and out of her scattered thoughts. She glanced up to see him staring down at her, his brows drawn together as he slid his cock from her mouth.

She flushed, guilty that she'd been caught out so easily. There was no hiding from Ash. He saw everything. He was in tune with her moods, her thoughts. It was scary to her that he read her so easily after only a week together.

"What are you thinking about, baby? Because it's definitely not my dick. Not that what you're doing doesn't feel good, but your head's not in it."

She sighed and rocked back on her heels, her fingers still wrapped around his length.

"Sorry, Ash. My fault. I was just thinking about a hundred different things."

She wondered if he'd punish her. It's certainly what Michael would have done. And his punishments weren't kinky pleasures. They hurt. They were meant to hurt.

Ash's gaze narrowed as he continued to study her. "What the hell is going through your head right now? Whatever it is, I don't like it."

She pursed her lips, almost allowing the word "nothing" to slip out. It would do no good to deny him. He'd only push her until she gave him the truth. He liked bluntness and honesty. He liked knowing what was going on in her head.

"I was wondering if you'd punish me for zoning out," she said quietly. "And I was thinking about Michael's punishments and the fact that he would absolutely have punished me for not giving him my full attention. And his punishments aren't kinky pleasurable punishments like yours. They . . . hurt. Just hurt. There's no pleasure in them."

There was a spark of rage in Ash's eyes that made her withdraw her hand instinctively. Darkness tracked over his entire face and she immediately regretted the fact that she'd been so honest. She shouldn't have brought up Michael. Not brought him into Ash's apartment. Into their lives.

She lowered her gaze, knotting her fingers together between her knees.

Above her, Ash swore but she didn't look up. Then his hands closed gently around her shoulders and lifted upward until she was standing right in front of him. He pulled his pants up and refastened the fly.

"This is one of those times when we're going to talk, but we're going to do it with you in my arms."

He didn't look angry, and relief coursed through her. Damn it, but it was hard navigating the waters of a new relationship. Always worrying about doing or saying the wrong thing was exhausting. She didn't want to screw this up. She was already half in love, okay maybe a lot in love with Ash, and she wanted to see where things would take them.

Ash turned her toward the couch and then sat, pulling her with him. His hands slid over her body, up her arms, before giving her another gentle squeeze. He cupped her face, thumbed the small area right at the corner of her mouth where there was still the faintest hint of a bruise.

"Told you before, I'm not your father. You aren't my daughter. We aren't playing daddy/daughter roles here. You're a grown woman, free to make your own choices. And if that sounds contradictory to the kind of relationship you and I have, it's not meant to be. You have a choice whether to submit to me. I can't make you. Can't force you to make decisions you don't want to make. Don't want to make you do that. Ever.

"Which means that I'm not into punishment for things you supposedly do wrong or to displease me. That just makes me an asshole, and that's not who I want to be with you. Now, when I feel like reddening your ass because it turns us both on? Yeah, I'm down with that. And it'll happen often if I have my way about it. But as for pulling out a crop and inflicting pain on you for no other reason than you did something wrong, or you pissed me off? Not going to happen. Ever. Because that would make me no better than the bastard who hit you because he was pissed that you dumped him."

She nodded, understanding where he was coming from.

"Do you really get it, Josie? It pisses me off to think of him meting out pain to you because of a supposed infraction. I am never going to touch you physically or sexually when I'm pissed. I may say shit that hurts you. I have a temper. But I'm not ever going to hurt you purposely."

Again she nodded, some of the tension lightening in her chest.

His voice lowered until it was soft, his gaze finding hers, warm and tender.

"Baby, what I need you to understand is that your relationship with Michael was not good. It wasn't healthy. And it's not indicative of the kind of relationship you thought you were getting with him. Maybe that works for other people, and if it does, more power to them. As long as both the man and the woman are down with it and the woman consents. If that's what she wants and needs from the guy she's with, then fine. But it doesn't work for me. I'm a demanding bastard. You and I both know that. But I'm not so egotistical and arrogant that it's all about me all the time. If there's something you don't like or something you don't want, then all you have to do is tell me. We'll talk about it. Figure out if it's really important. And we'll find a way to work around it."

She battled a smile but it broadened her lips and relief registered in his eyes.

"Was going to do this when I got here, but seeing you on your knees, naked and waiting for me . . . Let's just say I forgot all about what I was going to do. But you're here in my arms now, and I think this is the next logical step."

She cocked her head to the side and looked inquisitively at him.

"Let me go get it out of my briefcase."

He turned, easing her onto the couch, and then slid from underneath her. He strode toward his discarded briefcase, rummaged around for a moment and then returned carrying a long, rectangular box.

He tucked the box under his arm and resumed their earlier position. Him on the couch leaned against the arm with her on his lap, his arms firmly around her. He held the box in front of her so they could both see it and then he carefully opened it, revealing a stunning choker.

She gasped as he took it out and held it up. She knew what it was. He'd told her he was having one made. But she'd never imagined it would be so exquisite.

"I want you to wear this, Josie. I want you to understand what it means."

"I'd love to, Ash," she said softly.

He held it up, wrapping it around her neck. She turned so he could fasten it in back and then turned back to him, taking in his fierce expression.

"It's perfect," she said. And it was. "It's absolutely something I would have chosen for myself."

He smiled. "Yeah, it's you. It suits you. I wanted something to match your eyes, but I also wanted something that reflected your personality. Your vibrancy."

Tears bit the corners of her eyes and she sucked in a breath so she didn't lose the battle and let them fall.

He touched her cheek, stroking tenderly over her skin and then slipped his fingers down to trail over the collar resting at the hollow of her throat.

"Want you to understand what this means, baby," he said again. "I know it's fast, but just because it's fast doesn't mean it's not real. I saw my two best friends fall hard and fast. Very fast. I know it can happen and that it can last. I want you and me to last. Not saying we're there yet. But I want us to *get* there. And I want you to understand the significance of this collar. In some ways it's even more important than an engagement ring. Not that you won't have that too. When it's time, you'll have the rock and you'll have my commitment. But this collar is every bit as important as a ring and those formalities."

"I don't even know what to say," she said, her voice cracking as she stared down at him in awe.

"Say you understand its meaning and say you'll wear it. Then we'll get to the other parts of the conversation I want to have with you."

She nodded and then lifted her fingers to touch the collar. "I won't ever take it off, Ash."

Satisfaction gleamed in his eyes and then he pulled her down into a long, breathless kiss. When he pulled away, his eyes were half-lidded and smoky with desire.

"Now, to get back to your relationship with Michael."

She made a face but he put his finger to her lips.

"I get that it's not a good subject. I understand you not wanting to talk about it or even being afraid to bring him up when you're with me. But darling, this is you we're talking about. I'm not going to pretend that your relationship with him didn't happen and I'm not that much of an asshole to forbid any mention of your past and the things that affect you. You never have to be afraid to say anything to me. If it concerns you then it concerns me and we talk about it. Got it?"

"Yeah, I get it. I just didn't want him here, you know? Your apartment is our world and I hate bringing him here."

"I understand, baby. But here is where you should feel the safest bringing up shit from your past that hurts you. I don't want you ever holding out on me. Now, what I was going to add was that your relationship with Michael was all sorts of fucked up. And I'll tell you why I think that. I don't want you thinking I'm judging you or thinking you were an idiot for being with him. But what I'm going to say is important and it has bearing on what you and I have now."

God, she loved this man. If she hadn't already acknowledged that she was falling hard and fast for him, these words, completely and utterly sincere, amazingly awesome words, would have sealed the deal for her. Where else would she ever find a man like this? Someone who was so caring and considerate. So tender and gentle with her and yet rough and demanding when she needed it?

He was, in a word, perfect. And she hadn't thought perfect men existed except in fantasy land.

She settled into his arms, warm and content, waiting to hear what he'd say next.

"Michael took from you in your relationship but he didn't give shit back. And I know this from what you've told me. He expected things from you. He punished you when you didn't comply. But he didn't give you anything back. You said he was cold and distant. He was never affectionate. He didn't give you the things you needed. And he didn't reward you when you did something that pleased him."

She pursed her lips in distaste because Ash had nailed it right on the head. And the hell of it was she'd never seen it while she was in the relationship with Michael. She'd wrongly assumed that all relationships like the one she had with Michael were that way. Ash was fast proving her wrong.

"He didn't show you affection. He didn't do things for you because he knew you'd love them. And, baby, that's wrong. Your relationship with him was all about him. Not about you. It was about what he could take from you without having to give back. And that's ten sorts of fucked up. It's no way for a man to treat a woman he's supposed to cherish and protect."

"You're not like that," she whispered.

His eyes flared. "Thank fuck you feel that way, baby. I wouldn't be pleased at all if you thought I wasn't giving you back what you needed from me. And if it ever comes to that, I want you to let me know. Because I'll fix it. I won't ever consciously do it. But if it does ever happen, I expect you to give me a loud wake-up call."

She grinned. "No worries there, Ash. Now that you've shown me how it can be, I'm a greedy bitch and I'll never go back to the way it was with Michael. You've spoiled me for any other man."

His expression darkened. "It's a good damn thing because I have no intention of you ever finding out what it's like with another man. If I'm not giving you what you need, then you better be telling me what it is I'm not giving you because you going to another man for that . . . Not happening. You're mine, Josie."

"I'm yours," she whispered, tracing her fingers down his firm jawline.

"Now, let's talk about me letting you off the leash so to speak."

Her eyebrows shot up. "Leash? Ash, that sounds horrible! Is that what you think you've done? Put a leash on me?"

He laughed. "Was just joking with you, darling. Jace accused me of having a leash on you because I've been keeping you all to myself. And he's right. I've kept a pretty tight rein on you this week. It's me being selfish. I haven't wanted to share you with anyone yet.

And that's not fair to you. You've only been out once this entire week."

"I haven't minded, Ash. I've loved this week with you. And I've been working. So it's been fine."

"Yeah, but it'll get old after a while. I just wanted to make sure . . ."

He grimaced and broke off.

"Make sure of what?"

"Not important," he said gruffly. "The point is that I want you to meet my friends. They're the most important people in my life next to you. They're my family. My real family. Gabe and Mia are going to get in late Saturday and if they're up for it, I'd like to take you to meet everyone Sunday. I'd like you to meet my sister, Brittany, too. She's having a hard time of it and she's almost the same age as you. Mia and Bethany and Mia's girls are a bit younger but I think you'll like them too. Mia and Bethany have good heads on their shoulders and they both have hearts as big as Alaska."

"I can't wait," she said sincerely. "If they mean that much to you, I have no doubt I'll like them, Ash. And I want to meet the people you care about. I'm happy you want to share that part of yourself with me. I just wish I had that to share with you as well."

He squeezed her again. "Want you to have people to love and support you, baby. Hate that you're alone with no family and that you lost your mother. I'm sure I would have loved her if she's everything you've said."

She smiled and reached up to kiss him again.

"Bethany is different, Josie, and I want you to know that going in. She's had a hard life, so it would probably not be a good idea for you to ask her about herself. Before now I mean."

Josie's eyebrows came together in question as she stared up at Ash. "What do you mean?"

Ash sighed. "She was homeless when Jace and I met her. She

was working Mia's engagement party. We didn't know that at the time. We slept with her that night as I've already told you. But she bailed the next morning and Jace damn near turned the city over looking for her. He found her in a shelter and took her home with him. The rest is history, but even after that, she had some tough times. She had a foster brother who lived on the streets with her and he was mixed up in some shit. Bethany used to be addicted to painkillers and she'd worked past that, but the heaviness of her relationship with Jace nearly made her go back. And then her brother, Jack, drugged her hot chocolate and nearly killed her. We all thought she'd overdosed and that she'd tried to commit suicide. It was a cluster fuck because the night before Jace came home to find me with Bethany in his apartment and he flipped. Took it out on me and her and upset Bethany. So the next morning when this shit happened, it didn't look good."

"Wow," Josie breathed. "That sounds unbelievable! Like something you'd see on a television show or something."

"Yeah," Ash muttered. "Only it was all too real. Jack didn't mean to hurt her. He was the one going to commit suicide but Bethany picked up the wrong cup and ended up in the hospital fighting for her life. I just wanted you to know all of this so you don't ask the wrong questions or bring up shit that makes the situation awkward for you or for Bethany."

She bit her lip, a question burning, but she wasn't sure she should ask because it made her sound . . . jealous. Even if she still did feel a bit of the sting when he talked about Bethany. Because his expression changed when he talked about her. It was obvious that even if she did belong to his friend, he definitely cared a lot about her.

"What's on your mind?" Ash prompted. "I know that look. You're wanting to ask me something. Just ask, baby. You have to know by now you can ask me anything."

She sucked in a breath. "It's just that you said Jace found you and Bethany in his apartment and flipped out. But you told me it was just that first night . . ."

Ash's lips twisted. "It was nothing. I'd gone over to bring Jace stuff from work. We had a deal going south, which is why he was in such a pissy mood when he got there and immediately jumped to the wrong conclusion. I owed Bethany an apology. I came down on her pretty hard in the beginning. Didn't think she was right for Jace. Saw how he was losing his damn mind over her. I also wanted to move past the awkwardness of that first night and how we all met. So I apologized to her and told her I wanted us to be friends. That Jace was important to me so it meant now she was important to me. That was what Jace walked in on."

Josie nodded. "I understand."

Ash cocked his head, staring intently at her. "Does the thing with Bethany still bother you?"

Her shoulders heaved with a sigh but she was honest. She owed him that much at least.

"Yeah. I won't lie. It makes me a little nervous to meet her. It's not that I don't believe you at all. But I don't know a woman alive who likes being confronted by her man's ex-lover, even if it was just a one-night stand. And bad enough to have to meet her, but to have to spend time together long term. I'll get over it. But I'm honest enough to admit that when I meet her for the first time, I'll be picturing you with her and that won't be fun."

Ash didn't look happy with that statement.

"I don't want you torturing yourself over this, baby. It meant nothing. Or at least I should say it meant nothing to me. It meant a hell of a lot to Jace. And if he'd been honest with me from the start, that night would have never happened. I would have backed off because I wasn't into her. Not then and not now."

Relief settled into her chest. His words were absolutely sincere, and she believed him absolutely.

"I'm being silly. I won't let it bother me, Ash. I promise. And I won't bring it up. I won't bring up Bethany's past either. She sounds like a pretty amazing woman."

"She is," Ash said. "She's perfect for Jace. And you're perfect for *me*."

# chapter nineteen

Ash led Josie into the bedroom, his jaw clenched tight as he battled the urge to haul her onto the bed and thrust into her and ride her long and hard. He was on edge, the thing with Michael still bright in his mind.

And it only made his desire to possess Josie, to reassert his claim and possession, that much more fierce. It was inexplicable, this urge that came over him whenever he was near her. He wondered if it would ever dim with time. Somehow he didn't think so.

Something this volatile, this consuming, wasn't just a flash in the pan. It wouldn't go away next week, next month or even next year. He could well imagine himself feeling this way ten or twenty years into the future. Which told him he was already thinking long-term, no matter that he'd decided to take it a day at a time and not look beyond the present.

It was damn hard to only think about today when he was dead set on tying her to him on a permanent basis. Everything he did now was to convince her to remain with him. To show her how perfect she was for him and hopefully how perfect for her he was.

Josie turned, her naked body soft and warm against his. She gazed up at him, her eyes glowing with soft desire. He thought, at times, could swear, that he saw love in her eyes. But maybe it was what he wanted to see. She hadn't said anything, but then neither had he. It was too fast. No matter what he told her, it had only been a week. People didn't fall in love in a week.

Only they did. He'd seen it. Knew it happened. Knew it lasted.

Did he want Josie to love him?

Hell yeah he did. He wanted it, could taste it, would savor the sweetness of those words when they finally passed her lips.

"What would you like tonight, Ash?" she asked in a soft voice. "Tell me how you want me. You've had a long day. I want to make you feel good."

His heart softened. Sweet, darling Josie. So eager to please. So warm and willing. The darkness that had hung over him ever since he'd left the office building to go after Michael lifted under the ray of sunshine that was Josie. Some of the tension left his shoulders as her hands smoothed up his arms and to his neck where she cupped his jaw in her palms.

"Not going to mark your ass tonight, baby. I did that last night. Loved every minute of it. Loved those marks on your sweet ass. But it would hurt if I did it tonight."

And he didn't want the violence he'd meted out just an hour earlier to touch her in any way. He knew he wouldn't hurt her—intentionally—but he'd give himself no possibility of slipping beyond the here and now and back into that dark place he'd been when he'd beat another man.

He didn't regret what he'd done, but neither did he want it touching Josie. Ever.

"What, then?" she whispered. "Tell me. I'll do whatever you want."

He smoothed a hand down the side of her hair, staring down into her eyes awash with earnestness. So eager to please. So soft and submissive she made his gut ache.

"Want you on your hands and knees, baby. Not tying you up tonight. Want you to be able to hold yourself up. Going to fuck that pussy first and then I'm going to have your ass. Won't be as gentle as I was that first night I had your ass. Can you handle that?"

Her breath stuttered across her lips and her pupils dilated rapidly as desire swamped her face.

"I want whatever you give me, Ash."

He kissed her mouth, sliding his tongue in to taste her. He loved the way he swallowed her breath, breathed in the same air she expelled. There was something decidedly intimate about that. About taking the air she gave, sucking it in and savoring it before returning it.

"Go get on the bed," he said in a gruff voice. "Hands and knees, knees perched on the edge of the mattress."

She pulled away from him and he was reluctant to let her go even for the time it took her to position herself as he'd directed. He watched as she crawled onto the bed and presented her ass just the way he wanted. Then she glanced back over her shoulder, clear invitation in her eyes.

She wanted this. She was ready. He just had to make sure he didn't take things too far. She deserved gentleness. She'd already suffered far too much at the hands of a dominant man. Not that Michael could be called dominant. What he was was an asshole. An abusive dickhead who got off on controlling the woman in his life.

Not that Ash would be any less controlling, but it was all in the presentation. Josie would absolutely heed Ash's authority, but he'd give her all the things Michael had never given her. Love. Respect. Tenderness. He'd absolutely cherish her.

He quickly undressed and grabbed the tube of lubricant from the nightstand drawer, dropped it on the bed next to Josie's ass and then smoothed his hands over her behind, cupping and caressing. The marks from the night before were still there. Fading, but still visible, a stark contrast against her pale, soft skin.

His marks. Evidence of his possession. Arousal splintered hard and fierce through his body until his dick swelled, threatening to burst under the exquisite torture.

He slid his fingers through the folds of her pussy, testing her arousal. She was swollen and wet, more than ready for his entry, but still, he held off, wanting to stroke her to further heights.

She twisted restlessly, pushing back against his probing fingers, clutching greedily at him as he withdrew. He stroked again, going deeper, testing the plush walls of her vagina, seeking the spot where the texture was rougher, slightly different than the rest. He pressed in and she let out a cry. A burst of wetness coated his fingers and he smiled. Yeah, she was ready. And he couldn't wait to get inside her.

Grasping his dick with one hand, he spread her with the other, positioning himself at the mouth of her pussy before pushing in, slowly, inch by inch, until they were both vibrating with need.

When he gained his depth and strained against her, his balls flattened between her ass and his thighs, she let out a breathy sigh that he felt all the way to his soul. All the ways to take her swirled in the darkness of his mind. There was something about her that called to that darkness, like she was the one person with whom it would be okay to share that. She wanted it. She could take it. She needed it. Just as he needed it.

He leaned over her, blanketing her with his body as he remained tightly wedged inside her pussy.

"Tell me something, Josie," he said in a silky, entreating voice. "Did all the talk of my threesome with Bethany and Jace make you jealous?"

She stiffened and then turned her head, clear puzzlement and discomfort displayed in her expression.

"Ash . . . I don't understand . . ."

No, she wouldn't have. It came out all wrong. He cursed his tongue because it hadn't come out as he'd wanted.

"Just meant, did you picture yourself in that threesome? Is it something you thought about? Is it something that turned you on and you wanted?"

She shook her head, her eyes still perplexed. But there, just a flash. A hint of something in her eyes. He could barely see it because of the way she was turned.

"I think it did turn you on," he said huskily. "And I already said it wasn't happening. Did that disappoint you, Josie? Did you imagine what it was like to have two cocks at the same time?"

He reached underneath her to stroke her clit, feeling her body respond to his touch. She tightened around him, her sweet pussy fluttering and clenching, bearing down on his erection until he was near to exploding.

"Yes," she whispered. "I imagined what it would feel like."

"There's another way," he said smoothly. "Not quite as good as the real thing, but I can give you that sensation if nothing else. Have no desire to ever share you with another man, darling, but I can give you that experience at least."

"I don't understand," she said in a breathless, excited tone.

"I'll put in an anal plug. A bigger one so you're all snug and tight around it. Then I'll fuck your pussy with the plug inserted. You'll have the experience of two cocks inside you without there being another man in the picture."

"Oh."

That one word conveyed a whole host of things. Excitement. Arousal. Yeah, she wanted it. And he'd give her that. He might not give her another man—that was never happening—but he could give her that sensation. Having her pussy and ass stuffed full.

He eased back, lifting his weight off her, withdrawing slowly through engorged, silken tissue. Then he pushed forward again, not ready to leave her tight heat. Not yet. He'd tease her a bit more, get her so worked up that she'd be about out of her mind.

He thrust forward, back and forth, more clinically as he sought to rein in his control. She moaned and twisted restlessly, but he knew she wouldn't fall over that edge. Not unless his fingers were on her clit. That helped him because it meant she would only orgasm when he was ready for her to.

After a few more thrusts, he looked down, enjoying the sight of his dick sliding from her pussy, wet with her juices, so snug. So fucking tight. He couldn't even imagine how much tighter she'd be with that plug in her ass.

He pulled completely out and left her trembling on hands and knees on the bed while he went to retrieve one of the unopened plugs in his closet. His hands shook as he tore open the packaging. Anticipation. Desire, a razor's edge, boiling in his veins.

When he returned to the bed, Josie's hands were balled into tight fists, planted in the mattress, and she turned her head to look at him, her eyes widening when she took in the size of the plug.

He laughed softly. "It's no bigger than I am, love. You'll take it and you'll take me."

"It's going to hurt," she said dubiously.

"Part of the pleasure is the pain," he said softly. "Remember the marks on your ass from last night. I was a lot harder on you than I was that first time. But you took it and begged for more. Push aside the pain, Josie. Embrace it, because after the pain comes the pleasure. I'll give you that and a hell of a lot more."

She closed her eyes, throwing back her head, her glossy blond hair spilling like silk over her back. He wanted to twist his hands in the strands, pull hard and fuck her even harder. But that would come. For now he had to prepare her. Ease her into the situation. Then they'd both go over that edge together.

He applied a generous amount of lubricant both to the plug and to her ass, stretching her opening, sliding his fingers inside to coat her passageway. When he was certain there was enough to push the plug in with minimal effort, he tossed the lubricant aside and stepped back between her thighs.

"Breathe with it, baby. I'm going to go nice and slow and ease it in, but help me by breathing easy and pushing back when I tell you."

"Okay," she whispered, her voice breathy with excitement.

He inserted the tip, stretching her opening the slightest bit as he began to push inward. She moaned softly and he paused, withdrawing and then pushing forward in slow fucking motions as she continued to stretch around it.

For several long seconds, he played, teasing, pushing in and out, going a bit deeper with each thrust. Then he reached around, stroking over her clit as he began to press harder and deeper.

"Oh God," she cried.

"Too much?"

"No! It feels so good, Ash. Don't stop!"

He chuckled. "Not going to happen, baby."

He stroked gently over her clit, working her into a frenzy, before finally pushing the plug all the way home.

She cried out and arched her back, her legs trembling and shaking violently as breaths heaved from her chest.

"Shhh, darling," he crooned. "It's all the way in. Just breathe and settle. I'll give you a few seconds to come down. Don't want you coming yet."

She put her head down, resting it against the mattress, eyes closed as her body continued to shake. He wanted this to be good for her. It was all about her. No doubt he'd enjoy it every bit as much as her, but this was for her. He wanted her to come screaming her pleasure. His name.

He stepped back and her head immediately came back up,

turning toward him, her gaze seeking. He smiled and leaned down to kiss the small of her back, just above the curve of her buttocks.

"Give me a minute, baby. Want to make this good for you."

"If you make it any better, I'm going to die," she said with a groan.

He laughed again and then went to get the scarlet red sash at the top of his closet. He'd ordered these things the minute Josie had moved into his apartment. Wanted everything he used with her to be new. Never having touched another woman.

He carried it back and then gently pulled her around so she faced him. She was up on her knees, thighs splayed to alleviate the tightness of the plug. Her face was flushed with arousal, rosy, eyes glazed.

Her eyes widened when he began to lift the sash to put over her eyes. He paused only long enough to offer her an explanation.

"Going to blindfold you. It will heighten your other senses. Want you to trust me completely to give you pleasure."

"I do trust you," she said in a sweet, soft voice.

He smiled his approval and then placed the sash over her eyes. He tied it tightly in back, checking to make sure it completely covered her eyes, blanketing her in darkness.

"Now I want you to lie back," he directed. "On your back, legs over the edge of the bed."

Even as he spoke, he helped her into position, taking care to position her as he wanted. She sank onto the mattress, a soft smile curving her swollen lips.

"Wish you could see what I'm seeing," he said gruffly. "You're so fucking beautiful, Josie. All laid out in front of me. Blindfolded, that plug in your ass. Just waiting for me."

He knelt in front of the bed so his face and mouth were level with her open pussy. He licked over her opening and up to her clit, enjoying the shivers that cascaded through her belly.

"I won't last long this way, Ash," she said in a strained voice.

"Yes you will," he said calmly. "You come when I tell you and not before."

She made a sound of impatience that had him smiling. And he continued to eat her, savoring her like a delicacy, slow and sweet.

She writhed beneath him, bucking upward, each time she came back down, the plug pushing deeper inside her. She was panting, so close to her orgasm. But he knew her body well. Knew the signs of her impending release. And so he pulled back, leaving her precariously hanging off the edge.

She groaned, a sound of dismay and frustration, making him smile all over again.

"When I say, baby. When I say, and not before."

"You're killing me," she wailed.

"Oh, I haven't even begun yet," he said silkily. "Before I'm done, you'll beg me."

"I'm begging now!"

His smile broadened and he pushed her legs farther apart. Then he reached into the nightstand again, pulling out nipple clamps she couldn't see. He leaned over, licking one nipple and then the other, coaxing them into turgid points.

He sucked at both, setting a leisurely pace that would drive them both insane with want and need. When he had her nipples into rigid peaks, he flicked one last time with his tongue and then carefully applied the first clamp.

"Oh!" she exclaimed when the clamp bit into her nipple. "Ash?"

"Easy, baby. I won't hurt you. You know that. Just a little pain. Give you that edge. You'll like it."

He affixed the other and then leaned back to survey his handiwork.

She was a work of art. No corny statements. She was utterly magnificent. The intricate, colorful tattoo snaked over her right side. So reflective of who she was and what she was. He could honestly say before her he'd never been a fan of tattoos on women. It just wasn't something that did it for him. But from the moment he'd gotten a glimpse of hers, he'd been rabid with curiosity.

On her, it wasn't just a tattoo like so many others. It was her art. A reflection of herself. And it fit her to a T. He wouldn't have her any other way.

"You fascinate me, Josie. You have such a clean, wholesome, good-girl look going on. That blond hair, those gorgeous blue-green eyes. But underneath the clothes, there's that tattoo. It screams bad girl. I like it. I like it a lot."

A smile curved her lips again. A dreamy smile.

"Glad you like."

"Oh, I do, baby. No doubt there. I like everything about you. Everything that makes you you."

He stared a moment longer at the clamps pushing her nipples upward and then he let his hand drift down her midline, over her belly and to the wetness between her legs. Yeah, she was ready for him. No doubt there. But he didn't want to end it so soon. He would take his time. Savor her. Make it good for both of them.

He stroked his cock, holding it close to her opening as he stared down at what was his. *Mine.* She was his, absolutely. Never thought he'd have a woman who understood him so completely in his bed. And yet here he was, staring down at a woman so beautiful that it hurt to look at her. He couldn't look at her without a heavy ache in his chest. The knowledge and recognition that she was it for him. And he'd never look back. Never regret a single thing.

He pushed her knees upward, bending her legs so she was open wide to him. The base of the plug was lodged there at her ass. And he was ready to dive into that tight pussy.

Sweat beaded his forehead and his teeth clenched together as he pushed through her warm, damp folds to lodge himself at her opening. Oh hell, but she was tighter. So much tighter than before, that plug making her pussy opening that much smaller.

It wasn't going to be easy to get in, but it was going to feel fucking amazing.

He pushed the head farther in, eyes rolling back in his head at the exquisite feel of her tugging snugly at his dick. She moaned loudly, her hands coming off the bed and fluttering, almost as if she didn't know what to do with them.

Hell, he knew what to do about them. The idea of having her not only blindfolded, but bound, excited the visual side of him. Of being able to look down at his woman, vulnerable and helpless against his will. Oh yeah, that excited him.

He pulled back and she registered her complaint with a whimper. He caressed one leg, his imagination working overtime as he expanded on his earlier thought of tying her hands. Hell yeah. He'd tie her hands and legs. Spread her impossibly wide and secure her there. All he had to do was position her at the end of the bed where he could tie her ankles to the bedposts.

"Just a minute more, baby," he said, his voice rougher than he intended. "Going to tie you up."

She swallowed hard, but didn't make a sound. Her chest rose and fell with the exertion of her breaths. He knew it excited her every bit as much as it excited him.

He retrieved the rope from his closet and then went back to the bed. He helped her up and guided her toward the end of the bed and then surveyed his possibilities.

He lifted her arms up over her head and brought them together, binding the wrists with a secure knot. Then he pulled the long end of the rope up toward the head of the bed, pulled it taut so her arms were stretched high, and secured it, testing the tautness so that it didn't put too much of a strain on her shoulders.

Satisfied that it was perfect, he returned to the end of the bed, letting his hand wander lazily down her body, appreciating and savoring the fullness of her curves, the lean lines of her narrow belly and the flare of her hips. But this time he didn't touch her intimately, a fact that frustrated her judging by the groan she emitted. He grinned again. Yeah, this was going to be perfect and he was in no hurry. He was going to savor the delectable sight of her in restraints and fuck her until they both lost their minds.

Gently, he pulled one ankle up, wrapping the rope around it before stretching it to tie it to the bedpost. Again, he tested the tautness, wanting it to be tight and spread her wide but not wanting to hurt her or cause her too much discomfort.

By the time he got to her other leg, it shook and trembled beneath his touch. Her breaths were coming more rapidly now and perspiration gleamed on her skin.

"Ash?"

He paused in securing the last bond to the bedpost.

"Yes, darling?"

"Forget what I said about not being able to come without clitoral stimulation," she said weakly. "I think I'm about to get there anyway!"

He laughed and leaned down to kiss the inside of her calf. "Nuh-uh, baby. Not until I say. You're not going to leave me behind here."

She sighed and closed her eyes, her lips tightening as she battled the desire building within her.

Then he stepped back to survey his handiwork.

"Beautiful," he breathed. "You have no idea how turned on I am right now, Josie. I wish you could see yourself right now. Never seen a more beautiful sight than you tied to my bed, all spread out for me. I'm going to feast on you."

"Please, Ash. I'm begging. Please, I need you."

He'd promised her she'd beg, but he didn't want her begging.

No, he wanted to please her. To give her all the pleasure she was giving him.

His hands slid underneath her ass, lifting as much as the restraints would allow. He cupped and caressed the plump mounds as he moved in, ready to possess her.

He positioned his dick at her opening, pushing in just a bit to test the snugness. He let out a groan, one that was echoed by her when she stretched around him.

"So tight," he ground out. "Want you to feel this, baby. This is what it would be like to have two cocks inside you."

"It's wonderful," she breathed. "More, Ash. Please. Before I go crazy!"

He pushed in harder, nearly dying as her body fought his intrusion. The plug had made her pussy painfully tight. But it was pain he embraced because after that edge of pain came unimaginable pleasure.

He was sweating now, rigid as he sought to maintain control. He inched forward, pushing deeper into her snug passageway.

"It's too much!" she cried. "Oh God, Ash. I'm going to come!"

He stopped, gripping her legs, his fingers digging into her flesh. "Not too much, baby. Never enough. Hold on for me. Go when I go."

He glanced down, wincing when he saw he was only halfway in. He pulled back and then put one hand down over her mound, sliding his thumb in between her folds to her clit.

"Going to go hard, baby. I won't last and neither will you. Come with me now. Going to fuck you hard. It's going to hurt. But it's going to feel so damn good."

She moaned again, her entire body tightening around him. "Hurt me then, Ash. I want it. I need it. I need you."

The soft plea tore the last of his control. He pressed his thumb over her clit and then hammered forward, determined to get all the way in this time.

She cried out, her pussy convulsing around him. She went wet. Slick. So hot and velvety. He began to thrust hard and fast, and then she opened for him and he slid all the way home. But he didn't stop to savor the sensation of being completely immersed in her warmth. He was too close. She was too close. There was no stopping now.

His hips smacked against her ass, jostling her entire body. Her body swayed against the tight restraints and arched upward, bowing up off the bed.

Deeper, harder. His vision blurred. Her gasps sounded in his ears.

"Get there," he growled. "Now!"

Her cry splintered the room. Her wail went on and on as her body spasmed around him. His release was edgy and painful, boiling low in his balls and then exploding up his cock. He began coming in endless streams, the semen spilling from her pussy and onto the bed.

He thrust again, flicking over her clit with his thumb as she screamed again. Then he yanked himself from her pussy and grasped his pulsing cock in his hand. He pumped hard, directing the release onto her pussy and then her belly.

It jetted onto her skin, marking her. Streaming onto her flesh in thick spurts of white.

She was sobbing. His ears were roaring. And then he slid into her again, no longer able to bear being outside of her body. He went still against her, enjoying the last bursts. He closed his eyes and leaned into her, his body heaving with exertion.

Never had he been so gutted. Never had he felt more like his insides had been ripped out and laid bare. He lay there on her, his semen sticky and warm between them. Then he kissed just below her breasts.

"You undo me, Josie," he murmured. "Completely and utterly undo me."

## chapter twenty

When Josie saw the restaurant where she and Ash were meeting his friends, unease gripped her. It was a restaurant that Michael frequented with regularity. It was his favorite place to eat, a place he'd taken her many times.

Shaking off her momentary hesitation, she settled into Ash's side, his arm wrapped securely around her as they walked in. If she ran into Michael, and it seemed likely she would since he ate here almost every Sunday evening, she'd not act as though she was ashamed of anything. Certainly not of the fact that he'd attacked her. And she certainly wasn't ashamed to be out with Ash, no matter how quickly she'd fallen into a relationship after she'd broken things off with Michael.

"Is something wrong?" Ash murmured as they were shown to their table.

She shook her head and smiled brightly.

"Not nervous are you? Relax, darling. They're going to love you."

This time her smile came more easily. "I'm not worried, Ash. Really."

He squeezed her to his side. "Good. I want you to have a good time."

When they arrived at their table, situated in the far corner where they'd be afforded quiet and privacy, Josie saw that his friends were already there.

She blinked when she took in the two men who rose when she and Ash got to the table. Holy hotness factor. Individually, each of the three were gorgeous. But together? They were the epitome of rich, arrogant and devastatingly handsome.

She looked right past the two females sitting, because hello, she was female and how could she even see anything beyond the three alpha men gathered?

"Josie, I want you to meet my friends and business partners, Gabe Hamilton and Jace Crestwell."

The one he called Gabe stepped forward, a broad smile carving his rock-hard face. He extended his hand, and she shivered when their skin made contact.

"Very happy to meet you, Josie," Gabe said in a husky voice that just screamed sexy. "I've been looking forward to it."

"It's very nice to meet you too," Josie murmured.

She turned to Jace and swallowed. The man was Ash's polar opposite. Dark and brooding where Ash was lighter and seemingly less broody, but Josie knew that appearances were deceiving. Ash's looks were in direct contrast with his true personality. He might seem laid-back and carefree, but he was utterly serious. At least with her he was.

Jace leaned in and kissed either cheek before retreating with a smile that made his dark brown eyes warm and inviting.

"I've heard a lot about you, Josie. Glad Ash finally let you out of his apartment long enough to mingle with the rest of us."

She laughed and relaxed and then turned her attention to the two women she was now insanely curious about. Anyone who managed to capture and captivate two men like Gabe and Jace had to be pretty damn special. And according to Ash, they were very much captivated. Completely and unapologetically in love.

She wanted that. Craved it. She wanted it with Ash. And if Ash's words were anything to go by, they were on their way. It still baffled her that it had happened so fast, but then he'd explained that it had happened just as fast for his friends. In that context, perhaps it wasn't so unbelievable that she and Ash would become serious in such a short time.

"Darling, I want you to meet two very special women, Mia and Bethany. Mia is the newlywed and I'm sure if Jace has his way, Bethany won't be far behind on taking the marriage leap."

"Damn right," Jace growled.

"Hello, Josie," Mia said, her smile open and friendly. She was Jace's sister according to Ash and now Josie could see the resemblance.

"Hi," Josie returned. "I'm very happy to meet you both."

"Hello, Josie," Bethany said, her smile no less friendly than Mia's had been, but it was obvious she was shyer and more reserved than Mia.

Remembering everything Ash had told her about Bethany, Josie studied her, taking in the fact that the young woman sitting next to where Jace had retaken his seat had come a long way and had endured a very hard life.

And there was the fact that this woman had been to bed with Ash. Ash *and* Jace. Josie wasn't sure whether to be jealous of the fact Bethany had had Ash's hands on her or envious over the fact that Bethany had enjoyed a threesome with two unbelievably gorgeous alpha males.

She was teetering solidly in the direction of the latter.

"Hi, Bethany," Josie returned warmly. "I've heard so much about you all. You're all very important to Ash. His family as he calls you. I couldn't wait to meet you all."

Ash ushered her into her chair next to Gabe and across from Bethany and Mia.

"He is family," Jace said in a firm voice. "And we're his. Absolutely."

"I think it's wonderful he has such loyal friends," Josie said softly.

"So Ash says you're an artist, Josie," Jace spoke up once they'd all settled into their seats. "And that you design jewelry too."

Josie nodded, suddenly shy about having the attention focused on herself.

"She's amazing," Ash said. "Her work is beautiful."

Josie turned to Ash, surprised. "But you haven't seen it. Or not much of it. Not yet anyway."

Ash looked briefly uncomfortable but then smiled. "I've seen what you're working on now. It's very good."

Heat flushed into her cheeks and she knew she was blushing. What she was working on now was quite a bit more erotic than her previous works. But it was for Ash and Ash alone.

"Did you design the necklace you're wearing now?" Mia asked, leaning forward, her gaze riveted to Josie's collar. "It's gorgeous!"

Now she was really blushing. She was convinced of it. Ash squeezed her hand underneath the table, and she controlled her awkwardness. This was important. It was what he wanted. For her not to ever be ashamed for people to know she was his.

"No," she said in a husky voice. "Ash had it designed for me. It was his gift to me."

Mia's eyes widened with understanding, and to her credit she didn't press further or try to cover the awkwardness by hastily saying more.

Josie's gaze was drawn to the choker that Bethany wore. Her hand had automatically gone to it the minute Mia had commented on Josie's. Evidently, it was a collar as well. One given to her by Jace. Did all of Ash's friends share his sexual proclivities? She could certainly see Gabe and Jace in a dominant role. It was evident in the way they looked at Mia and Bethany. Evident in their body language. How protective they were even just sitting in a public restaurant.

Maybe others wouldn't notice, but Josie did. She was in tune with that aspect because it was one she lived. It was a need in her, just like it appeared to be a need for Ash, Gabe and Jace.

She had a million questions. Nosy questions that she'd love to be able to ask Mia and Bethany. But she held her tongue. She wouldn't want them prying into her relationship with Ash, and she'd offer them that same consideration. But it didn't assuage the burning curiosity she had. Perhaps in time, if they became friends, she'd feel more comfortable having those kinds of conversations with the other women. But still, she knew without a doubt she never wanted to get into a discussion with Bethany about the fact she'd had a threesome with Ash and Jace. There was only so much envy she could handle!

Gabe and Jace were looking at her, open curiosity in their gazes. They likely were as curious about her as she was about them. But if they knew Ash, were as close as Ash had hinted, there was little doubt they knew exactly what kinds of relationships he preferred and that Josie was . . . submissive.

But if she thought they'd look at her with "less" in their eyes, somehow looking down on her or thinking they were "more," she was wrong. There was nothing but interest. Concern for their friend, no doubt, and they were likely weighing whether they thought Josie was a good match for him.

Ash had said that in the beginning he hadn't thought Bethany was a good idea for Jace, and in fact he'd been vocal about it. Were his friends thinking the same thing about her?

She didn't want to be deemed unworthy. They didn't know her and she didn't want them passing judgment after only one glance.

"I'd love to see your work sometime," Gabe said. "Think we could use a little jazzing up in our office building. All we have is a bunch of boring abstract shit. Think you'd be up for taking a look sometime and see what you could do to color up the walls a bit?"

She smiled. "Of course. I'd like that. But I'll warn you now. My paintings are definitely colorful. I'm not into the dull, darker stuff. I like . . . vibrant colors. Themes. And I'd definitely have to shift gears. What I'm working on now would hardly be appropriate for a business setting."

Ash coughed, choking on a laugh.

Jace's eyebrows went up. "Oh? Do tell. What are you working on?"

She blushed again, knowing she'd stuck her foot in her mouth.

"The hell you'll see what she's working on now," Ash said in an even tone. "That is for my eyes alone. But you're welcome to see whatever else she'd like to show you."

"Oh, now I'm curious!" Mia exclaimed. "What is he talking about, Josie?"

She cleared her throat, mortified at setting herself up this way. Her mouth had always gotten ahead of her brain, unfortunately.

"Uh, well, they're kind of erotic." She blushed again. "Self-portrait stuff. I mean it's not like I had anyone else to use."

"Oh," Bethany said, her eyes twinkling with laughter. "Yeah, I bet Ash would go crazy if you showed them to anyone else."

"Damn right," Ash muttered. "No one's seeing that but me."

But someone else had seen them. Or at least the first one she'd taken to Mr. Downing. It had been sold with all her other paintings, and the others in that series that she'd taken to the gallery after the first sale. She wondered if it bothered Ash that some unknown person out there owned those paintings of her. She wished now she hadn't sold them. Wished they could be for Ash alone.

"Josie, we're planning a girls' night out this week and we'd love for you to come," Mia said.

Gabe and Jace promptly groaned and Ash grinned.

"What's with the groaning?" Josie asked.

Ash laughed. "From everything they've told me, I definitely think it's a good idea for you to go. But I'll be very disappointed if you don't come home shitfaced in a sexy dress and fuck-me shoes. It's all I've been tortured with ever since the last time they all went out. Now that I get to participate firsthand, have to say I'm looking forward to it."

Josie sent them all puzzled looks.

Gabe chuckled. "Let's just say when our girls go out, they get drunk, have fun, but then they come home and take advantage of us poor menfolk."

Bethany snorted. "Like you don't enjoy it."

"Didn't say that, baby," Jace said, amusement thick in his voice. But his expression and his eyes said it all. They'd grown positively smoldering as he looked at Bethany.

"So you're okay with that?" she whispered to Ash so the others wouldn't overhear.

Ash laced his fingers with hers underneath the table but then dropped her hand and wrapped his arm around her, pulling her in close so their chairs bumped and she was nearly in his lap.

Evidently he hadn't lied when he said he'd want to touch her, be close to her, and he didn't give a damn who saw it.

"Oh yeah, I'm okay with it," he murmured back. "If I get what Gabe and Jace get when their women go out and get drunk? Then yeah, definitely. I'll even go buy you the dress and the shoes for the occasion."

She laughed softly. "This warrants a new dress *and* shoes?"

"Definitely."

"I don't drink much, as I told you, but for this maybe I'll have to make an exception."

His eyes gleamed as he stared back at her. "Make an exception. I'll make sure you don't regret it."

They chatted about casual topics. Gabe and Mia's honeymoon dominated most of the conversation as Mia recounted their trip to Paris. After their meals were served and they'd eaten, the dessert menus were passed around and Josie excused herself to go to the restroom.

Mia and Bethany got up to accompany her and the three women headed toward the ladies' room.

Josie finished first and waited outside. She heard a door open and turned to see if it was them, but her mouth fell open when she saw Michael walk out of the men's room that was just across from the ladies' room.

He looked like hell!

Their gazes met and held a brief moment before his flickered and he looked hastily away.

"Michael?" she whispered. "What on earth happened to you?"

She could swear fear flickered in his eyes. He couldn't leave quick enough and Josie was too stunned to do more than stare after him as he hurried away.

There wasn't a spot on his face that hadn't been bruised. And it was ugly. Lip split, swollen eye.

"Josie?"

Josie whirled to see Mia and Bethany standing there, looks of concern on their faces.

"Do you know that man?" Mia asked. "Is everything all right?"

"I knew him, yes," Josie murmured. "And everything is fine. Let's go back for dessert. I'm sure it's there by now."

The entire way back to the table, Josie's mind was a whirlwind of what the hell. She hadn't imagined Michael's face or the fact that he'd damn near broken his neck getting away from her. And she hadn't imagined the fear in his eyes. Why would he be afraid of *her*?

Ash's gaze was sharp when she sat down. He didn't miss a thing and his eyes narrowed as he looked at her and then over to Bethany and Mia as if he thought they'd done something to upset her.

"What's wrong?" he demanded. "You're pale. Did something happen?"

"Not here," she said under her breath.

Without another word, Ash stood and reached for her hand. She followed openmouthed behind him as he dragged her out onto the patio to stand in front of the fountain. He pulled her to him, cupped a hand to her cheek and stared intently into her eyes.

"Tell me what happened," he said bluntly. "Did Mia or Bethany say anything to upset you?"

She shook her head, her thoughts still jumbled. She couldn't keep the one prevailing thought out of her mind, even though it was ludicrous. Wasn't it?

"I saw Michael," she blurted out.

Ash's face darkened with fury, his eyes sparking. "What? Did he say anything to you? Did that bastard follow you here? Why the hell didn't you immediately come to me, Josie?"

She held her hand up to halt the flow of questions. "This is his favorite place to eat. He and I ate here often. And he's always here on Sundays. I would have been more surprised if I *hadn't* seen him."

Ash swore. "You should have told me, Josie. We would have eaten somewhere else."

She swallowed and glanced up at Ash. "He looked terrible, Ash. He looked like someone beat the holy hell out of him."

"Did he? Couldn't happen to a nicer guy. Maybe now he won't raise his hand to another woman."

"Tell me something, Ash. Did you have anything to do with him getting the crap kicked out of him?"

It was a plunge. A reckless question spurred by the fear that had swamped her the minute she'd seen Michael. She remembered Ash's resoluteness that he'd take care of it. That she didn't have to worry about Michael anymore. She'd thought they were just words to comfort her. Spoken in the heat of the moment. Everyone had moments like that. It didn't mean they followed through on them!

His eyes flickered and he stared evenly back at her, his lips tight.

"I won't lie to you, Josie. So be careful what you ask."

"Oh God," she whispered. "You *did*. Oh my God, Ash. What did you do? How could you? And *why*?"

"You have to ask me *why*?" he bit out. "What the fuck, Josie. He hurt you. That son of a bitch had you on the floor. And you don't think that's reason enough to make sure he never does anything like that again?"

The blood drained from her face. She wavered, unsteady on her feet. Ash cursed again and then reached for her, pulling her against him once again. He stroked his hand over her cheek, pushing back her hair.

"You put yourself in my care, Josie. That's not something I take lightly. And when you gave that to me, when you submitted to me, it also gave me the right to take care of any threat to you. You need to deal with that. Accept it. Because it's not going away. I will not hesitate to do it again if you're ever threatened."

"Jesus, Ash. You can't do stuff like that. What if he reported it? You'd get arrested. For God's sake, you could go to jail!"

His expression softened. "Not going to happen, baby."

"How do you know?" she asked desperately.

"I took care of it. That's all you need to know. This doesn't touch you, baby. Wish to fuck you'd told me we had a good chance of running into him here. I would have never stayed. I want you to forget about it and him."

"How am I supposed to forget seeing him that way? Now I'm

not going to be able to sleep for worrying that the police will come and arrest you. Ash, this could fuck up the rest of your life! It's not worth that. *Nothing* is worth the rest of your life."

"You're wrong," he ground out. "Me making sure that son of a bitch never comes near you again is worth everything. I'm not going to argue with you over this, Josie. This was my call. We do it my way. You knew that going in. Rules don't change because you decide you don't like something."

"But you said . . ."

"What did I say, baby?"

She huffed in a breath, expelling it long over her lips. "You said it wasn't like that. That I have a choice. That you wouldn't do something I didn't want."

He sighed patiently, his gaze boring into her face. "Baby, it's done. You don't get a choice because the choice has already been *made*. And I'm not going to apologize for not discussing it with you beforehand. It was my choice to make. You belong to me. Told you from the start that I take that very seriously. That means I protect you. I do whatever it takes to make sure you're safe and well cared for."

"Would I have ever known if I hadn't run into him?" she whispered.

Ash immediately shook his head. Unapologetic. Gaze steady. Unwavering.

"No. Not something I'd ever want you to know or even think about. I'm pissed because you had to see him at all."

She closed her eyes and shook her head, trying to shake off the buzzing in her ears. This was crazy, wasn't it? Ash had taken a huge risk. For her. Not one she'd have wanted him to take. No way in hell. How could he be so certain nothing would fall back on him? The only thing he seemed annoyed about at all was that she'd run into Michael. It was obvious that Ash never had any intention of her knowing anything about it. And she wasn't sure how she felt about that.

The saying went that ignorance was bliss, and she supposed in this case it was. She wished she didn't know. Maybe she wouldn't feel so unsettled. And so uncertain of the man she'd committed to in a huge way.

"Josie, you're overthinking this," Ash chided softly. "This is why I would have never had you know about this. No good can come of you worrying or stressing over this. And if this brings us into question for you, then I can only tell you that I've been honest with you. I've been straightforward. Never tried to hide the kind of man I am from you. And I told you from the start that we do things my way. You're mine to protect. To care for. I can guarantee you that nothing like this will ever touch you. Don't want you thinking about it. Can you do that for me?"

She sucked in a deep breath as Ash watched her intently, waiting for her response. This was huge. He was basically asking her if she could get over it and move on. That she not freak out about this. That she trust him. Those were big things to ask. She'd assumed he was a businessman. A wealthy, powerful businessman. She'd never imagined for one minute that he was immersed in gray, murky areas or that he would even be capable of meting out violence to someone who'd hurt something he considered his own.

It shouldn't surprise her, and maybe that was what she grappled with. The idea that maybe it hadn't been as shocking to her as it should have been. It would explain why she was trying to muster up outrage. Or all the appropriate responses. Because she wasn't feeling them and she thought she should be.

"Josie?" Ash questioned quietly. "I need an answer from you, baby."

"Yes," she finally said. "I can do that for you, Ash."

He gathered her in his arms and pressed his lips to her forehead. She closed her eyes, melting into his embrace.

"It scares me, Ash. Not for the reasons you might think, and maybe I feel guilty over that. But what scares me isn't that you're this person who went out and beat the crap out of someone. I don't worry that you're capable of hurting me that way. But what scares me is the thought of losing you. Of you going to jail because you were protecting me. I don't want that. I never want that."

He smiled and lowered his mouth, kissing her lips.

"Don't worry about me, darling. I've got it covered. I didn't just go out on a whim and kick his ass. And I don't say this to freak you out, but I don't want you to worry about it anymore. After tonight, we don't talk about it. We don't bring it up. But I carried out a well-thought-out plan. I have an alibi and Michael was warned of the consequences of him ever coming near you and also of him going to the police. I don't think we'll have an issue with either. I made my point pretty clear."

She pressed her forehead to his chest, the top of her head brushing the underside of his chin.

"Okay," she whispered. "I won't worry and we won't talk about it again."

He squeezed her to him. "Thank you, baby. For trusting me. I won't let you down. Now let's go back inside and finish dessert. You have a girls' night out to plan and you and I have a dress and shoes to buy for you."

# chapter twenty-one

Josie walked ahead of Ash when the elevator opened into his apartment. The ride home had been quiet. They'd eaten dessert, conversed casually with Ash's friends and then Ash had made their excuses and he and Josie had left. She knew Ash watched her, was gauging her mood and her reaction to the issue with Michael.

What could she say? That she felt more shamed by the fact she *wasn't* outraged over what Ash had done than she was with the fact he'd exacted revenge on the man who'd hurt her?

She didn't want to think about the type of human being that made her. Or perhaps it just made her human. She hated Michael for what he'd done. Hated the fact that he'd made her doubt herself. That she'd been too shocked, ashamed and afraid to file charges against him. She also hated the fact that if she'd done what she should have, Ash would have never had to have involved himself in the mess. She could hardly blame him when her own inactivity contributed.

"Lot on your mind, baby," Ash observed as they stopped in the living room.

She turned to him, attempting a reassuring smile. "I'm good, Ash. Really. I don't want you to worry that I'm upset with you. Or angry. I'm mad at myself, but not you."

His brow lifted and his gaze sharpened. "Why the hell are you angry with yourself?"

She sighed, and then he wrapped his arm around her waist and pulled her toward the couch. He sat and tugged her down onto his lap, a position she was becoming all too accustomed to.

She loved that he wanted no distance between them. Loved that he felt the need to touch her often. That he wanted her close whenever they discussed an issue. She drew great comfort from that fact.

It was pretty damn hard to fear anything when she was surrounded by Ash. She knew, just as he'd done with Michael, that he'd protect her from anything that could possibly hurt her.

"Josie," he prompted. "Waiting, baby."

"If I'd had the guts to do what I was supposed to do, you would have never had to risk yourself the way you did by going after Michael," she said with an unhappy frown.

He put his fingers to her lips, his gaze fierce. He looked . . . pissed.

"That's bullshit," he bit out. "I would have still kicked his fucking ass. And in a lot of ways, my method of dealing with him is far more effective than if you'd had him arrested. He probably would have gotten out with a slap on the wrist, if that. And if you'd wanted to pursue anything further, it would have been hell on you. And there's no telling the lengths he would have gone to in order to discourage you from seeking punishment for him. This way—my way—he's scared shitless, and furthermore, he now knows what it feels like for someone to beat the shit out of him. I don't anticipate him ever being a problem for you again. Did he say anything to you when you saw him today? You never said."

She shook her head. "No. He looked . . . scared."

Triumph gleamed in Ash's eyes. "Good," he said fiercely. "So he said nothing? Did he look at you?"

"I ran into him, or rather he nearly ran into me when I was

waiting outside the ladies' restroom for Mia and Bethany. He came out of the men's restroom and I gasped when I saw him. He looked . . . horrible!"

"Good," Ash muttered again.

"I asked him what happened but he never said a word. He acted like he couldn't get away from me fast enough."

Ash smirked. "Guess my message got through then."

"Yeah, I guess it did," she murmured.

He stroked his hand through her hair and then pressed a kiss to her temple. "It still bothering you?"

"No," she whispered. "I think it bothers me more because it *doesn't* bother me. I know that makes no sense, but I feel guilty. I feel like a horrible person for not being appalled over what happened to him."

He kissed her again, leaving his lips pressed against her head. "You not feeling guilty over that scumbag getting what he deserves doesn't make you a bad person. He's an asshole, Josie. Think about the fact that not only will he not hurt you again, but he won't hurt any other woman. Having him arrested doesn't guarantee that. Me kicking his ass and threatening to ruin him if he ever so much as touches another woman wrong does."

She wrinkled her nose. "I'll get over it. He did deserve it. I almost wish I'd been there so I could hit him in the nuts just once."

Ash chuckled. "I got in plenty for you, baby. Don't ever want you involved in that kind of shit. Want you to shine. Not be dragged in the shadows with me."

"Sticking up for me doesn't mean you live in shadows, Ash. It means a lot that you'd risk so much. For me."

"Bet on that," he said in a low, serious tone. "Don't ever question it. Whatever you need, whatever you want, is yours. Never have to ask."

She leaned up to kiss him. "In that case, make love to me, Ash. That's what I really need and what I really want right now."

"*That*, you definitely never have to ask for," he growled against her mouth.

He shifted upward, leaned her forward before rising and lifting her into his arms. He carried her to the bedroom and gently, reverently laid her on the bed.

"Don't know what you have in mind tonight, baby, but what I want to give you is the sweet. You've had the pain. Don't want you thinking about pain tonight, not when you just saw the bastard who inflicted it on you. So tonight, I'm going to give you the sweet. Going to make love to you so you not only know how I feel about you, but you'll *feel* it too."

God, but she loved this man, and it grew increasingly harder not to let those words slip out. How easy it would be to tell him, but she wanted it at the right moment. Right now she wasn't sure what the right moment would be. But she didn't want him to think they were just words said in the heat of the moment. She wanted him to know with absolute certainty that she meant them and that they came from her heart.

He leaned down, fusing his mouth hotly to hers. Their tongues met and slid sensuously over one another. Rough then soft. Hot, damp, electric.

He wanted to show her, but she also wanted to show him. Wanted to make love to him. Let him feel what he meant to her.

She braced her palms on his shoulders and then slid them up to the column of his neck. She pulled him lower, meeting his tongue with hers, tangling them breathlessly. She tasted him. Wanted more.

Her fingers trailed down his shirt, tugging impatiently. "I want you naked," she complained.

He chuckled, the sound vibrating over her mouth. "I want you naked too. What do you say we both do something about that?"

"Race you," she challenged, a broad grin attacking her lips.

"Oh hell no," he said with a laugh when she rolled, tearing at her clothing. "Cheating little wench."

She laughed, yanking at her clothing while Ash ripped at his. She kicked the clothing away and stood by the bed, palms upturned as she smirked at him.

"Took you long enough," she taunted when he kicked away his pants.

He yanked her to him, hauling her into his arms. She landed with a thump against his chest.

"If you think that took a long time, wait to see how long it takes me to get you off," he said in a silky voice.

"You wouldn't," she breathed out.

He cocked an eyebrow. "Wouldn't I?"

"You said you weren't into punishments," she pointed out.

"Who said it would be a punishment? I can't think of anything more pleasurable than taking my sweet time teasing and taunting you, making you hold off until you're screaming my name when you come."

She moaned and leaned into his chest. "Stop. You're torturing me, Ash. No matter what you call it, that is most definitely punishment."

"Well, then, what do you say we do a little role reversal?"

Intrigued, she glanced up at him, cocking her head to the side.

"You on top. You calling the shots."

"Mmmm, I'm liking this idea. Definitely has merit."

"Then get to it, baby. Take your man to bed and ride him."

She leaned up to kiss him, palming his face in her hands as she held him for the lusty, hot kiss.

"Mmmm," he returned, mimicking her sound of pleasure. "My

beautiful little submissive likes the idea of being in charge for a night."

She loved those words from his lips. His beautiful little submissive. The way he said it. So much tenderness and affection in his voice. And she knew what he was doing. She loved him even more for it. He was wiping away the thoughts of Michael. Of her relationship with him. The fact that he never gave back anything he took.

Tonight Ash was offering her the most precious gift she could receive. Himself. His trust. Him relinquishing control to her.

This was not a man who ever handed over control or dominance. And she didn't delude herself. She was in charge but he would effectively be topping from the bottom. Because she knew he would still be in control. He would just be controlling her being in control.

"Get on the bed," she said huskily. "Flat on your back, head on the pillow. I want you to be comfortable."

"Baby, I have to say, you on top of me with me deep inside you? Doesn't matter where I am. I'll be comfortable."

She smiled and caressed his jaw before turning him toward the bed.

Who was she kidding? She had no idea how to do this. Didn't even have a strong desire to be the one in control. But it was what he wanted and what he wanted to give to her, so she'd do it without reservation.

He did her bidding, stretching his long frame over the bed. His cock jutted upward, reaching for his navel as he lay on his back. It was straining, utterly rigid, the head dark plum and liquid already seeping from the slit.

She crawled onto the bed between his legs and slowly made her way up his body on her hands and knees. She dipped her head and licked over his sac, rolling the balls with her mouth.

He moaned softly and twisted, adjusting his position so she had better access. She tongued the sac, sucking it lightly into her mouth before nibbling her way up to the base of his cock. Then she swiped her tongue up the underside, tracing the thick vein all the way to the head.

When she got to the top, she hesitated a brief moment, circling the tip with her tongue. Then she sucked him deep in one swift motion. His hips shot off the bed, arching up, pushing him farther into her mouth.

"Goddamn, Josie. Feels so good, baby. That mouth of yours is pure sin."

She grinned. "Glad you approve."

His hand tangled in her hair, holding her down to meet his thrust. Yes, he'd relinquished control to her, but he was still very much in command of the situation.

For several long moments she sucked and licked, enjoying the way he twitched and quivered beneath her. Then he pulled her head away, his hand still wrapped tightly in her hair.

"Baby, if you're going to get on, you need to do it now. I'm close, and I won't last much longer. Want you with me when I go."

She raised her head, freeing her hair from his grasp. Then she swung one leg over his, straddling him. She inched forward until his erection was nestled at the juncture of her thighs.

Leaning forward, she planted both palms on his chest and levered herself up.

"I need your help," she whispered. "Put it in me, Ash."

His eyes glittered brightly as he reached down to fist his cock. He stroked through her folds with his other hand, fingering her clit as he positioned himself. When he nudged the head of his dick against her opening, she lowered herself, capturing his erection.

He pulled his hands free and then curled his fingers around her hips, anchoring her to him as she slid farther down to fully envelop him.

With a contented sigh, she took him all the way in. The sensation of fullness was overwhelming. Even more so than when he'd fucked her with the plug in her ass. She felt unbelievably small and tight and he felt enormous stuffed into her pussy.

Every movement sent a twinge of unbelievable pleasure winging through her abdomen. She lifted up, moaning when he began to slide back the way he'd come.

"Jesus," Ash ground out. "So tight. You're clamped around me like a greedy fist, baby. Never felt anything like it."

She put more weight on her hands and pressed harder into his chest. He didn't seem to mind one bit. She watched his eyes, the way they swarmed with desire, pleasure, how they blanked and the pupils flared each time she took him whole.

His jaw was firm, as if his teeth were set hard. There were lines of tension around his eyes and across his forehead. A light sheen of perspiration glistened on his brow. He was the most beautiful man she'd ever laid eyes on. And he was all hers.

"Take me over, baby," he said. "Tell me what you need to get there and let's go together."

"Touch me," she whispered. "My breasts and my clit."

He smiled, those gorgeous eyes sparking fire. He cupped one breast and then slid his other hand between their bodies to stroke her intimately. She closed her eyes, threw back her head and waited a moment to let herself catch up to where he was.

When the stirrings of her orgasm rose, sharp and edgy, she began to move again. She rose up and then slid down. She rotated, grinding her ass into his groin. Ash's hands never left her. He continued to caress her breasts, alternating between them. He stroked over her clit, firmly, with just enough pressure, but still infinitely gentle.

"I'm almost there," she panted out. "What about you?"

"There," he bit out. "Don't stop, baby. Whatever you do, don't stop now."

She went wild atop him. Head thrown back, hair streaming down her back, her mouth open in a silent scream that eventually found its voice. His hands were seemingly everywhere. His cock driving deep.

Her orgasm rose higher and higher, out of control, spiraling like a skydive. And still, the pressure mounted, no relief.

Ash arched his hips, slamming into her from underneath. She went wet around him and then realized he was already coming, his release flooding her. Wet sucking sounds filled her ears, erotic. The scent of sex, tangy and musky, filtered through her nose.

He pinched her nipple between his thumb and forefinger. Just enough of an edge to the pleasure to finally, finally send her hurtling over the edge. It was a free fall like she'd never experienced. Powerful. Explosive. Painful and yet so oh-my-God good that all she could do was feel.

She dug her nails into his chest, knowing she tore his skin. He'd wear the marks for days, just like she wore his marks of possession. In a savage moment, she was thrilled by them. The idea that he was hers. That this was proof of her possession of him. By God, she may have chosen to submit to him, but he was every bit as much hers as she was his.

She collapsed forward, her arms no longer able to support her. Ash gathered her tightly against him, holding her as he whispered in her ear. She had no idea what he said. Couldn't hear it over the roaring in both ears. Her blood pounded. Her body was tingling from head to toe. She felt like she'd just been hit by lightning and all her nerve endings were fried.

Then she became aware of another pulse. The comforting, reassuring feel of Ash's heartbeat beneath her cheek. She sighed, snuggled deeper into his arms, and he squeezed her tighter, holding on as they both struggled for breath.

"Am I smothering you?" she asked weakly.

"No, darling. Don't want you to move. Just stay right here with me. Just like this. I'm going to stay inside you for as long as I can. We'll clean up in the morning."

She smiled as he stroked her hair with his hand. Nothing felt as good as right here, right now, sprawled atop her man after she'd ridden him long and hard. And him staying inside her for as long as he could manage it? Definitely a good way to sleep. What could be better?

Nothing could touch her here. No outside world. No crazy families. No abusive ex-lovers. No fears of Ash being arrested for meting out justice to the man who hurt her.

Just her and Ash.

*I love you.*

The words remained locked inside her. But she knew without a doubt that soon they'd find their way to the surface. Who cared if it was too soon? When the time was right, she'd tell him.

## chapter twenty-two

The next day, Ash sent his driver to pick up Josie from their apartment. She was having lunch with him and Brittany at the Bentley Hotel where Brittany now worked. After meeting his friends the night before, she wasn't as nervous about meeting Brittany, although she had to admit to being really curious about the other woman.

Ash had told her that until recently Brittany had played the dutiful bitch daughter, siding with his family in their scorn and revilement of him. But that she'd come to him in tears because she wanted out.

It took someone strong to stand up to the kind of family—and mother—Ash described. Especially after thirty years. And a marriage that her mother had pushed her into.

Ash was waiting outside when the car arrived, and he opened the door, extending his hand to help Josie out. He slipped an arm around her waist, keeping her snug against his side as they walked into the restaurant.

They were directed to the same table where she and Ash had eaten that first night, and there was a woman already seated. Josie soaked in the details from a distance so she wouldn't be staring once they got to the table.

She could definitely see the family resemblance. Brittany had the same blond hair with a variety of shades just like Ash. She also had the same green eyes Ash sported and the shape of their faces was very similar.

When they got close, Brittany looked up and a wide, welcoming smile curved her lips. Josie could swear she saw relief in the other woman's expression. Perhaps she'd been worried that Ash wouldn't come.

And when she smiled, Josie could see just how stunningly beautiful Brittany was. But then, Ash was a beautiful man. Brittany was more his feminine counterpart. She didn't have the hard edges that Ash had. She lacked Ash's intense gaze, his expression, the way he carried himself.

No matter how crazy or horrible his parents were, they definitely gave their children the beautiful genes.

Brittany rose but stood still, as if waiting to see how Ash would greet her. Ash circled the table and enveloped his sister in a big hug. He kissed her cheek and then took her hand, squeezing it. Brittany's reaction was sweet. She stared up at Ash, just like most sisters stared up at their big brothers when they'd done something huge and nice for their baby sisters. She looked at him like he hung the moon.

"Britt, I want you to meet Josie. Josie, this is my sister, Brittany."

"Hello, Josie," Brittany said in a cultured voice that just screamed money and privilege.

But there was no pretension about her. She grasped Josie's hand warmly and then, to Josie's surprise, Brittany hugged her and kissed her on the cheek.

"Hello, Brittany. I'm so happy to finally meet you. Ash has told me so much about you."

At that, her excitement dimmed, and her eyes grew cloudy with worry.

"It was all good," Josie hastened to say, regretting that she'd already put her foot in her mouth. "He said you were doing wonderfully in your job here. He bragged that you would end up running the entire thing before it was over with."

Brittany smiled and relaxed. Ash guided both women to their seats and then motioned for the waiter.

"I'm enjoying it," Brittany said, once the waiter took their drink order. "It's nice to be . . . useful. I'm remembering how smart I am. It just took a while because unfortunately I've become very adept at being dumb over the years."

Ash shook his head. "Cut yourself some slack, Britt. You'll get there. Rome wasn't built in a day."

Josie laughed at the old saying. "He's right, though. I've made my share of really dumb mistakes. But I'm through beating myself up over them."

Ash squeezed her hand under the table but then surprised her by dragging it up and over the table where he pulled it to his mouth and pressed a kiss into her palm.

"Glad to hear that, baby. About time."

Brittany looked inquisitively between Ash and Josie and then her eyes widened before a broad smile lit up her entire face.

Josie guessed it was pretty obvious that she and Ash were more than just a casual date. But then Ash had made it pretty clear that Josie was someone important to him. Why else would he bring her to lunch with his sister?

"Mom giving you any more trouble, Britt?" Ash asked.

Brittany made a face and then took a long swallow of the wine the waiter had served. "She came by that one time I told you about. After that she resorted to calling every day. I ignore the calls and let them go to voice mail. She called work one time, and I told her off. I haven't heard from her since."

Ash nodded approvingly. "That's good. You'll get there. Eventually she'll figure out that she can't get her claws into you anymore and she'll find another target."

"Like she did with you?" Brittany pointed out, a snort passing her lips.

"Okay, maybe she won't," Ash said ruefully. "But you'll figure out how to handle her and after a while it won't bother you as much."

"I envy you," Brittany said. "I know I've said it before, but I'd give anything to have your confidence."

The wistful tone in her voice made Josie wince with sympathy. But she sat quietly, not wanting to interrupt their conversation.

The waiter came and took their orders, and Ash leaned back, reaching for Josie. She slid into his side, their chairs mashed up against each other. His arm settled around her shoulders as he continued his conversation with Brittany.

"So how long have you two been dating?" Brittany asked.

Josie went still, her mouth suddenly unable to work. What could she say? They didn't date. One could hardly call what they'd done dating. They'd bypassed that stage all together. And somehow, the word *dating* seemed so tame. Not at all indicative of the intensity of their relationship.

"Josie and I have been together a while now," Ash said easily.

"Oh, that's good. You look so good together. Tell me more about you, Josie. What do you do?"

Apparently Ash hadn't spoken of Josie to Brittany. Josie licked her lips, suddenly feeling self-conscious in front of his sister. No matter that Ash had clearly outlined the difficulties Brittany had experienced, the woman still came from money. From a world Josie didn't fit into. She'd had a wealthy husband, rich parents. Hell, her brother Ash had more money than God.

"I'm an artist," Josie said in a husky voice. "I also design jewelry. But mostly I paint."

Brittany's eyes widened and Josie wasn't sure if it was surprise, judgment or what. Her nape prickled and she immediately felt defensive.

"I'd love to see your work sometime," Brittany said.

"I'm sure that can be arranged at some point," Ash said. "Right now she's busy working on something for me and she has a client who buys up all her work so she's pretty focused on that at the moment."

"You sound so successful!" Brittany gushed.

Josie ducked her head. "Well, yes, I suppose you could say that. It's a rather new development, though, so I still have a hard time thinking of myself that way. Someone came into the gallery where I exhibit and bought up all my stuff and demanded more. I have no idea what they're doing with it. I haven't heard anything about them doing a private exhibit. Perhaps it's for a private collection that will never be shown."

"But still, you must be thrilled. I'd love to be that independent," Brittany said wistfully.

"I am thrilled," Josie said. "It means a lot for me to be able to stand on my own two feet and support myself."

Brittany nodded, understanding bright in her eyes.

Ash had gone still beside her, his lips drawn into a firm line. Had she said or done something that displeased him? Surely he couldn't fault her for liking being able to support herself. It in no way interfered with her relationship with him. But it gave her the confidence to remain with him, submissive, because she knew she didn't have to. Didn't have to rely on him to support her. And that was important. It gave her much more power to *choose* to be with him rather than having no other option.

Their food came, breaking the current topic of conversation. For several moments, they ate, silence descending on the table.

Brittany looked up, her mouth open as she was evidently going to say something. But then her eyes flashed and her mouth snapped shut.

"Shit," she murmured.

Ash frowned and started to turn around to see what Brittany was looking at, but before he could, a woman strode into view, standing between Ash and Brittany at the table.

Without needing to be told, Josie guessed that this had to be their mother. It was also obvious that she was who both siblings got their looks from. She had long, blond hair that was probably helped by a bottle to cover the gray because Josie couldn't detect any sign of her age. At least not by looking at the healthy, glossy mane of hair.

For that matter, there wasn't a single wrinkle marring the other woman's face. No indication of her age. Her skin was smooth and free of blemishes. Her fingernails were immaculately manicured and expensive jewelry dripped from her wrists and fingers.

"Fuck," Ash muttered.

His mother sent him a look that would have fried a lesser man.

"Watch your language," she snapped. "There's no reason to be vulgar."

"What the hell are you doing here? In my hotel," he bit out.

The emphasis on it being his hotel wasn't lost on Josie or his mother.

Her eyes flashed with anger as she glared at Ash. Then her gaze turned to Brittany. Josie was just glad that so far the woman was ignoring her.

"When are you going to stop this silly game?" she demanded.

Color suffused Brittany's cheeks. No matter what the younger woman had said about handling her mother before, it was evident that she was still no match for her.

"And you," she said, rounding on Ash. She pointed her finger in an accusing manner toward Ash. "I know what you're doing and it won't work."

Her voice was like ice and the coldness of it made Josie shiver. These were her children and yet she treated them like they were people she *hated*.

"And what, pray tell, is it that I'm doing?" Ash drawled.

He hadn't moved his arm from Josie and in fact he'd tightened his hold around her shoulders. She could feel his fingers digging into her arm, but she made no move to get him to loosen it. She doubted he even realized how painful his hold was. It was her only indication of how his mother's impromptu visit was affecting him.

No matter what he might say about his mother, it still hurt him that she was so . . . bitchy.

His mother's eyes narrowed, fury spitting from the green eyes she shared with her children.

"Using Brittany to get back at me for some imagined slight. Really, Ash. Putting her to work in your hotel? How vulgar and common is that? Do you get a good laugh out of watching her work? Does it make you happy to know how it makes me feel?"

Ash sat forward like a shot, his face dark, anger gleaming in his eyes. Brittany cast a worried look in Josie's direction, but at least it didn't reflect hurt. She hadn't believed her mother's accusation. Josie gave her a look of support and sympathy, letting her know that she didn't believe it any more than Brittany did.

"I don't give a fuck how it makes you feel," Ash gritted out. "All I care about is how Brittany feels. But don't take my word for it, Mother dear. Ask her yourself. Ask her if she feels like I'm making a fool of her by giving her a real job where she gets paid a real salary for doing real work."

His mother never turned to look at Brittany. But Brittany spoke up, her tone even and unaffected.

"I asked him for a job. He gave me what I asked for. Now please go, Mother. You're making a spectacle of yourself and that's one thing you've always hated."

Fury sparked in the older woman's eyes. Josie was surprised that steam didn't rise from her ears. And then her gaze settled on Josie, almost as if she was looking for a new victim. Josie fidgeted uncomfortably underneath her gaze but refused to react. She kept her expression serene and unbothered.

"Is this your latest whore, Ash? How dare you take my daughter to lunch with you and your latest piece of ass."

Brittany gasped, her face turning red. Horror reflected in her eyes as she stared at Ash.

Ash stood, the clatter loud as he pushed back his chair. Then he motioned for security who were already hovering on the fringes.

"Escort this woman out," he said in a frigid tone. "Furthermore, she is never to be allowed back on the premises of any of my properties. You photograph her and distribute it along with her name. The person who allows her back will be terminated immediately."

His mother's face went white with shock. And then color invaded as embarrassment took over. She glanced right and then left, dismayed when she saw a security person on either side.

"Get out," Ash said, enunciating each word. "Stay away from Brittany and stay away from me. And stay the fuck away from Josie. She will be my wife and the mother of my children. I'll not allow any disrespect to be shown to her. Ever. Now get the fuck out of my sight. And tell dear old dad and the old man that Brittany and I are out. We have no desire to be a part of the family."

"Ash, wait," his mother begged. "I need to talk to you. Please. I let my temper get the best of me, but I came here today to speak to you. I didn't even know Brittany would be here. I was just caught off guard. But there's something I need to talk to you about."

"And I don't give a fuck," he said coldly. "I have no interest in anything you have to say."

Josie sat there, stunned by what Ash had said. His wife? Mother of his children? Holy shit but that was deep! They'd only known each other a very short time. He'd said nothing to her about marriage and babies. Not that she had anything against either, but shouldn't he have at least mentioned it to her before he blabbed it in a public restaurant?

His mother licked her lips as the security closed in. "I need to speak to you, Ash. It's important. It's about your grandfather."

"You aren't manipulating me like you manipulate everyone else in your life. I have no interest in you or the old man. Look around, Mother. I don't need you. I don't need him. I've made a success of myself without any of you. And perhaps that's the biggest reason you despise me so much."

She went white, but anger glittered in her eyes. Josie's heart ached for Ash. It didn't matter that he'd hardened himself to his family. This was his mother! Everyone needed a mother. She could only imagine how it made him feel to know his own mother despised him.

She reached up, not knowing if it was what she should do, but she curled her fingers around Ash's hand and then rose to stand beside him. Only he shifted so she wasn't exactly beside him but more behind him, nestled into his side. He was protecting her even now from his mother's judgment and vitriol. Josie just wanted him to know that she was here. Beside him. Always. He might be protective of her, but she sure as hell would protect him from whatever she could.

"Escort her out," Ash said to the two security officers.

"I know my own way out," she huffed, shrugging off the hand of one of the guards.

"I have no doubt of that. But then letting you walk out on your own would deprive me of the pleasure of having you thrown out," Ash said.

He nodded toward the two security guards and they grasped

his mother by the arms, one on either side, and began to lead her away.

Her shrieks of indignation filled the air. Josie flinched because every eye in the restaurant was on them. She'd even seen a few camera flashes. She had no doubt today's incident would be all over the tabloids. Ash was one of the wealthiest men in the city. He came from money, from people with connections in society. His grandfather was a well-known figure in politics. No doubt the papers would be tripping over themselves to report the estrangement between Ash and his mother.

What if Michael saw it? Would he try to cause trouble for Ash once he realized who Ash was?

More camera flashes, this time much closer. Josie flinched away, covering her face with a hand. Ash pulled her farther behind him and then flicked his hand toward the people taking pictures. In a moment's time, more security rushed forward, effectively shutting down the impromptu photo session.

Josie sagged into her chair. Brittany looked shell-shocked. She was pale and looked mortified as she sagged against the back of her chair. Josie's heart went out to her.

"I'm having a girls' night out Wednesday night," Josie said casually. "You should go with us. It'll be fun."

Brittany blinked in surprise as she stared back over at Josie.

Beside Josie, Ash had retaken his seat and he curled his fingers around hers, squeezing as she issued the invitation. She chanced a peek up at Ash and saw warm approval—and appreciation—glowing in his eyes. She smiled encouragingly up at him, as if to say, *It'll be all right.*

"I don't know," Brittany began.

"You should go, Britt. Josie is going with Mia and Bethany and their girls. You've already met Bethany. They're solid. You'd like them. No better women anywhere," Ash said.

Brittany's cheeks turned pink but delight simmered in her eyes. "I'd like that, Josie. Thanks. Tell me when and where."

Josie glanced up at Ash because she didn't know the when and where. Only that she was going Wednesday night and that she and Ash were shopping for a dress and shoes after lunch with Brittany.

"I'll send a car for you," Ash promised. "I'll warn you, though. They take girls' night out pretty seriously. You'll need a sexy dress and some to-die-for heels. It's the dress code, or so I've been informed."

Brittany laughed. "Well, I have plenty of those. Thank God I'll have a use for them. I took a look the other day and thought to myself that I'd never have a need of them again."

Ash smiled at his sister. "Be ready at seven. It's Jace's turn to ride herd so he'll be around in a car. I'll let him know to pick you up and to drop you back off when you're done."

Her eyes glittered with excitement. In that moment, Josie was glad she'd issued the impulsive invitation.

"Thank you for inviting me, Josie. It sounds like fun!"

Josie smiled warmly at Ash's sister and then reached across the table to squeeze her hand. "Us girls have to stick together, right?"

Brittany grinned back. "Yep. And with guys like Ash around, it's even more important not to let them get one over on us."

"Hey," Ash defended.

Josie elbowed him in the gut and he pretended to double over in pain.

"Let's finish eating. Not going to let that bitch ruin the meal for us," Ash proclaimed. "You have to get back to work, Britt, and Josie and I have some shopping to do."

Brittany's eyes rounded. "Shopping? You?"

Ash glared at her. "Some things are worth going shopping for. Like the results of this shopping trip."

Josie elbowed him for real, her face flaming with heat.

Brittany laughed and Ash grinned. Josie relaxed. The awkward moment was over and Ash and Brittany hadn't let it ruin their day.

Fifteen minutes later, Ash was guiding Josie into the car and they rode off toward the stores Ash was taking her to.

He pulled her against him, wrapping his arm around her shoulders. He kissed her temple and left his lips pressed to her skin for a long moment.

"Meant a lot that you'd invite Britt on your girls' night out," he rumbled. "That was sweet of you, baby. I won't forget it."

Josie smiled and then sobered. "You don't think Mia and Bethany will mind, do you? I didn't even think about asking them first."

Ash shook his head, pulling back from her temple. "No, they're the best. They won't mind a bit. Especially if I put a bug in Mia's ear about Britt. It was a nice thing to do, baby. It was something you didn't have to do, but I'm really happy that you're including Britt in your girls' stuff. She needs that. She needs good friends."

"I was happy to do it," Josie said softly. "Everyone needs friends. Brittany probably more than most. She looked so miserable and embarrassed when your mom showed up."

Ash's face darkened and he went stiff next to her. "I'm sorry for that. Sorry she ruined our lunch."

Josie shook her head. "She didn't ruin it, darling. You and Brittany didn't let her. I don't know the woman. Don't care what she thinks about me or that she doesn't think I'm good enough for you."

He went utterly still, his eyes blazing across her face. "You called me 'darling.'"

She blushed and looked away. "Sorry. It probably sounds stupid."

He took her face, not too gently, and forced her back to him. "I liked it. Liked it a hell of a lot. You've never called me anything but Ash."

"You do?"

He nodded. "Yeah. Don't give a fuck what other men like or don't like or what anyone thinks because you call me something sweet. I like it. Makes me feel like I mean something to you, so yeah, I like it a whole lot."

She smiled. "Okay then, darling. I'll remember that."

He kissed her, hard, long, breathless. His tongue pushed in, roaming through her mouth with sensual familiarity. When he finally dragged himself away, his eyes were dark with desire. He stroked her cheek, palming it with one hand as he stared back at her.

"Don't give a shit what my mother thinks about you either, baby. As long as you remember that it's bullshit you not being good enough for me. Don't want that ever on your mind. Doesn't even need to cross it. You're fucking perfect for me and you need to always remember that."

She smiled again and leaned up to kiss him, savoring the sweetness of his mouth against hers.

"I will."

# chapter twenty-three

After hearing all about the previous girls' nights out from Ash, Josie was determined to make sure he enjoyed it every bit as much as Gabe and Jace had on previous occasions. Which meant that she didn't let him see the dress. Or the shoes. Or, well, anything at all.

He'd protested the idea of her getting dressed at Mia's. He'd wanted a teaser of what was to come, but Josie had told him in a firm voice that the effect would be ruined if he saw her beforehand.

Oh, he'd seen the dress. He'd even seen the shoes. After all he'd gone with her to buy them. It had taken him twenty minutes to convince her to buy them because oh my God, they were ridiculously expensive! Clearly she was in the wrong line of work because that one pair of shoes cost three times as much as one of her paintings sold for. But he hadn't seen the dress or shoes on her nor had he seen her all made-up for the night out. She packed makeup, her dress and shoes, determined that she'd do her hair and everything over at Mia's.

Ash wasn't happy about it, but he saw her into his car with instructions for the driver to take her to Mia and Gabe's high-rise apartment in Midtown. She'd waved cheekily with a promise to see him much later.

When she arrived at Mia's building, to her surprise she found both Bethany and Mia waiting for her in the lobby. Bethany took one of Josie's bags while Mia herded them all into the elevator. When they reached the top floor, the elevator opened into a spacious apartment with a beautiful view of the city from the living room windows.

Gabe met them in the living room and Josie stood back, a little wary of him. He just looked so . . . formidable. Not that she thought he'd hurt her. Or Mia. But he was just this quiet, intimidating guy, and she had only been around him once, so she hadn't reached a level of comfort with him yet.

Gabe pulled Mia to him and planted a scorching kiss on her that made Josie's toes curl. Bethany just smiled and glanced at Josie, a teasing glint in her eyes.

"I'll leave you ladies to it," Gabe said. "The car and driver are waiting out front. Just call down and let the doorman know when you're ready to leave. Jace will get to the club a little later and make sure you all get home afterward. I'm going to head over to eat dinner with Ash."

Mia bestowed a devastating smile on her husband, one that earned her a sultry stare that told Josie Gabe was very much looking forward to later.

"You need me for anything," Gabe said as he tipped Mia's chin up with his fingers, "You call me. I'll have my cell. You run into any problems, you call."

Mia rolled her eyes. "You know I will, Gabe. Besides, Jace will be there, not to mention Brandon and all his bouncer friends. They keep a very close eye on us when we're at the club."

Josie was fast getting lost in this conversation.

"Brandon is our friend Caroline's boyfriend. Or rather fiancé since he popped the question recently. That's what we're celebrating tonight," Bethany whispered. "He works at Vibe as a bouncer and he always takes care of us when we're out getting drunk."

Josie nodded.

Gabe kissed Mia one last time and then he nodded to Bethany and Josie.

"Have a good time, ladies, but be careful, okay? Stay together at the club. Don't leave your drinks unattended and if one of you goes to the bathroom, take at least one other person with you."

"Gabe!" Mia exclaimed in irritation. "For God's sake, we aren't teenagers. We can take care of ourselves already!"

Gabe chuckled, had the grace to look abashed and then headed toward the elevator.

The women barely had time to head into the huge bathroom before Mia's cell phone rang. She heaved a sigh when she looked at who was calling. "For the love of God. He's not even gone yet and he's already calling me."

Bethany giggled and both she and Josie waited as Mia answered the phone. She said "okay" and then "I love you too," her voice going soft when she said the last.

Mia put her phone down on the counter and glanced up at Josie and Bethany. "Gabe ran into Brittany downstairs so he's sending her up in the elevator now. I'll go grab her. Bethany, get started on Josie's hair. She'll need to put on her dress before we do makeup or she'll get foundation all over her dress."

"We got this," Bethany said, making a shooing motion with her hands. "Go get Brittany so we can get this evening started."

An hour later, the four women rode the elevator down to the lobby and got off, Mia leading the way. Outside, as Gabe had promised, a driver waited to usher them into the waiting limousine.

When they were all settled, Mia pulled a chilled bottle of champagne from the ice bucket and poured four glasses.

"Caro's not with us. She'll meet us at the club. However, that doesn't prevent us from having a toast in her honor."

Bethany nodded solemnly as she raised her glass.

Brittany clinked glasses enthusiastically, her green eyes, Ash's green eyes, sparkled with excitement.

"Thank you so much for inviting me to come," Brittany said. "I've been doing nothing but working and going back to my apartment. I'm starting to feel my age!"

Mia sent her a look of horror. "We can't have that. Spend an evening with us. That'll fix you right up."

Brittany sobered and glanced Josie's way. "I'm really sorry about my mom and what she said about you. I was so horrified and embarrassed. Even more so because I've put up with her for so long. Ash has never let her walk over him and that's why she hates him so much. But me and my other brothers?"

She broke off, cringing.

Josie's heart went out to her and she reached forward to squeeze her hand. "You have nothing to be sorry for, Britt," she said, adopting Ash's pet name for her. Judging by the instant light in her eyes, she liked it. "I'm just so happy you aren't letting her run over you now."

Mia's nose crinkled in distaste. "Not to offend you, Brittany, but your mother is a bitch. And Ash is such a good guy. I have no idea how he managed it springing from that gene pool."

Brittany frowned. "You aren't offending me, Mia. I, more than anyone, know how much of a bitch my mother is. I don't know why she's the way she is. I wish I knew."

Bethany's eyes simmered with sympathy. "I don't know much, only what Jace has told me and the few times Ash has mentioned his family, but none of it sounds good. Jace worries about him. A lot."

"Let's not talk about them tonight," Brittany said in a bright voice. "We're supposed to be having fun, right? This is the first time I can honestly say I've looked forward to a night out with the girls."

"Agreed," Josie said. "And I need Mia's and Bethany's help because, uhm, obviously Ash is expecting something from this night, and I'm not entirely certain what it is. I don't want to disappoint him!"

Mia and Bethany both dissolved into laughter.

"Oh, we'll fill you in on all the juicy details," Mia said smugly. "I had to guide Bethany through her first night out with us, and let's just say, she had one happy man that night."

"You're killing me," Brittany muttered. "I have no hot guy to go home to, and I have to say, it's been way too long since I've had anything remotely resembling good sex."

Bethany's lips pinched together in thought. "What about one of Brandon's friends, Mia? There is a vast array of hotness working at that club. Surely one of them is single."

"I'll sic Caro on it when we get there," Mia said.

"I don't want to come across as desperate!" Brittany protested.

Bethany shook her head. "Of course not! Caro will fix you up. Maybe introduce you to one of the guys."

When they arrived at the club, the door immediately opened, and a pretty, younger woman stuck her head in, a broad smile on her lips. She shoved her hand in before anyone could get out.

"Look at it!" she squealed. "Isn't it awesome?"

Mia pounced on the woman's hand and then pulled her so she fell into the car with them.

"Oh my God, Caro, it's gorgeous! Brandon did so good!"

Caro grinned so big that it lit up the inside of the limo. Then she glanced Josie and Brittany's way and her smile got even bigger.

"I'm Caroline," she said, extending her right hand. "You must be Josie and Brittany!"

"I'm Josie," Josie said, returning her smile. "And this is Brittany."

"Brandon's waiting so let's get going," Caroline said enthusiastically. "He has our table, of course, and tonight we have two waitresses instead of our usual one. We're expanding, girls! Soon we'll have the entire club to ourselves on our nights out."

"Now there's an idea," Mia drawled. "Our own private club. It has a certain ring to it."

Bethany snorted as they piled out. "All you'd have to do is tell Gabe you want one and he'd buy it for you."

Mia grinned. "This is true."

"Chessy, Gina and Trish are already inside waiting at the table," Caroline explained.

Then a big, goofy smile attacked her face and Josie glanced up to see what she was looking at.

A tall, very muscular, very hot guy stood there, smiling indulgently. He had a goatee and he wore an earring in his left ear. It was obvious, judging by the way Caroline looked at him and the way he looked at her, that this had to be Brandon, the bouncer. He certainly looked the part.

"Ladies," he greeted. "If you'll follow me, I'll show you to your table."

"You did awesome, Brandon," Mia said, patting him on the shoulder. "Caro's ring is gorgeous!"

He smiled. "Glad you approve. I wanted her to have the perfect ring. It's only fair. I get the perfect girl so she gets the perfect ring."

"Oh damn," Brittany muttered. "That's the most awesome thing I've ever heard a guy say."

Josie had to agree. It was absolutely sweet.

Caroline's cheeks flushed but her eyes shone with love for Brandon. Two weeks ago, seeing this would have made Josie insanely jealous, because Michael would never ever make his feelings known in public. Or private for that matter. But now she had Ash. Ash who had no problem whatsoever with people knowing Josie was his.

They pushed their way to the front, bypassing the long line of people waiting to get in. Then Brandon led them through the noisy crowd toward a set of tables in the corner of the room just off the dance floor.

Music reverberated through the air, invading Josie's blood, pumping along in time with her pulse. Her feet were already hurting, and she knew there was no way in hell she'd dance with these shoes on. She'd probably kill herself. But the shoes were more for Ash's benefit. He'd actually been quite vocal about his choices when they'd gone shopping. She'd spare her feet for the evening, but when she headed back to Ash's apartment, they'd go back on.

When they reached the table, a waitress stood there with a tray full of drinks. Mia smiled and turned to explain to Josie and Brittany.

"She always brings us two drinks to start the evening. We drink one down immediately after a group toast and then we sip the second until she gets back with more. Bethany and I weren't sure what your preferences were so we went for girly drinks. Cosmos and amaretto sours. The sours are Bethany's favorite and one of the few things she can drink to the point of intoxication. If you let the waitress know what you like, she'll swing by with another round later."

"I like Cosmos," Brittany said over the music.

"I don't drink much," Josie said ruefully. "I'm kind of making an exception for tonight. Ash was so eager for me to go out that I couldn't disappoint him."

Bethany and Mia both laughed.

"That's because Gabe and Jace have tortured Ash with all the details of what the man gets out of girls' night out," Bethany said with a roll of her eyes.

"Try an amaretto sour, Josie," Bethany said, shoving one of the drinks into her hands. "I don't drink much either, but this one is really good. Sweet and fruity without too much alcohol. I still manage to get wasted on them though."

When everyone had their drinks, they gathered in a tight circle as Mia made introductions between Chessy, Gina and Trish and Josie and Brittany. Once they were done, they all held their drinks up.

"To Caro!" Mia yelled. "And that big ass rock on her finger!"

"To Caro!" the group chorused.

They clinked glasses, sloshing the drinks over the rims. Then they gulped them down, chugging until the glasses were empty. The waitress emptied her tray of the second-round drinks and with a smile left the tables to go get refills.

"Let's dance!" Caro yelled.

Josie allowed herself to be pulled toward the dance floor. She liked to dance. Was actually pretty good at it. It had been a while, though. Michael wasn't into dancing or clubbing. She could shake her ass with the best of them, and tonight was as good a night as any to let loose and have some fun.

She liked Mia and Bethany's friends. Brittany did too judging by her big smile and dancing eyes.

"We have a precedent to follow," Mia yelled.

"Oh?" Josie inquired.

"Yeah," Bethany interjected. "We get really sexy on the dance floor, make all the men's tongues hang out, and when whoever's drawn guy duty for the night gets here, we pull out all the stops and give them, Brandon and the rest of the guys a show they won't forget."

Josie burst into laughter. "Okay, I'm starting to see where Ash is coming from with the girls' night out thing."

Mia's eyes twinkled merrily. "Oh, Bethany and I will fill you all in after we've had a few drinks and are taking a break at the table."

That sounded fair enough. Until then? She was going to let her hair down. Just a figure of speech, however. Bethany had spent a lot of time upsweeping Josie's hair into an "elegant messy bun" as Mia had called it. The result was sexy if Josie had to say so herself.

Soft tendrils escaped the pins holding the bun in place. Mia had used a lot of eye makeup on her, for that matter a lot of makeup in general, but the effect was stunning. The entire package was pretty awesome. Josie wasn't vain, but she knew she looked hot tonight.

Bethany had called her a bronze goddess. The dress Josie had chosen was a bronze/gold color that went perfectly with her hair and skin color. Skintight, strapless and short. There wasn't much of it there, but it accentuated her legs and then with the four-inch heels she'd chosen? Yeah, her legs looked great.

The collar really stood out with her hair upswept and the dress being strapless. She'd seen both Bethany and Mia eyeing it on the ride over, a hundred questions brimming in their gazes. Josie wondered how long it would take before they started prying.

Brandon checked in with them often. He and three other guys Josie surmised were also bouncers. Though one of them looked too . . . Well, she wasn't sure what he looked, but he wasn't a bouncer. Of that she was certain. While Brandon and the others were dressed casually in jeans and polo shirts, this other guy was wearing an expensive suit, silk shirt, diamond cuff links that did not look fake.

The interesting thing was that while Caro had introduced Brittany to the three bouncers who worked with Brandon, the guy in the suit had walked over and asked Brandon to introduce him to Brittany. And now? Brittany and mystery guy were standing off to the side, talking. Brittany had a glow about her that could only mean one thing. The guy was interested.

Josie nudged Mia and dipped her head in Brittany's direction. "Who's that with Brittany?"

Mia followed her gaze and then frowned as she studied the couple. "No idea, but Brandon will know. I'll ask."

Before Josie could tell her it was okay, Mia gestured for Brandon to come over. He came, Caroline tucked into his side, his fingers splayed possessively over her upper arm.

"Who's the guy with Brittany?" Mia asked.

Brandon pursed his lips a moment before returning his gaze to Mia and Josie. "His name is Kai Wellington. He owns the club."

Josie's eyes widened. "He owns it? Like the whole thing?"

Brandon chuckled. "Yeah. He owns several. He's usually not here that much. He just opened one up in Vegas a few weeks ago and he's been spending all his time out there." He glanced down at Caroline and squeezed her closer to him. "He wants me to work out there. Take over security. If I go, I want Caro to go with me."

For a moment, Mia looked stricken and Josie's heart went out to her. Caro was her best friend. But Mia quickly got a grip on her reaction and she smiled broadly.

"Is that like a promotion or something?"

"Or something," Brandon said in amusement.

"I'm happy for you," Mia said, but Josie could see that her lower lip trembled.

Then Mia threw her arms around Caroline and hugged her tightly.

"I'm happy for both of you," Mia said in a rush. "Are you excited, Caro?"

Caroline pulled back from Mia, smiling broadly. "Yeah, I am. I'm so happy for Brandon. He's worked hard for this and it's huge that Mr. Wellington trusts him. But I hate to leave the city . . . and you," she finished unhappily.

Brandon pulled her back into his arms and then pulled Mia to his other side.

"Look on the bright side. Your girls' nights out can be relocated to Vegas. I'll make sure you're given VIP treatment from beginning to end. You can plan a couple a year."

"I like the way he thinks," Bethany said, speaking up for the first time.

"So, Brandon," Josie said, pulling the attention back to Brittany. "What does Mr. Wellington want with Brittany? Didn't he ask you to introduce her to him?"

Brandon glanced sideways again before looking back at the women. His eyes expressed regret. "I can't really say anything. Mr. Wellington is a very private man. But I'd say he was interested in Brittany. He never took his eyes off her the entire evening."

Very interesting. Josie glanced their way again and Brittany hadn't once taken her eyes off him either. Ash would probably find it interesting as well, although he'd most likely do a complete background check on Kai Wellington.

"We've got some drinking to do," Caroline said brightly. "The evening's going to waste and Jace will probably be here at any time. Bethany, he'll be so disappointed if you aren't completely shitfaced. He thinks you're the most adorable drunk ever!"

Mia burst out laughing and Bethany smiled, though she did reach for her drink.

"I'll have the waitress swing by and set you up," Brandon said. "Break's over for me. Time to make another pass around the club. If you all want a quieter place to drink and relax, I'll put you in one of the boxes overlooking the dance floor. There's a button you can push to silence the music and outside noise."

Josie smiled at his understanding. No doubt he thought that Mia and Caroline would want to talk about her impending move and they couldn't really do that on the floor.

"That sounds perfect!" Bethany exclaimed. "Can we move there for a bit? I need a break from dancing and standing on my feet, and I'd love a quieter place to drink and talk."

"Follow me. I'll have the waitress round up Chessy and the others. They're still on the dance floor. She'll let them know where to find you when they're done dancing."

The women followed Brandon, but Josie motioned them to stop when they got to where Brittany and Kai were standing. She wanted to check in on Brittany and make sure she was comfortable or see if she needed rescuing.

"Hi," Josie said, donning a bright smile as she greeted Kai. "I wanted to let Brittany know that we're going to one of the boxes. Didn't want her looking for us."

Kai's arm slid around Brittany's waist, anchoring her to him. Okay then, it would seem the man moved fast. He smiled, and it was a gentle, warm smile, but Josie did not miss the strength in those eyes. This was a powerful, intimidating man. She glanced at Brittany to gauge her reaction.

"Your concern is admirable," Kai said in a low voice she almost couldn't hear over the music. "But I'll take very good care of Brittany and I'll escort her to your box myself when she's ready."

"That okay with you?"

Josie directed the question just to Brittany because so far Kai had done all the talking.

Brittany smiled and Josie could see no strain or faking it. Her entire face was flushed.

"I'm fine. Thank you, Josie. I'll catch up to you and the girls in a minute."

"Take your time," Josie said with a smile.

"She will," Kai murmured.

## chapter twenty-four

Ash stretched on his couch, drink in one hand, as Gabe sprawled into the armchair across from him. The two had eaten takeout that Gabe had picked up on his way over after leaving the women at his apartment.

Ash checked his watch and grinned. "How drunk you think they are by now?"

Gabe grimaced. "I'm sure they're well on their way."

Ash chuckled, though he was willing the hours to pass. He wanted Josie back, drunk, cute, and he was dying to see her in that dress and heels she'd bought. She wouldn't even let him see them when she tried them on in the store. All she'd said was that she thought he'd like the end result.

Hell, he'd like her in a sackcloth or with a paper bag over her head. Didn't matter to him what she wore, because he'd get her out of it quick enough. It was what was underneath that mattered the most. But still, the image of her made-up, teetering on sexy heels and eyes cloudy with alcohol? Yeah, that did it for him. He'd listened to Gabe and Jace enough to know that girls' night out was not something to miss.

Neither man had any issue with their women going out and having fun because afterward they came home to them and the reward was pretty spectacular.

His cell phone rang, and he picked it up immediately, thinking it might be Josie. He hoped the evening was going well and that she was relaxed and having fun.

He frowned when he saw his doorman's name as the incoming call.

"Ash," he said shortly.

"Mr. McIntyre, you have visitors in the lobby. They wanted to go up, but I called first. They say they're your parents."

"Oh Jesus," Ash muttered. Just kill him now. They had to be here tonight of all nights? They'd never set foot in his apartment building, just as they'd never set foot in his office building either. Hell, before the lunch his mother had intruded on earlier in the week, he seriously doubted they'd ever stepped into one of his hotels either.

Such a move reeked of desperation. His mother had wanted to "talk" after making her scene in the restaurant and he'd let her know in no uncertain terms that he had no desire to discuss anything with her. He'd banned her from his hotel properties, but perhaps he should have broadened his parameters a bit. But he wouldn't have imagined that they'd come here. Making him come to them was more their style.

He glanced over at Gabe who was regarding him with a frown. He shook his head to let Gabe know it wasn't anything going on with the women.

"I'll be down. Do not let them up. In fact never let them up if they show up again. They aren't allowed here," Ash bit out. "I'll come down and take care of the matter personally, but in the future, if they show up, you're to show them the door. And you damn sure better not ever let them up when I'm not here and Josie is."

"Yes, sir."

Ash ended the call and then got to his feet.

"What the fuck, man?" Gabe demanded. "What's going on?"

"My parents are paying me a visit," Ash said dryly. "I'm going down to inform them they aren't welcome."

"Shit," Gabe swore. "I'll come with you."

"Not necessary," Ash said in a calm voice. "Just hang out up here. I'll be back in a few."

Gabe got up, ignoring Ash's response. "Didn't say it was necessary. But I'm going with you."

Ash shrugged. Most people wouldn't want their dirty laundry and family drama aired in front of others. But Gabe wasn't just anyone. He was Ash's real family. Just as Jace was. And Gabe knew everything there was to know about mommy dearest. Except her showing her ass at lunch. It wasn't that Ash hadn't wanted to tell him or Jace, but it had slipped his mind. He'd been too focused on other things.

"She showed her ass the other day," Ash said as they got into the elevator. "I was having lunch with Josie and Brittany at the Bentley and she strutted in making a scene. I had her escorted out and gave instructions that she wasn't to be allowed on any of our hotel properties."

"Jesus. Does she ever quit?"

Ash shook his head. "Evidently not. She insulted Britt and Josie. Then she wanted to talk. As if I'd give her the time of day even if she hadn't spewed her vitriol all over Britt and Josie."

Gabe shook his head as the elevator descended. "It's a sad fact but maybe you ought to look into a restraining order. Have their asses arrested the next time they come poking around. Maybe that would be a wake-up call and let them know just how serious you are about them staying the hell away from you and Brittany."

"I'll make my point face-to-face," Ash said, his face going hard over the impending confrontation.

Having it out with his parents in the lobby of his building wasn't his first choice, but no way in hell was he allowing them into his home. That was his sanctuary. And Josie's. He wasn't about to have it invaded by people he loathed. And he damn sure wasn't having this confrontation on their turf. He wouldn't give them the satisfaction of going to them. Ever.

When they got off the elevator, Ash saw his mother and father waiting in the lobby. Neither looked happy and when they turned and saw him, there was no welcome in their eyes. No recognition that he was their son. But then there'd never been. He didn't understand it. Couldn't fathom being so cold toward your own children. The hell he'd ever treat his own kids this way.

He strode up to them and halted several feet away, his face drawn into a glacier of ice. He stared at them both coldly until his father actually flinched and looked away, guilt edging into his eyes.

"Why are you here?" Ash demanded bluntly.

His mother's gaze flicked over him and then to Gabe, annoyance sparking in her eyes.

"Really, Ash, this is a private matter. Couldn't we speak privately? Perhaps in your apartment?"

"Gabe is family," Ash said in a flat tone. "Anything you have to say can be said in front of him."

She sniffed delicately and then schooled her features. He could swear she was actually trying to appear . . . nice. Beseeching even. His nape prickled because she resembled a bloodthirsty vampire closing in on the kill.

"I wanted to apologize for my unfortunate behavior earlier in the week."

Color rose in her cheeks and it looked as though the words nearly choked her. They probably had. Issuing an apology was not something she ever did.

"Apology accepted. Now if that's all?"

Anger flashed in her eyes briefly before she pushed it away, once again composing herself to look more congenial.

"Your grandfather would like to have us all for dinner. Brittany too. He—and I—would like it very much if you would come. Your brothers and their wives and children will be there too, of course."

Ash's eyes narrowed. "No chance in hell."

His father cleared his throat, speaking for the first time.

"I wish you'd reconsider, son."

Ash stared at him in disgust. "'Son'? When have I ever been your son? Suppose you cut the crap and tell me exactly what it is you want here. Because it sure as hell isn't some family quality time over dinner."

His mother's lips thinned and her eyes flashed. This time she did nothing to try and hide her annoyance.

"He's going to change his will. He's pissed because our family has gone to hell as he put it. He's not happy with Brittany's defection. Said if I was more of a mother then my children wouldn't all despise me. He's made noises about how we should start to support ourselves and that he's tired of dumping money into a nest of vipers. He said that if a mother and father can't even keep their family together then why should he reward us by leaving us everything."

Ash laughed and it only pissed his mother off even more.

"This affects you too," she hissed. "And Brittany! If he cuts us out of his will, he cuts everyone. You won't get a dime and neither will Brittany."

Ash shook his head, still chuckling. "Maybe you haven't been listening to me all these years, Mother dear. I don't give a flying fuck about the old man's money. I never have. It comes with too many strings. Just as everything with you has strings."

"If you don't care then at least think about how this will affect your sister. She won't get anything either."

"I'll provide for Brittany so she never has to give a fuck about the old man's money or strings either," Ash said icily. "She doesn't want to be part of this toxic family any more than I do. She wanted out. I gave her that option."

His mother's fingers balled into tight fists at her sides. Then she turned to his father and all but shouted at him.

"Do something, William! Don't just stand there like a coward. We'll be ruined if he changes his will!"

"There's nothing he can do," Ash said calmly. "There is nothing either of you can possibly say that will make me go play nice with the family. I don't give a fuck about my brothers or the fact that they can't support their wives and children. I don't give a fuck about you and dear old dad. You made your bed and you can fucking lie in it. Brittany and I will be just fine."

"I hate you," his mother hissed.

He flinched, even though he knew as much. But somehow hearing those words from the woman who gave him life cut deep.

"Elizabeth, stop it," his father snapped. "You don't mean that. He's our son for God's sake. Is it any wonder he won't have anything to do with either of us? Think about what you're saying."

But Ash knew she meant every word. It was there in her eyes. It had always been there since the day he'd brushed his family off and made his own way in the world.

"I think it's time you left," Ash said quietly. "And don't come back. You aren't welcome here. You aren't welcome on any of the properties I own. And here's a warning. Stay the hell away from Brittany. Stay the hell away from me. And you sure as fuck better stay the hell away from Josie and the rest of my family. You spread your poison to any of them and I'll come after you. I'll take everything away from you. Furthermore, I'll make certain that the old man *does* change his will and leaves you nothing. If you don't think I'm deadly serious, just try me."

"You're bluffing," his mother spat.

Ash raised one eyebrow and engaged in a stare down. He didn't say anything. He didn't have to. She blanched and then looked away, her face going pale as she realized just how serious he was.

When she glanced back at him, she looked . . . *old*. Haggard and defeated. She took a step forward, her hand going to his arm. It took everything he had not to flinch away.

"Ash, please. I'm begging you. Don't do this. If you want us to back off, we will. I'll never come around again. Not even to Brittany. If you'll get him to change his mind. If you'll just come to one dinner, I swear you'll never see us again unless you want to. I'll issue that promise in writing. Whatever you want. Don't let your hatred of me ruin your brothers' lives. Think of their children. Their wives. Think of your father and me. We'll have *nothing*."

"Don't let her fuck with your head, Ash," Gabe growled, speaking up for the first time.

Ash held up his hand. "I won't come to dinner. No way I'll expose Britt to that. Or Josie. And where I go, she goes. That's in stone."

Seeing that she might be making headway, his mother leaned forward eagerly. "You don't have to come to dinner. But meet with him, Ash. You can put a different spin on Brittany leaving. Tell him whatever you want. Tell him we've reconciled. Just do whatever you have to in order to convince him not to cut us all out of his will."

"Jesus," Gabe spat. "This is pathetic."

She sent Gabe a chilling look so full of hatred that Ash recoiled. What the hell was wrong with these people? How on earth had he come from these two self-absorbed malcontents?

"I'll call the old man," Ash offered.

Gabe shook his head in disgust.

"But that's all I'm doing," Ash continued. "And I'm telling you now, this shit stops. If I hear of you coming near Britt or Josie, if you make another appearance at one of my hotels, my office building and especially my *home*, I'll yank the rug out from under you so fast that it'll break your neck. Got it?"

She nodded quickly, her eyes filled with hope. Desperate didn't even begin to cover it. The fact that she'd humbled herself enough to beg for anything from him told him just how desperate and afraid she was.

He should walk way. Should wash his hands of the lot of them. But they were his family. His blood. Even if he never wanted a familial relationship with them, the idea of them being destitute left a bad taste in his mouth.

"Get out," Ash said. "I'm done with this. I'm not letting you ruin my evening."

"Thank you, son," his father said in a quiet voice. "This means a lot to your mother. To me. And to your brothers as well. Tell Brittany . . ." He broke off with a sigh and scrubbed a hand over his face. "Tell Brittany I love her and that I miss her and hope she's doing well."

Ash nodded and then looked pointedly at the door.

His mother, evidently satisfied that she'd won this round, whirled and stalked away, her nose in the air.

When Ash turned back toward the elevator, Gabe was staring at him, a grimace twisting his lips.

"Christ, man, that sucks. I knew they were bad, but until I saw that, I just had no idea."

Ash shrugged. "How's the saying go? 'You can choose your friends, but you can't choose your family'?"

# chapter twenty-five

Josie followed Bethany and Mia who followed Caroline and Brandon to a private room located above the dance floor. Though you could see out to the floor below, Brandon assured them that no one was able to see into the box, so they were afforded complete privacy.

"I'll be back to check on you in a little while," Brandon said to Caroline as he brushed a kiss over her lips.

Caroline flopped onto the comfortable couch next to Josie. Mia took the other side of Caroline and Bethany perched on the arm.

"So you're moving to Las Vegas," Mia murmured.

Tears filled Caroline's eyes. "Yeah. Brandon wants to get married before we go. We have six weeks to find a place to live there, get married and move out there before he starts his new job. Mr. Wellington is being fabulous about everything. He's paying for relocation and also helping with the down payment on the house. He's very serious about Brandon and wants him to consider this a long-term position. He's doubling Brandon's salary so we won't have to worry about money and I have plenty of time to find a job out there."

"That's wonderful, Caro," Mia said softly. "But I'll miss you terribly."

"We all will," Bethany amended. "Girls' night out just won't be the same without you!"

Caroline hugged them both and then rose. "I'm going to head to the ladies' room and see if the others are coming. I'll also snag the waitress and tell her we all want another round. Be back in a flash."

Mia watched her best friend go with an unhappy frown. When Caroline left the room, Mia sighed.

"Damn, I'm going to miss her."

"I know," Bethany said. "So will I. But you still have us, Mia."

Mia looked up and smiled and then impulsively reached for both Josie's and Bethany's hands to squeeze.

"Okay so we're alone now and I have to admit, Josie, that Bethany and I are bursting with nosy questions about you and Ash. I hope we don't offend you but we're dying to know all the details!"

Josie laughed. "I don't mind. But I'm afraid you're in for a disappointment. There's nothing really exciting about our relationship."

Mia snorted. "You'll forgive us if we don't quite believe that. The first thing you have to tell us is just how good he is in the sack. I suppose Bethany already knows, but I have to admit, I'm curious!"

Then she promptly clamped a hand over her mouth, her eyes rounding with horror.

"Oh my God, Josie! I'm so sorry!" A low moan escaped and Mia buried her face in her hands. "I'm so stupid. I swear. Gabe and Jace are always telling me how I just blurt out whatever I'm thinking without any consideration for what I'm saying."

Josie smiled wryly. "It's okay, Mia. Really. I know about Bethany and Ash." She glanced over at Bethany to see the other woman was even more mortified than Mia. Her cheeks were pink and her eyes were mirrors of discomfort.

"I hope you understand," Bethany said. "I mean that it didn't mean anything to Ash. Oh God, this is even more awkward than things were the first time Jace and I saw Ash together after that night."

Josie reached over to squeeze Bethany's hand. "Please don't. It's okay, really. I admit, when Ash first told me what happened, I dreaded meeting you. I wasn't crazy about having to spend time with a woman who'd had sex with Ash. I hated the idea of picturing the two of you together. But after meeting you it was okay. And I think in a lot of ways, seeing how Jace was with you helped cement for me that there was nothing between you and Ash except deep friendship."

"I'm glad," Bethany said sincerely. "I love Ash. I really do. But as a friend. I adore Jace beyond all reason."

"I suppose I've ruined any chance of us getting the dirt on you and Ash now, Josie," Mia said glumly.

Josie laughed. "Well, no, not if you give me return dirt. I'm dying of curiosity over your men too. Like for instance, is that a collar you wear, Bethany? Or is it just a necklace?"

Bethany's cheeks went pink as she fingered the diamond that rested in the hollow of her throat. "It's a collar," she said softly. "Jace wanted me to wear it. I never take it off."

"Is yours a collar too, Josie?" Mia asked.

Josie nodded.

"Well damn," Mia muttered. "I want one too. I think they're so cool. I'd love for Gabe to pick one out and put it on me. But he's not into collars. And to be honest, I never was until I saw Bethany's. The meaning behind it is pretty awesome."

Both Bethany and Josie nodded.

Josie downed the last of her drink and set it on the table in front of the couch. She had a pretty good buzz going, but she wasn't even close to being plastered. She slipped her heels off her aching feet and stretched her toes, nearly sighing in contentment.

"Oh look, there's Jace," Mia said.

She'd gotten up and walked to the glassed-in area of the box to look down on the floor.

She turned back to Bethany. "He's here early isn't he? Or have we not been drinking enough?"

"I don't think we've been drinking as much," Bethany said ruefully.

"Well damn. We have to fix this. And the only way I know to get shitfaced in a very short time is to do shots!"

"Oh hell," Josie said. "I've never even had a shot of anything."

"You'll be okay," Mia said. "After the first one, you don't really taste them anymore."

Just then the door burst open and the rest of the women came in noisily. The waitress was with them, and handed out drinks and then listened as Mia gave her the next series of orders.

"Shots?" Caroline asked. "Since when do we do shots?"

"Since we're not nearly drunk enough," Mia said dryly. "Jace is already here, which means we don't have much longer. We have to catch up!"

"Bring the bottle," Chessy called to the waitress. "Better make it two! We have a lot of women here tonight."

The waitress grinned. "You got it."

Everyone piled onto the couches and chairs, shoes going this way and that. A few moments later, the waitress returned and began lining up shot glasses on the table.

"Everyone got one?" Trish yelled.

After a chorus of yesses, Gina held up her shot glass in a toast. Everyone raised theirs and then amid shouts of "Go, go go!" they downed the first shot.

Fire blazed down Josie's throat. She coughed and sputtered so much her eyes watered. She could feel it in her belly. Hell, she could even feel it travel to her bladder. It was sitting in her bladder, hot and swirling. Already she needed to go pee.

"Let's do the next!" Trish encouraged.

They picked up the next shot glasses, held them up as they did the last ones and then tossed the contents back.

A low chuckle sounded from the door. Everyone jerked around to see Jace standing there with Brandon. Both men looked amused. Jace was outright laughing. Then Jace stepped aside and Brittany appeared in the doorway, her face pink, her eyes shining brightly.

Behind her, stood Kai Wellington. He had hold of her elbow, but he let it go when she started forward.

"Sorry I'm late," she said breathlessly. "Did you save any for me?"

Gina tossed a shot glass in Brittany's direction. Brittany caught it and then set it down so Mia could pour a shot from the bottle of tequila the waitress had brought. They were insane. All of them. Josie included. She had to be nuts to be doing this. She was going to be one hungover bitch in the morning. But for now? She was having a blast.

"I was so jealous of you guys," Brittany said wistfully.

Bethany cocked her head to the side. "Whatever for?"

"Because you all have a man to go home to. All you've talked about is how cute they think you are when you're drunk. How they'll tear your dresses off and fuck you in your heels." Her expression went dim. "I've never had a man who wanted to do that."

"You do now," Kai drawled from the doorway.

Brittany turned bright red, but warmth crept in to her gaze as she turned to look at Kai who was still standing in the doorway.

"Oh my," Mia murmured. "Brittany, girlfriend, I'd say you scored for the night."

Brittany grinned. "Maybe I did!"

"No maybe about it, babe," Kai said in a low growl. "Have

fun with your girls, but when you're done? You're coming home with me."

"I think I just came," Gina muttered under her breath.

"No lie," Trish said. "I need to change my underwear. Good God, Brittany. He is hot!"

Brittany's smile was one hundred watts. She reached for the full shot glass and promptly tossed it down.

"They do this regularly?" Kai asked, amusement thick in his voice.

"Yes," both Jace and Brandon answered in unison.

"How come the room is spinning?" Josie asked, her eyes crossing as she tried to keep up with the spins. "Kai, you own the club, Brandon said. Why does it spin?"

Kai chuckled. "No spin, babe. It's the alcohol making you spin."

"Then why do you serve alcohol that makes people spin?" Bethany asked in a perplexed voice.

Jace laughed this time.

"It gets worse," Brandon said with a sigh. "They're really only just getting started."

The waitress bustled back through picking up empties and replacing them with clean shot glasses. She did a quick check of the bottle she'd left and then set a new one down.

"She rocks," Caroline muttered as she picked up another shot. "We should totally take her to Vegas with us, Brandon."

"Drink up, girlfriends. The night is still young!" Chessy crowed.

Josie downed two more shots but her eyes bugged out the entire time. She was a lightweight. No way she'd be able to hold any more liquor without puking. The room was spinning. Like a merry-go-round from hell. And there were two of everyone, which made the already crowded room seem even more crowded.

"How about some music," Mia blurted. "Are we finished talking for a bit? Who wants to dance with me?"

Josie raised her hand. "I do! But someone has to help me up."

Josie was hoisted upward by no less than three sets of hands. Mia punched the button to allow the music through the sound system. The girls shrieked and then everyone was up, bumping and grinding in time to the beat.

"This is fun!" Josie yelled out.

"Bet your ass it is!" Mia yelled back.

"Thanks for inviting me!" Brittany exclaimed. "I've had so much fun, and oh my God, Kai wants me to go home with him after. Should I do it?"

Josie shot a fuzzy glance toward the door where the men were still standing and most assuredly heard Brittany's drunken question.

Kai's lips twisted with amusement. "Do I get a vote?"

Josie turned back to Brittany. "Do you want to?"

Brittany blinked. "Yeah. Yeah, I do."

"As long as he gives me contact info so I can check on you tomorrow and make sure he didn't murder you in your sleep then yeah, go for it," Josie urged.

There was more laughter by the door but Josie ignored them. She was having too much fun dancing with her new friends. And they were great. Just as Ash had said they were.

She closed her eyes and put her back to Mia's as they both swayed, arms up, asses shaking the entire time.

Ash's phone rang and he saw it was Jace calling.

"Hey, man, women giving you fits yet?"

Jace chuckled. "You ought to get up here, man."

Ash's eyes narrowed and he glanced over at Gabe who was also paying close attention to the conversation.

"What's going on?" Ash demanded. "Are they all right?"

"Oh yeah, they're fine. But I think we're going to have to go to plan B."

"What's plan B?"

"Well, plan A was for me to get them all in the limo and home after they got plastered and had fun. However, they're currently on the floor of a private box, staring up at the ceiling and talking about shit I don't have a clue about. If you have any hope of salvaging the evening, my suggestion is for you to come collect your woman and get her ass home."

Ash chuckled. "Gabe and I will be there in a few. Watch over them until then."

"Will do," Jace said as he rang off.

"What the hell?" Gabe demanded.

Ash laughed. "According to Jace, they're pretty shitfaced. He said they're lying on the floor of one of the boxes. He suggested we might want to go collect our women if we had any hope of later."

"I'll ride with you and call my driver on the way to have him meet us there."

Ash nodded. "Let's roll.

Twenty minutes later, they pulled up to the club. Ash directed the driver to park a short distance away and remain on standby. Then he and Gabe got out and walked toward the entrance.

Thank God Brandon was out waiting for them. The line was still long. They would have never gotten in if it weren't for Brandon.

"Do I even want to know?" Gabe asked Brandon as they headed in.

Brandon laughed. "No, I doubt it. They had a good night, though. Nobody messed with them. The club owner hung out with them most of the night and security is always tight around him."

"Who is this club owner and why the fuck was he hanging with our women?" Ash demanded.

Brandon laughed again. "Not women. Just one. He seems pretty interested in Brittany. He's been velcroed to her all night and that's not like him. He's never short on women to keep him company, but it's rare for him to seek a woman out like he did Brittany."

Ash scowled. The man needed to stay away from his sister.

Brandon led them up a short flight of stairs to the second level where many private boxes and open tables formed a semicircle above the dance floor. At the door, Brandon knocked softly and it opened, revealing Jace and a man Ash didn't recognize.

Jace looked up and saw them. His smile was instant and he nodded for them to come through. When Ash and Gabe stepped inside, Ash's eyes widened when he took in the sight before him.

There were women everywhere. Really beautiful women. This was any man's wet dream. A room full of gorgeous, very drunk women.

But his focus zeroed in on just one. Josie. She was sprawled on the end of the couch, her arm dangling over the side. Mia was lying below her, but the upper half of her body was between Josie and the couch so her head rested on Josie's hip. At the bottom, Bethany lay in the opposite direction so her feet were all but shoved in Josie's face.

On the floor, Chessy, Gina and Trish were lying down in various poses while Caroline was sprawled in a chair, her legs propped up over the arm.

They weren't passed out, but they were oblivious to anything going on around them.

Ash chuckled. Gabe sported a huge grin. The other men were no less charmed by the sight.

"What the hell do we do with them now?" Ash asked in a low voice.

Gabe sent him a smug, satisfied grin. "If I have to tell you that, there's no hope for you, man."

Josie looked up, apparently only just now hearing his voice. Her smile was dazzling, her eyes completely unfocused. Her head bobbed as she spoke.

"Hey darling," she sang out. "Did you know there are two of you? Who says you have to improvise to give me two cocks? There are two of you now. That would make an awesome threesome. Me, you and you! Just sayin'.'"

Gabe, Jace and Brandon cracked up.

Ash groaned and hurried over to cover her mouth with his hand. "Jesus, baby. You can stop talking now."

She smiled underneath his hand. When he pulled it away, she sent him a completely goofy, dazzling smile that took his breath away.

"Are you taking me home to fuck me in my shoes now? Mia and Bethany told me *all* about being fucked in their shoes after their dresses get ripped off. I'm going to be very disappointed if I don't get the same," she said in a solemn voice.

He leaned down and pressed a gentle kiss to her forehead. "I think I can accommodate you there, baby. You ready?"

She held up both arms. "Take me home," she said dramatically. Then she put a finger to her lips and said, "Shhhh! Don't tell Ash, but Brittany is going home with a badass-looking guy tonight. I'm not sure he would approve. He'll probably want to run a background check on him to make sure he's okay for his sister."

Ash scowled and then glanced at Brittany before looking toward the door.

"What the fuck is she talking about?" he asked in Jace's direction.

The man standing with Jace stepped forward. He was polished. Ash saw that right off. He had money. He had that quiet air about him that told Ash he had a lot of money but didn't necessarily go around screaming it.

Ash stared hard at him, not backing down an inch. To the man's credit, neither did he.

"I'm Kai Wellington," he said calmly. "I own the club. I've offered to see Brittany home tonight."

Ash continued to stare him down. "I don't want you taking advantage of her. She's shitfaced."

"I know. I won't be sleeping with her. Yet."

Ash cringed. No way did he want to get into a discussion about who his sister slept with.

"I'll ensure she gets home," Brandon spoke up. "You don't have to worry."

Kai sent Brandon an amused look. Ash could tell he didn't like Brandon speaking up for him or offering his services. But Brandon also knew how important these women were to Gabe, Jace and Ash. He'd been told in no uncertain terms what would happen to him if he ever let harm come to any of them when they were out at the club.

"See that you do," Ash said softly. "I'd like a phone call when she's home safely."

"Give me your card. I'll see that you get that call," Kai said.

Ash fished in his wallet, pulled out his business card with his cell number on it and then handed it over to Kai.

"If you want to head out with your women, me and the other bouncers will make sure that Chessy, Trish and Gina get home safely. Caro will stay with me until I get off," Brandon offered.

Gabe nodded his agreement.

"All right then. Let's get our girls and get the hell out of here," Ash announced.

# chapter twenty-six

"Huddle!" Mia called out belligerently. She stood in the center of the room and waved her hand urgently toward Bethany and Josie.

Josie and Bethany struggled up from the couch. Josie swayed precariously and stared down at her feet, baffled as to why they weren't working properly. She nearly went down, and a strong hand caught her elbow.

"Whoops!" she exclaimed before righting herself. She sent her "help" a dazzling smile and registered an amused male grin. Was it Ash? Hell, the room was spinning so much she couldn't tell who was who or where.

She teetered toward where Mia waited and caught Bethany's arm when the other woman stumbled on her way.

Giggling like fiends, they huddled with Mia.

"Okay, here's the deal," Mia said in a loud whisper. "We definitely have to meet up for lunch tomorrow and exchange details. I can't wait to hear how Ash reacts."

Josie frowned and then looked back over her shoulder to where the men stood, indulgent smiles on their faces.

"What about Brittany?" Josie hissed. "She's hooking up with Mr. Club Owner over there. We have to hear what goes down there, right?"

"Right," Bethany said solemnly.

"Brittany!" Mia yelled again.

Brittany scuttled over, breaking into the circle, her face flushed with excitement.

"Okay, lunch tomorrow," Mia said. "We have to get all the down-and-dirty details!"

A series of groans went up and Josie turned, silencing the males with a ferocious scowl. They laughed and Josie turned her attention back to the women.

Brittany bit her lip and then glanced over Josie's shoulder in the direction of Kai Wellington.

"I don't know, guys. Maybe I'm biting off more than I can chew."

"I'll take good care of you, Brittany," Kai said in amusement.

"They're eavesdropping," Mia muttered.

"Kind of hard not to, baby," Gabe said, laughter in his voice. "You're bellowing loud enough for the entire club to hear."

Mia scowled and then lowered her voice to a loud whisper.

"One o'clock. Isabella's. For all the girls' night wrap-up."

"Do they always do this?" Kai asked in the background.

"Hell if I know," Jace muttered. "Nothing like being intimidated by being rated the next day. That's a hell of a lot of pressure to put on a man."

The women giggled and then Mia put her hand in. "On three. Let's go get our men."

They slapped their hands in a pile in the middle. "One, two, three!"

They raised their hands, breaking away from the huddle. Josie stumbled away, scanning the floor for her shoes.

"My shoes! I have to have those shoes," she complained. "It will ruin everything if I don't have the shoes!"

"Looking for these, darling?"

She looked up to see Ash standing there, her shoes dangling

from his fingers. His eyes were bright with laughter, but his gaze smoldered appreciatively over her body. She did an experimental wiggle, hoping her dress covered everything it was supposed to.

His eyes gleamed brighter and he reached over to adjust the top, his fingers brushing over the swell of one breast.

"That sight is just for me," he murmured. "Not that you don't look delectable, that hint of nipple, but no one else gets to see that."

She slapped her hands over her chest in horror and then stared anxiously at the other men. "Oh my God. Did they see my nipples!"

Laughter went up and there was a series of shaking heads. Ash leaned in to kiss her, pulling her into his arms. His entire body shook with laughter.

"No, baby. Nobody but me saw."

As he spoke, he turned, sending a pointed glare in the direction of the other men who immediately shook their heads and donned expressions of complete innocence.

"I need to put my shoes on," Josie grumbled.

Ash eased her down on the couch and then gently slipped her heels back on her feet. There was something extremely decadent about having a man put her shoes back on. His hands were warm and soothing against her skin. He squeezed one foot before stepping back to offer his hand to help her up.

She rose, experimentally testing her legs. She hadn't worn the shoes for most of the drinkfest and the last thing she wanted to do was face-plant now that she had them on.

She was shaky, but Ash firmly grasped her elbow before pulling her into his side. She sighed and melted against him, savoring the heat and scent of this gorgeous male.

"Thanks for looking after them," Ash said to Brandon as they walked toward the door.

"Hey, what about me," Jace sputtered. "Just remember, it's your turn next time."

Ash grinned. "Looking forward to it."

Ash started toward the door, holding Josie tight against his side. She stumbled a bit and he slowed his pace, matching it to her unsteady one. She was melted against him, so soft and sweet that he wished they weren't so damn far from his apartment. He wanted nothing more than to strip her out of that dress and fuck her in those shoes until they both passed out.

Gabe and Jace had definitely not lied. He was insanely jealous of them for having experienced this before. But now he had Josie. Josie was a part of his circle of friends, just like he'd wanted. He looked forward with immense satisfaction, secure in the knowledge that from now on, he would have this.

Other guys might bitch about girls' night out. Some didn't like it when their women went out without them. Hell, if they had this to look forward to? There'd be an instant run on sexy dresses and sparkly fuck-me shoes.

He grinned again as he led Josie toward the ramp leading down to the dance floor. Brandon appeared with another bouncer, flanking Ash and providing a protective barrier so they weren't jostled by the other club goers.

When they got outside, he directed Josie toward the waiting car and helped her inside. When he slid into the backseat, Josie was already indelicately sprawled all over the seat, her legs extending sideways. One of her shoes dangled precariously from her foot, and he slid it back on, cupping her ankle as he did.

She opened her eyes and bestowed a goofy, sweet smile on him.

"Hi," she said huskily.

He laughed and leaned over to kiss her nose. She was so damn cute. And all his.

"Hi yourself. Have fun?"

"Oh yeah," she breathed out. "You were right. Mia and Bethany are the bomb. So are the rest of their friends." She frowned a minute and Ash looked curiously at her, seeking the source of that frown. "Caro is moving away though. That makes Mia sad. Caro and Brandon are getting married and moving to Vegas. But it's okay. She'll still have Bethany. And me," she said, pointing to her chest.

Ash chuckled. "Yeah, baby. She'll have you."

"And Brittany!" Josie said, brightening. "She had fun, Ash. She was sad because she didn't have a guy to enjoy fucking her drunk, but then she hooked up with Kai."

Ash frowned. "Not sure I like the idea of her picking up some stranger in a club."

"I think he's okay," Josie said slowly. "He seems really intense. But in a good way, you know? Like you."

Ash shook his head. "If he's like me, then I *know* I don't want my baby sister having a one-night stand with him."

Josie frowned again. "I don't think it'll be a one-night stand, Ash. He looked so . . . serious. Like he wanted to eat her up. He made me all shivery."

Ash scowled at that. "He made you shivery? What the fuck?"

She giggled. "S'okay. You know I only want you. But he's hot. And he thinks Brittany is hot. I'm happy for her."

Ash sighed. "I'll be the judge of whether we're happy for her or not. I'll have to do some checking on this guy. See if he's on the level."

But then what could Ash say about being on the level? It made him a flaming hypocrite. He'd done some not-so-great things. He didn't regret them, but they were there. He just wasn't sure whether he wanted his sister involved with a man steeped in gray. He knew his intentions were good. But Kai Wellington?

But enough of Brittany and Kai. He'd get a call later as Kai had promised or Ash would send someone out to check on Brittany. And then tomorrow he'd do some looking into Kai Wellington's background and see if he had any skeletons that would make him unsuitable for Brittany.

Right now he had a really drunk, really cute, sexy-as-hell woman he was dying to get home and out of that dress.

"Have to say, baby. That dress and those shoes are you."

She sent him another dazzling smile, teeth flashing, a dimple forming in her cheek. "You like?"

"Oh hell yeah I like," he growled. "I'll like them a lot better when I get you home and out of them."

Her nose bunched up and she frowned. "But not the shoes, Ash. Mia and Bethany said they always get fucked with the shoes on. We can't mess the system up. It's the girls' night out creed."

He laughed. "Oh yeah, baby. The shoes definitely stay on."

When they pulled up to his apartment building, he got out and then reached in to help Josie out. After he was sure she had her legs underneath her and wouldn't take a header, he guided her toward the door, his arm securely around her.

On the elevator ride up, she put a hasty hand to her stomach and turned green as the elevator rose.

He pulled her into his arms. "Deep breaths, baby. Can't have you getting sick on me now."

"I'm fine," she said faintly. "The elevator just made me a little queasy."

The doors opened into his apartment and he helped her out, immediately heading toward the bedroom. His cell phone rang, and he glanced down to see an unfamiliar number. Knowing it could be Wellington calling about Brittany, he kept hold of Josie with one hand and answered with the other.

"Ash McIntyre," he said

"This is Kai Wellington. Brittany is home and safe. You don't have to worry, Mr. McIntyre. Your sister is in good hands."

"Thanks," Ash murmured. "Appreciate the call."

They rang off and Ash made a mental note to make sure all was well with his sister the next day. Then he turned his attention to Josie, easing her onto the edge of the bed.

"Okay, darling, we're home and you're in charge of the girls' night out seduction. What do you want your man to do?"

Her eyes glowed, almost neon in the faint light of the bedside lamp. Her lips parted and he almost let out a groan. God, but the woman was going to drive him insane.

"First you have to tear off my dress. Then you have to fuck me long and hard."

She looked so hopeful that he chuckled. "Anything you want, baby. Don't ever let it be said I disappointed my girl."

She smiled, letting out a blissful sigh. "I like that."

"What do you like, baby?"

"When you say 'my girl.' It sounds so sweet and sexy."

"You are my girl," he said, letting his voice go deep and low.

She held up her arms. "Then tear off your girl's dress and fuck her until she passes out."

He laughed but moved in, pulling her to her feet. "That I can do, love."

She sighed again, teetered unsteadily before regaining her balance. "I love all the things you call me. They're so nice."

He grinned, turning her around to unzip the dress. He let it fall to her feet and then helped her disentangle her shoes from the material. He sucked in his breath when his gaze traveled back up her body.

"Holy hell," he murmured. "Where did you get the lingerie?"

"I've had it," she said smugly. "Michael never saw it so don't worry. You're the only man who's seen me in it. I was saving it for a special occasion. I'd say this qualifies."

"Oh yeah. It definitely qualifies."

She turned, leaning into him, her eyes big, and she whispered as though she were imparting a huge secret. "It has a slit in the bottoms. You don't even have to take them off to fuck me."

His body shook and he cupped her chin, leaning down to fuse his mouth to hers. She tasted of tequila and something fruity. Her tongue, hot and wild, met his in a clash. He sucked it deep, wanting to devour her whole.

She whimpered against his mouth. She kissed him lustily, her body writhing against his in need. Already he could sense that she was precariously close to her release. It wouldn't take much at all to tilt her over.

But he didn't want it done so soon. If she came now, she might very well pass out in a sated alcohol-coma. He'd looked forward to this for too long to have it all over in five minutes.

"Going to fuck you hard, baby," he said, purposely inflecting an edge of steel into his voice. She shivered against him just as he knew she would. "Your mouth, your pussy and your ass. Going to have them all before it's over with."

"Ash."

His name came out in a needy wail that had him grinning. Oh yeah, she was hot and worked up. Her entire body was flushed with heat. She was rubbing her body against his like a cat in heat.

"Get on your knees," he ordered brusquely.

He held onto her as she slid down his body and perched on her knees. He grabbed a pillow and tucked it underneath her before he finally let go of her. He stood a moment making certain she wouldn't pitch over and then he stepped back, unzipping his fly.

His cock surged into his hand, protesting the fact that his hand was wrapped around it and not her mouth. He pushed his free hand into her hair, pulling her roughly forward as he pressed his dick to her lips.

She opened around him with a breathy sigh that sent tingles

racing down his spine. His balls drew up tight, aching as his erection slid over her hot tongue. She closed her mouth around him, sucking him deep. He let out a harsh groan, thrusting all the way to the back of her throat.

"Fucking beautiful," he rasped out.

The wet sucking sounds she made were loud and erotic in his ears. Each time he pulled back, he met resistance as she attempted to suck him back. Her cheeks hollowed with each pull and then puffed out when he thrust forward again.

He loved the sight of his cock sliding through her lips and then retreating, wet with her saliva. She made a smacking sound that damn near had him coming on the spot. For several long moments, he enjoyed the feel of her tongue sliding over the underside of his cock. Then she circled the tip, teasing the sensitive head when he pulled out.

No way he was going to last if this kept up. Reluctant to leave the sweetness of her mouth, he withdrew and pulled her to her feet. Her eyes were glazed, a mixture of the alcohol and intense desire. They glowed, warm and bright, full of the sweet he associated with her.

He laid her back on the bed, pulling at her bra, wanting to feast on her breasts. He leaned over her, between her splayed thighs and ran his tongue over the swell before capturing her nipple and sucking it strongly between his teeth. Then he nibbled a path up to her neck, devouring the supple flesh before tugging at her earlobe, nipping with just enough bite to make her cry out. He licked the shell, sliding his tongue over the contours of her ear before dropping down again to suck at the lobe.

"A-ash," she wailed, drawing his name into two syllables. "You're killing me."

He chuckled. "That's the idea, baby. Want you so worked up and crazy that you take me in your ass without any effort."

She shivered uncontrollably, her body arching helplessly into his.

"I'm already there," she panted. "I reached the crazy point about two minutes ago."

"Good."

He took his time, licking and devouring her nipples until they were red and straining into rigid peaks. Then he let his mouth roam lower, kissing the softness of her belly, and then lower still, nuzzling through the slit in her panties and into her velvety, plush folds. He licked over her clit, making sure he didn't spend too much time there or she'd come. He sucked and kissed his way lower until his tongue found her entrance, sliding inside just like his dick would soon do.

"Never get enough of you," he said hoarsely. "You taste so sweet. Addicting."

He continued his sensual assault on her most intimate flesh, until she was shamelessly begging him to end it. She was bucking upward, her motions frantic and needy. He grasped her hips, holding her in place as he continued fucking her with his tongue.

"Ash! I'm going to come!"

He drew away, leaving her dangling on the edge. He stood there a long moment, his breaths coming just as harshly as hers. Then he positioned himself between her legs, pulling her ankles up so he could grasp the heels of her shoes.

Her eyes widened, excitement bursting in the aquamarine depths. He pushed her legs even farther up until they were doubled against her body, her knees spread wide. He didn't wait. Didn't prolong the agony. Making sure the slit in her panties was parted, he pushed hard and deep on the first thrust, instantly filling her to the hilt.

She let out a cry. Her pussy swallowed him up in a heated rush that had him baring his teeth as he fought to maintain control. He knew he couldn't do this long so he thrust rapidly, working them both into a frenzy. Deep. Hard. Just as he'd soon do in her ass.

When he felt her quiver more urgently around him, he went still, buried balls-deep inside her. He sucked in steadying breaths, closing his eyes as he got it together. Then he withdrew, still holding on to her heels with both hands.

He let one go, hastily tearing away the silky panties he'd just fucked her in. He wanted her ass, and as sexy as the lingerie was, there was only one slit that gave him access to her pussy. He slid his hand underneath her now bare ass, pushing upward so her ass was presented. Her eyes widened when she realized he meant to take her this way. Usually when he fucked her ass, she was on her hands and knees. But this way, she was a lot more vulnerable. Completely open to him, her legs hiked high in the air, her ass curved upward just ready for him to dive in.

He guided his cock to her ass, taking only a moment to reach for the lubricant.

"I'm not using much this time, baby. Just enough to get inside you. I want you to feel it. Feel me pushing inside."

Her breath hiccupped over her lips. She licked them in anticipation and he damn near lost it on the spot. His jaw clenched, he hastily applied lubricant to his straining erection and then tossed the tube aside as he positioned himself. The minute he lodged the head against her opening, he removed his hand and wrapped it around her heel so both hands were holding her shoes, spreading her wide for his invasion.

He pushed in, not hesitating. She opened for him, her eyes growing even wider as she stretched to accommodate him.

"That's it, baby," he said in an approving tone. "Let me in. I'm going to fuck you hard until we both come. I want you to use your hand because I'm going to be holding your shoes the entire time I'm fucking you. But don't come until I tell you, okay?"

"'Kay," she said in a dreamy voice.

She slipped one hand between her thighs and over her clit, emitting a moan when she stroked.

Using that moment of inattention, when she was focused on her own pleasure, he surged forward, opening her in one ruthless thrust. She bucked upward, her cry splintering the air.

He was balls-deep, pressed against her, straining to get deeper still.

"Oh hell," he groaned. "Not going to last long, baby. You need to get there because I'm going to go hard and I'm not stopping until I come."

"I'm there," she said breathlessly. "Don't stop, Ash. I'm so close."

Needing no further encouragement, he began to thrust hard into her. His thighs slapped against her ass, jiggling her entire body. She closed her eyes and arched her neck upward as he began the race to completion.

She came first, her sharp cry washing over him, urging him on to his own orgasm. He began coming, jet after jet of his semen shooting deep inside her body, easing his way. Her fingers worked furiously over her clit as he rammed harder and deeper. Then she let her hand fall away, her chest heaving, eyes wild and unfocused.

He lunged into her one last time and held himself deep as he finished emptying himself into her body. Then he lowered himself onto her, carefully letting her heels go and allowing her legs to fall limply onto the bed.

They were both struggling to catch their breath, to suck in enough air into their burning lungs. He closed his eyes, gathering her tightly against him, holding her close so he felt the beat of her heart.

It had never been like this. Never before. Only with Josie. His heart was so full, it felt near to bursting. So much he wanted to say. That he wanted to tell her.

Her fingers stroked through his hair, caressing gently before they fell away, her body going lax beneath him. He picked up his head, staring down at her, a broad smile curving his lips upward.

She was out cold.

Chuckling, he gently extricated himself from her body and then he went into the bathroom, returning with a warm cloth to clean her up. After ensuring she was clean and comfortable, he pulled her heels off, then rid himself of the rest of his clothing before picking her up and positioning her on the bed. He crawled in beside her, reaching to turn off the lamp.

The room was doused in darkness and he pulled her close, into the shelter of his body. He stroked her body, enjoying the feel of her warm and sated next to him.

Yeah, girls' night out definitely needed to be a regular event. There wasn't anything better than having a gorgeous, very drunk, cute-as-hell woman come home to him wanting nothing more than to be fucked in killer heels.

He made a mental note to go and buy her a dozen pairs of sexy, sparkly heels. And while he was at it, he'd definitely be buying more of the naughty lingerie, complete with access slits.

# chapter twenty-seven

"Is Brittany coming?" Mia asked when Josie slid into the booth next to Bethany.

"She texted right when I was leaving the apartment and said she'd meet us here," Josie replied. "I'd think she'd be here any minute."

"Did she say anything about her night?" Bethany asked.

Josie grimaced and shook her head. "Nothing. She said she'd fill us in when she got here."

"At least she's off today and didn't have to deal with a hangover at work," Mia said. "Those shots kicked my ass! Gabe was sweet and babied me before he left for work, but I went back to bed and stayed there until it was time to meet up for lunch."

Bethany snickered. "Yeah, Jace was sweet too. Amazing the gratitude they show for drunk sex."

Josie laughed. "Ash brought me coffee and what he called a hangover cure. I don't even know what it was. Several pills. But it did the trick. After a shower, I actually felt human again."

"Oh look, there's Brittany now," Bethany said, raising her hand to wave.

Brittany navigated the busy restaurant and then slid into the booth next to Mia.

"Hey, gang," she said brightly.

"Now there is the face of a girl who got some," Mia said dryly.

Brittany blushed bright red, but her eyes were glowing.

"Spill!" Josie demanded. "We're dying to hear all about Kai Wellington."

Brittany laughed. "Oh my gosh, you guys. He is amazing. I don't even have words. He has this dark, mysterious thing going on with him. He doesn't say a whole lot, but when he talks, you just listen, you know?"

"Get to the good part," Mia said impatiently. "What's he like in bed?"

Everyone burst into laughter.

"Uhm, well, we didn't have sex last night," Brittany hedged. "He brought me to my apartment, tucked me into bed. I don't remember anything after that. But this morning, I woke up and he was in bed next to me. He'd stripped down to his boxers, and let me just say, that man is built! I was drooling all over my pillowcase, for God's sake."

Josie chuckled at Brittany's animated description.

"He was sooo sweet too! He made me breakfast in bed then he took me into the bathroom to shower."

"He took you into the bathroom?" Bethany asked. "As in got in the shower with you?"

Brittany blushed. "Yeah. It was sweet. But also hot. I mean all that gorgeous naked male flesh. I thought I was going to have a heart attack."

"So what happened then?" Mia said.

"After the shower, we went back to bed, and *then* we had sex."

Brittany wore a smug, satisfied smile. Yeah, the sex must have been really good judging by her expression.

"And?" Bethany demanded. "Come on, don't leave us hanging!

He just looked like he'd be a beast in bed. So dark and brooding. A lot like Jace!"

"Okay stop," Mia said with a shudder. "We can talk about hotness all we want, but can we please leave Jace out of it?"

Josie pulled a face. "You're no fun, Mia. Can't you forget he's your brother just for a little while?"

Mia shook her head adamantly.

Brittany laughed and then leaned back in the booth, sighing a dreamy sigh that told Josie she was in deep already. But then who was she to judge? It hadn't taken any longer for Ash to completely reel her in. She'd been a goner the minute he'd dragged her out of her apartment. If she was completely honest, she'd admit that she'd been a goner that very first day in the park. It had just taken her longer to realize that.

"It was awesome," Brittany said. "And yes, total beast in bed. So demanding and possessive." She shivered, chill bumps breaking out over her skin. Then her expression dimmed and her lips twisted into a grimace. "Nothing at all like my first husband. Ugh. Not even in the same universe!"

"Forget him," Josie ordered. "He's in the past. Move on. Now tell us more."

The others burst into laughter again. They were drawing attention from the other tables, but Josie didn't care. Normally she'd be appalled over being the focus in a public setting, but she already loved these girls and she was having fun.

"I orgasmed three times," Brittany said in a loud whisper. "Three times! That's three more times than I ever came with my husband."

"Yay!" Bethany said, a broad smile on her face. "So what now? Was it a one-night thing? Did he get your number? Is he going to call?"

"One question at a time, Bethany," Mia scolded. "She can't keep up! But yes, Brittany, tell us everything."

Brittany smiled and Josie saw just how beautiful she was. Her eyes shone and the shadows that had haunted them were gone. She seemed more sure of herself. She seemed . . . happy.

"Oh, he got my number. Made me program all his numbers into my cell. Wanted to know what I was doing today. Where I was going and with whom. Then he told me that this was not a one-night stand and that I better get it out of my head now if that's what I was thinking."

"Wow," Mia whispered. "That sounds intense!"

"He didn't even ask if I *wanted* to see him again," Brittany continued, a goofy grin plastered on her face. "He told me he'd be at my apartment this evening to take me to dinner and that I was staying over in his hotel."

Josie frowned. "So he doesn't have an apartment here?"

Brittany shook her head. "No. He's been in Vegas getting the new club ready to open. Now that it is, he's planning to spend a lot of his time out there, or at least for the first few months. He travels a lot, going between his clubs, so he doesn't maintain a permanent residence anywhere."

"How long will he be here then?" Bethany asked, her lips turning down into a frown that mirrored Josie's own.

Brittany shrugged. "I don't know. I guess we'll have to take it one day at a time and see what happens. Who knows? Maybe I'm just an itch he wants to scratch while he's in town. I know better than to read more into the situation. Good way to get my hopes crushed."

"He could scratch his itch with me," Mia muttered.

Bethany died laughing. "I'm so telling Gabe you said that."

Mia glared at her. "No you won't. Girlfriends' code. What's discussed with girlfriends stays with girlfriends."

"True," Bethany agreed. "But it's fun to tease you."

"Besides, I've got more than I can handle with Gabe. I can look. Nothing's wrong with my eyes—or my hormones for that matter. But I have no desire to touch another man," she said cheekily.

"Is it possible to fall in love at first sight?" Brittany asked wistfully. "I'm thirty years old and I've never been in love. I certainly wasn't in love with my husband. I'm worried that Kai just overwhelmed me and that I latched on to him because he was so attracted to me. I just wonder if I would have responded to any guy the way I responded to Kai."

Josie reached over to squeeze Brittany's hand. "Absolutely it is possible. It happens more than you'd think. And you need to stop beating yourself up over your first marriage. Shit happens. But you got out. Now it's time to move on and give yourself a chance at happiness."

"I couldn't have said it better myself," Bethany said. "And Jace swears that he fell for me the first time he laid eyes on me. And from what you say, it certainly seems that Kai fell pretty hard himself."

Mia slung an arm around Brittany's shoulders. "Go for it, girlfriend. Have a great time. If it works out, great. But if it doesn't? You'll have us to fall back on. Not to mention Ash and the guys will beat the crap out of Kai if he fucks you over."

Bethany grinned her agreement. Even Brittany's eyes sparkled with amusement. Josie didn't say anything since she well knew that Ash would do just that. Mia's words were just that. Words. But Ash wouldn't hesitate to go after someone for hurting someone he cared about. He'd already proven that much.

"You're right," Brittany said. "I should just go with it. Have a good time. I'm reading too much into it. He probably just wants some action while he's here. And since he's the bomb in bed that's not a hardship. I just hope I don't get all whiny when he leaves."

"Maybe he won't," Josie said with a shrug. "He looked pretty into you last night and from what you've said about him, this doesn't look like just a pussy call for him."

"Pussy call!" Mia cracked up. "I'm so going to steal that from you. That's hilarious!"

"I think you're right," Bethany agreed. "I mean that's all I thought I was to Jace that first night. I never dreamed he'd turn the city over looking for me! And let's just say once he found me that was it. Not that we didn't have issues. But he was in it for the long haul."

"So what about you and Ash?" Brittany asked, turning the attention to Josie. "I've never seen my brother this intense over a woman. Not that we spent a lot of time together, mind you, but I would have known if he'd been with the same woman for a long time."

"Long time!" Josie exclaimed with a laugh. "We've only been together like two weeks."

"He's a goner," Mia said solemnly. "Trust me, I know. He and Jace always fucked the same women, and it wasn't always pretty. I met their last piece of ass." She winced and cleared her throat. "Not you, Bethany. Before you. Ah shit, but there goes my foot into my mouth again."

Bethany's cheeks turned pink, but Josie laughed. "Don't Bethany. It's okay. Really. I love that we can talk about it and not let it be all awkward between us. Really it's better that way."

Brittany looked thoroughly confused but they didn't fill her in.

"Anyway, as I was saying," Mia said. "Before I inserted the foot. Was that I met up with Jace and Ash's last chick. They took me out to eat and I swear she followed us there. No way she just happened to be in the same place we were. Totally wasn't her style if you know what I mean. We were in a pub munching down on nachos and other yummy lowbrow stuff. And she marches up like a woman scorned and made a scene. Insulted me in the process because she assumed I was her replacement."

She shuddered delicately as she said the last.

"Didn't go over too well, huh," Bethany said with a grin.

Mia winced. "No. Uh, let's just say she didn't take the 'it's the end' message very well. And my point in bringing this up was that Jace and Ash were banging the same chicks for a long time. And then suddenly Jace met Bethany and that was over. And then Ash met you and it's obvious that his banging random chicks is over too. I've been around him a lot of years, and he never hung on to the same woman for as long as he's been with you, Josie."

"Glad to know that," Josie murmured.

"So, are you in love with him?" Brittany asked. "Should I be asking what your intentions toward my brother are?"

Everyone laughed and Josie held up her hands. "I was gentle last night. Promise!"

"You didn't answer the question," Mia said pointedly.

Josie sighed. "Yes, I'm in love with him. I haven't told him. I wanted to make sure I told him at the right time. It sounds so stupid, but I don't want to scream it out when we're having sex or caught up in the moment, nor do I want to tell him when he's doing something really sweet for me because I want him to know I mean it and that I'm not just spouting something in the heat of the moment."

"Has he told you he loves you?" Bethany asked softly.

Josie grimaced. "No."

"He does," Mia said resolutely. "No doubt in my mind. Holy hell, the way he looks at you? Totally makes me shiver."

Brittany nodded her agreement. "Not to mention the way he went off on Mom when she made that scene at the restaurant and said that crap about you. I thought he was going to choke her. I wouldn't have tried to stop him either!"

They all laughed again and then were interrupted by the waiter bringing their orders. For the next several minutes they shoveled food in and laughed and talked about the guys, sex and well, more sex.

Josie couldn't remember when she'd had a better time. Everything was so . . . perfect. She had Ash, and really, if that's all she had, she'd be one happy bitch. But now she also had really good girlfriends. She really liked them. They were genuine, had huge hearts and there wasn't a fake bone in their bodies.

What more could she ask for? She was now a successful artist—her work was actually in demand! So what if it was only one person. It only took one. Whoever it was had loved her work enough to scoop everything of hers up as soon as she brought it in. And now she had great friends and a man she adored. And she was pretty sure he adored her too.

Maybe they hadn't said the words yet, but Josie was confident that Ash was the one. The words would come. He'd already talked about their future like it was a done deal. He'd even told her she'd get the rock! He'd even mentioned their children! No man who wasn't thinking long term talked about engagement rings and babies.

She sat back with a sigh, indulging in a glass of wine with the others. She had someone to drive her home. Why not?

An hour later, the girls said their good-byes and got into their respective cars to head home. Josie offered Brittany a ride since she'd walked to the restaurant and the two chatted all the way to Brittany's apartment.

"Today was fun," Brittany said when they pulled to the front of her building. "Thanks so much for inviting me today and last night, Josie. I really enjoyed myself."

"You're welcome," Josie said with a warm smile. "I had fun too. We absolutely have to make this a regular event."

"Absolutely!" Brittany said as she climbed out of the car.

"And keep me posted on Kai!" Josie yelled after her.

Brittany turned and gave her a thumbs-up and an exaggerated smile.

Josie settled into the backseat and texted Ash on her way back to the apartment. She'd told him she was having lunch with the girls and he'd told her to have fun and let him know when she was headed back. Maybe he'd even get to come home early from work.

Anticipation licked up her spine as they drove through the city. She couldn't remember the last time she'd been so . . . happy. So carefree and utterly satisfied with the direction of her life.

When they arrived at Ash's apartment building, she got out and thanked the driver. As she headed inside, the doorman, who was on the phone, put his hand over the receiver and called from across the lobby.

"Miss Carlysle, a package came for you while you were out. It's on my desk. Shall I have it brought up to the apartment?"

Josie smiled. "No, that's okay. It's small, right? I'll take it up with me."

She'd ordered some new brushes and knew they were coming in today.

"It's in the office. Give me just a sec and I'll get it for you."

"Oh no need," she called. "Finish your call. I'll just get it and bring it up with me."

"Miss Carlysle!" he called after her.

She pushed inside the small office that housed deliveries and glanced at the desk where a small package was sitting. With a smile, she went over and tucked it underneath her arm. When she turned to go back out, her gaze caught on several covered paintings resting against the far wall.

She frowned because one of them wasn't fully covered and it looked an awful lot like hers. But what would they be doing here of all places?

She hurried over, unrepentant about snooping. She pulled back the covering and gasped. They *were* her paintings!

# chapter twenty-eight

Josie quickly rummaged through the others, her stomach knotting as she took in every single painting she'd sold in Mr. Downing's art gallery.

What on earth?

She let the covering fall and stepped back, the knot in her stomach growing bigger. Oh no. No, no, no. It couldn't be. He wouldn't have.

But he had. The evidence was staring her right in the face.

"Miss Carlysle, please. You shouldn't be in here," the doorman said from the door.

"No, I don't suppose I should," she murmured.

She pushed past him, ignoring his calls for her to stop. What on earth could he possibly say?

She shoved into the elevator, tears stinging her eyes. How could he have done it? She felt like the biggest fool on earth. She'd never dreamed that Ash had been the one to buy all her paintings, but it shouldn't have surprised her. He'd orchestrated every aspect of their relationship so far.

Desolation settled over her. She wasn't successful. She wasn't independent. Everything she had came from Ash. She was living off his money, in his apartment. Nothing had been bought with her money. Her earlier sensation of rightness, that she'd found her place in the world, was gone with the discovery of those paintings.

She swept out of the elevator so agitated she couldn't even think straight. Her gaze settled on the boxes, most of which had already been unpacked. She walked right by them and sagged onto the couch, covering her face with her hands.

She was utterly humiliated. Every single time she'd excitedly exclaimed to Ash over the success of her work came back to her in waves of embarrassment. And he'd let her!

He'd lied to her, something she wouldn't have imagined. No, he hadn't come out and denied buying the paintings, but then she hadn't asked. She'd never dreamed that he'd been behind it. His was a lie of omission. So huge, so monumental that she couldn't even fathom.

What else had he kept from her?

Tears burned her eyelids but she refused to give in to them. She also refused to believe she was overreacting. This wasn't something small. Her success had enabled her to say yes to Ash's demands. She'd felt like she could agree because she felt capable of supporting herself. No way would she have gone blindly into a relationship with Ash with such a huge disparity between them. She'd been willing and able to submit because she'd been strong enough to come to him as an equal. Not that there'd ever been true equality between them, but her success as an artist, having money in her bank account and the means to support herself, had been very important to her and it had evened the odds between them. At least in her mind.

What she hadn't realized was just how unequal things were between them.

She was living in his apartment. All the money in her bank account was his. Not hers. Oh God, he'd even paid her double. She should have questioned her good fortune. People didn't just walk into an art gallery and magnanimously offer to pay more than asking price for art.

She was so stupid. Naïve. A complete and utter moron.

She'd actually believed that someone had been awed by her work. She'd believed she had real talent even though Mr. Downing had refused to display more of her art because it wasn't selling. Now she knew the truth.

She closed her eyes, devastated by her discovery. She'd trusted him. Had kept no part of herself from him. And he'd shit all over that gift.

All his words about cherishing her gift, about protecting it and appreciating it, meant nothing. He'd made a gigantic fool of her. God, she'd even told the others about the sale of her artwork. She'd been so proud. So excited. Did they all know that Ash was her benefactor?

Ash apparently operated on a need-to-know basis. What else had he decided she didn't need to know?

She picked her head up, grief welling in her chest until she couldn't breathe. She sucked in ragged breaths, trying to assuage the burning in her chest. But nothing worked.

She loved him. She'd thought he loved her.

She rubbed at her temples, weariness assailing her. What was she supposed to do?

She glanced toward the boxes, anger replacing some of her devastation. The hell she'd just stay here and pretend that she didn't know what he'd done. How could she? She was living a complete lie. And now she was faced with the knowledge that she wasn't successful. There was no demand for her work. And she'd been lax with her jewelry design business ever since she'd moved in with Ash. She'd been too caught up in other things to design new pieces and put them up for sale. She'd been comforted by the knowledge that she was selling her artwork as fast as she could get it to the gallery and those pieces made her far more money than her jewelry did. Or at least they had.

Sucking in a deep breath, she forced herself to her feet. To action. It wouldn't take long to repack her belongings. And really all she wanted was her art supplies and the clothing she'd brought with her. Everything else belonged to Ash. They were things he bought for her and she wouldn't bring them with her.

Mechanically, she stuffed everything in the boxes, not taking the care she had when they'd been packed before. After thirty minutes, they were full, her overnight bag filled with her toiletries and her clothing. She stood surveying the room, knowing it would take several trips to get all the stuff to her apartment. Thank God she hadn't terminated the lease and still had a place to live.

Squaring her shoulders, she pulled out her phone and Googled a local mover. After a phone call, and a hefty bill for a last-minute job, all she had to do was wait. Wait for the people who'd remove all traces of her presence in Ash's apartment.

It hurt. *She* hurt. There wasn't a part of her heart or soul that wasn't sick. But how could she stay with a man who'd so blithely manipulate her? He might not have ever physically hurt her as Michael had, but right now Josie would take that kind of pain over the gut-wrenching agony she was experiencing over his deception.

An hour later, the movers arrived and began taking the boxes down in the elevator to the waiting truck. Josie remained in the apartment until the last box went down. She silently urged them to hurry. She wanted no chance of Ash coming home from work while she was still moving out. He hadn't called yet, so she should have plenty of time.

By the time he made it home, she'd be back in her apartment. And this time, she wouldn't be swayed by pretty words and hollow promises.

Damn him for making her love him. And damn him for pulling

her into his world. She liked his friends. Loved Bethany and Mia and Brittany and all the others. But they were his friends. Loyal to him. She was accepted because of him. And now she'd have nothing at all.

It was on her way down that she realized two things. One, she didn't have a ride to her apartment and Ash's apartment wasn't convenient to public transportation. She could take a cab, but she'd have to have the doorman call for one and it could take a while. Especially at this time of day when all the taxi drivers went off duty.

The other thing she realized was that she needed to confront Ash. She couldn't just move out and hide in her apartment. Not that she owed him anything, but she didn't want to go home, dreading the moment when he realized she was gone and the inevitable confrontation that would ensue. It would be better if she went to his office, said her piece and made it clear they were over. That way she wouldn't have to worry about him showing up at her apartment.

For that, she would use Ash's driver. After all, he'd have to pick up Ash from work anyway. A quick check of her watch told her the driver would likely still be here. If he wasn't, she'd just take a cab to Ash's building, even if it meant waiting. From his office, she'd just take the subway.

She rummaged for her phone in the big bag she'd thrown over her shoulder. After waving off the movers and providing the keys to her apartment so they could start unloading, she called Ash's driver, who as luck would have it, was just a block away.

A few minutes later, she was on her way to Ash's office building, silent tears trailing down her cheeks.

# chapter twenty-nine

Ash leaned his head back against his chair, still holding the phone to his ear as the conference call droned on and on and on.

Christ, all he wanted was to get the fuck off the phone so he could head home to Josie. She'd had lunch with the girls today and he was looking forward to hearing about her day. Afterward he'd take her to dinner. Somewhere quiet and intimate. They'd talk some more and then he'd take her home and make love to her until they both dropped from exhaustion.

A knock sounded at his door and Eleanor stuck her head in. Ash frowned over the interruption, but then, if she'd poked her head in, it must be important. She was too efficient not to know he was on an important call.

Temporarily muting the call, he lowered the receiver and looked questioningly in Eleanor's direction.

"Sorry, sir, I know you're busy but Miss Carlysle is here to see you."

It took him a moment to realize Miss Carlysle was in fact Josie. He straightened, ending the call without hesitation.

"Josie's here?" he asked sharply. "Send her in immediately."

Eleanor disappeared and Ash was already on his feet striding toward the door to meet Josie when she came in. Josie hadn't been to his office before. Hell, he didn't even remember if he'd told her where he worked.

A moment later, the door pushed open and Josie walked slowly in, her face pale, eyes swollen. Like she'd been fucking *crying*.

He was in front of her in seconds, pulling her into his arms. She went stiff and rigid and utterly unyielding.

"What's wrong?" he demanded. "What's upset you, Josie?"

She pried herself away from him and walked by, toward the middle of his office where she just stood, back turned, her spine stiff.

His gaze narrowed. "Josie?"

When she didn't respond he reached for her, turning her to face him. What he saw in her face he didn't like one bit. Dread gripped him by the balls as he took in her lifeless eyes.

Josie always shined. That was just her. She could light up a room just by walking into it. She sparkled, had a gorgeous smile and her eyes were always bright and sunny. Like every other part of her.

But not today. She looked worn. Sad. She looked devastated.

When she pulled away from him again, his lips came together in a tight line.

"Remember what I said, Josie. When you and I are talking and *especially* if you're upset about something, we do not discuss it with a room between us. You're pushing me away, and that is *not* an option."

When he would have pulled her to him, she put both arms out, effectively blocking him.

"You don't get an option," she said tightly. "We're over, Ash. I've moved my stuff back to my apartment."

He couldn't even control his reaction. Of the hundred different

things she could have said, he would have never imagined her saying *this*. What the ever-loving fuck?

"The *hell* we're over," he bit out. "What the fuck is going on,
Josie?"

"I saw the paintings," she said hoarsely. "All of them."

*Fuck.*

He blew out his breath and ran a hand raggedly through his
hair. "Not the way I wanted you to find out, baby."

"No, I guess it wasn't," she said scornfully. "I don't imagine you
wanted me to find out at all."

"You're not moving out and calling it quits just because I didn't
tell you I was the one who bought your paintings."

"Watch me," she said in an icy tone that was just not her.

"Baby, you need to calm down and let me explain. We'll talk this
out and then we'll move on. But I'm not having this goddamn conversation in my fucking office and I'm damn sure not having it with
you four feet away from me and you building a fucking wall between us."

"Calm down?" she demanded. "You lied to me, Ash. You *lied*.
And I'm supposed to discuss and move on?"

"I never lied to you," he bit out.

"Don't give me that crap. You did lie and you know it. Moreover
you made a gigantic fool out of me. All those times when I was so
excited over selling those paintings. You let me talk about it with
your friends. You let me feel like I'd done something great. That I
was able to support myself. That I had money. Options. A future.
God, you really did a number on me, Ash. And every single part of
it is and was a *lie*."

"Jesus," he swore. "Josie that is not what I intended at all."

She held up her hand. "Do you know why I didn't argue with
you about moving in? Why I let you talk me into it so easily? Be-

cause I felt like I could. Because I had options. Because I didn't *need* you. But I *wanted* you. I thought I was self-sufficient. Able to be somewhat equal, although I'll never have all the money you do. But it was important to me to be able to contribute something to our relationship. Even if it was just a sense of self. Me having confidence. I was on top of the world, Ash. Because I felt like for once I had everything. A career. You. Really great friends. And none of it, *none* of it was real!"

Every single one of her words sliced through him like a knife. Her face had grown even paler, her eyes more stricken. He hadn't thought about her sense of value, of self-worth. Of her feeling like she had options. Of her not having to depend solely on him, even if that's what he wanted. But damn it, neither had he ever wanted to hurt her. That wasn't why he'd done it at all.

"You manipulated every aspect of our relationship," she said painfully. "You orchestrated every point. Every move was calculated and thought out. You played me like an instrument and I fell right into your lap. I should have known better when you blackmailed me into dinner. Hell, the fact that you had me followed, that you knew about me pawning my mother's jewelry. But I didn't pay attention. I didn't think those were huge warning signs, though it makes me a complete idiot for not recognizing them for what they were. You are so used to being God in your world that you thought nothing of playing God in *mine*."

"Josie, stop," he ordered. "That's enough. I'm sorry I hurt you. For God's sake, that's the last thing I ever wanted to do! We can work this out, baby."

She was already shaking her head, and fear curled in his belly, spreading to his chest and into his throat, grabbing him, squeezing until he could barely breathe.

"Goddamn it, Josie, *I love you*."

She closed her eyes and a tear slipped down her cheek. When she reopened them, both were shiny with moisture and there was such hopelessness reflected that his stomach bottomed out.

"I would have given *anything* for those words," she said softly. "I'd even convinced myself that you *did* love me but just hadn't said the words yet. You have no idea how much I wanted to hear them from you. But now? How can I even believe you? You've proven what lengths you'll go to in order to manipulate the circumstances so you get your desired outcome. So how can I believe that's not what you're doing now, trying to play on my emotions?"

He was speechless. Completely and utterly speechless. He'd never given those words to another damn woman in his life. And she thought he said them to manipulate her emotions?

Anger burned in his veins, sizzling until he was certain he'd lose his grip. He turned to the side, panicked and frustrated because he had no idea what to say, what to *do*. She was breaking up with him and he'd been planning *forever* with her.

Her hand shook as she lifted it to the collar she wore around her neck.

"No!" he said hoarsely, turning fully back to her as she unfastened the clasp.

She let it fall into her hand and then she held it out to him, pressing it into his palm.

"I moved everything out of your apartment," she said in a low voice. "I left the keys on your bar. Good-bye, Ash. You were the best—and worst—thing that ever happened to me."

He held up his hand, trying to stop her because no way in hell was he going to let her just walk out that door.

"Wait just a goddamn minute, Josie. We're not finished. No way in fuck I'm giving up that easy. We're worth fighting for. *You're* worth fighting for and I hope to fuck you think I'm worth it no matter how upset you may be right now."

"Please, Ash. I can't do this right now," she begged. Her eyes were filled with tears and more slipped rapidly down her cheeks. "Just let me go. I'm too upset to form a coherent argument and the last thing I want is to say things I'll regret."

He closed the short distance between them, pulling her against his chest. He tilted her chin up with his fingers and stared down into her eyes.

"I love you, Josie. That's a fact. No manipulation. No hidden agenda. I. Love. You. Period."

She closed her eyes and turned her face to the side. He cupped her cheek and thumbed away one of the silver trails.

"Just tell me why?" she whispered. "Why did you do it? Why didn't you tell me? Why hide it from me?"

He sighed. "I don't know," he admitted. "Maybe I thought you'd react just like you have and I didn't want that. I loved the paintings, Josie. It pisses me off that because you found out I bought them you think you have no talent and that no one wants your work. That's bullshit."

She tugged herself away from him and presented her back, her shoulders shaking.

"I'm too upset to have this conversation with you, Ash. Please, just let it go."

"I'm not fucking letting it go when you just told me you moved your shit out of *our* apartment. You honestly expect me to just say okay, have a nice life? Fuck that. The only nice life I want to have is with *you*."

She curled her arms around her waist, hugging herself. "I'm going back to my apartment. My stuff has already been moved. I can't stay. I promised the movers I'd meet them there."

Panic clawed at his throat. Helplessness gripped him. She was actually walking away. Over those goddamn paintings. He knew it was more than that. He understood why she was pissed. He'd never looked beyond the fact that he'd bought them to see how it would make her feel once she discovered it was all a lie. He got that. But how the fuck was he supposed to make it up to her, to make her realize how much she had to offer, if she was sleeping in another bed in another part of the city?

She started toward the door, him staring after her, utterly paralyzed, his heart in his stomach.

"Josie, stop. Please."

At the "please" she stopped but didn't turn around.

"Look at me, please," he said softly.

Slowly she turned, her eyes awash with fresh tears. He cursed softly because he never wanted to be the reason for those tears.

"Swear to me you'll think about it. And us," he said in a choked voice. "I'll give you tonight, baby. But if you think I'm going to give up and let you walk away then you don't know me very well."

She closed her eyes and sucked in a deep breath. "I'll think about it, Ash. That's all I can promise. I have a lot to sort out in my head. You pulled the rug out from under me. I have to figure out what I'm going to do from here. I knew when I entered this relationship with you that you promised to take care of me, to protect me, to provide for me. And I was okay with that because I didn't *need* you to. Can you possibly understand the difference? I didn't have to be with you. I *wanted* to be. If I'd had no other choice, no place to live, no money, then how could you ever be certain I wasn't with you for your money? I never want that between us. It's important to me to be independent and able to provide for myself even if that's *not what I end up doing*. But I want that choice. I want to be able to look at myself in the mirror and know that I have value. That I can support myself and make my own choices."

He closed his eyes because so much of what she said made sense. It's how he'd feel in her situation too. And he'd looked right past that. Never considered how it would make her feel for him to buy the paintings and hide that from her. He fucked up. And now he could lose her because of that fuck-up.

"I get it," he said hoarsely. "I do, baby. I'll give you tonight. But I don't have to fucking like it. And I'm not giving up on us, so prepare yourself for that. No way in *hell* I'm giving you up."

She swallowed, her face still pale, her eyes still wounded. Then she turned and walked away, taking his heart and soul with her, leaving him standing there holding the collar she'd taken from around her neck.

# chapter thirty

Josie spent a miserable night tossing and turning before she finally gave up and immersed herself in her painting. For the first time, the vibrant colors didn't come. There was nothing vivid about the scene she painted. It was dark, gray. There was a sadness to it that seeped onto the canvas without her realizing it was there.

At dawn, her shoulders sagged, stiff and sore from the hours she'd spent on the painting. When she took it in, she winced. It was a clear image of her mood. Miserable.

She nearly splattered paint on it to ruin it but held back, her hands trembling before she finally affixed her trademark *J* in the lower right-hand corner.

It was honest. It was also very good. It was just different from any of her other work. Perhaps this would be something more along the lines of what others wanted. Maybe people didn't want bright, cheerful, sexy fun.

As she stared at the painting, the title came to her. *Rain in Manhattan*. Not particularly original, but it suited her mood, even if it was a perfect spring morning outside. The buildings in her painting were tall and gloomy, outlined by rain and overcast skies. She also realized that the building on the canvas was Ash's.

She sighed and rose, stretching her stiff muscles. She stumbled into the kitchen to make herself coffee, thankful that she still had an old canister in the cabinet. She would have to restock her apartment. All of the perishables had been thrown out when she'd moved and only a few items remained. One of them being the coffee. She needed to bypass a mug and go straight for an IV infusion of caffeine.

Holding the steaming cup in her hand, she went back into the living room and opened her blinds to let the early morning light in. Outside, the streets were quiet, only just now starting to come alive with the traffic of the day.

She'd always loved her apartment. The rent for the brownstone was costing her a mint, though, and the realization hit her that she would have to move somewhere cheaper. There had been no unexpected windfall. No customer who loved her work and would buy whatever she brought in.

She needed to make a trip to the art gallery and speak to Mr. Downing. Make it clear that if she were to continue displaying her work there that he couldn't sell it to Ash. He probably wouldn't allow her to bring in anything else since she was refusing what had to be his best customer. How could she trust that Ash wouldn't simply buy it under a different name, one she'd never be able to trace back to him?

Yes, she would have to move, reorder her priorities and think about her options. She needed to create more jewelry and put it up for sale on her site. The site had languished since she'd moved in with Ash, all her focus going into her art. But she needed the money from the sale of her jewelry. When she produced regularly, she sold regularly. Her art would have to take a temporary backseat until she built up enough reserves to give her time to think about a new direction in her artwork.

Mr. Downing had said she lacked vision and focus. That she was too scattered and all over the board. Evidently he was right. But what would her new focus be? If people didn't like the cheerful, colorful works she created then she had to rethink her vision.

It shouldn't be too hard to come up with more of the depressing, gloomy paintings that she'd done this morning. She wouldn't get over Ash in a day, a week or even a month. She loved him. She'd fallen hard and fast without a safety net. The old adage about playing with fire came to mind. She'd definitely played, throwing caution to the wind, and as a result she'd been burnt.

Shaking her head, she finished off her coffee and set the mug on the coffee table. She needed to get back to work, perhaps draw a companion piece for the *Rain in Manhattan* painting. She could then take both to Mr. Downing and see if he thought they'd sell better than her previous offerings. If not? Plan B. Whatever that was.

She eyed her cell phone, which she'd put on silent, debated whether she should check for calls or messages. Then she sighed. No one would be calling her. Except maybe Ash, and she didn't want to think about him right now. Resisting the temptation to look at her messages—if there were any—she went back to work, driven to complete another piece.

Her paintings usually took days. She tweaked endlessly, frowning over every little detail. But today she put paint to canvas and didn't stop until it was done. So what if it was imperfect? It wasn't like all that attention to detail had gotten her very far before.

She shook her head. God, she sounded like a whiny, feeling-sorry-for-herself nitwit. This wasn't her and she wasn't going to let it be her. She wasn't one to give up. She'd never given up her dream. Her mother had made her swear that she wouldn't. No way in hell she was going to let herself or her mother down.

For hours she worked steadily, the sun rising higher and more sunlight shining through her window. At one point she closed her blinds because she felt too exposed to the passersby on the sidewalk. She'd noticed a couple of guys walking back and forth on the street outside, seeming like they were trying to get a glimpse of her painting. Painting was private. Even moreso now that she was spilling her heart and her devastation onto the canvas.

She'd just put the last touches on the painting when a knock sounded at her door. She froze, dismay coursing through her veins. Was Ash here? He'd been blunt about the fact that he'd give her last night but that he wasn't giving up on her or them. He'd wanted her to think about it but she'd shoved the whole issue solidly from her mind and immersed herself in work.

She rose, hands shaking. She could ignore the door, but she wasn't a coward. And if Ash had come all this way, the least she could do was tell him that she needed more time. Space.

Her heart beating a mile a minute, she wiped her hands and went to the door. Taking a deep breath, she opened it. Blinking in surprise, she took in the fact that it was not Ash at her door. Was it disappointment she felt? She shook that idea off and stared wordlessly at Mia and Bethany who wore determined expressions on their faces.

"You look awful," Mia said bluntly. "Have you slept at all?"

"Stupid question, Mia. It's obvious she hasn't," Bethany said.

"What are you doing here?" Josie asked faintly.

"To answer what will likely be your next question, no, Ash didn't send us," Mia said firmly. "To answer your first question, we're here because we're dragging you to lunch with us and don't even think about telling us no."

Josie's mouth fell open. Bethany laughed.

"You may as well give in gracefully, Josie," Bethany said, laughter still in her voice. "Mia is very determined and she's kind of scary when she sets her mind to something. I'm sure Gabe will attest to that fact."

Mia elbowed Bethany and scowled. Despite herself, Josie smiled, relief settling over her shoulders.

"Can you give me just a minute to clean up? I've, uh, been working," she finished lamely.

"Sure," Mia chirped.

"Come in," Josie said hastily. "Have a seat. It's kind of a mess. I haven't unpacked or anything and as I said, I've been working."

"Is this your new stuff?" Bethany asked softly when they entered the living room.

Mia and Bethany were staring at the two paintings she'd just finished. Josie rubbed her hands down her pants legs and nodded.

"They're really good," Mia said. "So much emotion in them." She turned sympathetic eyes toward Josie. "And it's obvious you're very upset."

Josie didn't know how to respond to that.

"I'll, uh, just be a minute, okay?"

Mia and Bethany nodded and Josie hurried into her bathroom to make herself more presentable. When she got a look at herself in the mirror she winced. No wonder they'd told her she looked awful. She *did*.

She splashed water on her face and hastily applied foundation and powder. She brushed her lashes with light mascara and then swiped on lip gloss. She wouldn't win any beauty pageants but at least she didn't look quite so washed-out and hollow. No amount of makeup in the world was going to fix the dark shadows under her eyes.

When she returned to the living room, Mia and Bethany were waiting and quickly hustled her outside and toward the car parked just down the street.

The two guys Josie had noticed earlier caught her attention once more and she frowned. No doubt, they were Ash's men. Watching her. Even though he'd sworn to give her at least last night. She shook her head. Trust Ash to do things his own way. Just as he'd always done. In the back of her mind she supposed it was good that he was still protecting her, but her trust in him had been shattered. Now what should seem like protection was just one more sign of how controlling Ash was.

"We would have invited Brittany too but we worried it might be a little awkward since she's Ash's sister," Mia said in a low voice once they were inside the car.

Josie winced. Okay, obviously they did know about her breakup with Ash and they weren't just inviting her to lunch as if everything was normal.

Bethany slid her hand over Josie's and squeezed. "Don't look like that, Josie. Everything will be fine. You'll see."

Tears burned her eyelids and she battled fiercely to keep from breaking down. "I'm not sure anything will ever be okay again."

"It will," Mia said fiercely. "You can tell us all about it at lunch. Then we'll figure out how to kick Ash's ass."

Bethany laughed and Josie just looked at her in bewilderment.

"But Ash is your friend," Josie said. "Aren't you mad at *me* for breaking up with him?"

"You're *our* friend," Mia said. "Ash isn't our only connection to you, Josie. And women have to close ranks and stick together! I'm sure whatever the problem is that it's Ash's fault."

"Absolutely," Bethany said loyally. "Gabe and Jace messed up plenty of times so it's certainly par for the course that Ash would too. He is a man after all."

Josie laughed even as tears welled in her eyes." Oh God, I love you guys."

"We love you too," Mia said. "Now let's get something yummy and fattening to eat and bitch about men."

Ten minutes later, they were seated at a small pub not far from Josie's apartment. They placed their orders and then Mia all but pounced on Josie.

"Okay, give us the dirt. All Gabe and Jace have said was that you broke up with Ash and moved out and that Ash got shitfaced drunk last night."

Josie winced and put her face in her hands. "Oh God. I don't know what to do. On one hand I'm pissed and hurt and a whole host of things. And on the other, I wonder if I've overreacted."

"What happened?" Bethany asked softly.

Josie sighed and then recounted the entire story from beginning to end, leaving nothing out. Not the fact that Ash had her followed, him buying her mother's jewelry and him insisting on her moving in with him after what happened with Michael, and then her discovery that he was the one who bought all her paintings.

"Wow," Mia said, sitting back in her seat. "I would say I was surprised but that so sounds like something Ash would do."

"Gabe and Jace too," Bethany pointed out. "They're very determined when they want something."

"True," Mia admitted. "They're persistent if nothing else."

Bethany nodded her agreement.

"Did I overreact?" Josie asked. "Part of me says yes while the other part of me is hurt. I mean I'm pissed too, but more than that I'm devastated."

"You didn't overreact, Josie," Bethany said.

Mia sat forward again, her gaze earnest as she stared at Josie. "I understand why you're upset. But listen to me, Josie, and I don't say this to hurt you. I'm saying it to make a point. Ash could have any woman he wanted. There are literally thousands of women who'd line up to have a chance with him. But he wants *you*."

Bethany nodded rapidly.

"I absolutely get what you're saying about taking away your independence and how what he did negated a lot of what you'd worked very hard to achieve. But here's the thing. Men are thick. Thick as a brick! Ash wanted to help you. Men like Ash only know one way. Their way. But, Josie, he was so proud of you. He bragged to Jace and Gabe and even to me and Bethany about how talented you are. I don't think he ever in a million years meant to hurt you the way he has. He saw a way to help you, to provide for you and to give you a sense of accomplishment. He may not have done it in the best way, but his intentions were good. I absolutely believe that. Ash is just so intense. But he has a huge heart, evidenced by the fact that he helped his sister who was a bitch to him for years. And despite the fact that his family are huge assholes, he still can't quite turn his back on them."

"I had a lot of issues with the fact that Jace wanted me," Bethany said quietly. "It baffled me that he turned the city over looking for me after that first night and that he went to such lengths to help me, to provide for me. He, like Ash, could have any woman he wanted. But he wanted me. Just like Ash wants you. We can sit here and analyze it and try to understand it, but at the end of the day, they want who they want and that happens to be us. And Jace made plenty of mistakes along the way, but we worked past those issues and I'm so glad we did because he makes me so happy. I'd never have this with another man. I wouldn't want to."

"So you think I'm making too big of a deal out of this," Josie said ruefully.

Mia shook her head. "No, honey, I don't. I think it's obviously important to you and I absolutely think Ash should know that and recognize what he did was wrong. But at the same time, is it something you can't forgive him for? Because really, what did he do that was so bad? His heart was in the right place even if he went about it all wrong."

And there it was. In a nutshell. Was it really so unforgivable? Sure, she had a right to be angry, but moving out? Breaking up? That was so . . . permanent.

She dropped her face into her hands. "Oh God. I did overreact."

Bethany slid her hand over Josie's back.

"I should have confronted him, absolutely, but I completely overreacted. I shouldn't have done what I did. Now he's going to be so pissed at me, and I don't blame him!"

"He won't be pissed, Josie," Mia said softly. "He'll just be glad to have you back."

She shook her head miserably. "It's worse than what you think. He said . . ." She sighed. "He said he loved me and I threw it back at him. I said some pretty horrible things. Like that I couldn't trust that he wasn't saying it to manipulate me."

"Was it the first time he told you?" Bethany asked gently.

Josie nodded.

"Then it's understandable that you would have reacted the way you did," Mia said. "Do you love him?"

"Oh yeah," Josie breathed. "Completely and utterly in love with him."

Bethany beamed. "There. You love each other. You can work this out. He'll forgive you and you'll forgive him."

"You make it sound so easy," Josie muttered. "I was such a hysterical twit. I can't believe I marched into his office and said the things I said. I wish there was a Rewind button and I had it to do all over again."

"Love isn't perfect," Mia said. "We've all made mistakes. Gabe, Jace, me, Bethany. And now you and Ash. It's not supposed to be perfect. It's what you make it. And you can make it really special, Josie. Go and talk to him. Or call him. Make things right and give him the chance to make things right."

Some of the heavy weight lifted off Josie's shoulders. Hope crept in and with it the realization that this wasn't the end. Nothing Ash had done was unforgiveable. She'd make mistakes. There was no doubt she would. But she absolutely believed that Ash would be a lot more forgiving of her mistakes than she'd been of his.

"Thanks, you guys," she said, smiling with relief. "I'm going to go home, take a shower and call Ash and hope he's not too pissed to listen to me apologize."

Mia smiled back. "Oh, he'll listen. Come on. Let's go. We'll drop you back by your apartment."

Josie shook her head. "Thanks, but I'll walk. I need some time to get my thoughts together. I want to get this just right."

"You sure?" Bethany asked.

"Yeah, I'm sure. It's not that far and it will give me the chance to work up my nerve to call him."

"Okay, but you have to swear to text me and Bethany and let us know how it goes!" Mia demanded.

"I will. Promise! And thanks again. This means a lot to me. That you'd be willing to kick his ass when we've only known each other a short time."

Mia grinned. "What are friends for?"

Josie rose, hugged both of the women fiercely and promised again to text them the minute she got things worked out with Ash. Then she walked out with them and waited while they got into the car and waved as they pulled away.

Slinging her purse over her shoulder, she started walking in the direction of her apartment. Her thoughts were a whirlwind, but excitement and relief replaced her earlier gloom.

Now she just had to hope that Ash would forgive her and that he really did love her.

The walk took longer than she'd thought and by the time she reached her apartment she was tired from not having slept the night before and she was impatient to get inside, take a shower and call Ash.

She cursed the fact that she'd left her cell phone in her living room. She could have already read her texts and listened to her voice mails. They would give her a good idea of Ash's mood and whether it would be a simple matter of apologizing to him.

She put her key in the lock, frowning when she realized she must have forgotten to lock it on her way out. But then the last thing on her mind hadn't been whether she locked up or not. She really needed to be more careful. Of course if she and Ash reconciled, she wouldn't have to worry about that because he always made certain she was protected. For that matter he had still made sure she was protected, even though she'd left him. But then she hadn't noticed her two shadows when she returned to her apartment. Had they given up? Had Ash given up?

A frown tugged at her lips as she pushed inside, closing and locking the door behind her. The minute she stepped inside her living room she realized she wasn't alone.

Her breath caught when she saw three men standing, waiting, grim expressions on their faces. She recognized two of them from before. What she'd assumed were Ash's men. For her protection. In that instant, she knew she was terribly wrong. These men weren't here to protect her at all.

Before she could react, one moved in quickly behind her, barring her pathway to the door. Not that she would have had time to escape anyway since she'd locked her door on the way in.

"Miss Carlysle," one of the men said in a tone that sent shivers down her skin. "There's a message I want you to deliver to Gabe Hamilton, Jace Crestwell and Ash McIntyre."

Before she could demand to know what he was talking about and that they get the hell out of her apartment, pain exploded through her body. She lay sprawled on the floor, utterly bewildered.

And then pain. More pain, agonizing, splintering through her body as they meted out violence. Blood smeared her nose. She could taste it in her mouth. She couldn't breathe right. It hurt too much. She couldn't even scream.

She was going to die.

That thought hit her and, oddly, she didn't fight it because it meant escape from the horrific agony she was enduring.

Then it went silent. A hand dug into her hair and yanked her head painfully upward. A man leaned into her face, his nose just inches from her own.

"You tell them that nothing they hold dear is safe from me. I'm coming after them. They will regret the day they ever fucked with me. They ruined me. And by God, I'll ruin them before I'm done."

He shoved something into her hand and then dropped her head back onto the floor. Pain shot down her spine. She heard footsteps and then her door opening. And then it closing.

A low whimper stuttered past stiff, swollen lips. Ash. She had to get to her cell phone and call him. Had to warn him. He'd come for her. Everything would be all right if she could just get to her phone.

She tried to push herself up and shrieked in agony when she put weight on her right hand. She stared down at it, her vision fuzzy, one eye nearly swollen shut. What was wrong with her hand?

Using her elbow to prop herself up, she dragged herself toward the coffee table where she'd left her phone. She reached up for it, knocking it onto the floor and then praying she hadn't broken it.

With her left hand she fumbled to push the right button to bring up her contacts. Then she changed her mind and hit recent calls because his would have been the last. She hit his name and with a whispered prayer as she waited for him to answer.

# chapter thirty-one

Ash sat in on the staff meeting with Gabe and their executives, but his mind was anywhere but here in this room. He had a hangover from hell after getting roaring drunk the night before. Gabe and Jace had poured him into a car and then brought him home and tossed him on his bed. He'd woken up the next morning feeling like he'd been run over by a truck, but the pain of the headache was nothing compared to the pain of losing Josie.

No, he hadn't lost her. Not yet. He wouldn't let himself go there. She was upset—rightfully so—and he'd given her last night. Time to spend apart from him and hopefully decide when she got over her initial anger that this was something they could work through.

At any rate, he'd given her all the time he was going to. As soon as this fucking meeting ended, he was out of here. He was going to Josie's apartment and would get on his knees if he had to. Whatever it took to get her back home. To their apartment. In his arms and in his bed. And then he was never going to let her go again.

His phone vibrated and he glanced down, his heart clenching when he saw it was Josie calling. Without saying a word, he abruptly got up and walked out of the meeting, the phone already to his ear.

"Josie? Baby?" he cut in before she could even say anything.

There was a long silence and at first he thought she'd hung up. But then he heard it and the sound froze his blood. A low whimper. Of *pain*. His heart dropped into his stomach.

"Josie, talk to me," he demanded. "What's wrong? Where are you?"

"Ash . . ."

His name came out barely a whisper and it was obvious that she was in a lot of pain.

"I'm here, baby. Tell me what's happened. Where are you?"

"Need you," she whispered. "Hurt. It's bad."

Panic froze him in place. He couldn't think, couldn't act, couldn't process anything but the agony in her voice.

"Where are you?" he demanded.

"Apartment."

"I'm on my way, baby. Hold tight, okay? I'll be there in just a minute."

He turned in the hallway, having gotten no farther than the door where the meeting was being held and ran solidly into Gabe.

"What's wrong?" Gabe demanded. "I heard you on the phone with Josie. What's happened?"

"I don't know," Ash choked out. "She's hurt. I have to go. She's at her apartment."

"Come on. I'll go with you," Gabe said grimly, even as he started striding down the hall toward the elevators.

Not arguing, Ash ran after him, his heart beating like a hammer.

"Did she say what happened?" Gabe asked when they'd gotten into the car.

"No," Ash clipped out. *"Fuck!"*

"It's okay, man. We'll get to her. She'll be okay. You have to believe that."

"You said Mia and Bethany had lunch with her. Have you heard from Mia? What could possibly have happened? They can't have finished that long ago."

Gabe paled and then immediately dialed Mia's number.

"Are you okay?" Gabe asked bluntly.

Then his shoulders sagged in relief. Mia must be fine. But Josie wasn't. What the fuck could have happened?

"When did you and Bethany leave Josie?" Gabe asked.

He listened a moment and then said good-bye without telling Mia anything about Josie.

"Well?" Ash demanded, silently urging the driver to go faster. They were already driving recklessly.

"She said Josie walked back to her apartment after they had lunch. That was an hour ago."

Ash closed his eyes. He should have kept a man on her. What if Michael had gotten to her? He'd refused to put anyone on her, not wanting to upset her even more than she already was. He'd promised her space and now that space had cost her.

A few minutes later the car squealed to a stop in front of Josie's brownstone and Ash jumped out, Gabe close on his heels. The first thing he registered when he burst through her door was the smell of blood. His own went cold, freezing in his veins. He tore into the living room, his heart seizing as he took in the sight before him.

"Sweet mother of God," he choked out.

Josie lay in a bloody heap in front of the coffee table. Blood was smeared on the floor where she'd evidently dragged herself to the phone.

"Call an ambulance," Ash barked to Gabe.

God, he should have already called one but he hadn't been *thinking*. His only thought had been to get to her as fast as he could. And maybe he'd denied that it would be this bad.

He ran over, dropping to his knees beside her, afraid to touch her because oh God, the blood. Her face was a mess, eyes swollen, lips split and bleeding.

"Josie. Josie, darling, I'm here. It's me, Ash. Talk to me, baby. Please. Open your eyes and talk to me."

He was pleading with her even as he put a shaky finger to her neck to feel for a pulse.

She stirred, emitting a soft moan that seared his heart and cut straight to his soul.

"A-ash?"

Her words were slurred, distorted by her swollen lips. He smoothed a hand over her forehead because it was the only place she wasn't bruised or bleeding.

"Yes, baby, it's me. I'm here. Tell me what happened, Josie. Who did this to you?"

"H-hurts to b-breathe," she said and then she stopped, coughing and choking as a stream of blood trickled from the corner of her mouth.

Oh God. Oh God. She was hurt badly. Someone had beat the ever-loving hell out of her. Rage exploded through his chest until he couldn't breathe either. His vision went dim, his pulse about to beat out of his head. He was coming apart. Unraveling at the seams. His hands shook so badly that he had to pull them away from her skin so he didn't risk hurting her.

She tried to lift her left hand and he saw she was holding something. He gently pulled it away, frowning when he saw it was a picture. Bile rose in his throat as he stared in disbelief. It was a picture of Mia. Dear God. She was naked, tied up and spread out on what looked like a coffee table. The man in the picture was Charles Willis and he was trying to shove his dick inside her mouth.

He quickly stuffed the picture into his pocket before Gabe could see it. Gabe would lose his fucking mind, and right now the only thing Ash was worried about was Josie and getting her to a hospital. They'd deal with the picture later.

"Is she okay?" Gabe asked as he dropped down beside Ash. "Jesus. She's obviously not okay. Ambulance is on the way. ETA is five minutes. What the fuck happened?"

"I don't know," Ash said, his voice still shaking with fury.

He leaned down and pressed a kiss to Josie's forehead, too afraid to do what he most wanted and gather her in his arms. She obviously had internal injuries and he didn't want to cause her further injury.

"Who did this to you, baby? Can you tell me?" he asked her gently.

Tears gathered in her eyes and slid silently down her cheeks. Each one broke his heart. He wanted to cry with her, but he refused to break down. She needed him to be strong. He would be strong. No way he was going to let her down again.

"He had a message," Josie whispered. "For you. And Gabe and Jace."

Gabe and Ash exchanged quick *what the fuck* looks.

"What was the message, Josie? Don't try to talk if it hurts you, though. We have plenty of time to talk later when you're not in pain."

She licked her lips, her tongue bright red with blood. Ash was shaking from head to toe now as his reaction set in. This was bad. If she was coughing up blood it meant she was fucked up on the inside. People died from internal injuries!

"Said nothing . . ." She broke off and choked, more blood seeping from her lips. Ash was panicking now. Where was the goddamn ambulance?

She took a long moment and for a second Ash thought she'd slipped into unconsciousness.

"Josie. Josie! Stay with me, baby. Fight it. Stay awake. Can you do that for me? Open your eyes, baby. I'm right here. I'm not going anywhere. The ambulance is on its way. They'll be here soon and they'll take care of you. I'll take care of you," he choked out, tears knotting his throat.

Her eyelids fluttered and she trained her unfocused eyes on him, pain glittering brightly in their depths.

"Said nothing you hold dear . . . is safe. S-s-said you r-ruined him . . . and now he's going to ruin y-you."

Gabe went white even as he grabbed his phone. He stepped back and away from Josie and Ash, but Ash could hear him talking to Jace, telling him to make sure Mia and Bethany were safe. Then he told Jace to meet him and Ash at the hospital.

The sound of a siren sent relief coursing through Ash's veins. He jumped to his feet but Gabe stopped him.

"I'll get them in. You stay with Josie," Gabe bit out.

Ash dropped back down, bending over Josie so she'd know he was here.

"The ambulance is here, baby," he soothed. "They'll get you to the hospital and I'll be with you every step of the way. You'll be okay, darling. I won't let you be anything else. Stay with me. I love you. I love you so much."

She tried to lift her right hand and then whimpered in pain. "H-hand h-hurts. What's wrong with it?"

He stared in horror at the obviously broken fingers. Son of a bitch! They'd broken her fingers! He was precariously close to losing his composure. He wanted to get his hands on the sons of bitches who did this to her. He'd kill the bastards with his own hands.

Forcing himself to focus on her and pushing everything else from his mind, he captured her wrist, holding it gently so she wouldn't let it fall back to the floor and hurt herself even more. Then he kissed the swollen fingers ever so gently as tears gathered in his eyes.

"Just some broken fingers," he said shakily. "Nothing the doctor won't fix right up."

"My painting hand," she said as more tears squeezed from her swollen eyes.

"Shhh, it's okay, baby. You'll be back to painting before you know it."

Even as he spoke, his gaze caught on the two paintings propped against the wall. Dark. Full of turmoil. He'd done that to her. He'd taken her vibrancy away. The essence of her work. These weren't the Josie he knew and loved. This was Josie hurting and expressing her emotions in the only way she knew how.

The EMTs burst through the door and into the living room, immediately assessing Josie's condition. Ash moved back so he didn't interfere, but he stayed close, hovering anxiously as they went through the assessment.

"Decreased breath sounds on the left side," the paramedic said grimly as he pulled his stethoscope away. "Get the O2," he barked at his partner.

"How bad is it?" Ash demanded.

The paramedic shook his head. "No way to know without x-rays. I'm guessing she has several broken ribs. Probably punctured a lung."

"Be careful with her hand," Ash said. "It's broken."

"She's a mess," the medic said bluntly. "We need to load and go. I'll get a c-collar on her and bag her on the way."

Ash went pale. The words sounded so grim and utterly serious.

"Will she live?" Ash whispered, voicing his darkest fear.

"Not my call, but she sure as hell isn't going to die on my watch."

A stretcher was brought in and the medics worked quickly, securing the c-collar and then giving her oxygen. She was just as quickly wheeled out and loaded into the ambulance. Ash barely had time to jump into the back before they roared away in a rush of sirens and lights.

He slid his hand into his pocket, feeling for the photo Josie had had in her hand. Gabe had a hell of a lot to answer for, and then Ash was going after the son of a bitch who'd put his hands on Josie.

# chapter thirty-two

"What the fuck is going on?" Jace demanded as he strode into the ER waiting room.

Ash turned and then motioned Gabe and Jace into one of the smaller private rooms where doctors met with families.

"We have a serious problem," Ash said grimly.

"What the hell happened to Josie?" Jace asked. "Gabe called worried about Mia and Bethany, told me to lock them both down and make sure they were safe. I called Kaden Ginsberg and now I have two very pissed-off women because I made Kaden sit on them both and they're scared and want to know what the fuck is going on, which I couldn't tell them because I don't know myself!"

Ash held up his hand and then reached into his pocket with the other. He pulled out the photo that was in Josie's hand and held it out to Gabe.

Gabe's face was a mixture of shock and rage. And then, oddly, *guilt*. He went gray and then staggered back to sit in one of the chairs. He buried his face in his hands, the photo crumpled in his fist.

Jace snatched the photo from Gabe and then he went pale as he stared at his sister naked, tied up, another man trying to force himself on her.

"What the *fuck* is this?"

Jace's explosive demand echoed through the room.

"Josie was holding that when I got to her," Ash said quietly. "And then she told me the man who beat the crap out of her had a message for me, you and Gabe."

*"What?"* Jace said in disbelief.

"He told her that nothing we held dear was safe from him. That we ruined him and now he was going to ruin us. I'd say Josie was probably the first target because she was the easiest. She was alone and vulnerable. It would be a lot harder to get to Mia or Bethany."

"I want to know what the fuck that picture is about," Jace said in a furious tone. "That was Charles Willis in that photo. Is he the one who hurt Josie and is threatening us now?"

"Yes," Gabe said bleakly.

"What do you know that you haven't told us," Ash asked in a dangerously low tone. It was obvious by the look on Gabe's face that there was a *lot* that Ash and Jace evidently didn't know.

Gabe rubbed a hand wearily over his face, his eyes sick.

"What I have to say is going to piss you both off. I thought it was behind me and Mia. I was wrong, apparently."

"Yeah, I'd say so," Jace bit out. "What the fuck did you do, Gabe?"

"When Mia and I were together, before, when we were keeping it a secret from you, right before we went to Paris on business, my ex-wife came into my office saying all sorts of crazy shit. Then she accused me of being in love with Mia. Accused me of being in love with her when I was still married to Lisa. It hit me all wrong. I wasn't ready to admit my feelings for Mia. And in an effort to distance us, to prove to myself that she was just sex, I set up a thing in Paris."

"What kind of thing," Ash growled.

Gabe blew out his breath. "Mia and I had discussed, before, her interest in being with another man. With me, I mean. I guess kind of like you and Jace sharing women. So I set it up that Charles Willis and two other men were in our hotel room. Jesus, this is complicated."

Jace stared stonily at Gabe, his eyes glittering with anger.

"Things got out of hand. I was going to let them touch her, nothing else. I made it clear they weren't to do anything but touch, which meant keeping their dicks in their pants. But as soon as it began, I knew it was wrong. I realized what I was doing, but before I could put a stop to it, Charles got rough with Mia. He was trying to shove his dick down her throat and then he hit her when she protested."

"Son of a bitch!" Jace swore. "What the fuck, man? How could you do that to her? What were you *thinking*?"

Gabe held up his hand. "There's more. It gets worse."

"Jesus," Ash muttered.

"When we got back, Charles confronted Mia outside the office building when she went out to get us something to eat. He tried to blackmail her into giving him information on the bids. He knew I had no intention of doing business with him, but he figured if he bid low enough we wouldn't have a choice. He showed her that picture and said that if she didn't give him what he wanted that he'd go public with it."

"Un-fucking-real," Jace growled.

"Mia came to me instead of caving in, and I took care of the matter. Or at least I thought I had," Gabe said wearily.

Ash's jaw bulged. Rage smoldered through him like a wildfire.

"I'll handle it," Gabe said quietly. "I fucked up. I'll make sure that son of a bitch doesn't get his hands on Mia or Bethany and I'll make sure he pays for what he did to Josie."

"No," Ash said, the word whipping through the room like a gunshot.

Gabe and Jace both looked at Ash with narrowed eyes.

"You had your chance," Ash said in an even tone. "I'll take care of the little bastard."

Jace's face flashed with alarm. "Don't think that's a good idea, man. Your emotions are running high. Let me and Gabe take care of this."

"I said no," Ash snapped. "This is mine. Gabe had his chance. He fucked up. I'm not leaving this to him."

"Ash," Gabe began but Ash silenced him with a look.

"If it were Mia or Bethany lying in a hospital bed, bruises, broken bones, punctured lung and God only knows what else, would you just sit back and let someone else take care of the asshole who did that to her?"

Jace's lips twisted and then he sighed. "No. I wouldn't. But Jesus, man. After what went down with Michael, this is too risky. You got away with the first. You won't get away with this. Charles Willis has nothing to lose. He's not going to sway under threats. You touch him and he'll have your ass in a sling."

"Who said anything about threats?" Ash asked calmly. "In my world, threats are meaningless unless you do something to back them up. I have no intention of threatening Charles Willis. But I have every intention of taking him down."

Gabe and Jace exchanged worried looks but Ash ignored them. They'd try to talk him down but in this he would not be dissuaded.

"This won't touch you. It damn sure won't touch Mia, Bethany or Josie. Not ever again. You don't have to worry. You won't be remotely tied to this."

"Oh fuck you," Jace said rudely. "The hell I'm letting you take this shit on by yourself. We've already been over this. You never have to ask. We'll always have your back."

"Means a lot," Ash said quietly. "But I'm not pulling my family down. You and the girls mean far too much to me. I'm not going down either. You can take that to the bank. No way in hell I'm leaving Josie to survive on her own. I'm going to be there for her every step of the way and she will never have to worry about some asshole with a grudge against us using her to get to us. That will *not* happen again."

"What are you going to do?" Gabe asked quietly.

"You're better off not knowing," Ash replied.

Gabe ran a hand through his hair. "Jesus, man. This is on me."

"You had your shot," Ash said carefully. "Not saying you did wrong, but whatever you did was not enough. I'm going to make sure that this time it is. He didn't beat your woman half to death, even if she was the intended mark. He fucked Josie over, and I'm going to make damn sure that never happens again."

"Why the fuck didn't you tell us this before?" Jace said to Gabe. "Can't believe you kept this from us. Especially if you didn't make damn sure Charles wouldn't be a threat in the future."

"I couldn't tell you when it happened," Gabe said between his teeth. "Mia was freaking because she didn't want her brother to know what kind of relationship we had or that we even had a relationship. And then after, it didn't seem so important. He went away. Months passed and he seemed to disappear off the face of the planet. I thought he wasn't going to be a problem any longer."

"What you did was piss him off to the point that he beat the shit out of Josie and now he's gunning for Mia and Bethany," Jace said in a furious tone.

"You need to close ranks around the girls," Ash said, veering the subject away from Jace's fury. He had a right. Mia was his sister. But that wasn't what was important right now. The women's safety was all that mattered.

"Hell yes," Gabe growled. "They'll go nowhere until he's taken care of."

Ash nodded. "And I'll let you know when the issue has been resolved."

Jace's expression was still uneasy but he kept silent, though it was obvious that he and Gabe weren't finished with their conversation.

"Mr. McIntyre?"

Ash whirled around to see a nurse standing in the doorway. He rushed forward.

"How is Josie?" he demanded. "Can I see her yet?"

The nurse smiled. "The doctor will see you now. She'll update you on Josie's condition and then you can ask her if you can go back. Stay right here while I let her know where you are."

Ash fidgeted with impatience. It had been too long with no word and he was slowly losing his mind. He didn't like that Josie was alone. Or at least surrounded by strangers. She'd wonder where he was. He'd sworn to her that he wasn't leaving her, that he would be with her every step of the way. How could he keep that promise when he'd been barred from her room while they gave her treatment?

A moment later a woman dressed in scrubs walked in the door. She looked young, the ponytail her hair was pulled back in contributing to her youthful appearance.

"Mr. McIntyre?"

"Yes, that's me," Ash said, stepping forward.

She extended her hand and firmly shook his. "Dr. Newton. I'm the ER doctor handling Miss Carlysle's care."

"How is she?" Ash asked anxiously. "When can I see her?"

The doctor's expression softened. "She's pretty banged up. Of most concern is the traumatic pneumothorax. I've inserted a chest tube to help suck out the air trapped between the lung and the chest cavity and it will also help the lung reinflate. We're going to be closely monitoring her for infection as well as seeing how the lung heals. Right now I don't think she requires surgery, but a surgeon will be consulted and he'll make the final determination.

"She has several broken ribs, a concussion and broken fingers on her right hand. She also has a hairline fracture of her right wrist. Numerous contusions and other more minor injuries. She was badly beaten, Mr. McIntyre. She's lucky to be alive."

Ash blew out his breath while Gabe and Jace swore softly behind him.

"Can I see her?"

"You can go in. She's back from x-ray and she'll be moved to ICU as soon as the paperwork gets done on her admission. I can't say with any authority how long she'll remain in ICU. That will be up to the internal medicine physician assigned to her care. But you can stay with her until they move her up to the unit. They're usually pretty lenient about letting family members back even when it's not the scheduled hours."

"I'm not leaving her," Ash bit out.

The doctor's expression was sympathetic. "I understand. And as I said, they're usually pretty lenient. Unfortunately when she's first moved, you'll have to wait until they get her settled, but they'll let you know when you can go back."

"Thank you," Ash said in a low voice. "I appreciate all you've done for her."

"That's my job, Mr. McIntyre," she said in a cheerful voice. "Now if you'll excuse me, I have other patients to attend. If you like I'll walk you back and show you which room she's in."

Ash turned to Gabe and Jace. "Are you going to let Mia and Bethany know what happened? They'll be worried about Josie."

"We'll let them know," Jace said. "I'll have Kaden drive them here and they'll stay with us until we leave."

Ash nodded and then turned back to follow the doctor to Josie's room.

When he walked into the small cubicle where Josie was, he sucked in his breath and tears burned the corners of his eyes. It hurt to breathe. His chest was so tight that his hand automatically came up to rub it, trying to rid himself of the discomfort.

"Jesus," he whispered.

It gutted him that she was lying in a hospital bed all because some asshole had an ax to grind with him and Gabe and Jace. He went to her bedside and tentatively reached out a hand to stroke her forehead. He smoothed her hair back and then leaned down to brush his lips across her brow.

"I love you," he murmured. "I'm here. With you, just like I said I'd be. I'll always be here, Josie. You and me are forever, baby. Not letting go of that."

She lay perfectly still, the only sound the low hum of the machine that made oxygen flow through the mask over her face and the steady beeping of the heart monitor. She looked so fragile, bruised and swollen. The blood had been cleaned away, but the dark purpling of the bruises was already vivid against her pale skin.

He touched her neck where the collar he'd given her had rested. It looked bare. He wanted that collar back around her neck. Wanted his ring on her finger and her promise to marry him. He wanted to tie her to him in ways she'd never escape. But they'd be the most loving, silken ties in the world.

He'd pamper her, cherish her, adore her every single day of his life.

He stood at her bedside for two hours, only moving when one of the nurses came in to check on her. And then finally, they came to move her to ICU.

To his frustration they told him it would be a while before he was allowed back to see her. But that was okay because he had the problem of Charles Willis to take care of. The sooner he was out of the picture, the sooner they could all relax and not worry that Mia or Bethany would be next.

After updating Gabe, Jace, Mia and Bethany on Josie's condition and exacting a promise from them to stay with Josie until he returned, he strode out of the hospital, determined to seek vengeance on the bastard who'd put Josie there.

## chapter thirty-three

Pain. It came to her piercing like a nail being driven into her head by a hammer. She hurt everywhere. It hurt to breathe. It hurt to open her eyes.

There were voices, or at least one voice. It was hard to tell because there was a roaring in her ears she couldn't make go away.

And then a warm, gentle hand on her forehead. A kiss. Sweet, soft words whispered over her skin. She gave a little sigh and promptly regretted it because pain speared through her chest.

"H-hurts," she said in a pitiful voice that she wasn't even sure was actually audible.

"I know it does, baby. The nurse is coming to give you something for pain."

"Ash?" she whispered.

"Yes, darling, it's me. Open those pretty eyes and you'll see me right here."

She tried. She really did. But her eyes wouldn't cooperate and it *hurt* to try and force the issue.

"Can't," she managed to get past stiff, swollen lips.

Again he pressed his lips to her brow and she felt his hand in her hair. That felt nice. The only part of her that wasn't hurting.

"It's okay," he soothed. "Don't try too hard. Just know that I'm with you and you're going to be all right."

But still, she wanted to see him. Wanted to make sure her imagination wasn't playing nasty tricks on her. So she braced herself against the pain and tried harder. A small sliver of light seared her eyeballs and she promptly shut her eyes again. She lay there, nearly panting with exertion and the agony such a small movement had caused. Then she tried again, this time prepared for the light.

At first all she saw was a blurry haze. And then he moved into her line of vision.

"Hey, gorgeous," he said softly.

She tried to smile, but that hurt too, so she just lay there slowly blinking to bring him into sharper focus.

"Hi," she returned just as quietly.

To her utter shock, his eyes were glossy with moisture and he looked like hell. He hadn't shaved, his hair was rumpled and his clothes looked like he'd slept in them.

She licked her lips and moaned softly. "W-what happened to me?"

Ash frowned, his eyes going dark. "You don't remember?"

She concentrated hard but it was all a blur. "How long?"

He touched her hair, his expression worried. "How long what, love?"

"Have I been here."

"Two days," he said.

Her eyes widened in surprise despite the discomfort it caused her. "Two days?"

"Yes, baby. You've been in ICU for two days. Gave us quite a scare."

"Am I going to be okay?"

It was a question she was afraid to ask but she had to know. She wouldn't hurt this much if it wasn't bad.

His face softened, his eyes going warm and loving. "You're going to be fine. I won't allow any other possibility."

"Sorry," she said with a sigh.

His head came back in surprise. "What the hell are you sorry for?"

"I overreacted," she said. "I shouldn't have done it. I'm sorry. I was going to call you but then . . ."

And it was then she remembered everything that had happened. She sucked in her breath at the impact the memories had. Her terror, her pain, the worry that she was going to die. Tears welled, burning her eyes.

"Oh, baby," he said in an aching voice. "Don't cry. And don't apologize. You have nothing to be sorry for. Nothing at all."

"Who were they?" she whispered. "Why did they do this? Why do they hate you and Gabe and Jace?"

He closed his eyes and then leaned down, touching his forehead to hers. "Let's not talk about this right now, darling. I don't want to upset you. I'd rather talk about how much I love you and what I'm going to do to pamper you and spoil you while you recover."

She had to ask another question, had to know where they stood and if she'd screwed up any chance of them being together.

"Are we back together?"

He smiled. So sweet and tender it warmed her to her toes and took away some of the overwhelming pain. Relief shone in his eyes.

"Bet your ass we are."

Her own shoulders sagged in relief. "I'm glad," she said softly.

"God, baby, it's torture being so close to you and unable to hold you and kiss you the way I want."

"I'm just glad you're here."

"I wouldn't be anywhere else."

She closed her eyes as fatigue and the pain grew stronger. It was becoming overwhelming and she had so many questions. She needed answers. She needed to know exactly how serious her injuries were. For that matter she didn't even know exactly what they were.

"The nurse is here, darling. Bear with me a few more seconds and the pain will be gone."

"Talk to me," she begged. "I just want to hear your voice. Stay here and tell me what happened and how bad it is. I need to know."

He wiped a hand over her forehead as the nurse injected pain medication into her IV. She felt the slight burn travel up her arm and then, right on its heels, blessed relief. A feeling of euphoria enveloped her. She felt light and floaty like she was on a cloud. The ceiling suddenly seemed right on top of her and she gasped.

"Okay?" Ash asked in concern.

"'Kay."

He went silent and her eyes fluttered open in panic as she tried to see where he'd gone.

"I'm right here, darling. Not going anywhere. I promise."

"Talk to me," she said again, woozy and sleepy. But she didn't want to go to sleep. Not yet.

He kissed her brow. "Give me just a second, baby. I want to talk to the nurse about you but I'll be right back. Can you stay awake for me?"

"Uh-huh."

She felt him move away and she was suddenly cold. She hated that feeling. Fear and panic seeped all the way to her bones. Her lips chattered but they were so swollen that it felt weird, like they were ten times their size.

Or maybe it was just the medication.

Why did it hurt so bad to breathe? It was then she became aware of the oxygen blowing through her nostrils. Her chest was so tight and her muscles ached from head to toe.

Had they wanted to kill her? But no, that couldn't be the case. They'd given her a message to give to Ash. Had she given it to him?

Panic flared all over again. She had to tell him! Mia and Bethany were in danger, and she'd never forgive herself if they were hurt because she hadn't warned Gabe and Jace.

"Ash," she called out as loudly as she could.

"Right here, baby. What's wrong? You need to slow down your breathing. You're going too fast. Can you do that for me?"

She sucked in a deep breath and tried to steady herself. The pressure building in her chest was intense. She dragged in another breath, blew it out and then tried again.

"What is it, Josie? What are you afraid of?"

"Mia. Bethany," she croaked out. "He'll hurt them like he hurt me. Have to tell Gabe and Jace."

"Already done," he soothed. "You told us. Gabe and Jace are making sure that Mia and Bethany are safe. You don't have to worry about them. I've taken care of Britt too. You'll be happy to know that Kai has her under lock and key."

She tried to smile. She may have even managed half of one judging by Ash's look of delight.

Then she sobered because the big question remained unanswered. And she was getting groggier and groggier. It was getting harder to stay awake. She wanted nothing more than to drift off into oblivion where there was no pain, no worries. Nothing but a black void of nothing.

"Why?"

Ash sighed. Didn't even try to misunderstand her.

"They hurt you because of me," he said, pain thick in his voice. "Because of the business. Me, Gabe and Jace. He's an asshole who hurt Mia before. I didn't know it, but he and Gabe have history. He was retaliating because we shut him down and refused to do business with him. It's not going to happen again, Josie. I swear to you it won't."

The resoluteness of his words worried Josie. It was the same matter of fact way he'd spoken of Michael and the fact that Michael would no longer be an issue.

"What did you do?" she whispered.

"Nothing you need to worry about," he said as he brushed another kiss across her forehead.

She frowned, her eyes half-closed already. She struggled to remain awake and focused.

"That's not an answer," she slurred out.

"It is," he insisted. "I don't want you to worry about anything but getting better. This doesn't touch you, Josie. It never will."

"Don't want to lose you," she whispered.

He stroked her hair, his eyes soft with love. "You won't lose me. Never that. I'm always going to be here."

"'Kay."

"Rest now, baby. You're about to go under. Go to sleep. I'll be here when you wake up."

She fought only as long as it took to whisper the words. Words she'd never given him before.

"Love you."

This time there were tears in his eyes. Turning the green to aqua pools. His breath caught and stuttered over his lips as he stared down at her.

"I love you too, darling. Now get some rest. I'll be here watching over you while you sleep."

She gave in, closing her eyes, surrendering to the pull of the medication. But she was still aware of the warm hand cupped over her brow. And of the lips against her temple.

## chapter thirty-four

"How is she?" Mia asked anxiously when Ash walked into the ICU waiting room. "Has she woken up yet?"

Ash gathered Mia in a hug and then put an arm around Bethany, who wore the same worried, grim expression. He hated that this touched them. That they'd been threatened and now had to live with that knowledge.

More than that he hated that Mia's past had been dragged into the present. Shame burned bright in her eyes. She carried guilt she had no business carrying. It wasn't her goddamn fault that Charles Willis was a fucking coward who preyed on women to get his point across. He was pissed beyond belief that Charles had put that fear in Mia and Bethany's eyes. More than that, he was enraged that Josie bore the bruises and broken bones from Charles's attack.

The man would pay. It was only a matter of time.

Gabe and Jace also looked expectantly at Ash as they waited for an update on Josie's condition. None of the men had slept since this all began. They were too worried that Mia or Bethany could be next and so they'd taken steps to ensure neither woman would ever be at risk.

Mia and Bethany weren't thrilled, but neither did they object.

"She woke up for a few minutes," Ash said.

"Oh, that's wonderful," Bethany breathed. "How was she doing?"

"She's in a lot of pain. They gave her pain medication and she slipped back under. She managed to say a few things. She's confused. She was very worried about Mia and Bethany. She didn't remember that she'd already warned us so she was frantic to tell Gabe and Jace that he'd threatened Mia and Bethany."

"Son of a bitch," Jace muttered. "What has the doctor said?"

"When will we be able to see her?" Mia asked anxiously.

"Maybe the next time she wakes up," Ash said. "And the doctor said she's making remarkable progress. They were able to take the chest tube out and she's breathing on her own with the aid of oxygen. They'll likely move her to a step-down unit tomorrow if she continues to do well and shows no sign of infection."

"That's wonderful," Bethany said.

"I'm so pissed this happened to her," Mia said tearfully.

Gabe immediately went to her, wrapping his arm around her waist and pulling her into his side.

"It's my fault," she continued, tears slipping down her cheeks. "It should have been me not her."

Ash scowled and Gabe didn't look any better. Guilt weighed heavily in Gabe's eyes. He looked haggard and gray, suddenly older than his thirty-nine years.

"That's bullshit," Jace growled. "It's not your fault, Mia. I won't have you saying it."

"We all know it's my fault," Gabe said grimly. "If I'd taken care of the asshole the first time, we wouldn't be standing here and Josie wouldn't be lying in a hospital bed."

Ash wasn't going to refute that. If it had been him and the situation with Mia had happened to Josie, Ash would have taken care of the issue then and there. But assigning blame did none of them any good. Gabe was kicking himself enough without Ash and Jace piling more on.

Jace sent Gabe a dark look that said he still hadn't forgiven the other man for what had gone down in Paris and then afterward when Charles had tried to blackmail Mia. But Jace remained silent, his lips pressed together in a tight line.

"It doesn't matter. It's been taken care of," Ash said. "There are other more important things right now."

Jace shot a worried look in Ash's direction but Ash ignored it. He wasn't about to get into specifics in front of Mia and Bethany. They had enough to deal with as it was.

"I have a lot of making up to do with Josie," Ash continued. "Apart from the fact that she's lying in a hospital bed in horrific pain, there's also the issue of the paintings I bought. I hurt her by doing that and keeping it from her. I need your help."

"You know we'll do anything," Bethany said.

Ash squeezed her to him, his arm still wrapped around her. "Thanks, sweetheart. That means a lot."

"What do you need us to do?" Gabe asked.

"I want to arrange an art show for her and I want to go all out. I need you to call in every favor owed you to make this huge. We can use the ballroom at the Bentley for the showing. Make sure everyone who is anyone is invited and that the show is hyped as the must-attend event of the year. Politicians, celebrities, the whole nine yards. I want Josie to have a venue where her art will shine and prove to her that she has incredible talent. She just needs the right exposure."

"Okay, when?" Jace asked.

"It will have to be in a couple of months. I want to make sure that Josie is recovered enough to enjoy her big night. The last thing she'd want is to show up to her own event with bruises and a cast. But we need to start working on it now so everything goes off without a hitch."

"You got it," Gabe said.

"Thanks," Ash murmured. "Means a lot you always having my back."

Mia moved from Gabe's hold and hugged Ash fiercely. "We love you, Ash. And we love Josie too. We'll be happy to help. Just let us know if you need anything else."

Ash's lips curved into a half smile. "As a matter of fact there is."

"Name it," Bethany said.

"Need you to stay here in case Josie wakes up again. I have a ring to buy."

Mia's and Bethany's delighted smiles warmed his heart. He squeezed both women to him and dropped kisses on their temples.

And then he went to Tiffany's to buy Josie's ring.

## chapter thirty-five

Josie managed to sit up in bed propped on several pillows, no small feat considering the pain in her ribs. But after several
days and a move from ICU to a step-down unit and finally to the
floor, she was able to sit up and actually move some. More importantly, she was able to eat!

Not that they'd busted out the real food or even something remotely palatable, but she'd been so hungry she had fallen on the
jello and pudding like it was manna from heaven.

Ash had gone out to meet Gabe, Jace, Mia, Bethany and even
Brittany and he was bringing them all in to visit with her. She was
extremely self-conscious about the fact she looked terrible. But she
was so anxious to have company she didn't care. All the makeup in
the world wouldn't hide her face, but hopefully the bruising would
heal quickly.

Already some had faded from the purple, almost black, to green
and yellow. She didn't even want to know what the rest of her body
looked like. She'd made it a point not to look when Ash had helped
her shower.

The door opened and she eagerly looked up to see everyone spill
through the door. Ash led the way and right behind him were Mia,

Bethany and Brittany. They swarmed her bed, giving gentle hugs and exclaiming how much better she looked. They were total liars but she loved them for it.

To her surprise, Kai Wellington came in with Gabe and Jace. She arched an eyebrow in Brittany's direction and Brittany blushed like a schoolgirl getting caught making out with the quarterback.

"He insisted on coming," Brittany whispered. "He hasn't left me alone since this happened."

"Damn right," Kai growled. "Not going to let some fucker get to you and hurt you. Bad enough he got to Josie."

"He sounds so possessive," Josie whispered to Brittany. "I take it things are going well?"

Brittany's eyes glowed and she nodded vigorously. "Oh yes. Definitely."

Josie squeezed her hand with the fingers that weren't casted. "I'm glad."

"How are you feeling?" Mia asked anxiously.

"Better," Josie said.

At Ash's skeptical look, she flushed. "Okay. Not wonderful, but I *am* better. I can sit up now without feeling like my chest caught on fire. And I can breathe normally again. They took the oxygen off this morning."

"That's wonderful, Josie!" Bethany exclaimed. "We've been so worried about you."

"How are you guys?" Josie asked in a low voice. But her question was mainly directed at Mia. Ash had told her about Mia's history with Charles Willis.

"We're okay," Mia said, but her eyes were haunted. "I still feel like it's my fault. I mean I'm the one who pissed him off."

Josie shook her head and winced at the pain it caused. "He's an asshole, Mia. You aren't to blame for his actions."

"Got that right," Ash growled.

"I hate that I share a last name with him," Bethany said, pulling a face. "I don't want anyone thinking we're related!"

Mia rolled her eyes. "Like Willis isn't a common last name?"

"You won't have to worry about that much longer, baby," Jace said, satisfaction written on his face. "Your last name will soon be Crestwell."

Bethany's face flushed with happiness and she automatically stared down at the ring on her left hand. And it was a gorgeous ring. Huge diamond but it didn't look gawdy at all. It was tastefully expensive and it suited her perfectly.

"Speaking of, have you set a date yet?" Josie asked.

Jace looked unhappy and Bethany laughed. "We're working on it. I wasn't planning anything until you're completely recovered and can stand for me at my wedding."

Josie's heart warmed and she smiled big, allowing her pleasure to show.

"I wouldn't miss it," she said. "Even if I'm still in a cast. Don't wait on me! I don't want to delay your big day."

"It wouldn't be the same without you," Bethany said, putting her hand on Josie's. "I want you all there. Brittany too! All the girls will be there. Caro has promised that she'll come even if it means flying in from Vegas."

Kai cleared his throat. "That won't be a problem. If Brittany and I are in Vegas by then we'll fly in on my jet and bring Brandon and Caro with us."

Josie's eyes widened and her gaze went to Brittany. "You're going to Vegas with him?"

"Yes," Kai cut in before Brittany could answer.

Ash's eyes narrowed but he kept silent. Josie had no doubt he'd be talking to his sister later. And Kai as well.

"Thank you," Bethany said to Kai, ducking her face in shyness. "It means a lot that you'll make sure they get to come."

"Wouldn't miss it," Kai said, a smile on his ruggedly handsome face. "Maybe seeing you get married will entice Brittany to take the plunge again. Her last husband was a fool to let her go, but I won't make that same mistake."

Whoa. This guy was moving fast! Josie risked another look at Brittany to see her face drawn in consternation. It seemed as though Kai wanted to move fast and that Brittany wasn't quite on board yet. Her money was on Kai, though. He struck her as being a very determined man when he wanted something. Just like every other man in this room.

"I don't suppose you all brought food with you?" Josie asked hopefully. "I'm starving and all they'll give me is clear liquids, which means lots of jello and chicken broth."

Ash sent her a look of reprimand. "No real food yet, baby. Not until tomorrow, and even then you'll start out slow."

She sighed. "It was worth a try. Maybe the girls will smuggle me in something when you're not looking."

As she said it, she sent a pleading look in the women's direction that had everyone laughing.

"We're on it," Mia said firmly, shooting Ash a glare.

Ash shook his head and rolled his eyes. "Just remember you have to get by me."

"You have to sleep sometime," Bethany said lightly. "If the smell of food just happens to wake you up, I'm sure it will be from the next room."

They all laughed and Josie felt lightness enter her chest. Things were going to be okay. She'd get through this. The doctor had even said she could go home in the next day or two if everything continued to improve as it was doing currently. After so many days in the hospital she was ready to scream.

She hadn't even been able to get out of the bed except to shower and pee. She was dying to get up and stretch. Anything but lying here in this bed all day.

They talked more, laughing, joking and chatting until Josie began to yawn, fatigue settling over her. Ash noticed and sent a not-so-subtle look in the others' direction. They immediately took the hint and announced they were leaving.

They crowded around Josie's bed, giving her gentle hugs and kisses. Even Kai dropped a kiss on her cheek before stepping back to anchor Brittany to his side.

"I hate that you all are going so soon," Josie said mournfully. "It gets boring just lying here all day. I'm about to climb the walls!"

"We'll be back soon," Mia promised. "And we're bringing food!"

Mia sent Ash another warning glare as she said the last.

"I'll be looking forward to it!" Josie said.

Ash bent over her bed and kissed her softly on the mouth. "I'm going to walk them out, darling. But I'll be right back, okay? Want me to bring you something hot to drink? Doctor said you could have coffee or hot chocolate."

"Oh, that sounds heavenly," Josie sighed. "Coffee would be perfect. I don't suppose you could bring me a latte?"

Ash grinned. "Anything for you. I'll see what I can do."

"Anything except food you mean," Josie grumbled.

He caressed the side of her head and gave her an affectionate pat. "Anything except food."

She waved him away and settled back against her pillows, sagging precariously to one side. The visit had exhausted her. Maybe she wasn't quite as recovered as she wanted to think. But she was glad they'd all come.

Everyone filed out of the door and Ash turned back, sending her a look so filled with love that her breath caught in her throat. Then he turned, quietly closing the door behind him.

She sighed and closed her eyes, taking the opportunity for some rest. She'd just drifted off when she heard her door open. Surely she hadn't slept that long. Ash hadn't had time to go down with his friends, get her coffee and get back so soon.

Two men in suits appeared in her doorway and she recognized them as the detectives that had questioned her right after she'd been hospitalized. She didn't remember a whole lot about the interview. She'd been groggy, in pain and doped up on pain medication. But maybe they'd arrested Charles. This time she'd done what she should have done when Michael assaulted her. She was pressing charges. She wanted Charles to go to jail for what he'd done because she was terrified of what Ash might do to him.

"Miss Carlysle, we'd like to ask you a few questions, if you don't mind. Do you remember my partner, Clinton? I'm Detective Starks. The last time we saw you was right after your attack. I wasn't sure how much you'd remember."

"I remember you, Detective Starks. And no, I don't mind. Have you made an arrest yet?"

"That's what we want to discuss with you," Starks said in an even tone.

The looks on their faces put Josie immediately on guard. She glanced between them, trying to gauge what was going on.

"Charles Willis was found brutally murdered this morning," Starks said bluntly. "We'd like to know who killed him."

## chapter thirty-six

Josie stared at the two policemen in shock. Fear raced through her veins. Oh God. Surely Ash hadn't . . . He wouldn't. Would he? Panic clutched her stomach and she had a hard time breathing, pain jolting through her chest with the effort.

"Are you all right, Miss Carlysle?" Clinton asked with concern.

"Of course I'm not all right," she said faintly. "You just told me that the man who assaulted me was murdered." And then another thought occurred to her. She glanced sharply at both detectives. "You said you want to find out who killed him. Surely you don't think I'm a suspect. I'm hardly capable of killing a man in my current condition."

But Ash would be a suspect. He'd made no secret of his rage over what had happened. And worse, Josie couldn't immediately discount the notion that he *could* have done it.

"You're not a suspect, now," Starks in a bland tone. "But Mr. McIntyre is. Can you tell me if you know of his whereabouts last night between seven and ten P.M.?"

Relief surged, making her light-headed. She gripped the bed rail with her left hand because it felt like she'd pitch right over the side. If that was the time they were asking about then Ash couldn't have done it because he had been with *her*.

"He was here with me," she said firmly. "You can ask any of the nurses who were on duty. He sat with me the entire night and slept on the couch over there."

Clinton was busy scribbling notes on a pocket notebook while Starks continued to stare at her until she shifted uncomfortably.

"Pretty convenient that the man who attacked you turns up dead wouldn't you say?"

"What are you getting at, detective?" she snapped. "If you'd done your job and arrested him, he wouldn't be dead now, would he? I've already told you that Ash was with me. If you don't believe me, there are plenty of other people who can support his alibi."

Starks nodded slowly. "We'll be checking, absolutely. But what about Mr. Hamilton and Mr. Crestwell. Did you see either of them last night?"

The blood seeped from her face. "Are you crazy? Why would either of them kill Charles Willis?"

"You didn't answer the question," Clinton interjected.

"No," she said. "I didn't see them, but I'm sure if you ask them they'll be able to tell you where they were."

"Oh, we will," Starks said grimly.

The door opened and Ash walked in, abruptly halting when he took in the two police officers. Evidently he saw something on her face he didn't like because his expression became thunderous.

"What the fuck is going on here?" he demanded.

"Mr. McIntyre," Starks acknowledged with a dip of his head. "We're questioning Miss Carlysle in the murder of Charles Willis."

Ash blinked, no expression betraying his thoughts. "He's dead?"

Clinton nodded.

"Good," Ash said savagely.

Josie gasped. He wasn't helping matters any with his declaration. Now they'd be convinced that Ash had something to do with it.

"They think you had something to do with it, Ash!"

Ash arched one brow. "Do they?"

"You don't seem too torn up over the fact he's dead," Starks commented.

Ash turned his furious gaze on the detectives. "Take a good look at her. Now you tell me, if that was your woman that he nearly beat to death, would you be upset that someone killed the bastard?"

Clinton shifted uncomfortably and Starks had the grace to look abashed.

"Not saying what I think," Starks replied. "What I think doesn't matter and it doesn't change the fact that a crime was committed. I have to investigate it as I would any other murder."

"You do that," Ash said flatly. "But you leave Josie the fuck alone. You aren't to so much as look at her unless she has a lawyer present. Are we clear? Furthermore, if you want to speak to her again, you'll call me and set up an appointment and it won't be when she's in pain and about to drop from exhaustion. You've upset her and that's the last thing she needs right now."

"Then perhaps you wouldn't mind stepping outside with us to answer a few questions," Starks said in a clipped tone.

"I would mind," Ash bit back. "I'm not leaving Josie. If you want to talk, I'll give you my lawyer's number and you can arrange an interview through him."

"It doesn't have to be this difficult," Clinton broke in. "Just answer a few questions for us and we'll be on our way."

"And I've already told you what you need to do if you want to talk to either of us again," Ash said flatly.

He fished in his wallet and then pulled out a card, handing it to Starks. Neither detective looked pleased, but they backed off.

"We're going to be investigating you, Mr. McIntyre. If you had anything to do with Charles Willis's death, we'll find out," Starks said grimly.

"My life is an open book," Ash said in a calm voice. "Though if you look into Charles Willis's business practices, you'll find your suspects. There is plenty of motive there. Do yourself a favor and spend your time looking into his dealings and not wasting it by looking into mine. You won't find what you're looking for investigating me."

Clinton and Starks exchanged sharp glances.

"We'll be in touch," Starks said to both Josie and Ash.

Then they turned and walked out. Ash followed, closing the door forcefully behind them.

He turned back, striding toward the bed, his expression fierce.

"I'm sorry about that, baby. Never thought they would have come in here like that. I'm sorry I left you alone to deal with that. It won't happen again. If they show up, you aren't to talk to them without a lawyer present. If for some reason I'm not with you, you call me immediately."

Her hand was shaking despite the grip she still had on the bed rail. Ash carefully pried her fingers away and cupped them in his hand, stroking soothingly with his thumb.

"They asked where you were last night between seven and ten," she said, her voice quivering. "They think you did it."

"I was here with you," Ash said in a soft voice.

"I know. I told them that. But they still think . . . and they asked about Gabe and Jace. Ash you have to warn them. They think one of you did this. You didn't, did you?"

Her voice had a pleading note she couldn't control.

Ash slowly shook his head. "I didn't do it, baby. I was here with you."

"But did you have it done?" she whispered.

He leaned over and kissed her brow, leaving his lips there a long moment.

"I didn't have to. He stole from a lot of people. Fucked over a lot of people—the wrong people—in his business dealings. Once they found that out, his life wasn't worth a dime."

She gave him a perplexed look when he stood back up. "How did they find out?"

Ash smiled, but it wasn't a warm smile. She shivered at the darkness in his eyes. This was a man you didn't fuck with. No matter how he appeared. Laid-back, charming and easygoing, underneath that carefully constructed façade was an intense man with unbreakable determination.

"They may have had a little help," he said in a dark tone.

She sucked in her breath as she stared back at Ash. "So you *did* have something to do with his murder."

Ash shook his head. "No. I didn't. If you're asking if I have blood on my hands then yeah, no doubt. I slipped the right information to the right people. What they did with it was up to them. I didn't kill him. Didn't have him killed. But I made it possible with the information I provided. I guess you have to decide if you can live with that. And me."

Slowly she nodded, a little numb, but relieved too. She couldn't face the idea of Ash going to jail because of her. Of it ruining both their lives. Not when she planned a life with him.

"He deserved to die. He wasn't a good man. And that goes against everything I've ever believed in. It's not for me to judge. Before I would have been appalled over justice being taken this way."

"And now?" he asked quietly.

"You've changed me, Ash. I don't know if it's all good. Or all bad. I don't know that it's either. It just is. You've changed me. Made me better in some ways. Murky in others."

"I don't want you to ever be touched by the gray areas I'm immersed in, baby. I want you clean. I want you to shine, just like you always do. We'll never talk about this again. Don't ask and I'm not going to say. You may know things—I will not lie to you—but you will not be confronted with them. Ever. Can you live with that?"

"Yeah," she whispered. "I can live with that."

"I love you, baby," Ash said in a tight voice, filled with emotion. "I don't deserve your love or your shine, but I want it because with you I can feel the sun. I don't want to go back to those shadows."

"You don't have to," she said quietly. "Stay in the sun. With me."

"Always, darling. Nothing will touch our children, Josie. You have my word. Nothing ever touches you or our kids. Gabe or Jace, Mia and Bethany. You're my family. I'd die for any one of you and you'll all stay in the sun where you belong."

"You belong there too, Ash. And I want you there with me."

She broke off, frowning as she realized what he'd said.

"Wait, are we having children?"

He smiled, slow and sexy, his eyes knowing. Arrogance and male confidence radiated in waves. "You're having my babies, Josie. Bank on that. How many is up to you. I want boys first. And then a little girl. Because she'll need big brothers who'll always look out for her. They'll be different from my brothers. They'll give a shit. We'll be a real family."

Josie sent him a tender smile, full of her love for him. "Yeah. We'll be a real family. I want six. Think you can handle that?"

Ash looked dumbstruck. "Six? Holy shit, woman. That's a hell of a lot of knocking you up I gotta do."

She nodded solemnly. "Don't you think we should get started?"

"Hell yeah," he muttered. "Don't want to be an old bastard when you have the last one. But you have to get well and out of the hospital before we start working on that first baby."

He reached into his pocket and pulled out a tiny box.

"I wanted to do this at just the perfect moment," he said gruffly. "But I can't think of a more perfect time than when we're talking about our kids and how many we'll have."

He opened the box and Josie gasped as she stared down at a gorgeous diamond ring. It sparkled and caught the sunlight streaming through her window, dazzling her with its brilliance.

He lowered himself to one knee beside her bed and gently took her left hand in his.

"Will you marry me, Josie? Have my babies and put up with me for the rest of your life? No one will ever love you more than me and I'm going to spend every day for the rest of my life making sure you know that."

The ring wobbled and went blurry in her vision as he slid it onto her finger.

"Yes. Oh yes, Ash! I'll marry you. I love you so much. And I want those babies. Lots of babies."

He smiled and pushed himself back up so he could lean over, gathering her carefully in his arms. He kissed her tenderly, her heart melting.

"I love you too, Josie. Never want you to doubt that. I have a lot to make up for and I'm working on that right now. But it'll wait until you're out of the hospital and home where I can fuss over you and spoil you rotten."

She reached up with her left hand to cup his cheek, her ring sparkling on her finger.

"I'm looking forward to that, my love."

# chapter thirty-seven

"I can't believe you did this for me," Josie said in awe as she stared at the very full ballroom of the Bentley Hotel.

Ash wrapped his arm around her and squeezed her tightly against him. "I didn't do anything, baby. It's all you. They love your work. You're going to sell out in the first half hour. A bidding war has begun over your erotic series of paintings."

Josie took in the glittering array of people who were admiring her work while drinking very expensive champagne. Everyone was here. The mayor, oh my God. And there were celebrities everywhere! She was agog at the names of some of the people in attendance. And they were here for her paintings!

She glanced back up at Ash and leaned further into him. "Do you hate that they're seeing those paintings of me? I know you didn't like showing them and wanted to be the only one to see them."

He smiled and dropped a kiss on her upturned lips. "I have the real thing. What do I need the paintings for? They only get to *imagine* what they can't see in those paintings, but I get to see it and touch it every night. That's only for me. No one else will ever have that."

She smiled back, delighted at his response.

"Now, if you ever venture into something more revealing, then yeah, I'm going to buy those. I don't care what you say. Nobody but me gets to see you completely naked."

She grinned and elbowed him in the ribs. "Don't worry. That's the extent of the bravery I have concerning me in the buff."

"Thank fuck," he muttered. "Don't want to have to beat the asses of any men who drool over you in a painting."

"Oh look, there're the girls!" Josie exclaimed, breaking away from Ash to go and greet them.

"Josie!" Brittany cried, engulfing Josie in a huge hug. "You're famous! Have you seen all the people here going bananas over your paintings?"

Josie hugged her back and smiled up at Kai who stood indulgently to the side while Brittany attacked Josie.

Mia and Bethany shoved past Gabe and Jace the minute Brittany let Josie go and hugged her fiercely.

"Oh my gosh, you guys look gorgeous!" Josie said, surveying the cocktail dresses worn by each. "And your shoes!" Her voice dropped to a whisper. "I know what you guys will be doing later!"

They all laughed and then Mia said, "Hey, where's the champagne! We need to get our drink on!"

The men groaned but there wasn't a single one who didn't have a smug gleam in his eyes. Yeah, they knew what they were getting later. Josie hoped to have her own after-party romp between the sheets with Ash.

He'd been exceedingly gentle and patient during her recovery. She'd eventually had to jump *him* because he'd refused to so much as touch her, much less have sex with her, until he was absolutely certain she was healed. And he still hadn't done more than make sweet, exquisite love to her, not that she was complaining. But she was eager to resume a normal sexual relationship with her dominant man.

She could see in his eyes the desire not to remind her of what had happened. He'd been extremely careful, worried that he would somehow be correlated with the assault on her. But she loved that edge, that fine line between too far and not enough. She wanted it back. Wanted him to lose his tightly held control and to unleash his dark hungers on the both of them.

She shivered just thinking about it. Tonight. Definitely tonight she'd give him no option. She wanted everything he could give her. Wanted to feel the snap of leather against her ass. Wanted him to tie her up and have his wicked way with her. She wanted Ash back!

"I'm going to steal Josie and take her around the room. I want to introduce her to a few people. Drink up and we'll be back in a few minutes," Ash said.

The girls waved and then turned back to their own men who were more than happy to get them back. Ash led her through the crowd, stopping and introducing her to people she could barely stammer hello to.

She was tongue-tied and had no idea what to say to the people who gushed about her work. She'd never dreamed that anyone would be that excited over her paintings. And she had Ash to thank.

"Thank you," she whispered, slipping her arm around his waist as they threaded back through the crowd. "This is the most awesome night of my life!"

"Glad you're enjoying yourself, darling. This is your night to shine. But don't worry because there will be many more. Judging by how fast your paintings have sold, you're going to be in high demand. I may regret doing this because you're going to be spending all your time painting and you'll forget all about me."

She laughed and hugged him tighter. "No chance of that. You'll always come first, Ash."

He kissed her, long and lingeringly, uncaring of the people in the crowded ballroom. She sighed, blissfully happy. So much had happened over the last two months. She'd been released from the hospital after having to stay for nearly two weeks. The police had questioned her and Ash, this time with his lawyer present. They'd also questioned Gabe and Jace and had combed through Ash's life, leaving no stone unturned. But there had been nothing to find.

Then they'd turned their attention to Charles Willis's business practices and it was there that they'd struck a gold mine. He'd stolen from numerous people. Embezzled money. Set up fake accounts. He'd billed for work never done, and at least three offshore accounts had been discovered with millions of dollars in stolen money.

Worse was the people he'd stolen from. They weren't exactly the legitimate businessmen that Ash and his partners were. They were not the kind of people you steal from because, if discovered, it wasn't jail time you had to worry about. As Charles had no doubt discovered far too late. He even had ties to the mob, and Josie hadn't even realized the mob still existed outside of books and movies.

The police had investigated one man in particular, convinced that he was behind Charles's murder, but had been frustrated by their inability to pin anything on him. As a result, the case was still open, but Ash was no longer a suspect.

Josie had breathed much easier when the police backed off. She knew Ash hadn't been directly behind Charles's death, but he had been involved to an extent. But as he'd promised that day in the hospital, they never spoke of it again, and she didn't ask.

Maybe that made her just as murky and gray as Ash thought he was himself, but she couldn't spare any real remorse over Charles's death. He'd hurt a lot of people and she could have died from the beating she'd received. She was ready to move on with her life. With Ash.

"Have something I want to ask you, baby," Ash murmured next to her ear.

She looked up, curious as to why he sounded so serious all of a sudden.

"Jace and Bethany have asked if we want to get married with them. A double wedding. I told them I'd discuss it with you. It's something they'd really like. Jace is impatient and wants the wedding to be soon. But I don't want us to do it with them if you want or need more time. If you want your own big day separate from theirs, I understand. I want it to be special for you."

"But what about you?" Josie asked softly. "What do you want?"

Ash smiled. "All I want out of the deal is you. Nothing else matters. Don't care where it happens or when, though I'm not a fan of waiting very long. I want you to have my name. For me to know you're legally mine. How we do it doesn't matter."

"I think it would be really special to share a wedding with Jace and Bethany," she murmured. "He's your best friend and I adore Bethany. Let's do it!"

"You okay with getting married soon?" Ash asked. "Jace wants it done as soon as possible. He thought about hitting a beach somewhere. Maybe go to Bora-Bora and get married on the sand."

"That sounds so romantic," she sighed. "I don't care when or where either, Ash. I just want to be married to you. Anything else is just icing on the cake."

He kissed her again. "Let's go tell them, then. We need to celebrate."

She hooked her arm through his as they made their way back to where their friends stood together across the room. Their friends. Not just Ash's. These people were hers too and it filled her heart with warmth.

Brittany was over the moon with Kai. She'd already moved to Vegas with him but they visited the city often. Josie was glad that Ash had at least his sister. The rest of his family had backed off after he'd called his grandfather. He still didn't know what the old man was going to do with his will, but Ash had done what he'd promised and then washed his hands of them all.

But Brittany and he were close now and she spent a lot of time with Josie and Ash. But his real family stood just a few feet away. Gabe, Jace, Mia, Bethany. Her family too.

They erupted in cheers when Ash announced that he and Josie would be getting married with Jace and Bethany. Then champagne was passed around again.

"Hope you'll also come to mine and Brittany's wedding," Kai interjected with a smug grin. "Only just talked her into it today."

Brittany held up a huge diamond engagement ring that Josie hadn't noticed until now. Her face was flushed with happiness and her eyes glittered brightly.

"A double toast, then," Ash said, holding his glass up. "To Josie and her success. And to Brittany and Kai."

Everyone held up their glasses, noisily clinking them together before downing the bubbly liquid.

"To girlfriends," Mia called out, holding her glass up to Josie, Bethany and Brittany.

"I'll drink to that!" Bethany exclaimed.

"And here's to us providing the guys many more girls' nights out," Josie said with a grin.

"*I'll* drink to that," Ash said.

"Me too," Jace put in.

"And me," Gabe said, grinning.

"I'll definitely fly Brittany in for the occasion," Kai said, his eyes twinkling with amusement.

Josie pulled Brittany and Bethany to her side, hugging them both while Mia slid in next to Bethany. They raised their glasses.

"To girls' night out!" they chorused.